M000231351

"Sara Davison has written a unique and powerful story of love, loss, and redemption that will touch your heart and feed your spirit. I highly recommend The Watcher."

~*Nancy Mehl, author of the Quantico Files Series*

"When I say this is a beautiful story of God's grace, forgiveness, and love, it must also be said that it is a book where things happen that necessitate God's grace, forgiveness and love. The subject matter is sensitive and may have triggers for some. That said, Sara Davison has woven a story with multiple characters including Beings from the spirit world. Biblical Beings. Spiritual Warfare is something we are hearing more about these days, and Davison has used her Bible and her God-granted writing skills to give us a look at what some of that might look like. She weaves a complex story that draws you in even as it gives us a better chance to understand and love the God we serve. He is magnificent. I highly recommend *The Watcher*."

~*Linda K. Rodante, author of the Spiritual Warfare Series and the Dangerous Series*

The Watcher

The Watcher

By

Sara Davison

The Watcher
Published by Mountain Brook Ink under the Mountain Brook
Fire line
White Salmon, WA U.S.A.

The website addresses shown in this book are not intended in any way to be or imply an endorsement on the part of Mountain Brook Ink, nor do we vouch for their content.

This story is a work of fiction. All characters and events are the product of the author's imagination. Any resemblance to any person, living or dead, is coincidental.

Scripture taken from the Holy Bible, Berean Study Bible, BSB Copyright ©2016, 2018 by Bible Hub. Used by Permission. All Rights Reserved Worldwide.

ISBN 978-1-943959-96-9

The Team: Miralee Ferrell, Alyssa Roat, Nikki Wright, Cindy Jackson
Cover Design: Indie Cover Design, Lynnette Bonner

Mountain Brook Fire is an inspirational publisher offering worlds you can believe in.
Printed in the United States of America

Dedication

To Michael, because if you hadn't looked up from an early draft and said, "This just has to be a book, that's all there is to it," it might never have been.

Thank you for doing this life with me.

And always and above all to the One who gives the stories and who watches—and watches over—us all.

As I lay on my bed, I also saw in the visions of my mind a watcher, a holy one, coming down from heaven (Daniel 4:13).

Chapter One

The knock that rattled the screen door startled me awake. I bolted upright, clutching the arms of the wooden rocking chair on the porch and muttering to myself as I groped my way out of a dream. The murkiness thinned and gradually cleared like the last vestiges of fog blown away by the morning breeze. I blinked, not entirely sure for a few seconds whether the image in front of me was real or a remnant of the half-world I'd been pulled from.

I'm not certain how tall I would be if I actually materialized, perhaps a foot or two. In any case, the man standing on the porch towered over me like Gulliver next to the Lilliputians. If I absolutely had to be torn from my slumber, I suppose this wasn't the worst sight to see upon waking. Although he couldn't see me, I primped my hair a little. It never hurt for a girl to look her best.

I glanced through the screen door into the kitchen of the old farmhouse. At the sound of the knock, Kathryn Ellison had pushed herself away from the counter she'd been relaxing against while she talked on the phone with her only daughter, Tory.

Still chatting away, Kathryn strolled around the island and over to the door, blissfully oblivious that her life was about to change completely. And not for the first time. For my part, I couldn't suppress a shiver of excitement. A perfect metaphor always does that to me. And her pushing open the screen to see the man waiting on the other side, thereby flinging open a door she had long ago wedged a shoulder against—figuratively speaking—*was* such a metaphor.

I held my breath, anticipating a strong reaction. She didn't disappoint me.

"Nick." The phone she'd been holding to her ear slipped down her cheek.

"Mom?" The concern in her daughter's voice called her

back, and she lifted the receiver.

"Tory, I'll talk to you later. Someone's here."

In spite of the extraordinary abilities I possess, I had to lean forward to catch the words, they came out in such a breathless whisper. Not waiting for a response, she pressed the off button and dropped the phone onto the small wooden table inside the door.

Nick might not have noticed the way Kathryn's legs trembled and her fingers gripped the door handle until they turned white at the knuckles, but I certainly did. I planted my palms on one arm of the chair and hauled myself to my feet, groaning as my long idle bones and muscles clicked into place. Balancing on the seat, I peered over the edge. The wooden slats of the veranda seemed miles away, but I took a deep breath and launched myself from the chair. Thankfully, my non-material state prevented any injuries as I landed softly on the porch.

I couldn't miss this meeting. Not for anything. This was the moment I had been waiting for since that day in the courthouse seventeen years earlier when Kathryn had first laid eyes on Nick Lawson.

Pressing her shoulder to the wood, Kathryn leaned against the frame as though she would sink to the porch in a quivering heap without its silent support. Neither of them spoke.

This is an interesting phenomenon I have noted about humans in intense situations—the words are the first thing to go. Frankly, I am uncomfortable with this. Silence rarely sends you hurtling toward me, so I usually attempt to fill in the empty air—when I don't forget myself and become caught up in the drama of the moment—with dialogue of my own. Whenever that happens, I will take the opportunity to fill you in on what has happened in the life of Kathryn Ellison to bring her to this point. Only I and one other Being— my good friend Faith—can do it, as we have been with

Kathryn since the beginning, or very nearly.

At times both of us have packed to go, thinking we would soon be ordered away or lost forever. We never have been. Not quite. I'm still here, and so, somewhat battered and bruised, is Faith. Over there, in the corner of the porch where she has climbed up on the railing and sits, swinging both legs in front of her and watching the encounter taking place with as much interest as I am.

Which is all either of us can do—watch and wait, with a newly piqued interest, to see if Nick and Kathryn will find me, or if either of them will even have the courage to try.

"I shouldn't have come by without calling." When he did break the silence, Nick's voice was as unsteady as Kathryn's. I took a step toward them so as to not miss anything. "But I needed to see you."

"You know you don't have to call." His eyes hadn't left hers, and Kathryn could barely hear her own words past the pounding in her ears. *He's come, finally.* "Do you want to sit down?"

He wore a black T-shirt and jeans, and his light brown hair curled a little around his ears. Nick Lawson had been born after his time. His bearing and the look in his eyes revealed a man completely at home herding cattle on the open range. He was a cowboy, at heart and by profession.

"Sure." He sank onto one of the white wicker chairs on the porch.

"Can I get you something to drink? Lemonade, maybe?" *Please say yes.* A cold drink would help, as Kathryn was in desperate need of something to wrap her trembling fingers around.

Nick managed a grin, although his dark brown eyes churned with as much emotion as she felt. "Lemonade would be great, thanks."

3

I watched her through the screen as she opened the refrigerator door and withdrew the pitcher.

Get a hold of yourself, Kathryn.

I grinned at her self-admonishment. As I had the ability to hear her thoughts, I'd listened in on a lot of that over the years, and it never failed to amuse me, particularly as she rarely followed her own advice.

Her hand shook as she poured them both a tall glass of lemonade. *It's been three years. He could be here to let me know that he's with someone else now.* She set the pitcher on the counter and pressed a hand to her chest. *Breathe.* Clutching a glass in each hand, she returned to the veranda. After handing Nick a drink, she lowered herself onto the wicker chair beside him.

He took a sip and raised his glass. "That's good. Not from a can."

"Oh, no." Kathryn's eyes widened in feigned horror. "My mother would die before she'd allow lemonade—or anything else for that matter—to be served from a can in this house."

His laugh was infectious, and she couldn't help smiling in return. Nick took another swallow of lemonade then set his glass on the small table between their chairs.

I glanced over at Faith, well aware of the magnitude of this conversation. Lifting her head, she winked in my direction before shifting a little on the porch railing and returning her attention to the pair in front of us.

Kathryn was drawn to Nick's eyes. They were an even darker, richer brown than she'd remembered, and she felt, when they were directed at her, as though he could see right through her. She swallowed hard. "How have you been, Nick? I've thought about you and James often and wondered how you were doing."

A shadow crossed his face. "We had a rough time after Halyna died. I think we're better now. The pain isn't as sharp, and I can go a whole day here and there without thinking about her, but it hasn't been easy. We all miss her."

My grin faded. Nick's sister had died three years earlier, and I'd accompanied Kathryn to the funeral so she could pay her respects to Halyna's husband, James. And to Nick. That had been another time when I had watched Kathryn and Nick and wondered whether it was the beginning or the end for them. Rarely had I been involved with two humans where it was so hard to tell.

"I'm sure you do." An ache of grief for all that he'd been through settled in her chest. For all they had both been through.

She set her glass next to the one he'd left on the table and raised her gaze to meet his. He was studying her intently. When she didn't speak, Nick drew in a deep breath. "I've tried so hard to put you out of my mind."

"Me too." Kathryn nodded, making the admission to herself as much as to him.

"I hope it's worked as well for you as it has for me." He reached over and brushed a strand of her long, dark hair from her face before taking her hand in his. "I know the timing has never been right for us and, like I told you I would, I've prayed and waited to feel a peace about when it would be. Not very patiently, I might add. I haven't felt it, until now, although I've had to get James to hide my truck keys occasionally to keep me from driving over here and taking you in my arms anyway."

She tightened her fingers around his. "I'm not sure I would have objected if you had."

A smile broke across Nick's face. "Now you tell me." He sobered as he leaned forward, their clasped hands resting on his knee. "I know you've been hurt, Kathryn, so it's natural for you to be scared. I'm scared too. I'm still dealing with the loss of a person I loved deeply, and the thought of getting close to someone again is a bit terrifying. The thing is," he ran his thumb over the back of her hand. "I don't think I have a choice with you anymore. I'm not sure I ever have, to be honest."

I waited for her to bolt. It was her MO. I'd seen it happen almost every time they had been together over the years. I realized suddenly that I had the porch railing in a white-knuckled grip. I yanked my hand away as though the wood was burning hot. I was becoming far too involved with this one. Kathryn Ellison had been through so much since That Night. I wanted her to find me, more than I ever had with anyone else. So much so that on more than one occasion I had almost jumped in front of her, waving my arms to let her know that I had not, as she supposed, abandoned her entirely.

It was strictly forbidden, of course. My job was to watch and to make myself available, not to interfere in any way. Sometimes, the watching and waiting—mostly because it occurred during those unbearable silences I referred to earlier— required almost inhuman strength. Fortunately for all concerned, I am inhuman, but still...

"I don't have a choice, either." The words floated from her mouth and hung in the air like the last notes of a particularly haunting song do, even after the instrument has been put away. Joy flared inside her but was immediately banked. Her eyelids flickered. They'd waited so long to be together—why did Kathryn feel a sudden check, as though someone had grabbed her arm to prevent her from taking another step forward?

Nick didn't seem to notice. A bright light ignited in his eyes. "Kathryn." He said her name as though it were a rare treasure in his hands that he needed to handle with reverent care.

Hope helped straighten my old bones. Maybe he'd be able to convince her to let go of whatever held her back. If anyone could, it was him. If only a cloud neither of them could see—the only other thing to disturb my slumber that week, hadn't recently formed over the horizon, they might have a real chance this time.

A sudden apprehension swept through Kathryn. She couldn't be with him. Not yet. "But..."

Oh dear. Too many clouds blocking the sun now, a storm obviously brewing. I shot a glance at Faith. Her legs had stopped swinging, but otherwise she did not exhibit any of the trepidation I was experiencing. Not surprising. Faith is a lot hardier than I am. She doesn't dread storms. In fact, I sometimes wonder if she doesn't wish for them to come along. Easy for her. She usually comes out of the battering wind and rain stronger than ever. For me it can go either way. If I emerge at all, I am either in better shape than before, or limping badly and in need of some sort of metaphysical assistance. Not that it mattered. Neither of us could do anything now but watch and wait for the hurricane to blow in.

The light that had been glowing in Nick's eyes flickered and went out. I shivered as the cold wind that had extinguished it blew through me. He gripped her hand tightly. And uselessly, as it turned out. "Kathryn, no. Don't do this. Not again."

"I'm sorry." Her voice broke, but she tugged her fingers from his and stood, backing toward the house until she reached the cold stone side of it. "There's something I have to do first. I need time."

"How much time?" His gaze followed her, pinned her to the wall.

"I'm not sure. A few days."

Nick pushed to his feet and strode toward the porch stairs. Thinking he was going, I took a couple of steps forward, prepared to follow, but he stopped at the post and clutched it in both hands, resting his forehead on the smooth, white-painted surface. Kathryn waited, twisting her fingers together in front of her as though she could feel me leaving on his heels and was struggling to hold on.

When he turned around, the light had returned to his eyes, but a hot red glow now. "Hasn't this thing kept us apart long enough?"

The same red glow leapt into her eyes as she straightened, the rough stones scraping against her back. "This *thing* almost destroyed my life."

His shoulders sagged, and he crossed the porch toward her and pressed the palms of his hands against the wall on either side of her head. "Don't you think I know that? I've watched it eat you up for years. And I've felt the prick of every tooth that ripped into you gnawing away at me too."

His words didn't dredge up the tears that welled in her eyes. It was the pain that laced through them, like the yarn on a child's sewing card, outlining and defining each one.

Nick searched her face in the soft glow of the porch light. Then, with a heavy sigh, he lowered one hand, trailing his thumb across her cheek to wipe away the tear that had started down. "Well, it's been seventeen years. What's a few more days?" He made an attempt, which failed miserably, at a smile.

Kathryn did no better when she tried to return it. A few days were a lot. Except for Faith and me, no one understood better than Kathryn and Nick did what could be gained—or lost—in a few days.

A few hours.

A few seconds.

"This isn't like the other times. I promise."

Nick studied her, his jaw tight. "A few days. Then I'm coming for you." He spun around and started for the stairs.

"I'll be here." The words were soft, almost under her breath. Still, he heard them, and took Hope along with him. I could see it in the set of his shoulders.

I'd started to follow him, but the quiet promise reined me in, and I climbed up onto my wooden chair in the deeply shadowed corner of the porch once again.

When he came back, she would be here. And so, apparently, would I.

Chapter Two

For a long time Kathryn stood, her back chafed by the rough stone of the farmhouse, watching the taillights of Nick Lawson's truck disappearing down the road in a cloud of dust. Even after the lights had gone and the swirls of dirt had settled on the rough gravel road, she didn't move.

Fortunately, I possess virtually limitless patience. I know about waiting. I wait years, sometimes lifetimes, for people to turn around and discover me. Even when I know they likely won't, I wait. So I stayed in my chair in the corner, my gaze fixed on Kathryn's face, curious to see what she would do now.

When she did finally push herself away from the wall, she grabbed the glasses of lemonade from the little white wicker table and moved mechanically toward the door. I jumped to my feet and slipped through the screen behind her. When she reached the sink, she set her glass on the counter but held Nick's in her hand for a moment. A small shudder passed through her as she ran her finger around the rim and touched it to her lips—a reminder of the rare kisses the two of them had shared.

Her finger lingered there a moment. Then, with a soft sigh, she opened the dishwasher door, set both glasses upside-down on the top rack, and slammed the door. Given my penchant for the metaphorical, I had to admire the gesture, although I knew it would do nothing to shut off the thoughts of him that spun through her mind like snowflakes swirling from a leaden sky.

Squaring her shoulders, she marched out the back entrance of the kitchen into the hallway that led to the stairs. I trailed after her. I was tired, worn out from the emotional exchange I had witnessed on the porch. If I had any common sense at all, I would have stayed in my chair and taken a nap. Sadly, Common Sense and I have never been very close. Some have even suggested, on more than one occasion, that we are incompatible, but I believe that is going a bit far.

In any case, I gathered up the few reserves of strength I possessed and rested a foot on the bottom step. Fortunately for those limited reserves, Kathryn had already started toward me, a cream-colored shoebox clutched in both hands. My eyes narrowed. I knew that box well. I had watched her on numerous occasions shove a pile of soft wool sweaters out of the way to extract it from its hiding place at the very back of her closet shelf. She did it each time she received a letter from *him*, to be exact.

He was David Henley, a minister, a pastor, a man of the cloth, take your pick. Not that he was one when he and Kathryn first met. At that point he was as far away from God as he was from me.

Kathryn headed for the living room. I scrambled after her. I hated missing anything. Not, as I have sometimes been accused, because I am nosy, but because it is my job to be there when needed, and I never knew when that might be.

When I arrived, the box rested on the large, glass-topped coffee table in front of the brown leather couch. Kathryn had dropped to her knees before the woodstove and was crumpling up paper and shoving it and several small pieces of kindling inside. Normally I love a good, roaring fire. I've been able to get pretty close to Kathryn many evenings when she has relaxed on the couch in front of the woodstove with a good book and a steaming cup of tea.

Tonight, I strongly suspected there was not going to be any book. Or any tea. And the way every muscle in her body was stretched taut and quivering did not bode well for the relaxing either. I caught myself about to heave a sigh. There'd been enough of that around here in the last hour to do us all for a while.

The soft whooshing sound of a match flaring to life drew my attention to my charge. For several seconds Kathryn stared, mesmerized, at the bright flame. My own muscles tightened as the fire worked its way along the wood toward her fingers. Right before the orange of the fire melded with the pink of her fingertips, she flung the match into the stove. Two matches later, neither coming in contact with her skin, to my relief, flames leapt high behind the glass door. She pressed a palm to the coffee table and pushed to her feet.

I was right. No tea. She walked around the coffee table and sank onto the couch. I waited for her to reach for the shoebox, but she only bent her knees to her chest and folded her arms on top of them, staring at the box in front of her.

My fingers tapped the back of the couch.

All right, I may have been exaggerating about my limitless patience. In point of fact, I tend to be much more comfortable with action than with stillness and silence. And this had been an evening of long periods of both. My nerves were stretched nearly as taut as Kathryn's, which was saying something.

I studied the shoebox. Such an innocuous object. It was hard to believe that so much emotion could be contained within its four little cardboard sides. And not only because of David Henley. The actions of others had also affected Kathryn deeply, changed the course of her life. But it was his letters and the night that precipitated their correspondence that had affected her most of all.

My thoughts, with nothing happening in the living room to keep them transfixed, began to wander. I'd known David most of his life. When he was a young boy, we were close, practically inseparable. As he grew older, our encounters became much more sporadic. It wasn't him that drove me away as much as his father, although David allowed it to happen. I was still available in case he needed me. And I always thought we would renew our acquaintance someday. At least, until *it* happened …

I remember it well, the night that Kathryn Ellison and David Henley met. If I closed my eyes, and really—I threw my hands in the air as I cast another glance over the shoulder in front of me— I might as well, I could see him getting ready. I could hear the crash of the keys hitting the floor. Watch him making plans that all but ensured the two of us would never reconcile. I watched, and I knew, and I shuddered in fear and contempt.

But there was absolutely nothing I could do to stop it.

Chapter Three

"Okay, Walker. Got it." David Henley's fingers tightened around the cell phone pressed to his ear. "*Yes*, I wrote everything down. It's not that complicated. I can handle it." He listened for a moment then took a breath, deliberately toning down the sarcasm. "I *know* there are plenty of people who'd be happy to do this job. I appreciate you calling me."

Henley clenched his jaw and propped a hip against the kitchen counter. The voice droned on until he couldn't take it any longer. "It'll get done. All you need to do is show up at the cabin and bring the cash with you."

He slammed the device onto the countertop, sending the half-eaten apple he'd been working on when the phone rang spinning across the dingy quartz surface. "Maybe you should do your own dirty work if you're so concerned." He let out a short laugh. "Of course, with all your daddy's money, I'm sure you've never had to get your hands dirty in your life." Holding his fingers out in front of him, he studied them a moment before clenching them into fists. "Well, some of us haven't had the luxury of that kind of *sanitized* lifestyle."

An empty Styrofoam cup sat on the counter, and Henley picked it up and crushed it in his hand. He'd been small-time long enough. Now he wanted a piece of real action—and a piece of the pie that went with it. He tossed the crumpled cup toward the garbage can in the corner. It landed on the floor where he left it. This wasn't the job he would have chosen, but at least it was a foot in the door of the world where he belonged.

He reached for the apple and took a bite. Was that true? He'd never really felt as though he belonged in this world, lurking in the shadows outside the well-lit shelter of the law. Did anybody really belong here? *Kevin Dylan, maybe.* A chill passed through him. Kevin Dylan. Not his partner of choice, with those cold, dead eyes. But he couldn't mess this up.

David Henley knew himself. Knew that, when it came right down to it, he might not be able to follow through with a job he had no stomach for. Kevin Dylan would have no such qualms. And when it was over, David would be on his way up and Dylan would hopefully be on his way out. Out of the country, anyway. The farther the better.

But was it worth it? Worth risking the life of another human being? Henley shook his head, not wanting to have this conversation, even with himself. He stared at the phone for a minute, fingers tapping on the counter. Then he tossed the apple into the sink, snatched the phone off the counter, and punched in Dylan's number.

"Talk to me."

The arrogance in the man's voice set David's teeth on edge, as though he'd bit down on a piece of tinfoil. "It's me. Everything's set for tonight."

"Where?"

"Langley. Some place called Toby's."

"And he's sure she'll be there?"

"That's what he told me. Meet me at the cabin in an hour and we can go over it all."

Henley slammed the phone on the counter without waiting for a reply. The piece of paper slid across the surface. He grabbed it before it could drift to the floor and shoved it in the pocket of his jeans. Talking to Dylan made his blood run cold, and he tugged on his tan corduroy jacket. A vague sense of foreboding settled around him like a damp mist—the feeling that after tonight nothing would be the same. He shook off the sensation.

What was the matter with him? This was the chance he'd been waiting for. He didn't *want* things to be the same anymore. Another chill rippled through him that the heavy jacket could do nothing to dispel. Henley grabbed the duffle bag he'd packed with enough clothes and supplies to last him if he needed to disappear for a few days. When he reached for the keys lying on the table in the hallway and knocked them to the floor, he cursed himself, the keys, and all the lousy breaks that had driven him to this life in the first place.

Then he yanked open the door and headed to work.

A note of caution before I continue. As you know, David Henley is about to meet up with his partner, Kevin Dylan. If my relationship with Henley had been sporadic and volatile over the years, my encounters with Kevin Dylan were non-existent. His choice, by the way. And I have found through experience that it is best to avoid those who deliberately choose that kind of life. The decision may be entirely theirs, but they tend to want to inflict the consequences on everyone with whom they come in contact. Fair warning.

Dylan's Harley was already parked around the side of the building when Henley drove his rusted-out F-150 up the long, rutted lane. He sat for a minute, staring at the building. "You've got to be kidding me." When Walker, the man who had hired him, had said a cabin, he'd pictured a rustic cottage on a lake. This shack appeared as though the next breath of wind would send it crashing to the ground. He flung the door of the truck open so hard it rocked back and forth on its hinges. "Whatever. I'm not planning to move in."

When Henley walked through the front door, Kevin Dylan sat at a rough wooden table along the wall, hands clasped behind his head, booted feet resting on a chair pushed out to the side. Even from ten feet away his cold, hard stare pierced Henley's layers of clothing and slammed into his chest like shots fired from a gun.

Henley didn't think, in the four years he'd known him, he'd ever seen Dylan smile. He wished he would—once—so Henley would know there was a human being in there somewhere.

"Welcome to the Ritz-Carleton." Dylan unclasped his hands and waved his arms around the room.

Henley snorted. "Let's discuss the details on the way. The less time spent in this place the better."

The boots dropped to the floor with a thud. Grabbing a navy backpack off the table, Dylan stood and slung it over his shoulder.

Henley headed for the door, drawing in a deep breath as they left the rank air of the cabin. He slid behind the wheel of the gunmetal blue truck.

Dylan pulled open the passenger door and tossed the backpack on the floor. He climbed in after it and slammed the door. "Show time. Let's go."

Henley shot him a sideways glance as he started the engine. He'd seen this before. Dylan, normally emotionless, grew more and more animated as the starting time for a job approached. Shaking his head in disgust, Henley steered the truck down the long lane. That was why he didn't belong in this world. Nothing about a job excited him—it was a means to an end. And the sooner the end came, the better. Fortunately, Dylan's antsiness wouldn't last long. He'd be cold as ice once things got going. A real professional.

David Henley tugged the paper out of his pocket and tossed it onto the seat. He stared out the front window in silence as Dylan studied the information. A block from downtown Langley, Henley pulled over to the curb and shoved the transmission into park.

"Sounds pretty straightforward." His partner folded up the paper and stuck it in the pocket of his denim jacket. "I can do this myself. You head to the cabin and wait for me there."

"But—"

Dylan raised his hand. "It'll be a lot easier to pull this off alone. Two people are way too conspicuous. Besides, she'll be driving that dark green Accord. That's how we'll know it's her, right? I'll bring her to the cabin in that and you take your truck, since we don't want to leave either behind for the cops to find. Relax in that lovely resort and I'll be back before you have time to miss me."

It was eerie the way Kevin Dylan could display a sarcastic sense of humor without a sliver of ice melting in those cold blue eyes. Henley guessed the levity—like the long, blond, Brad-Pitt style hair—was intended to disarm his victims, making them all the more vulnerable to whatever plans he had for them.

Maybe a little less time in his company wouldn't be such a bad thing. Henley shrugged. "Fine. But make sure everything goes smoothly."

Dylan grabbed the navy backpack from the floor and set it on the seat beside him. He unzipped the bag and reached inside. When he withdrew his hand, a .38-calibre Derringer lay in his palm. Henley's stomach tightened to the point of pain when he saw the gun.

He lifted his gaze to his partner. Kevin Dylan was smiling now. Henley went cold. *What have I done?*

Dylan shoved the gun into the back of his jeans before climbing out of the truck. "Get some rest. It's gonna be a long night." The door slammed behind him.

Henley shook his head. "Didn't *I* call *you* in for this?"

Dylan kept walking, back ramrod straight, all business. The smile would be gone now.

"I almost feel sorry for ..." Henley murmured. His head shot up and he reached for the key. *Knock it off.* He could not let emotion get in the way of finishing this job.

Expelling a deep breath, he shoved the truck into gear and pulled a U-turn. Spending a minute more than necessary at that cabin was not appealing, but he couldn't risk not being there when his partner got back. One hand ran through his short sandy-brown crew cut. Crazy or not, Dylan had been right about one thing.

It was going to be a very long night.

Armed with the knowledge of all that would happen in the next few hours—having lived through them twenty years ago, if barely—I managed a cynical smile at that thought. Because, as it turned out, David Henley had no idea.

Chapter Four

Tuesday

A movement on the couch caught my attention. Kathryn had finally reached for the box and moved it onto her lap. Gripping the lid with both hands, she slowly lifted it off. The thin cardboard might have been lined with gold, it seemed so heavy in her hands. Its removal appeared to exact every last ounce of her strength—which it likely did, emotionally speaking. She set it gingerly on the couch cushion beside her and stared at the contents of the box.

I craned my neck to see over her shoulder. Not exactly ethical, but also not something new. I'd watched over her shoulder each time she had written David Henley a letter. Over his too, for that matter, every time he had written her back. All part of the job description. At least, that's how I defended my actions on the odd occasion my guilty conscience woke me in the night with a sharp jab to the ribs.

The contents of those envelopes had a great deal to do with the future of the two individuals involved. If pressed, I likely wouldn't be able to tell you why or how. Call it a hunch. In any case, I was convinced enough to continue reading over her shoulder, waiting until the moment when all would be revealed.

Which—long-forgotten excitement tingled along my extremities—might come sooner than I had thought.

Kathryn riffled through the pile of envelopes and tugged something out of the box. Not a letter like I had expected. A photo. Absently sliding the box onto the couch, she leaned against the cushions, clutching the picture in both hands. Ty Stuart. I pressed a hand over my mouth to keep from gasping. Not that she would have heard me. Still, it's a point of professional pride to me that I keep my emotions, if not under check, at least to myself. The picture had caught me by surprise.

I'd almost forgotten about Ty—the memory had been buried under other, darker and more powerful ones. Kathryn obviously had not forgotten. The fingers that clenched the worn photo trembled, and I longed to cover them with mine.

I clasped my arms behind my back. I'd come close over the years to ignoring the proper decorum with her, to breaching the non-involvement clause in my contract. Even now my heart thudded painfully against the wall of my chest and I had to struggle to draw in breath. It wasn't my place and I knew it. Somehow she had to work her way through all this to find her way to Nick. And to me.

I studied the picture that rested against her knees. A shudder gripped her thin shoulders. She was thinking about That Night. The night she thought her whole life was about to begin.

What she couldn't have known then, of course, was that the exact opposite was true.

April 1999

Kathryn Ellison stopped at the curb and turned off the engine of her car. She waited for it, then smiled at the sharp crack of the engine backfiring. Her beloved Clover Green Pearl 1978 Accord shuddered once and was still.

"You're starting to show your age, girl." Kathryn patted the dashboard. "Still get me where I want to go, don't you?" Grinning, she climbed out of her brother Aaron's hand-me-down car, careful not to slam the door too hard.

The street was quiet as she walked toward downtown Langley, British Columbia. She loved this city. Less than half an hour from the Surrey area, where she'd grown up and where her family still ran a ranch, this university town had become a second home for her as she'd attended school.

Tall oak trees lined the sidewalk, the spring air drawing out the buds that lined the overhanging branches. The smell of damp earth and the sweet light scent of flowers poking through the ground filled the air and she took a deep breath.

20

In those days, Kathryn Ellison wore me close, wrapped around her shoulders like a long cape fastened at her throat with a brooch. She couldn't see, as I could, that the clasp was loose and I was in serious danger of slipping off and falling in a crumpled heap in the dust behind her. It wouldn't have even occurred to her to check to see if I was securely fastened. I'd simply always been there, flowing around her, so much a part of her life that, even if I had been able to warn her, she would never have believed I could be stripped away.

That she could be torn from the light and the warmth that had surrounded her since the day she was born and left shivering in a cold darkness she had never experienced and knew nothing about.

A darkness that, sadly, she was about to become intimately acquainted with.

Deep in thought, she turned the corner and nearly ran into a tall, dark-haired man in a Trinity Western leather jacket.

"Hey. Watch it, lady." The man grabbed Kathryn by both arms.

"*Me* watch it? You were the one barreling along the sidewalk without watching where you were going. You could have knocked me off my feet."

A grin flashed across his face and ignited in his deep blue eyes. "I thought I already did that." He leaned in and kissed her on the lips before pulling her into his arms. "How's my girl?"

Kathryn rested her cheek on his chest. "Good now, Ty. Weren't we meeting at Toby's?"

"I got there a bit early, so I figured I'd walk this way and run into you. Which I did. Literally."

"Let's head there now. I'm starving."

Ty draped his arm over her shoulders as they turned and walked a couple of blocks to their favorite restaurant. Bells jangled when he opened the door, and Kathryn smiled in anticipation. She was about to step into the doorway when a man in a jean jacket with wavy blond hair pushed past her on the sidewalk. Ty caught her as she stumbled toward him.

"Hey!" Kathryn craned her neck to peer around the door, but the blond man had disappeared.

Ty tipped up her chin with his fingers. "He's gone. Are you all right?"

"I guess so." Kathryn rubbed her right shoulder and threw one last glance down the street before stepping into the restaurant. "Seems to be my night for crashing into men I don't see coming." It didn't take long for her good humor to return. Walking through the door of Toby's was like being wrapped in the enthusiastic embrace of a friend. The pulse of the place—the beat of the music, lively conversations, the loud clinking of dishes—infused her with energy and excitement.

Ty slid into the brown leather booth across from her and grabbed her hands. "I've missed you." He lifted one to his mouth and kissed the back of it. Even sitting, Kathryn's knees went weak. "It feels like forever since I've seen you."

"Ty, I saw you in class yesterday morning and then we had coffee together in the cafeteria. It's been like thirty-two hours since we've been together."

"That's thirty-one too long." He squeezed her fingers then let go as the server arrived and set two glasses of ice water in front of them.

Kathryn watched him as he chatted with the woman. *He is so cute.* Her gaze dropped to his arms, resting on the table. The rigorous workout schedule his hockey coach had him on was paying off. Muscles bulged along the length of them. *I'd be content to stay in those arms forever.*

"Kath?" Yanked from her daydream, she realized Ty had already ordered, and he and the server were watching her expectantly. A sudden flush warmed her face. She gripped her drink, resisting the urge to lift it and press the cool wet glass to her cheek.

Ty grinned as if reading her thoughts. "She'll have the deluxe burger with the works and a side of fries."

Their server scratched the order on a pad of paper before gathering up their menus and hurrying away.

When Kathryn's eyes met Ty's, one corner of his mouth turned up in the half-smile she loved.

"What?"

She lifted a shoulder. "It's nice when someone knows your usual."

His eyes softened. "I want to know everything about you, Kath."

The air appeared to have been sucked from the room. Ty held her gaze for a moment, then picked up his glass of water and took a sip.

Kathryn relaxed against the leather seat, grateful he had broken the intensity of the moment. She took a deep breath to slow her heart rate, drawing in the smell of frying grease that would always remind her of this place.

"How's your shoulder?" he asked.

She touched it lightly. "A little sore. No big deal."

"You handled that well. I thought I might get to experience the Ellison temper I've heard about but don't think I've seen yet."

Kathryn grinned. "If you don't think you've seen it, you probably haven't, or you'd know it."

"Just as well that guy took off so fast then. Things might've gotten ugly."

"Yeah, and he better hope we don't run into each other again." She raised both hands in front of her chest like a boxer and jabbed at the air with her fists.

"Remind me never to cross you."

"Don't cross me. Consider yourself warned."

Ty laughed and set down his glass. "Hey, what are we doing to celebrate our graduation?"

Before she could reply, the waitress returned with their food.

Between bites of cheeseburger, Kathryn told him about her day and asked about his. She watched his face as he spoke, trying hard to focus on what he was saying and not on his incredible blue eyes. The stained-glass chandelier above their heads dropped a soft golden circle around them, as though they were the only two people in the room.

"What do you think?"

Kathryn popped one last fry into her mouth and pushed away her plate. "About what?"

"About our graduation. What should we do to celebrate?"

She bit her lip.

"What is it? You're looking awfully guilty about something."

"No, not guilty." She wiped her fingers on the paper napkin. "But I do have something to tell you, and I'm not sure how you're going to feel about it."

Ty pushed his own plate away and contemplated her.

Kathryn tossed the crumpled napkin on her plate. "I've been thinking about doing something big to celebrate, like ..."

"Like?"

"Taking a trip to Europe."

Ty's eyebrows rose as he reached for her hands again. "You're going away?"

"We're thinking about it. I mean, you only graduate from university once. We want to do something memorable."

"Who's we?" Before she could reply, he shook his head. "Never mind, I know who. You and Meg and Claire."

Her eyes narrowed at his tone, and she tugged her hands free and clasped them in her lap. "Come on, Ty. They're my best friends."

"I know that. And you know how I feel about them. Meg's a sweetheart and Claire ... well, Claire's fun." The teasing was back in his voice. "You know, like a tornado whirling through the room is fun."

It was useless to try and stay mad at him, especially when he scrunched up his face as though berating himself for his reaction.

"I'm sorry." He swirled his straw through the last of his chocolate milkshake. "You caught me by surprise. It's a great idea. In fact, I'd love to go with you and sleep on your hotel room floor or something. Although I guess your parents wouldn't really go for that. Or Aaron." He glanced around the room as though her big brother might be lurking in a corner, watching them.

Kathryn winced. "Ultimately he wouldn't have a say in it, but he'd probably make it clear what he thought of the two of us sharing a hotel room thousands of miles away."

"Where are you planning to go?"

"We haven't decided for sure. Paris, of course. London. Rome." A shiver of pleasure rippled through her at the thought of cafés, cathedrals, palaces, and canals winding through ancient Italian cities. She rested her chin on one hand and sighed.

Ty let out a short laugh. "Seems like you've got your heart set on this trip. As long as you don't meet some handsome French guy and forget about me, I'll try to be happy for you."

"Somehow I don't think that's going to happen."

His gaze was intense, and for a moment she couldn't tear her eyes away. *I really should go.* Time seemed to defy all laws when she was with him and fly mercilessly by. She glanced at her watch and wrinkled her nose.

Ty's shoulders slumped. "No. Tell me you don't have to leave."

"I'm sorry."

"I'm going to take this away from you." His fingers circled her watch, and her heart skipped a beat. "You're always leaving me to go to a meeting or basketball practice or to work on an assignment. It's Saturday night—what could you possibly have to do?"

"I need to work on my lesson for tomorrow. Those nine-year-old girls in my Sunday school class will be all over me if I'm not prepared."

Ty groaned. "Tell me again why you agreed to teach that class?"

"I like it. The girls are great. They're always asking me questions I really have to think about." Kathryn slid to the end of the bench and stood. If she didn't leave now she might not leave at all.

Ty shook his head, then reached for the wallet in his pocket and dropped a credit card on top of the bill.

"You don't have to go." Kathryn lifted her jacket from the back of the chair.

"That's okay. I'll walk you to your car. I should head home too. As long as you're going to put your nose to the grind-stone…"

Kathryn rolled her eyes. "Nice image."

Ty tapped the end of her nose.

A flash of school pride shot through her as she slid her own Trinity Western University jacket on over her red shirt. It had been a great four years, and in spite of her excitement about the upcoming trip to Europe and then grad school, part of her was sad to be leaving. She gathered her long dark hair in one hand and tugged it out of the collar of her jacket, then let it drop before grabbing her backpack.

Ty reached for her hand as they walked down the quiet street. Kathryn lifted her head to let the cool evening air brush past her face, the soft scent of lilacs on its breath. Although the sun had sunk low in the sky, the streetlights hadn't come on yet. The Accord waited for her, deep in shadow from the tree she'd parked under.

Ty brushed his hand over a patch of rust above the rear window. "Tell me again why you drive this old clunker?"

"Old clunker! This car is a classic. She keeps going and going."

"Like you do whenever the subject comes up." Ty laughed and took a step toward her.

Heart beating rapidly, Kathryn gazed up at him. A serious expression replaced his half-smile. "You're so beautiful." Taking her face in his hands, he pressed his lips to hers.

Kathryn closed her eyes and wrapped her arms around his neck.

Both thumbs stroked her cheeks as he lifted his head. "I love you."

26

"Really?" Surprise rippled through her as the words he'd said—for the first time—lingered on the air.

"Yes, really." He kissed her on the forehead. "Now get going before I decide I can't share you with those nine-year-old girls."

Kathryn sighed. "All right. Thanks for dinner, Ty."

He patted his back pocket. "Shoot. That reminds me. I left my credit card with the bill. Are you okay here or do you want me to wait?"

"No, go. I have to find my keys and then I'll be off."

"Okay. See you tomorrow." Trailing his fingers across her cheek, he turned to head to the restaurant.

Kathryn slid the backpack off her shoulder and gripped it in one hand, feeling around the front pocket for her keys. She yanked them out and fumbled to fit the right one into the passenger side door. The dying daylight made it difficult to see much. *Come on. Come on.* The locks disengaged. She yanked open the door and tossed her bag onto the back seat, then slammed it and walked around the front of the car. The clicking of her high-heeled boots on the pavement echoed along the quiet street.

She sat behind the wheel for a moment, staring out the front window. A slow smile crossed her face. "He loves me." She patted the dashboard. "What do you think of that, old girl? And I'm heading to Europe and then grad school. Could my life be any more perfect?"

I winced. Even now footsteps she couldn't hear over the thudding of her heart and her own voice tracked along the sidewalk toward her car. Maybe her life couldn't be any more perfect than it was in this moment.

But it could—and was about to—become a whole lot less so.

Chapter Five

With a small shake of her head, Kathryn leaned forward to insert the key into the ignition. Before she could, the door opened and Ty slid onto the passenger seat. A thrill shot through Kathryn as she straightened. "Did you miss me al—?"

It wasn't Ty. The jean jacket was familiar, though, and the wavy blond hair. The man's cold, hard stare hit her as forcefully as his shoulder had a couple of hours before. Her cry was choked off by the terror that lodged itself in her throat like a tangible object. Kathryn lunged for the door handle.

Before her shaking fingers could close around it, the man pressed something round and hard to the side of her head. "Don't." His voice was as cold as the barrel of the gun. "Start driving."

Her lungs felt caught in a vice. The stranger's terse commands increased the fear building in her chest until she gasped for breath. *Do what he says. Everything will be fine.* The keys jangled in her hand as she tried to insert the right one into the ignition.

Not fast enough to suit him. Drawing back the gun, he hit her on the side of the head. Stars exploded before her eyes.

"Now."

A stabbing pain shot behind her right eye. Kathryn blinked back tears. She managed to shove the key into the ignition and turn it. Worship music filled the car, a track from the praise CD she'd been listening to on the way to the restaurant. With a muttered oath, the man hit the button on the stereo with his fist until the music stopped. His eyes and the weapon never left Kathryn.

"Let's go." He gestured down the street with the gun.

No. I can't go with him. But if I refuse ... Kathryn slid the car into gear. She'd driven down this street a hundred times, but now all the familiar landmarks appeared strange and slightly out of focus, as though she'd put on someone else's glasses by mistake.

"This is not happening," she murmured through trembling lips.

"Shut up!" The blond man pulled the gun back in warning. Kathryn pressed her lips together. "Take the next right."

As they approached the end of the quiet street, Kathryn glanced in her rear-view mirror. The streetlights had come on, and a warm glow, reflected in the mirror, suffused the spot where she and Ty had stood.

She clung to the sight until her car rounded the corner and the light faded away.

As you know, there is almost nothing I enjoy more than a good metaphor. In this case, I draw no satisfaction from the dying of the light. Kathryn would not, as it turned out, go quietly into the night. Still, sometimes a person can rail against it all she wants but the darkness comes anyway, blanketing and suffocating and impenetrable.

Tuesday

I was pulled into the present by the sound of a not-quite repressed sob. Kathryn sat with her forehead pressed to the photo she'd set on her knees. I couldn't stand it. My hands slipped from behind my back and I reached for her, tentatively resting the tips of my fingers on the sleeve of her pale blue sundress.

A distant rumbling rippled through the air. A stern warning that even the watcher was being watched. I snatched my hand away but wasn't as quick to repress the slightly rebellious hope that my touch, even if she hadn't actually felt it, had been of some small help to Kathryn Ellison.

Because I had the distinct feeling that in the hours and days to come, she was going to need as much of that as she could get.

Chapter Six

The squeaking of the woodstove door drew my attention. Kathryn had lowered herself to one knee in front of the fire, still holding the picture of Ty. For a few seconds she stared into the flickering flames. Then she took a deep breath, inhaling courage, and flung the picture into the fire. Something deep inside of her shriveled up with the photo, but she didn't make any attempt to grab it, only shut the door with a decisive clang.

The shrill ringing of her cell phone startled us both. Kathryn pushed to her feet and rounded the coffee table, grabbing the device as she dropped onto her seat. I took the opportunity to cross the room and sink into the armchair next to the fire, feeling old and worn out and in as much need as I had ever been of a nice long snooze in front of the woodstove.

"Hello?" The word came out dry and raspy, and Kathryn cleared her throat.

"Mom? Is everything okay? I've been going crazy here, waiting for you to call me."

"Oh, Tory, I'm sorry. I got busy doing something and forgot."

"What's going on? Who came to see you?"

Kathryn hesitated. The two of them shared everything that happened in their lives, every detail of their day, their present. The past, however, she guarded fiercely, kept it hidden and locked deep away in, well, a shoebox in the hidden recesses of her closet. Ty and David were locked up in that box and rarely let out. Even Nick, who had been a shadow in the background of her life for so long and had shown up now, very much in the present. He was so tied up with her past—with everything that had happened That Night and the months and years that followed— that she was clearly having difficulty separating the two. When she lifted her chin, I knew she had managed it.

"Nick Lawson."

I could hear the quick intake of breath through the phone and managed a grin, in spite of the emotional turmoil still swirling through me. Tory was good that way. No matter what you were going through, she could almost always make you smile, whether she meant to or not. "Really? How did that go?"

"It was interesting."

"Interesting? What does that mean?"

In contrast, Kathryn's breath was a soft exhalation. "I'm not exactly sure. He … wants us to be together."

"Mom!"

I winced at the loud squeal. Kathryn moved the phone slightly away from her ear.

"Finally. I knew the day I met him in the coffee shop that the two of you were meant to be together."

She pressed the phone to her ear again. "Tory. How could you? You were only a kid."

"It was so obvious. I've never understood why you didn't get together before now."

Kathryn bit her lower lip. "It's never been the right time for us."

"Why not?"

"You know. Life stuff." She picked up a square coaster with a picture of the Eiffel Tower on it—the closest she ever came to seeing the real thing—and absently tapped the edge on the end table.

"Mom, you do know I'm not still a kid, right?"

Kathryn sighed. "Yes, my darling daughter. I am very well aware."

"Tell me you said yes."

"I haven't said anything yet. I told him I had a few things I needed to do first." She set the coaster on the pile with three others.

"What things?" Tory sounded incredulous. Of course, she was nineteen, still at an age where nothing in the world was big enough to come between two people who were meant to be together. She had a lot to learn.

I was sure that, in spite of my best efforts, she would do so soon enough.

"Some things from my past that I need to work through." Kathryn kneaded the afghan flung over the arm of the couch.

An uncharacteristic silence fell at the other end of the line. My stomach tightened. Kathryn pressed her eyes shut, clearly suspecting that the topic she had studiously avoided since Tory was old enough to start asking questions was about to come up once again.

"Do these *things* have anything to do with my father?"

The question was hard and cold and laced with pain. Her mother didn't answer.

"Mom?"

Kathryn's eyes opened, hazel pools of fear. "That's part of it, yes."

My own eyes widened in shock. That was as much of an admission of willingness to open the door on the past as I had ever heard her make to her daughter. Nick Lawson's arrival on the front porch had obviously set major changes in motion. I shifted on my chair and crossed my legs, settling in. Things were getting mighty intriguing around here, that was for sure.

Tory must have been as shocked as I was, because her mother's words were met with another long silence. I couldn't remember there ever being two in any conversation involving Kathryn's daughter—one of the many reasons I liked her so much.

When she did speak, the words pushed her mother against the pillows on the couch, dread and resignation flitting across her face.

"I'm tired of waiting, Mom. I'm coming home on Sunday so we can talk. I need to know who my father is, and I'm hoping you'll help me find him. If not, I've decided to do everything I can to find him on my own."

Kathryn set the phone on the end table and got up. I watched as she crossed the room, hoping she wasn't going far since I didn't particularly feel like getting up to follow. She stopped in the doorway and braced herself with a hand against the frame. Her shoulders sagged, as though all that had happened in the hour since she had seen Nick Lawson on the other side of the screen door had settled there, threatening to drive her to her knees. After a few seconds, she pushed herself away and disappeared into the kitchen. I could hear her moving around, opening cupboard doors and setting something on the counter with a soft clink. A mug, likely. I knew her well enough to know that she wouldn't be making anything to eat, not when she was so upset. Tea then.

So I'd been wrong earlier. In my defence, everything was turned around and flipped over and backwards around here tonight, so my discombobulation could certainly be excused. The kettle whistled, followed by the gurgling sound of hot water being poured into the pot. Good, she'd be coming back soon and—

The screen door creaked and my heart sank. Kathryn was taking her tea out to the porch.

With a heavy sigh, I uncurled myself from the soft chair and rose to stand on weary legs. When I stepped outside, Kathryn stood, steaming mug in hand, at the top of the porch stairs, a shoulder propped against the post. Darkness had crept across the ranch since we'd gone inside. Her head was tipped back, her eyes fixed on the bright crescent moon, its soft light streaming through the branches of the big oak tree in the front yard to fall, dappled and dancing in the cool evening breeze, at her bare feet.

As a general principle, I avoid listening in on prayers. Occasionally I am even blocked from overhearing them, which I understand—the conversations are too intimate, too personal. Tonight I caught the fervent thoughts as they streamed upwards and the gentle responses as clearly as if the two of them were sitting on the white wicker chairs on the porch carrying on a conversation. I leaned against the stone wall and crossed my arms over my chest, content to stand back and listen as Kathryn wrestled with her thoughts and with her God.

What should she do? If Tory tried, she could find out what happened that night. She was so determined, eventually she'd think to research newspaper archives online. Someone on a computer could find out pretty much anything in five minutes these days. Kathryn rubbed her free hand hard across her forehead. Had she been wrong to keep this from her daughter? Maybe she should tell her the truth, tell her about her father.

She dropped her hand and stared at the moon. A cloud drifted across the face of it. Instead of obscuring the orb, the light emanating from the moon was so strong that the cloud glowed, its edges shimmering with gold. The dread that had tightened around her heart since she'd talked to Tory began to lose its grip.

A tear slid down her cheek. *Even if I did decide to tell her, I couldn't. I don't know who her father is.*

Ask him.

A wave of pain gripped her, and she pressed a hand to her stomach. *I can't.*

Ask him.

She lifted a fist to her mouth. Talk to David Henley? She couldn't. She'd have to go see him, turn his life upside-down. And hers. There had to be another way.

Silence.

Kathryn closed her eyes. *I know. There is no other way. But I can't do it alone.*

You are never alone.

Like an arm sweeping across a cluttered table, the words cleared away the last of the fear and anxiety that had been tying her insides into knots.

She opened her eyes. Through the branches of the tree, the moon burned so brightly the night around it seemed to have relinquished itself to the day.

The light always overcomes the darkness somehow, doesn't it?

Always.

Resting the side of her head against the porch post—I couldn't help wondering how many weary heads that old wooden post had supported over the years—she nodded in surrender. *All right, I'll go. If you're sending me, I know it's the right thing to do.* One last thought passed through her mind as she gazed up at the brilliant moon, a satellite reflecting a much greater light onto her.

I only hope and pray that David Henley will feel the same way.

Chapter Seven

Tuesday

Kathryn couldn't see it, of course, but the cloud that had risen over the horizon was growing darker.

Kevin Dylan. Ever since That Night, the awareness of his continued presence on the planet had buried itself in the back of her brain like a malignant tumor whose reaching, grasping tentacles did their best to choke out the possibility of her ever finding me.

Even when news of his arrest reached her through Olivia Drayton, the investigating officer who had become a close friend throughout Kathryn's long ordeal, the paralyzing fear had never gone away completely—fear that, although she had been rescued from the cold darkness and returned to the warmth and light she had been surrounded by all of her life, she still wasn't safe.

And now it appeared as though that fear might be justified.

Fear is no friend of mine, let me tell you. In fact, he may be my greatest enemy, so when my charges wrestle with him it is usually me that ends up the worse for wear. I had gotten pretty beaten up over the years whenever Fear and Kathryn confronted each other, and I couldn't suppress the thought that the biggest battle was yet to come. One in which I may be annihilated completely.

Maybe not. Maybe everything would be fine. So you don't think I'm withholding valuable information from you regarding what will happen to Kathryn, the truth is that I honestly don't know. I am incapable of seeing the future. I'm not God, you know, as Faith is very fond of reminding me. He and I *are* on excellent terms, in spite of the fact that, although I have pleaded with Him to do so,

He steadfastly refuses to promise me to anyone, even His own.

As Faith explains to me, on the many occasions that I ask her about it, it's the way things are on this planet. Too many shadows stretch across its surface, too much darkness hovers over it like a second layer of charred atmosphere. In spite of the darkness, this world and its inhabitants continue to be dear to God's heart, which I understand. There is something about humans—their strength and vulnerability, their ability to love and overcome and reach out to each other—that draws one in and makes it impossible to turn away. In spite of their weaknesses, which are considerable. Vast even.

No offense.

I do have the blessing—or the curse, I've never quite decided—of being transported, virtually instantaneously, from one place to another. I can be taken anywhere that something is happening that could affect the future of my current charge. And, at the moment, that includes a prison in Wyoming. Death Row, to be exact. The current home of Kevin Dylan who, for better or worse—and given his history, it's almost certainly for the worse—very definitely wields the power to affect my relationship with Kathryn. I resist this transportation, as that dark hole is the very last place I want to be, but to no avail.

A damp cold seeps through my bones as I settle onto a hard, plastic, institution-issued chair.

A far cry from the soft armchair in front of Kathryn's fireplace, I reflect with no small degree of bitterness.

Tuesday

"Move along, Dylan." The tall man in the white jacket, small paper hat perched on his head, gestured down the line with a ladle dripping globs of stew.

Dylan made no attempt to hide his disgust as he stared at the contents of the bowl. He pushed his tray along the rollers toward the man holding a set of tongs in one hand and standing behind a pile of soggy toast.

"Looks like pig-slop," Dylan said. "They feed us like animals in here."

"If the shoe fits."

Dylan's dark glare sent the smart-mouthed server stumbling back a step, his face pale. *Good. Haven't lost my touch yet.*

Throwing his tray on the table with a loud clatter, Dylan slouched onto a chair and took a bite of the lukewarm food. He grimaced and tossed his spoon onto the tray, a string of curse words spewing from his lips.

"Play your cards right, Dylan, and you could be stuffing your face with prime rib and gravy by the end of the week."

Irritated, he glanced up from his meal. Matt McGregor, an inmate he played poker with a few nights a week, leaned down and spoke the words out of the corner of his mouth before sliding onto the chair across from him.

"What are you talking about?"

McGregor surveyed the empty tables around them, then picked up a piece of toast and took a bite. "How are you set?"

"What do you mean?"

"Financially."

Dylan studied the tall, red-headed man. He didn't trust him, of course. Only a fool would trust anyone in this place. Still, something in his manner made Dylan want to stay and finish the conversation, which didn't happen to him often. And what difference did it make if someone found out he had money hidden away? It was useless to him now. His eyes narrowed. Or maybe it *wasn't* useless.

"I've made a few bucks over the years, I guess." He picked up the spoon and swirled it through the greasy mess in his bowl. "Socked most of it away. It's not like I had a family to support or anything."

McGregor nodded. "That's what I figured." Another furtive look around.

Dylan alternated between intrigued and impatient. Against his better judgment he was leaning toward intrigued. "What about it?"

"Something might be in the works."

"What?"

"Someone on the inside has indicated he might be available, for a price, to help a couple of us get out of here."

"Who?"

"I can't tell you that," McGregor said. "All I need to know is who's in. He'll only take two besides me. Something told me you might be more interested in getting out of here than most of the others, now that your date's set. It'll cost you, of course."

Dylan let out a short laugh. "Of course. Everything does." He absently separated a kernel of corn from the gravy. "But yeah, I'm in."

McGregor studied him. "Seems like there's something else you want out for, other than saving your neck. You got a hot girl on the outside?"

"That's not your business. You get me out of here and I'll pay whatever it takes."

McGregor shrugged. "Fair enough. That's all I care about anyway." Shoving the last bite of toast into his mouth, he grabbed his tray and stood. "I'll be in touch."

"When?"

"Soon. In the next twenty-four hours. Be ready."

Dylan tapped the spoon against the side of the bowl. *Well, whaddya know?* Without thinking about it, he shoved the utensil into the mound of congealing stew and took a bite. He nearly spit it into the bowl, but managed to swallow it and throw the spoon onto the tray again. Whatever. Seemed he might be eating anything he wanted to in the next few days. He shook his head and picked up the tray. Not that he'd believe anything until he saw it, but it was an interesting prospect. He got up and walked over to Toast Guy, who took the tray Dylan shoved at him without meeting his eyes.

Back in his cell, Dylan reached under the mattress and took out the piece of paper he always kept there. *Unfinished business, McGregor. That's what I want out of here for.* Running his fingers over the ripped and yellowing newspaper clipping, a cold smile almost imperceptibly turned up the corners of his mouth.

And there was nothing he wouldn't pay to get out of this place and finish it.

I shuddered as Kathryn opened the screen door of the old farmhouse, unaware of what was happening twelve hundred miles from her home. In a way, I envied her. If ignorance was bliss, then it followed that too much knowledge must be absolute misery. And I felt about as miserable now, watching what was unfolding, as I had ever felt before.

Something, or someone, was coming. And I had a terrible feeling that nothing good could possibly come of its arrival.

Chapter Eight

Tuesday

Kathryn dumped her untouched tea into the sink and rinsed out the mug before returning to the living room.

> I will refrain from any smug comments about how I had been right about her not drinking tea after all, since pettiness is a weakness I refuse to indulge in. Faith might tell you differently, but I maintain that what she regards as pettiness is merely a reflection of how deeply acquainted I am with my charge. And I should be deeply acquainted with Kathryn Ellison, after all these years. I certainly know when the woman feels like a cup of tea, and when she does not.
>
> There is nothing petty in that, is there?

Kathryn stumbled over to the couch and dropped onto it. Her thoughts whirled, but when she stretched out and tugged the afghan off the back of the couch to drape over herself, exhaustion dragged her eyelids closed. In moments, her breathing had deepened. I made myself comfortable on the armchair next to the fire. My own eyelids were heavy, but I propped my elbow on the arm of the chair and rested my chin on my hand, wanting to keep an eye on her to see if she was okay.

Good thing I did. Before long, she moaned in her sleep and then flopped onto her side. Distress flitted across her face. This was more than a nightmare. Kathryn had gone back to That Night and was reliving the experience all over again. I didn't have the strength to get out of the armchair and go to her, but she wasn't alone. Terror and Horror—Fear's bigger, meaner cousins—had shown up and slipped under the afghan with her.

April 1999

Kathryn gripped the steering wheel until her knuckles gleamed white in the deepening twilight. She risked a sideways glance at the man beside her. The eyes that met hers were as cold as ice. They narrowed to menacing slits, sending shivers of terror rippling up and down her spine. *You have to do something.* All she could think of was to obey the commands thrown at her. And pray.

Even that was hard to do. Words and thoughts whipped through her mind, but she could only grasp hold of one of them. *Jesus.* Kathryn clung to the word like an outstretched hand, knowing if she lost her grip she'd hurtle into the black nothingness below.

As they drove through the quiet streets of Langley, the man leaned against the passenger door, half-turned to face her. The gun rested on his bent knee, pointed at Kathryn. "That was a very touching scene back there."

Her fingers tightened on the steering wheel.

"Of course you know he's lying." The stranger laughed. "Every man in the world eventually tells you he loves you. Funny how those warm fuzzy feelings disappear as soon as he gets you into—"

"Hey." Kathryn glared at the man. "You don't know him and you don't know me. And I'm not about to take relationship advice from a guy who has to use a gun to get a woman to go with him."

When his eyes narrowed, she bit her lip and shifted her attention to the road. Had she pushed him too far? The car had started to cross the center line, and she jerked to the right. Lucky there wasn't anything coming.

When the stranger spoke, every word was an icy finger trailing up and down her spine. "If I were you, I'd keep my mouth shut, lady. You do *not* want to make me mad."

"Maybe you don't want to make me mad either." Defiance

was useless, given the odds, but she drew strength from it anyway.

The man snorted. "Oh, I think I've already done that. The difference is," he bent forward and stroked her cheek with the barrel of the gun. "If I get angry, I can do something about it."

Infuriated, Kathryn swiped the gun away with her right hand. His arm shot out and his fingers closed over her wrist. He squeezed until a sharp pain snaked all the way to her shoulder. She bit her lip to keep from crying out.

"You are really pushing your luck, girl." Warm breath dampened her cheek as he hissed the words into her ear. "In fact, I'm starting to think you might be too much trouble." The barrel of the gun pressed into her head, behind her ear.

She struggled to take a breath. Neither of them spoke or moved for several seconds. Then the man let out a cold, humorless laugh and let her go. Kathryn desperately wanted to rub her throbbing wrist, but she refused to give him the satisfaction.

He shrugged and slumped against the passenger door. "Do whatever you want with my *relationship* advice. It doesn't matter anymore."

Her chest constricted. "Who are you and what do you want with me?" She hated that her voice trembled when she spoke.

His eyes remained ice-cold, but a mocking smile twisted across his lips. "I don't want anything with you, sweetheart," he drawled. "I'm only the delivery boy."

"What's that supposed to mean?" She glanced at him. "Who are you delivering me to?"

His grin was taunting, and she gritted her teeth. "I'm sure you can figure that out. Who would want you badly enough to go to all this trouble?"

No one Kathryn could think of would do this to her. A light began to dawn. "I think you have the wrong person."

The mirthless smile died. "No more talking." Steel returned to his voice. "The Fraser Highway east exit is next. Get on it." He waved the gun to underscore the terse order.

Shaking her head in disbelief, Kathryn pulled onto the ramp. She picked up speed as she merged with the highway traffic. Terror spun itself around her like a spider enveloping its still-living victim. *This is it.* Despair sucked the breath from her body. *I'm going to die.*

The relief came slowly. A sharp blade of anger working its way through the fear, cutting away the layers until she was able to gasp in air. An idea niggled at the back of her mind. Kathryn tried hard to pin it down. Lucky there wasn't anything coming. The pounding in her chest intensified. If she swerved into the lane of the car next to her, enough to cause a minor accident, they'd have to stop, or someone would call the police at least.

Gripping the steering wheel, she edged the car over the line. The drawn-out honk of the vehicle in the fast lane alerted her abductor. Diving across the seat, he grabbed a handful of hair and jerked her toward him and against the cold barrel of the gun. This time she couldn't keep from crying out as white-hot pain shot across her scalp.

His mouth an inch from her ear, the man spoke in a cold, calm voice. "If you do that again, I will kill you. Then I will kill every person who comes over to this car to see if we need help. Do you hear me?"

Terror robbed her of speech. She nodded her head as slightly as possible. Even that small movement caused stabs of pain where he still held her hair in his grasp. The man pushed her head away and trained the gun at her ribs. "That was your last warning. Any more trouble from you and I swear I'll put a bullet through your head and throw you into the ditch." He inclined his head toward the side of the road. "I'm not getting paid enough to put up with a woman who doesn't have the sense to shut up and do what she's told."

No, she'd never been very good at that. Kathryn bit her lip until she tasted blood. What did that mean, he wasn't getting paid enough? Who would pay him to do this to her? The throbbing in her head made it difficult to think.

I will never leave you. Words from one of the Sunday school lessons she'd prepared for her girls whirred through her mind like ticker tape.

I want to believe that. But why can't I feel you? As aware as she was of the other person in the vehicle, Kathryn felt completely and utterly alone. What about Ty or her family at home on the ranch? Would any of them realize she was missing and call the police? Her heart sank. Her roommates from school had all gone home for the weekend. Ty and Aaron and her parents believed she was busy getting her Sunday school lesson ready and wouldn't expect to hear from her until tomorrow.

It's you and me then. She lifted her chin and blinked back stinging tears. *Please don't leave me.*

"Get off here."

Kathryn jumped, then signaled and moved into the exit lane. Where was he taking her? They were getting pretty far from anywhere. They stopped at the end of the ramp for a red light. The only sound was the incessant clicking of the signal.

"Almost there, gorgeous." The mocking tone was back.

Fresh terror coursed through her. *Don't leave me.*

Houses lined the road they traveled on. Light poured from every window. Kathryn caught a glimpse of a family sitting around a dinner table, gesturing and laughing. She felt oddly disconnected from that world now—what was happening to her was the only reality that existed. Glancing into the windows of the homes they passed was like fixing her eyes on a flickering TV screen, as though the images she was seeing were only the product of someone's imagination. She turned her wrist and checked the time. 8:20. Aaron would be feeding the horses now. She blinked back tears. Would she ever see him again or breathe in the comforting smell of her horse Bonnie, her sides warm and heaving after a long run?

The houses grew farther and farther apart. Kathryn peered through the fog that swirled in front of the headlights. The row of streetlamps ended fifty yards ahead. After that, a heavy blackness loomed. *I can't go into that dark.* Her heart pounded. She had to stay in the light.

She lifted her foot from the gas pedal then closed her eyes at the sharp click of the gun being cocked. Reluctantly, she pressed on the accelerator again. The thick night soon swallowed the car, extinguishing the dim glow behind them.

After several minutes, the stranger's cold voice broke the silence. "Turn here, that road to the right."

Kathryn eased the car along a bumpy gravel road. The man straightened in his seat. They must be close. Her stomach clenched. What now? When the man gestured with the gun, she turned off the road onto a long driveway with deep ruts that jostled the car as they drove.

"Stop here."

She braked in front of a dilapidated old building and shifted into park. Before the headlights went out, Kathryn caught a quick glimpse. The old cabin leaned precariously to one side. A jagged crack ran down the middle of the front window and the bottom corner had fallen out. Dim light shone through gaping holes in the uneven curtains.

Kathryn tensed her muscles, prepared to run while her captor was getting out of the car. Clouds covered the sliver of moon. If she could get a few feet away from him, she was sure she could get lost in the darkness.

That faint hope vanished as the door of the cabin flew open. A tall, lanky man came out, the screen door slamming behind him. In the dull light of the cobweb-encrusted bulb dangling beside the door, she watched in trepidation as he stepped over the missing boards on the porch and strode toward the car.

"Where have you been?" He jerked open the driver's side door. "I've been waiting for hours."

"She wasn't alone when she got to the restaurant." The blond man sounded disgusted. "I had to wait until she came back out. I was beginning to think I'd have to spend the night in that alley."

"Couldn't be any worse than this place."

Kathryn bit her lip to keep from crying out as the tall man grabbed her elbow. He yanked her from the car.

This is my last chance. She ground the heel of her leather boot into the top of his foot. The man yelped and stumbled forward, loosening his grip on her arm. One hard pull and she was free.

But only for a couple of steps. He lunged forward, grabbed her wrist, and spun her around. The loud smack of his palm across her cheek split the silence of the night.

"Don't do that again," the man warned in a low, hard voice. The stranger who had brought her there laughed.

Kathryn had never been struck in anger before. Pain exploded across her face and neck. Rising fury draped a veil of red over her vision. *How dare you ...*

The tall man twisted her arm behind her until the muscles and tendons in her shoulder felt as though they were being torn out of place. He shoved her up the steps and through the doorway. Kathryn glanced around the desolate room. Then something hit the back of her head with a force that snapped her chin to her chest, and everything went black.

Chapter Nine

Tuesday

Impenetrable gloom cloaked the living room. The drapes hanging on either side of the windows were open, but as they had the night Kathryn had been taken, thick clouds had slid across the moon and the tiny golden sliver didn't have the strength to try to penetrate them. *The light always overcomes the darkness. The light always overcomes the darkness.* I tried to cling to the promise, but my joints were weak and sore and it slipped through my fingers like water.

A cold mist the dying fire could do nothing to dispel crept across the floor, swirling around my feet and up my legs. "Faith?" I croaked the word, my throat dry and raw. I knew she was there, somewhere, but she didn't answer me. The mist was too thick for my straining eyes to make out her form. I sagged against the chair, helpless to do anything but watch as my strength waned.

April 1999

The cold was excruciating. Kathryn clung to the murky world between asleep and awake, terrified to open her eyes. Her hands were drawn over her head. She tugged hard, desperate to free herself. Fire raced along her arms. Her wrists chafed and burned. Kathryn's eyes flew open, and she twisted her head. Her hands were bound with rope to the metal headboard of a bed. A wave of nausea washed over her, and she squeezed her eyes shut.

Don't move. Don't move.

The smell of whiskey hanging heavy in the air stung her throat. Throbs of pain shot from her right temple and the base of her skull. Even in the meager light she winced as she cracked open her eyes, trying to get her bearings.

She lay on an old, musty-smelling bed in one corner of the

room. The quilt covering it may have been colorful once, but now it was worn and faded to a dull gray. When she shifted, trying to ease the discomfort in her arms, puffs of dust wafted into the air. Kathryn risked a glance around her in the dim moonlight trickling through the torn curtains.

The two men sat at a rough wooden table, a half-empty bottle between them. The man with the long blond hair was carving something in the wood with a sharp knife. Kathryn caught her breath at the sight. The other man stared into his drink.

The cabin was one large room. The furnishings were sparse—an old brown couch with several springs poking through the stuffing and two wooden chairs, one missing an arm and the other held together with duct tape. Someone had made a futile attempt to brighten the room by framing pictures of flowers cut out of magazines.

"What time's he coming, Henley?"

Kathryn jumped when the man who'd brought her spoke. *Henley.* She filed the name of the tall, thin man away.

"All he said was late morning."

"Well, he better have the cash with him. Nothing I'd like more than to stick a knife in the gut of that psycho. No one would find him out here for years."

Henley nudged his glass aside and reached for her backpack.

Her fists clenched as he rooted through it and withdrew her wallet. *Hands off. That's mine.* Seething, Kathryn watched as he riffled through her cards.

"Dylan!"

Every nerve in Kathryn's body stretched taut at the sudden outburst.

Dylan's head shot up. "What?"

"It's not her. You picked up the wrong girl."

A surge of hope rose in her. If she wasn't the one they wanted, maybe they would let her go. Her shoulders slumped. More likely they'd kill her rather than risk her going to the police, especially now that she knew both of their names. Her forehead wrinkled. Who did they think she was and what did they want with that other woman? None of this made any sense.

Dylan grabbed for her driver's license. "Let me see that." He stared at the picture for a few seconds. His arm swept across the table, sending the backpack and its contents clattering across the floor.

"How did that happen?" Henley's fist smashed onto the table. "You had the description of her car, and you knew where she was going to be. She was practically handed to you and you couldn't get it right."

Dylan shoved his chair away from the table and rose unsteadily to his feet. Slamming the knife on the table so hard that whiskey sloshed out of both their glasses, he leaned across the table until his face was inches from Henley's.

"Look at her!" Dylan said. Kathryn flinched as he thrust his arm in her direction. "She has long, dark hair, like he said. How was I supposed to know there'd be two women like that at the restaurant who happened to drive the same make and color of car?"

The two men glared at each other until Henley lifted a hand. "All right, calm down. Let's figure out what we're going to do now."

Prickles of shock skittered across her flesh when Dylan spun around to stare at her.

"I know what I'm going to do." A smirk twisted his face as he drew the knife out of the tabletop. He took one last swig of his drink, then lowered the glass to the table and wiped his mouth with the back of his hand. He started across the room toward her, the knife in one hand, the other hand unbuckling his belt.

"Let's go, Henley. Psycho-boy's not going to want this one anyway. We might as well have some fun with her."

Henley hesitated.

Kathryn shifted her head on the pillow to meet his eyes. *Don't do this.* Fingers of terror gripped her throat. *Don't do this.*

"Come on. Be a man for once," Dylan called over his

shoulder.

Henley tore his gaze from hers and drained the last of his whiskey. He set the glass too close to the edge of the table. It thudded to the floor and rolled against the wall. He stood and staggered toward her.

Her heart pounded violently against her breastbone. Ropes cut into her wrists as she struggled to free herself. Stabbing pain, like electrical impulses, shot up and down her arms.

Dylan slashed at her clothing with the knife. She bent her leg and kicked, experiencing a second of satisfaction when her heel connected with his knee. He cursed and punched her hard in the stomach.

Kathryn gasped for breath. Every attempt at resistance was met with a hard fist until she gave up trying to protect herself. Terror and rage warred within her as she realized the helpless position she was in.

A picture fell from the wall, shattering on the floor. In the distance she heard a mournful keening. She didn't realize it was coming from her until someone slapped her hard across the mouth and the sound stopped.

Help me.

It no longer mattered whether God stopped the attack or let her die. Anything but this.

Don't leave me. Don't leave me.

Like hot coals slowly consuming a piece of firewood, peace worked its way through her. In the midst of the dark violence, a tiny ray of light, the knowledge that she was not alone, broke over the horizon. Strong arms circled her and held her tight.

Finally, both men finished with her and returned to their bottle. Kathryn huddled on the twisted sheets, her tangled hair spread across the dingy pillow. She pressed her face into her arm to muffle the sobs that wracked her body. Every part of her throbbed with pain, so she lay still, terrified to move, until exhaustion overcame her and she slipped into unconsciousness again.

Tuesday

As I had That Night, I fell with her, deep into a black pit. On my hands and knees, I gasped for air and inhaled only a thick murky fog that filled my mouth, my throat, and my lungs and squeezed the last agonized breaths from my body. I collapsed to the ground and let the waves of damp mist flow over me, sure now that I would not live to see the morning light.

Chapter Ten

Sometime in the night the plates of the earth had shifted dramatically. Tremors had shaken the ground, wreaking havoc and destruction.

Kathryn lay in the rubble.

Heavy objects pinned her down, pieces of wood and concrete from the building that had collapsed around her. Torn from the places that grounded them, electrical wires sent showers of sparks hissing through the air. Searing shocks pulsed through her with every breath.

Memories of the assault, heavier than concrete and wood, crashed in upon her and the ground beneath heaved again, ripping her from her nightmare.

Her eyes flew open.

Bright sunshine poured into the room. Eyelids, heavy with swelling and tears, dropped against the bolt the light sent shooting through her pounding head.

They were still here. She stifled a moan. What was she going to do? Screwing up her face, she attempted another glance.

Henley sat at the table, his head resting on both hands.

The door opened, and Dylan strode into the cabin. The screen door slammed behind him.

Henley winced. "Do you have to make all that noise?"

Dylan laughed and set a cardboard tray with two cups of coffee on the table, then tossed a box of donuts beside it. Henley shoved the box away but reached for the coffee. With a grunt, Dylan slouched onto his chair, resting one booted foot on top of the other as he took a sip from his cup.

Disgust twisted Henley's face. "How can you drink so much and not get hung-over?"

"Good genes." His partner shot him a sardonic grin. "I come from a long, proud line of alcoholics."

Henley snorted and sipped from his steaming cup.

Kathryn fought the nausea threatening to sweep over her. *I have to get out of here.* Thinking felt like slogging through knee-deep mud. The fog in her mind wouldn't clear long enough to plan any kind of escape.

Henley lowered his cup. "We don't have a lot of time. We need to figure out what we're going to do."

"Do?" Dylan's snicker was as cold as his eyes. "There's only one thing to do. Kill the girl, dump the body, then get out of here."

She froze. In the ensuing silence, scattered scenes flashed across her muddled consciousness like a box of photographs dropped and spilling out across the floor.

Her parents, gazing at one another and smiling like they were in the wedding photo that hung above their bed. Aaron, clinging to the rope that swung out over the lake in front of their cottage before he dropped, arms and legs flailing. She and Meg and Claire, posing for their high school graduation photo, heads thrown back in laughter, hair blowing around their faces.

And Ty, blue eyes glowing as he told her for the first time that he loved her. Would he feel the same way when he found out what had happened last night? She couldn't suppress a groan.

The picture changed, still familiar, but now more daydream than memory. She'd had this dream before—Ty leaning over her and the tiny baby she rocked in her arms. Her eyelids flickered in confusion. The scene was the same as she'd always imagined, but now the man's face was hidden.

The picture began to crack and shatter. Kathryn tried to hold onto the pieces as they fell away, but a blank sheet dropped over the screen in her mind. She squeezed her eyes shut. Salt tingled on her lips as warm tears slid along both sides of her face.

Henley hadn't said anything. She opened her eyes and glanced over at him.

He stared at Dylan, biting his lip as though contemplating his partner's words. He shot her a look but turned away quickly when their eyes met.

"Kill her? I don't know about that." He shook his head. "I didn't sign up for murder. It was supposed to be a simple drop and grab. If everything had gone as planned," he glared pointedly at Dylan, "we'd be about to get paid, and then we'd be out of here. No one would be hurt."

"Well, sometimes things don't go as planned," his partner shot back. "Then you do what you gotta do and move on. As far as I'm concerned, the only questions are who's gonna do it and how." He set the knife on the table and yanked the gun from the back of his jeans. When he laid them side by side, the sunlight filtering into the room glinted off both weapons.

Kathryn shut her eyes again. *God, help me.* The terror coursing like blood through her veins kept her from forming any other thought. That one was enough. As it had the night before, peace flowed through her.

"Look at me."

She pushed open her eyes. Dylan stood over her, holding his knife. The blade, as he turned it over and over in his hand, mesmerized her. "God, help me," she whispered.

"Shut up."

Dylan dropped to one knee on the mattress and reached behind her. Grabbing a handful of hair, he yanked her head back, exposing her throat. The steel pressed into her skin.

A sharp pain shot through her. She groaned as warm liquid trickled down her neck. "Take me home," she begged the presence surrounding her. "Please let this end."

"I said shut up!" Dylan's once lifeless features twisted in rage.

Kathryn's eyes shimmered with tears, but she didn't take them from his. "God help you too."

His gaze jerked toward the ceiling. All the color drained from his face. Without warning, he let go of her and stumbled backward. The knife clattered to the floor.

She twisted her head in the direction he'd been staring. What was it? What was he looking at? Nothing hovered near the ceiling. Nothing that she could see, anyway.

Dylan staggered backwards across the room. When he hit the table, he slumped against it, supporting himself with both palms pressed to its rough wooden surface. Even from across the room, Kathryn could tell he was shaking.

Henley had been focused on the ceiling as well, but now he lowered his chin and his eyes connected with hers. Something arced between them that she couldn't put a name to, although it reverberated all through her. He pushed past his partner, the gun glinting in his hand. "Get out of here, Dylan, before I kill you myself."

"Did you see that?" Dylan's voice was hoarse.

"See what?"

Dylan shook his head and shoved away from the table. "Nothin'." He stalked across the room and grabbed his backpack off the floor, then smacked his palm against the screen door. Seconds later, the roar of a motorcycle engine revving broke the silence. The tires spun through the dirt, gravel clattering as the vehicle sped away.

Henley stooped to pick up the knife from the floor. Kathryn flinched, but he reached behind her and cut the ropes binding her wrists. He grabbed the blanket at the end of the bed and tossed it to her.

Clutching it to her chest, she sat up.

"We need to get out of here." He whirled around and started for the door. "I'll wait for you outside."

What just happened? Head swirling in confusion, Kathryn crawled off the bed. The blanket reeked of cigarette smoke but, long past caring, she wrapped it around herself and made her way across the room. She pushed open the door that led into the cramped washroom. One tap was missing, but she twisted the other and splashed cold water on her face, trying to clear the fog. A cracked mirror hung on the wall above the sink and she leaned forward.

Horror pushed her back a step as she stared at the stranger in the glass. Both eyes were ringed with black, the edges tinged with blue. Her cheeks were a mass of bruises and blood had dried at the corner of her mouth where one of the men had slapped her.

Kathryn gripped the sides of the sink. Nausea welled and she spun sideways and bent over the iron-stained toilet bowl, retching long after her stomach had emptied. Her head pounded as she sank onto the edge of the iron-stained bathtub. She rested her arms on the sink in front of her. The cool porcelain soothed the sharp, tingling sensation of blood beginning to flow again. *I have to get out of here.*

Kathryn struggled to her feet and moved into the larger room. The contents of her backpack were scattered across the floor. She gathered them up and shoved them in her bag before crossing the room and opening the screen door. Her eyes squinted against the brilliant sunshine.

Henley leaned against the door of a dark blue pick-up. Hands stuck deep in his pockets, he kicked the stones at his feet with his boot. "Can you drive?" He didn't look at her.

"Yes." *Just go.*

With a nod, Henley pushed away from the truck and opened the driver's side door. Her heart leaped into her throat when he stopped and started to turn around, but he shook his head and hauled himself into the cab.

She watched as he drove along the laneway and turned onto the road. On impulse, Kathryn stepped over the threshold. She braced herself against the counter as she made her way along it. Where were they? The matches were in the last drawer, and she withdrew a box and slid open the tray. Three broke in her trembling fingers before the fourth one flared to life. Limping around the room, she touched the lit end of several matches to anything flammable she could find. The torn curtains were the last to go up in flames before she staggered out of the building.

With a groan, Kathryn slid behind the wheel of her car. Every few seconds she glanced in the rear-view mirror as she drove. The flames engulfing the shack glowed orange in the mirror. When she reached the road, she sat for a few moments until the building collapsed with a crash. An eruption of sparks shot toward the sky.

A gray mist swirled before her eyes as she made her way to Langley. All she wanted to do was lay her head on a pillow and sleep. Not yet. She urged herself to keep going. *You have to get somewhere safe.* In Langley, Kathryn drove to Douglas Crescent, searching for the police station. She lurched to a stop in front of the door. A wall of darkness slowly moved across her vision.

A uniformed officer strolled toward the door of the police station and grasped the handle. *Help me.* Unable to move or cry out, she watched in despair as he started to open the door. He stopped and glanced over at her vehicle. Bending down, he squinted and peered through the front windshield. His eyes widened as he straightened and ran toward her.

As help approached, Kathryn was only able to manage one coherent thought.

She never wanted to see her old car again.

Tuesday

And so, miraculously, we both lived to see the light again, although it had gone dull and gray, barely penetrating the thick clouds that hung so low above her she could have reached out and touched them if she tried.

The clouds had lifted, slowly, over the years. This long, dark night had brought them rolling in again. Desperate, I clung to the arms of the rocking chair, reminding myself over and over that Kathryn had made it through this disorienting fog before. And she would do it again, all the way through to the end this time.

My brief spurt of confidence dissipated in the roiling mist. I had no idea whether she would make it through or not. All I could do was work to keep drawing in one ragged breath after another in the hopes that, if she did finally stumble out of the thick fog, I would still be here for her to find.

Chapter Eleven

Wednesday

When Kathryn jerked awake, still on the couch in the wee hours of the morning, thoughts of David Henley and the possibility of seeing him again after so many years consumed her. Even if I couldn't read her mind, I would have known that. Her face was filled with that curious mix of pushing away and pulling toward that it always displayed when she read his letters or thought of him. As I felt much the same way about the man before two long days in a motel room twenty years ago that changed everything, I understood completely.

That, incidentally, was a rare instance when my prediction was wrong. As is inevitably the case when I am mistaken, it was Grace, another good friend, who messed me up. This time she stepped in to completely reverse the direction David Henley's life had been heading. In the process, she opened up the possibility that he and I could actually reconcile.

And I freely admit that was something I hadn't seen coming at all.

April 1999

David Henley drove straight to the guy he always used when he needed to get rid of a vehicle. He couldn't help wincing as he slid behind the wheel of the forest green Taurus. It hurt to give up the F-150, but in his line of work it didn't pay to get attached to anything.

Along a deserted stretch of highway south of Vancouver, Henley stopped and climbed out of the car. Only a flock of seagulls watched, their cries of reproach echoing off the rocks, as he flung the knife and gun far out into the pounding surf of the ocean.

"That better be the last I see of them—and of Kevin Dylan."

Getting rid of the evidence should have eased his mind, but as he drew closer to the border, the vehicle seemed to slow of its own volition. An unseen force tugged him north like a magnet, keeping him from crossing the border and losing himself in the States.

Henley slammed on the brakes and veered over to the side of the road. He raked a hand through his hair in frustration. "What is the matter with me?" His fist pounded the steering wheel.

Turn around.

Henley's head shot up. Great, now he was hearing voices. Exactly what he needed. "I don't think so." He shoved the transmission into gear. "And on the off-chance that's you, God, you can *back off*. Like I told you years ago, I don't want anything to do with you."

Spinning his tires on the gravel shoulder, he accelerated onto the highway. Every sign he passed depicting the distance left to the border increased his uneasiness. Finally he drove over a crest in the road and saw the sign announcing the crossing. He joined the long line of vehicles, drumming his fingers on the steering wheel as he waited.

Turn around.

He shifted in his seat and punched on the radio with his thumb. Loud, pulsing rock music filled the car.

"That's more like it." Nodding, he slapped the steering wheel with his palm to the beat of the music.

Turn around. Turn around. Turn around.

"Shut up!"

The driver in the next lane peered over, a startled look on his face, but he glanced away when their eyes met. Henley rolled up his windows.

Turn around.

"I can't." He moaned. "If I stay in the country, I'll go to prison for years. Maybe for the rest of my life. You don't know what I've done."

The ludicrousness of that statement hit him immediately.

Expelling a deep breath, he rubbed his forehead hard with the side of his hand. "Okay, to review my options ..." A familiar bitterness began to burn like acid in his throat. "Either I'm sitting in my car talking to no one, in which case I am clearly losing my mind. Or ..." He was hesitant to even contemplate the second possibility. "I really am having a conversation with God." Who, if He did exist, would know exactly what David had done with his life. Nice choices.

Three cars idled in the line in front of him. He sat frozen, staring across the bridge at the new life he could envision on the other side. Two cars. He smacked the button to turn off the music. Rotating one shoulder and then the other, he attempted to relieve a little of the tension that had settled there. One car. His hands gripped the steering wheel so tightly that his fingernails dug into the palms of his hands. The stinging pain helped to clear his mind.

Turn around.

"I don't believe this." Henley twisted the wheel hard to the right and vacated the line, then swung his car around and headed in the direction he had come. Every few seconds he glanced in the rear-view mirror. Pulling out of a border crossing line wasn't exactly the best way to be inconspicuous. He half-expected to see flashing lights behind him as he drove away.

"I hope you're happy." No audible response reached his ears, but somehow he felt the presence more strongly than ever. The feeling left him cold. "This was your brilliant idea," he called into the dark night. "What am I supposed to do now?"

Silence filled the vehicle.

"Oh, *this* decision you're going to let me make on my own, are you? Thank you very much." The miles spun beneath his tires, every rotation taking him farther from freedom. On the outskirts of Vancouver he spotted a motel. Several letters had burned out on the sign, but he could make out the word *vacancy*. The parking lot was surprisingly full, but he found an empty spot in the front of the building and steered the sedan into it. Tugging his ball cap over his eyes, he sauntered into the office.

A television mounted high in one corner blared out a Seattle Mariners game. A large, round man with thick glasses managed to check him in and take his cash payment for three nights without taking his eyes off the screen.

"Sports fans," Henley murmured, shaking his head in bemusement as he returned to his car. "That guy has no idea he just put a roof over the head of one of British Columbia's Most Wanted."

After grabbing his duffle bag, a box of groceries, and a six-pack of beer from the trunk of the car, he made his way past several rooms before finding the one with the number five on the door, dangling by one screw so it more closely resembled a two. He shoved the door open with his shoulder and dropped everything on top of the dresser, then shut and locked the door behind him.

The heavy orange and brown floral curtains were hideous, but they served his purpose—blocking the view of any nosy passersby. Henley grabbed a beer out of the case and sprawled onto the bed. After flipping through all the channels on the TV two or three times, he switched it off. He took a long swig from the can and changed positions, trying to get comfortable.

The problem wasn't the bed, but the presence that had followed him here. He glanced around the room. "I told you to go."

No response.

Henley waved a hand through the air. "Fine. Stay. Go. Whatever. You're God, I guess you'll do as you please. Don't expect me to talk. I have nothing to say to you."

Desperate for a diversion, he yanked open the drawer of the bedside table and spotted a Bible. "You've got to be kidding." He grabbed the book and flung it as hard as he could against the wall. It landed upside-down on the floor, several pages bent beneath it.

Henley took another long drink. His eyes shifted to the book then away. When he'd finished the can, he crumpled it and tossed it in the general direction of the wastebasket. He punched up the pillow behind his head and reached for the remote again.

Every few minutes, he caught himself glancing over at the Bible. Unable to concentrate, he threw the remote on the bedside table, dragged himself off the bed, and headed into the bathroom, stripping off his navy T-shirt and jeans as he went.

Steam filled the tiny room as he stood under the hot water of the shower. He scrubbed hard with the bar of soap, hoping to rid himself of the grime coating his skin. The more he scrubbed, the worse he felt. The weight of what he'd done pressed in on him from all sides, suffocating him.

"What do you want from me?"

Read it.

"Forget that." Whirling around, he flattened his hands against the shower stall, letting the hot water course over his back.

When the steam hung so thick in the room he couldn't breathe without drawing droplets into his throat, Henley banged at the tap with his fist. He tugged on his jeans, grabbed another beer from the case, and dropped onto the bed again. Automatically, he flipped on the television then shut it off without even glancing at it.

The crisp, cool taste of his favorite beer usually refreshed him, but tonight the liquid was flat and stale in his mouth. He set the can on the bedside table and rolled onto his side. Tomorrow he would get in his vehicle, drive to the States, and disappear like he should have done today.

Nothing and no one would stop him from crossing the border this time.

Chapter Twelve

When Henley woke the next morning, the single, sparse beam of light that managed to work its way around the edge of the floral curtain and fall across his face ignited a roaring headache the second he opened his eyes. The book lying on the floor was the first thing he saw.

Read it.

Groaning, he pulled the spare pillow over his pounding head.

Read it.

"Fine." He tossed off the pillow and leaned over the edge of the bed to grab the book. Clutching it tightly, he shook it at the ceiling. "I have heard all this before, you know. As I'm sure you're aware, my father read it to me instead of nursery rhymes at night. It did nothing for me then, and it will do nothing for me now. I'll read it anyway if you will leave—me—alone."

David turned the thin pages so violently that one ripped in his hand. He was still enough of a preacher's son for fear to ripple through him as he stared at the paper. With shaking fingers, he placed the torn page into the Bible. As he did, the word *sin* caught his eye, and he let out a curt laugh. "There it is. Dad's favorite word." A chill passed through him. "I am *not* going there again. I heard enough preaching—or should I say ranting and raving—my first sixteen years to last me several lifetimes."

He slammed the Bible shut, but the torn piece had fallen halfway out, so he flipped it open and shoved it into place.

Read it.

His gaze rested on the hated word. Exhaling in frustration, he pushed past his aversion and read, "... where sin increased, grace increased all the more ..."

David stopped reading. His eyes were scratchy and he

rubbed them with his thumb and forefinger before focusing on the words.

"Well, sin definitely increased in that cabin. But grace? I doubt it. Some sins are beyond grace, aren't they?"

Silence.

David glanced around the room. "Well, aren't they?"

Again, no response.

"Exactly what I thought." He laughed coldly. "Pretty anxious to condemn me, but not so quick to let me off the hook, are you?"

The Bible hit the floor again, but when he shut his eyes the words were burned into the back of his eyelids and he opened them quickly. Whatever it was, it was still there, waiting.

Which meant it was time to get out of this place and leave behind the book, the presence, and whatever else that might be hanging around that dank motel room.

After shoving his clothes into the duffle bag, he stepped over the Bible, stalked to the door, and yanked it open. On the way to his car, he started to pass by the side window of the office. Something caught his eye, and he stopped and peered through the glass, his heart beating out an uneven staccato rhythm in his chest. The announcer on a twenty-four-hour news station glared down at him from the monitor attached to the wall high in the corner. Had his name and picture shown up on the screen yet? That woman—Kathryn Ellison, according to her license—had to have gone straight to the police after he let her go yesterday.

He tried clawing through the events of the day before in his mind. Had they used their names with each other? After a few seconds, he gave up. Other than a few horrifyingly clear images that stood out starkly in his mind—moments he'd rather forget or, better yet, travel through time to stop from happening—no clear details would emerge from the thick sludge in his brain.

Henley risked a glance at the man working behind the desk. He wasn't paying any attention to the TV. It was a different clerk than the night before, and that guy hadn't even glanced at Henley. Even if they had posted a photo of him, likely neither of them would connect the story to their guest staying in room five, especially since he'd used an alias when he signed in.

Even so ... Henley pressed his back to the dull gray siding of the L-shaped, one-story structure. What should he do? His car was parked at the front of the building, in full view of the check-in area. If he tried to get to it now, it was highly unlikely he'd be able to slip into the vehicle and drive away without drawing the gaze of the guy standing behind the desk and maybe other guests as well. If the story had aired, he might be offering himself up on a platter, strolling around in broad daylight like this.

A bead of cold sweat slid between his shoulder blades, and he silently cursed the voice that had caused him to turn away from the border the day before. Now it was probably too late. If his name and photo were already on the news, no way he'd be able to drive across to the US. He'd have to change course, head farther north or maybe east to lose himself in the prairies. If he'd kept driving the day before, he'd already be far away from the scene of the crime.

Crimes.

He shoved away the thought—and the sick feeling that accompanied it. He needed to stay focused, to think clearly. Maybe it would actually work in his favor that he hadn't gotten very far yesterday. No doubt they'd be targeting places well beyond this area by now. He shot a look toward the front of the building. Either way, he couldn't leave until dark.

Muttering another curse, he returned to his room. Everything in him wanted to slam the door, maybe three or four times, but that would definitely draw the attention he needed to avoid if he wanted to stay out of prison.

The Bible lay on the floor where he'd left it. Henley lifted his foot, intending to kick it under the bed, out of sight. For several seconds he stood like that, his foot poised in the air, then he lowered it to the floor. Shaking his head, he skirted the book and flopped onto the mattress. He lost track of how much time he sprawled there, staring up at the water-stained ceiling, trying to keep his thoughts from wandering to the events of the day before.

His head pounded and he licked his lips, his mouth pasty. He needed a drink. Something a lot stronger than the bottle of water he'd stuck into the box with his groceries.

Henley flopped onto his side. He wasn't normally much of a drinker, but being around Kevin Dylan drove him to it. He wasn't sure he'd ever drunk as much as he had yesterday. Enough to make much of what had happened pretty hazy. Not so hazy that he could forget what he'd done, or how terrified that woman looked when Dylan had goaded him into crossing the room toward her.

With a loud groan, Henley swung his legs off the side of the bed. He was going to go crazy stuck in this room by himself—the absolute last person on the planet, other than Kevin Dylan, that he wanted to be alone with. For several long seconds he stared at the book on the floor.

Read it.

He glanced at his watch. One in the afternoon. This time of year, it wouldn't be fully dark before nine pm. Eight hours to kill while trying not to think about anything at all. Piece of cake. Dark thoughts crowding into his mind, he headed for the shower again. Like the day before, the harder he scrubbed, the dirtier he felt. Finally he tossed the soap onto the tiny plastic ledge and rested his head against the side of the shower, lukewarm water streaming down his neck. "Oh God, what have I done?" he moaned.

His head came up sharply. What he'd meant as a meaningless expression of frustration had come out sounding a lot like a prayer. Which was the last thing he'd intended. He had no desire to talk to the overbearing old man in the sky who'd never done anything for him but make his life miserable. That would mean acknowledging the existence he'd devoted the last ten years of his life to denying—since the fateful day he'd stormed out of his parents' home for the last time.

Henley shoved the door of the shower with his palms, hard enough that it swung wide and cracked against the wall. Grabbing the towel—still slightly damp after his last attempt to cleanse his body and soul—he rubbed himself vigorously before tossing it into the corner.

After dressing and stretching out on the bed, he mindlessly flipped through channels for another hour or so, then flung the remote against the wall. Should he eat something? The thought of food turned his stomach. He fumbled in his duffle bag, found the bottle of aspirin he'd tossed into a side pocket, and took a swig of warm water from the plastic bottle to wash down two tablets.

For the rest of the afternoon, he dozed a little, fitfully, dark dreams wrenching him awake every few minutes. The last time he woke up, the thin beam of light that had disturbed him that morning had faded and a stifling gloom hung over the room. He folded his arms behind his head and stared at the ceiling, entertaining himself by concentrating on one crack or water stain at a time as it criss-crossed over several others, trying to follow the entire length of it to its source.

The pounding in his head had receded a little, which wasn't good. As the pain cleared, so did his thoughts. He would have thought he'd been drunk enough for the memory of that disgusting cabin—and everything that happened in it—to be impossible for him to recall. Instead, as objects in the room faded in the twilight, his recollection of the look in the woman's eyes when they met his, pleading with him, came into sharper focus.

Henley propelled himself off the bed and stalked across the room. His shoulder to the wall, he moved the heavy drapes aside a couple of inches and peered out. Dusk had fallen, but it wasn't dark yet, not as dark as it was inside the dingy room. He let the drapes swing into place. The movement released a cloud of dust and he coughed and turned away. Light. He needed light. He crossed the room, heading for the tall brass lamp with the cream-colored shade on the table beside the bed. Right before he reached it, his foot connected with something lying on the floor and he glanced down. The Bible. That old familiar twinge of guilt-ridden fear shot through him.

Bending down, he pressed the switch on the lamp before scooping the book off the floor. Soft light filled the room, driving away a few of the shadows.

Read it.

With a heavy sigh, he sank onto the edge of the mattress and opened the book. He flipped through the thin pages with trembling fingers. Without making the conscious decision to do so, he kept going until he reached John 3:16, the first verse he remembered learning as a kid. He scanned the familiar words, ones he'd heard countless times in countless boring sermons throughout his childhood and teen years.

His mom had helped him learn them when he was six, the two of them going over and over the lines after school every day until he could recite it to her without cheating and glancing at the page. A vision of her face, beaming with pride when he made it through without help—including the reference at the end—drifted through his mind. Even as a soft smile crossed his lips, a pain so intense shot through him that he let go of the book with one hand and rubbed his palm over his chest.

His mother. She was the most remarkable woman he knew. Not for one minute had he doubted her love for him, not even when he lashed out at his father and the world and broke her heart over and over. She didn't deserve what he had put her through. Or what he was about to put her through.

The weight of that thought sent him to his knees on the floor, the Bible clutched in one hand. Henley groaned as the verse echoed in his mind. *Whoever believes.* Those words couldn't be for him. He'd strayed too far. If he hadn't erected an insurmountable barrier between himself and God before entering that cabin, he certainly had now.

Whoever believes.

Whoever was pretty all-encompassing. Which begged the question, *did* he believe? He had believed, as a kid. When he was learning that verse, it never occurred to him to question any part of it. God did love the world, enough to send His only Son to die in the place of every human being who had ever sinned. Even at six years old, David had known that included him. He believed with all his heart that he'd been forgiven and would live with

God forever. When had he stopped believing?

Had he stopped? Or had he only been angry with his father—who preached those words every Sunday but lived a different way entirely outside of his pulpit. Had his early belief that God loved him and had forgiven him become so entangled with the messenger that he'd rejected the message at the same time? Either way, it was too late now to claim the truth of it again.

Wasn't it?

The memory of those hours at the cabin pressed down on him so hard that, with a groan, he set the Bible aside and lowered himself to stretch out on the dirty carpet, his hands clasped on the floor in front of him, his forehead resting on his upper arms. He knew with absolute certainty that he needed a higher power in his life. He'd tried to make it on his own for more than a decade and it had all gone horribly, horribly wrong. Years of bad choices, of rebellion, of self-reliance, had culminated in that heinous act in the cabin. Every attempt to better himself, to carve out a successful life, had only sent him spiraling further and further into darkness.

"Oh, God," he moaned again, meaning it this time. At the end of himself and unable to see any other way to climb out of the deep pit he'd flung himself into years ago, he cried out, "Forgive me."

No voice answered him, but David felt the presence that had hovered in the room since he'd entered it the night before surrounding him. Only now, instead of repelling him, he was drawn to it, desperate for it. "Help me to believe."

Warmth tingled across his skin. Was it possible? Could he be forgiven? How could he be?

The words from the torn page penetrated his consciousness. *Where sin abounded, grace increased.*

Breath squeezed from his body. Grace. The vastness of the word overwhelmed him. In the shadow of it he felt dirty and small. David bent his arms, pressing his clasped hands to the back of his head. The presence pulsed around him. His entire body shook. How could he survive this? How could he, after everything that he had done, stand—even lie on his face—before the almighty God of the universe and live?

"Help me." The whispered words were pushed out between trembling lips.

The presence surrounded him, not crushing like a python, as he'd half-expected, but enfolding him like warm bath water.

"I do believe."

He squeezed his eyes tighter as the burden of his guilt was wrestled from him. The weight pressing his face into the carpet lifted. In its place a rising heat spread along both arms and tingled in his fingertips.

It had been so long since David Henley had experienced peace that he hardly recognized it when it came. The sensation spread through his body like shafts of sunlight working their way through thick billows of cloud.

For hours he lay there, the faint odors of smoke and mold drifting up his nostrils. The carpet scraped his cheeks and forehead and tears dampened the coarse fibers brushing against his skin. Finally, he climbed to his feet. He set the Bible reverently into the drawer of the bedside table before sinking onto the edge of the bed. In the soft glow of the lamp, he turned his arm, covered in a thin sheen of sweat, to glance at his watch. Almost three in the morning. Time for him to go.

David propped his elbows on his knees and lowered his face into his hands, his mind spinning. God may have forgiven him, but he still had to face the consequences of what he'd done. He would turn himself in to the authorities. Before he did that, he had something even more difficult to do.

He had to go home.

See? How could I have known that would happen? It did, and I know, because I was there. I made a mistake and for once in my existence I was perfectly happy to be wrong.

Unfortunately, I wasn't mistaken the next day

when I set out with David to return to the place he had grown up and that he hadn't gone anywhere near in ten years. I knew, not because I could predict the future, but because I had spent enough time in that home, that it was not going to be pretty.

Another time I wouldn't have minded being wrong.

Chapter Thirteen

April 1999

"That can't be my old school." David drove the Taurus through the streets of his hometown of Abbotsford. "It's so small." He stopped and gazed at the yellow brick building. He could still remember his first day, walking along the sidewalk holding his mom's hand. If he narrowed his eyes he could see them, the boy and his mother, as she took him to kindergarten.

"Come on." The boy tugged her along the sidewalk. David smiled as they walked up to the door of the classroom. "Let go, Mom." The child yanked his hand out of the woman's and bounded into the brightly decorated room without a backward glance.

The smile faded. She looked so sad. An unfamiliar feeling of regret twisted his insides. He'd always been so eager to grow up, to move away from his mom and dad. He couldn't remember ever bothering to check with them to see how they felt about their only child leaving them behind.

David shoved the car into gear and drove until he reached a city park. He slowed the Taurus as he drove by, seeing them there, in the early-morning light. The boy's mother pushed him on a swing and laughed as he squealed with delight. "Higher, higher." A stab of grief pricked his chest. Where had that carefree little boy gone?

When he turned left at the next corner, his features hardened. There it was. The red brick church where his father had been the minister. Still was, as far as David knew. A wave of resentment swept over him and he glared at the building. Tomorrow at this time he would be behind bars, and David was pretty sure he wouldn't be as miserable there as he'd been in that church every week. He turned his head as he drove past, his eyes following the brick pathway lined with the purple, pink, and yellow flowers that led up to the curved, white front doors. His teeth clenched. Fresh new paint. It was as beautiful on the outside as he remembered and no doubt as cold on the inside as it had always been. He stepped on the gas.

David took the next right then stopped the car at the curb. Across the street and down a few doors stood the house he'd grown up in. White clapboard siding with green shutters and roof—the house hadn't changed since the last time he'd seen it. He swallowed hard at the memory.

Through the car window he saw himself at sixteen, returning home after six months in detention to find his father waiting for him. Sick with dread, David pictured the young man dragging himself up the walk and stopping at the bottom of the stairs.

The minister, his imposing six-foot-three-inch frame taking up much of the doorway, stared at him, arms folded across his chest.

A tremor passed through David. "Watch out, buddy," he warned his younger self. "You're about to get kicked in the teeth."

The teenager stared at his feet, swiping at a rock with his shoe.

"Look up," David hissed, gripping the steering wheel. His breath came in short gasps. "Be a man."

The kid didn't move. Even now he could feel his father's gaze boring into the top of his head.

"What do you think you're doing?" The memory was so vivid that his father's shout seemed to echo inside the car.

"I'm ... coming home?"

"This is no longer your home." The words had slapped him across the face. "Get out of here and don't ever come back."

In David's imagination, the boy looked like David felt now, as though he was about to be sick. He'd known his father would be furious with him for what he'd done, for embarrassing him in front of his congregation. Somehow he'd never considered the possibility that his dad wouldn't let him come home.

The teen finally raised his chin. "Don't worry," he sneered.

"I'll never set foot in this place again." He picked up the bag with his meager belongings and stormed along the sidewalk, throwing a glance over his shoulder at an upstairs window. When he whirled around, his face was twisted in pain and disbelief.

David followed his gaze, visualizing his mother's face disappearing as the curtains swung into place. She'd seen him. Instead of helping him—he swallowed the lump forming in his throat—she backed out of sight, refusing to face him like she'd always refused to face his father.

I shouldn't have come here. His hand fell to the key in the ignition. If his father saw him—

He froze as his mother came around the side of the house, captured for a moment against a background of pink and orange sky.

She wore gardening gloves and a straw hat tied on with a kerchief. A basket of flowers swung from her arm as she strolled up the stairs and opened the screen door.

Exactly like he remembered. Blinking away sudden tears, he glanced at the driveway. No car. He pushed open the door of the Taurus and climbed out, pressing his hand to the hood to steady himself. *Calm down.* He wasn't that scared kid anymore. He could do this. He had to do this before—

David crossed the street and headed up the front walk. He took a deep breath before knocking on the frame of the screen door.

"Yes?" His mother peered out, then drew in a sharp breath. "David." Her face lit up.

"Is he—?"

"He's not here. He's gone for coffee, but he won't be long." She opened the door and grasped his elbow to tug him into the house. She threw her arms around him and held him for a moment before stepping away. "Let me look at you." His mom rested her hands, still wearing the gardening gloves, on his arms. Her short hair, whiter than he remembered, framed a face that radiated warmth.

A sudden ache in his chest surprised him. Until he saw her

again, David hadn't realized how much he'd missed her.

"My goodness, you're skin and bones. Let me get you something to eat." She took a step toward the kitchen, but he laid a hand on her shoulder.

"Mom, I can't stay. I just need to talk to you for a few minutes." His voice shook. "Could we sit down?"

With a quick glance at the door, she walked into the living room, pulling off the gardening gloves. She sat in a soft white suede armchair and set the gloves on the table beside her.

David maneuvered the footstool closer with his foot before settling on it. He took his mother's hand in his. His chest constricted, and he struggled to draw a breath. "I came to see you because I've done something ..."

A mist rose in his mother's soft blue eyes, but her gaze never left his.

Now that he was here, in front of her, David couldn't find the words to tell her, couldn't bear to see the pain on her face that he'd put there so many times before. It didn't matter. He could see in her eyes that she didn't need any details. She only wanted him to be there. Like he never really had been, not since he was a child.

"I'm going to Vancouver this afternoon to turn myself in. But I had to see you before I went."

She squeezed his hand. "I'm glad you came, son." Her eyes probed his. "There's something else, isn't there?"

He nodded. "I ran for the border, but I kept hearing this voice in my head telling me to go back. I tried to ignore it, but it wouldn't stop. Finally I turned around and returned to Vancouver. I checked into a motel and spent the last two days fighting with God until I couldn't fight him anymore."

Tears spilled over his mother's cheeks. "Oh, David, you have no idea how many years I've waited to hear you say those words. I've been praying for so—"

"I told you never to come back to this house." The preacher's voice boomed across the room.

David froze. His mother's slight nod, when he met her eyes,

gave him the courage to rise and turn around.

His father stalked across the room toward him.

"Don't worry, Dad. I'm going."

A large hand smashed across his cheek, so hard that he stumbled backwards. "Do *not* call me that. You are no son of mine."

Bitterness and rage rose in David's throat so thick and strong that he thought he would choke on it. His fists clenched.

"Jack!" his mother cried.

"Elizabeth, stay out of this. You don't know what your precious boy has done now." A newspaper landed on the coffee table. Except for a splotch of heat on one cheek, all the warmth drained from David's face. His own image stared at him from the front page.

"I'm calling the police." His father's words were ground out between clenched teeth as he pushed past David and reached for the telephone on the end table.

"No."

Both men shifted their gazes to his mother. David had never heard her raise her voice before. He certainly had never seen her stand up to his father.

Now she moved toward her husband, her face a mask of fury. "Put down that phone."

After a moment's hesitation, he returned the receiver to the cradle.

She touched David's arm. "Go, son. Do what you have to do. Don't forget that you are always in my prayers." Her voice broke, but his mother stood tall, her chin thrust forward.

He studied her face, trying to commit every detail to memory.

She brushed his throbbing cheek. "Go, David."

With a nod, he headed for the door. When he glanced over his shoulder, his mother was still watching him. Head hanging low, his father slumped on the couch.

David shoved open the screen door and bounded down the

stairs. He strode across the street and hopped into his car. A stinging pain thrummed across one side of his face. His stomach twisted at the thought of what was to come. In spite of that, his heart was light as he guided the Taurus through the streets of Abbotsford.

"She did it!" David smacked his palm against the steering wheel. "I can't believe it. She stood up to him. For me." Shaking his head, he went over the events of the past few minutes. "And he crumbled. He was probably more shocked than I was."

David had no idea whether he'd see his parents again. Somehow he knew that, if he did, things would be very different.

He merged his car with the traffic on the Trans-Canada Highway, for the second time in three days drawn to Vancouver when all logic told him to turn and head the other way. This time, however, the presence surrounding him did not send cold chills up and down his spine. "So you know," he said to the empty air, "you're coming with me."

One word filled his mind, giving him the strength to keep driving, to do what had to be done.

Yes.

Chapter Fourteen

April 1999

David's heart thumped erratically as he wheeled into the parking lot of the Vancouver police department. He pressed a palm to his chest. Then the presence wrapped around him like a cloak and the pounding subsided.

The sidewalk from the parking lot to the front door of the police station wasn't long, but his feet felt weighted down and each step took so much effort it seemed like hours before he stood in front of the heavy glass door. He raised a leaden arm and grasped the handle. *Stay with me.*

A uniformed officer stood and circled his desk, studying David's face. His eyes narrowed as his gaze flew to a piece of paper tacked to a bulletin board on the wall. A hand dropped to the gun in his holster. "Don't move."

Not taking his eyes off David, the officer picked up the phone. Within seconds, four more officers had come through a door to the left of the front desk and surrounded David.

"Hands behind your head."

David complied. Someone moved behind him and patted the pockets of his jeans and his tan corduroy jacket. *You won't find any weapons there, boys. I've worked with Kevin Dylan before and know he always comes fully equipped.* A sickening lurch in the stomach cut off his grim smile.

A policeman pulled the car keys from David's right jacket pocket and tossed them to his partner. The room began to spin, and David closed his eyes as another officer yanked his hands behind his back.

"You have the right to retain and instruct counsel." The rest of the words were lost in the haze drifting through his mind. It didn't matter—he'd heard them often enough to be able to repeat them as smoothly as he'd recited John 3:16 for his mother that day.

stairs. He strode across the street and hopped into his car. A stinging pain thrummed across one side of his face. His stomach twisted at the thought of what was to come. In spite of that, his heart was light as he guided the Taurus through the streets of Abbotsford.

"She did it!" David smacked his palm against the steering wheel. "I can't believe it. She stood up to him. For me." Shaking his head, he went over the events of the past few minutes. "And he crumbled. He was probably more shocked than I was."

David had no idea whether he'd see his parents again. Somehow he knew that, if he did, things would be very different.

He merged his car with the traffic on the Trans-Canada Highway, for the second time in three days drawn to Vancouver when all logic told him to turn and head the other way. This time, however, the presence surrounding him did not send cold chills up and down his spine. "So you know," he said to the empty air, "you're coming with me."

One word filled his mind, giving him the strength to keep driving, to do what had to be done.

Yes.

Chapter Fourteen

April 1999

David's heart thumped erratically as he wheeled into the parking lot of the Vancouver police department. He pressed a palm to his chest. Then the presence wrapped around him like a cloak and the pounding subsided.

The sidewalk from the parking lot to the front door of the police station wasn't long, but his feet felt weighted down and each step took so much effort it seemed like hours before he stood in front of the heavy glass door. He raised a leaden arm and grasped the handle. *Stay with me.*

A uniformed officer stood and circled his desk, studying David's face. His eyes narrowed as his gaze flew to a piece of paper tacked to a bulletin board on the wall. A hand dropped to the gun in his holster. "Don't move."

Not taking his eyes off David, the officer picked up the phone. Within seconds, four more officers had come through a door to the left of the front desk and surrounded David.

"Hands behind your head."

David complied. Someone moved behind him and patted the pockets of his jeans and his tan corduroy jacket. *You won't find any weapons there, boys. I've worked with Kevin Dylan before and know he always comes fully equipped.* A sickening lurch in the stomach cut off his grim smile.

A policeman pulled the car keys from David's right jacket pocket and tossed them to his partner. The room began to spin, and David closed his eyes as another officer yanked his hands behind his back.

"You have the right to retain and instruct counsel." The rest of the words were lost in the haze drifting through his mind. It didn't matter—he'd heard them often enough to be able to repeat them as smoothly as he'd recited John 3:16 for his mother that day.

stairs. He strode across the street and hopped into his car. A stinging pain thrummed across one side of his face. His stomach twisted at the thought of what was to come. In spite of that, his heart was light as he guided the Taurus through the streets of Abbotsford.

"She did it!" David smacked his palm against the steering wheel. "I can't believe it. She stood up to him. For me." Shaking his head, he went over the events of the past few minutes. "And he crumbled. He was probably more shocked than I was."

David had no idea whether he'd see his parents again. Somehow he knew that, if he did, things would be very different.

He merged his car with the traffic on the Trans-Canada Highway, for the second time in three days drawn to Vancouver when all logic told him to turn and head the other way. This time, however, the presence surrounding him did not send cold chills up and down his spine. "So you know," he said to the empty air, "you're coming with me."

One word filled his mind, giving him the strength to keep driving, to do what had to be done.

Yes.

Chapter Fourteen

April 1999

David's heart thumped erratically as he wheeled into the parking lot of the Vancouver police department. He pressed a palm to his chest. Then the presence wrapped around him like a cloak and the pounding subsided.

The sidewalk from the parking lot to the front door of the police station wasn't long, but his feet felt weighted down and each step took so much effort it seemed like hours before he stood in front of the heavy glass door. He raised a leaden arm and grasped the handle. *Stay with me.*

A uniformed officer stood and circled his desk, studying David's face. His eyes narrowed as his gaze flew to a piece of paper tacked to a bulletin board on the wall. A hand dropped to the gun in his holster. "Don't move."

Not taking his eyes off David, the officer picked up the phone. Within seconds, four more officers had come through a door to the left of the front desk and surrounded David.

"Hands behind your head."

David complied. Someone moved behind him and patted the pockets of his jeans and his tan corduroy jacket. *You won't find any weapons there, boys. I've worked with Kevin Dylan before and know he always comes fully equipped.* A sickening lurch in the stomach cut off his grim smile.

A policeman pulled the car keys from David's right jacket pocket and tossed them to his partner. The room began to spin, and David closed his eyes as another officer yanked his hands behind his back.

"You have the right to retain and instruct counsel." The rest of the words were lost in the haze drifting through his mind. It didn't matter—he'd heard them often enough to be able to repeat them as smoothly as he'd recited John 3:16 for his mother that day.

Cold steel encircled his wrists.

A uniformed officer on each side of him, David was led away. They stopped outside a closed door, and one of the men twisted the handle and pushed it open. Tugging on his elbow, the officer directed David inside and shoved him onto a hard metal chair.

"Make yourself at home, Henley. You won't be going anywhere for a while." The door clanged shut behind them.

David sat in the warm room for almost an hour, doubts about his decision to turn himself in weighing on him like the corduroy jacket he'd have given anything to take off. Where was Kevin Dylan now? Probably lying on a beach somewhere down south. David let out a bitter laugh. Not that Dylan struck him as a lying around on a beach kind of guy.

David shot a glance at the ceiling. *You're here, right? 'Cause I am a lying around on a beach kind of guy, and that's exactly what I'd be doing right now if you hadn't dragged me here. The least you can do is stick around and go through this with me.* Knots dissolved from his shoulders as the warmth that had filled him the night before spread through his chest.

Finally the heavy metal door scraped open, and two plain-clothed officers entered the room. David swallowed and looked up. The first one, a heavy-set man in his mid-fifties, took off his jacket and hung it on the back of the chair across from David. A blond man with a thin moustache followed the first cop into the room, closing the door behind them.

"I'm Detective Alderson, and this—" the large man jerked his head toward his partner, "—is Detective Collins." A piece of paper landed on the table. "And you've moved into the big leagues, Henley. Kidnapping. Forcible confinement. Sexual assault. Assault. Did we miss anything?"

David's throat was dry. "Could I get a glass of water?"

Alderson's eyes narrowed. "How about you give us something first?"

He glanced at the paper. The charges were what he'd expected, but reading the words, seeing his guilt laid out in black and white, made it all so real that he had to look away.

"Well?"

The events of the last forty-eight hours whirred through his mind like silent pictures in an old home movie. It took him a moment to remember how it had all started. He cleared his throat. "Two weeks ago, I got a call from this guy, Jeff Walker. I didn't recognize the name, but he said he was the friend of a friend who'd told him to call me to—"

"What friend?" interrupted Collins.

"Just a friend." David had no desire to drag anyone else into this mess. All he wanted was to come clean about his part in it.

The men exchanged a look. "We'll come back to that." Alderson shrugged. "Let's hear the story."

"Walker was this real psychopath. Some girl had dumped him, and he'd been stalking her ever since. He had an old cabin outside Langley that he wanted her brought to, and he asked if I could do the job. It sounded pretty simple, and Walker told me he'd make it worth my while, so I agreed."

"How much?" Collins held his pen above the notepad he'd been scribbling on.

"Ten thousand."

Collins whistled and wrote on the pad.

"I wanted to make sure nothing would go wrong, since I hadn't done that type of work before, so I called up a guy I knew and asked him if he wanted in."

"His name?" Collins tapped his pen on the notepad.

David hesitated. As much as he hated ratting anyone out, it would be better to get his former partner off the streets than to leave him out there to hurt anyone else. Besides, Kathryn Ellison had given him up. No doubt she'd done the same with Dylan.

"Kevin Dylan." Turning his head, he coughed into his shoulder.

Alderson jerked his head toward the door. Collins shoved his chair away from the table, its legs scraping along the floor. He flipped the notepad closed and threw it and the pen on the table, then crossed the room and went out the door.

David took several deep breaths, hoping to slow the wild beating in his chest. It didn't help much. *I know this is the right thing to do.* The presence in the room was as real to him as the officer staring at him from across the table. Even so, he wasn't looking forward to finishing this conversation and finding himself on the wrong side of a wall of metal bars.

The door to the interview room opened, and Collins returned carrying a Styrofoam cup. When the officer held it to his mouth, David gulped the tepid water, suddenly realizing he hadn't had anything to eat or drink other than a few drops of water since that stale beer in his motel room two nights earlier.

"All right, break time's over." Alderson circled a finger in the air. "What happened the night of the abduction?"

A few drops of water had dripped onto his chin, and David swiped the side of his face against his shoulder. "Walker told me which restaurant she'd be at and gave me a description of her car. I met Dylan at the cabin and we drove into Langley. He insisted on doing the job alone, so I went back to the cabin to wait.

"They pulled in around 8:30. After we took her into the cabin, Dylan hit her on the back of the head with his gun and knocked her out. Then we dragged her to the bed and tied her up."

The water he'd drunk wasn't sitting very well. A wave of nausea swept over him.

"You're turning a little green, Henley," Collins jeered. "Not coming down with an attack of conscience all of a sudden, are we?"

Alderson tapped his fingers on the table. "Let's get on with it. What happened then?"

Dread tightened his chest at the thought of rehashing the events that came next. David swallowed hard. "We were sitting around the table, drinking pretty heavily and waiting for morning so we could hand her over and get out of there."

"And?"

"And I was bored and started going through her bag. When I

saw her driver's license, I realized we had the wrong girl."

He clenched his teeth at Collins' derisive laugh. "You've got to be kidding."

David waited in silence. At Alderson's raised eyebrows, he cleared his throat. "I yelled at Dylan for making the mistake, and he got really mad. I told him to calm down so we could figure out what to do next. He turned to the girl, grabbed his knife, and said he knew what he was going to do."

Neither of the cops was laughing now. David's stomach lurched as he described what happened then. As soon as he finished, he croaked, "Bathroom," and they jumped up and came around the table. Each of them grabbed an arm as they took him across the hall to the men's room, moving toward the door as David fell to his knees and retched into the toilet.

When he staggered to his feet, they took him to the tiny room and pushed him onto his chair again. Collins held the cup up to his mouth and David drained it.

"Can you continue?" Alderson asked dryly. David nodded. "Okay then, why didn't you go back and get the right girl?"

"Walker hadn't given us her home address, only told us where she'd be that night." He let out a short laugh. "Besides, neither of us would have stayed on the road five minutes after all we'd had to drink."

"So it's the next morning. What happened then?" Collins asked.

"Dylan said the only option was to kill the girl. I hadn't planned on murdering anybody, but he was adamant. I could see his point. If we freed her, she'd go straight to the police. She knew too much about us for that. Still, I couldn't bring myself to do it. Dylan had no problem with the plan. In fact, he seemed pretty keen. He grabbed his knife and headed to the bed." David's throat tightened.

"Well?" Alderson lifted a hand. "What happened? Did you stop him?"

"No." *You better help me here.* He had no idea how to describe what happened next. "It was the girl. Even knowing she

84

was about to die, she wasn't hysterical. There was this kind of ... peace, I guess, on her face. She started talking to God like he was right there with her. It freaked Dylan out."

"What did she say?"

"'God help me.' Dylan had the knife pressed to her throat, and blood was trickling down her neck. She stared right at him and said, 'God help you too.'"

"What did he say to that?"

"Nothing. That was the weird part. He dropped the knife and backed across the room, staring at the ceiling like he'd seen some kind of ghost. I grabbed the gun and told him to get out of there or I'd kill him, and he took off."

Complete silence filled the room. Then Collins let out his breath. "And you let her go." He waved his arm through the air. "That's the craziest story I've ever heard. Dylan dropped the knife and ran out of the room for no reason?"

David exhaled. The story *was* implausible. If he hadn't been there, he probably wouldn't believe it himself. "I don't know what else to tell you. That's what happened."

Another look passed between the two officers.

"Why don't you read the woman's statement?" David twisted his wrists, trying to relieve a little of the pressure from the cuffs. "I'm sure her story will match mine."

Alderson's fist slammed onto the table, and the Styrofoam cup tipped over. "We don't need you telling us how to do our job, Henley. Answer our questions and keep the suggestions to yourself."

With another jerk of his head toward the door, Alderson stalked out of the room, Collins on his heels. David sagged against the chair, hoping he wouldn't have to tell that story too many times.

After a few minutes, the door flew open. Collins strode across the room, grabbed David's arm, and hauled him to his feet. "We'll need to talk to you again, but we have enough to book you. Time to smile nicely for the camera." Alderson met them at the door and took his other arm. After David had been photographed and fingerprinted, the cops directed him through a hallway past several holding cells.

"Hey, pretty boy." A man with long, stringy blond hair reached through the bars as they walked by. Other voices joined in, jeering and hollering as the officers led him past the cell doors to the last one. Collins shoved him inside and removed the handcuffs.

Standing with his back to the door, David rubbed his wrists and listened for the sound he'd been dreading all day—metal scraping along the floor followed by the clanging of the door as it locked behind him. The wave of peace that washed over him when he heard it surprised him. He sank onto the bare cot in the corner of his cell.

David swung his legs around and stretched out on the hard bed. He knew he deserved whatever punishment was given to him, and was equally sure he didn't deserve the grace he'd already received.

At this point, however, he would gladly take them both.

Chapter Fifteen

Wednesday

Kathryn was dreaming again. The eastern sky had barely begun to lighten when she'd given up trying to do anything more than doze on the couch and trudged up the stairs. I settled on the rocking chair in the corner of her bedroom, arms crossed, watching her as she crawled under the blankets on her bed. The sun rose above the horizon outside her window, casting long rays of soft, pink light across the farmyard. I hoped she would fall into a deep sleep, a fortification for the testing to come. Instead, she tossed and turned, her desperate moans sending chills—like the long, cold fingers of Fear—up and down my spine.

That's a nasty trick, by the way, and I've told Fear that often, but still he amuses himself by doing it every time he enters a room.

May 1999

Kathryn settled herself against the pillows as the movie started. The front door slammed and a minute later Aaron ducked into the room. Grabbing one of the bowls of popcorn, he lifted her feet, sat on the other end of the couch, and set her feet on his leg.

He leaned forward and ruffled Claire's hair, earning a "Heyyy!" of mock indignation. Her brother smiled at Meg, his eyes holding hers a little longer than they used to. *Interesting.* With a wink at Kathryn, Aaron adjusted the blanket over them both.

It would take a while to really feel better. Years, maybe. But evenings like this were like warm oil being poured over her. Kathryn relaxed into the sensation as she focused her attention on the television. By the time the movie ended, she was almost asleep and didn't have the energy to respond when Meg leaned down and kissed her on the cheek. She and Claire tiptoed out of the room.

Kathryn felt Aaron's eyes on her for a moment before he reached over and switched off the lamp on the table next to the couch. Every muscle in her body tensed at the sudden darkness. She swallowed hard, pushing away the suffocating fear. *Relax. Aaron is here and you're safe at home. Nothing can happen to you.* He tugged the blanket toward him a little and stretched his long legs out in front of him. Soon his breathing slowed and, soothed by the rhythmic sound, she drifted off to sleep.

A noise in the middle of the night woke her. It was so dark. Panic swept over her and she struggled to sit up. A shaft of moonlight streamed through the window, glinting off something metal. Kathryn's heart slammed painfully. The quiet creak of a wooden floorboard sent her groping for the lamp, icy fingers of terror closing around her throat. She pressed the switch and the room flooded with soft light. A scream rose, but when she opened her mouth, no sound came out.

Kevin Dylan stood in front of the window, turning the long, sharp knife over and over in his hand.

Kathryn tried to scramble to her feet, but her body was paralyzed, refusing to obey the commands her mind was sending it. *Aaron!* The desperate cry was trapped by the constriction in her throat. Her brother continued to sleep beside her.

Dylan crossed the room. He planted one foot in front of the other, drawing out the moment. The blade caught the light from the lamp. As they had been the last time, her eyes were drawn to the flashing weapon. The instrument of her death mesmerized as it advanced.

When he reached her, Dylan dropped to one knee on the couch. Tangling his hand in her hair, he yanked her head back. She screamed then—a blood-chilling sound that rent the silence of the night. Strong arms pinned her. She fought to free herself, pounding her fists on the chest that pressed against her.

"Kat, it's me. It's Aaron. I've got you." Her brother's voice was soothing, gradually breaking into her consciousness. Tears continued to flow down her cheeks and dampen his denim shirt as she stilled in his arms. He held her, rocking back and forth and whispering words of comfort. After a few minutes, he smoothed the damp tendrils of hair that curled around her face, then pressed her head to his chest and leaned against the arm of the couch.

Although terrified to close her eyes, the horror of the nightmare had drained her, and she couldn't fight the exhaustion. Aaron's eyes closed too, and they both slept, bathed by the gentle light of the lamp left on to dispel the blackness of the night.

Wednesday

After That Night, Kathryn had dreamed almost every time she slept, terrible nightmares so real to her that only Aaron could bring her out of them. They had waned as the years passed, and it had been a long time since she had gone to that cabin in the night. Not surprisingly, the events of the last couple of days had dragged her there again, kicking and screaming. Literally.

I glanced toward the open window. If things got out of control, I sincerely hoped that Aaron would hear her and come running from the smaller house on the property where he and Meg lived. I had no desire for Horror and Terror to show up again. Their idea of a good time is to wrap corpse-like fingers around your throat and choke you nearly to death before dropping you into a weeping, shivering huddle on the floor. Nice.

Aaron could keep them at bay, but if he didn't hear her, as in her dreams, it would only be the two of us. Like that night in the cabin all over again. Except we weren't alone then, and we weren't alone now.

I stared hard into the shadowy corners of the room. Fear was here. But other Beings were as well. Faith. Courage. Even Love, still hanging around waiting to see what would happen. Like I said, the guy was tenacious. I guess I was too. He appeared as tired and weak as I felt, but at least neither of us had given up and gone home. Not yet.

Fear clung to my back like a pesky little brother. I gave my shoulders an impatient shake to toss him off and settled in to wait.

Chapter Sixteen

In spite of being awake most of the night, Kathryn was up and showered by 9 am. Thankfully, the first thing she did when she went downstairs was brew a fresh pot of coffee. I inhaled deeply as I meandered into the kitchen to see what she was up to. A piece of toast sat on a white china plate in front of her, a tiny corner of it missing. Otherwise, her breakfast appeared to be untouched. An envelope lay on the table.

She reached out and I raised my eyebrows in anticipation, but she ran her fingers lightly over the scrawled handwriting and then, with a soft sigh, pushed her chair away from the table. Grabbing her mug, she headed to the coffeemaker. A picture stuck to the fridge with a little ladybug magnet on each corner caught her eye, and she stopped to study it. My morning boost delayed by her detour, I ambled across the room to join her. A small smile played across her face as she stared at the picture of a tiny Tory standing in her crib, gripping the rails and no doubt hollering to be set free. That girl had always known what she wanted, and once she set her mind to something it was nearly impossible to turn her from her course.

Which explained the dread on Kathryn's face when they spoke on the phone yesterday. Tory had talked for years about finding out who her father was, but always in passing. That last call was the first time she had sounded like she'd truly made up her mind to find out. Maybe she somehow knew without being told that the door had been cracked open by Nick Lawson's visit, and if she didn't push through now to find out what was on the other side, she may never have another chance. As much as I would have liked to have sided with her mother on this, I had to admit Tory might be right.

I filled my lungs with the rich scent of mocha then checked on Kathryn. Pain swam in her eyes. The sound of waves crashing onto the sand filled the air and my heart sank. She was remembering the day at the ocean, the day both her and her daughter's lives had nearly ended. That was the second time in her life Kathryn had become convinced that I was as far away from her as the distant horizon and that she would never find me again.

At the risk of sounding immodest, who would want to live with that?

June 1999

Kathryn was running. Where she was running to she didn't know and didn't care. All she knew was that she couldn't stop until she'd outrun the sound of the doctor's voice in her head. When the ground gave way beneath her feet, she lifted her head to see a vast expanse of silver-white sand leading down to the ocean she'd always loved. Salt-laden air coated her throat as she drew in one ragged breath after another. She closed her eyes and let the sound of the breakers pounding against the shore wash over her as she slowed her pace to a walk, both hands low on her hips.

Pain shot through her leg as she stumbled over a large rock at the water's edge and nearly fell. When she caught herself on its jagged edges, her hands scraped across the surface. Kathryn was grateful for the pain when it hit her. For a moment, it took her mind off the news she'd been given an hour earlier.

When the stinging in her shin and hands eased, she lowered herself onto the stone, drawing her knees to her chest. It would be so easy to walk out into the cool, dark waves. To keep going until the sound of the surf and the crying of the seagulls faded away. To wade into a world where there was no more sound, no more pain.

Her eyes scanned the surface of the water, locking on a point far out in the sea where the tips of the waves broke. Whitecaps beckoned to her as though the outstretched hands of all those who over the centuries had found peace in the water's soft embrace summoned her to join them.

Kathryn nodded.

She climbed off the rock and made her way to the water's edge. The waves rolled onto the sand, lapping at her shoes. She bent down and tugged them off, never taking her eyes off that point in the distance. The ocean was cool and refreshing on her feet. The water called to her like a siren, the force stronger than her will to survive. She took several more steps. The waves rose above her ankles and splashed up her legs. Suddenly a sharp pain shot across her shin. She glanced down. The salty water had reached the open gash. The unbearable stinging jolted her out of her trance.

Kathryn threw back her head and wrapped both arms around her waist as waves of agony washed over her. "Oh, God. Why? Will this never end?" Tears dripped from her chin to disappear in the dark, swirling water below.

For several minutes she stood with her face lifted to the sky, the ocean waves splashing around her knees. Bumps rose on her arms and legs. When her teeth began to chatter, she waded to shore, rubbing both arms to stop the shivering. With a heavy sigh, she climbed onto the rock again and stared out at the expanse of blue water. The curling whitecaps flowed away from the shore as though refusing to wait for her any longer. A stab of regret shot through her at the lost opportunity.

Her gaze traveled to where the sky reached down to meet the ocean. Wisps of red and orange blazed across the horizon as the sun dipped lower, dropping splashes of color onto the surface of the water. Kathryn drew a deep, shuddering breath. Her nose and mouth filled with the damp, heavy air that hung at the edge of the shore. One hand lay across her stomach. She pressed her other hand to her mouth.

The memory of her doctor walking into the room, eyes filled with compassion, played across her mind. A baby. How often had she longed for the day she would hear those words? She squeezed her eyes shut. Somehow she never imagined they'd be accompanied by this overwhelming horror.

Wrapping her arms around both knees, she rocked back and forth. *What should I do? Can I get rid of it?* Her eyes flew open. Never in her wildest dreams would she have believed that she could even consider ending the life of her unborn child.

Dreams. She laughed bitterly. She had no more dreams. No Europe. No grad school. No life. Everything important to her had been torn away, against her will, by two brutal strangers. Her chin dropped onto her folded hands. *Not that my will has had anything to do with this.* Eyes hardening, Kathryn glanced up. Darkness edged across the sky like thick paint spreading across a palette, blotting out the colors underneath.

"What about *your* will?" She glared at the sky. The wind sprinkled cool droplets of salty water across her flushed cheeks. "Is that what this is?" She slid her arms from her knees to tighten them against her stomach. "Could this really be what you want? Do you have any control whatsoever over what happens on this planet? Do you even care?" She clenched her fists and ground them against her forehead. Her voice rose as she flung the words toward the heavens. "I don't even know whose baby this is."

Both hands dropped down to rest on the rock as a warm wind blew across the surface of the ocean. Like fingers passing over her, a soft breeze dried the tears that had made tracks to her chin. Kathryn lifted her face to the sky as the wind circled her, wrapping her in its soothing embrace.

In the soft sighing of the breeze as it swirled around her, her heart finally stilled as three words were pressed into her heart.

She is mine.

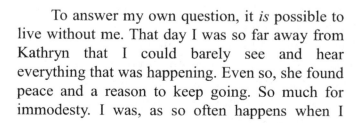

To answer my own question, it *is* possible to live without me. That day I was so far away from Kathryn that I could barely see and hear everything that was happening. Even so, she found peace and a reason to keep going. So much for immodesty. I was, as so often happens when I forget myself and overinflate my own importance, humbled at the reminder. Still, I wasn't about to leave her entirely, not now.

Because, as dark as things seemed to her at the moment, the light was about to dim even further.

Chapter Seventeen

June 1999

Kathryn brushed the side of the gray, dappled mare Bonnie, the horse her parents had given her when she graduated from high school four years earlier. The slightly sweet scent of alfalfa hung in the air, and she breathed deeply. Aaron stopped outside the stall and flung a pitchfork of straw in her direction.

"Hey," Kathryn protested, swiping the straw off her pink T-shirt. Particles drifted on the air and she sneezed.

"Sorry." Given the laughter in her brother's voice, she suspected he wasn't one bit sorry. She couldn't bring herself to be too irritated. For twelve terrifying hours a couple of months ago she hadn't been sure she'd ever see this barn, her horse, or Aaron again. Every time she came out here she remembered that and was filled with a renewed sense of how precious life was. She'd never take a minute of it for granted again.

The gleaming saddle hanging over the top of the stall caught her eye and she contemplated it, resting her chin on the back of the horse. The tightness in her chest had nothing to do with breathing in the particles of dust hanging in the air in the barn. The last time she'd ridden she'd been with Ty. A tear slid down her cheek, but she swiped it away.

"Hey."

Kathryn lifted her head. Aaron stood in the opening of the stall, still clutching the pitchfork. His yellow T-shirt and jeans were covered in a thin layer of straw particles. "What is it?"

She resumed brushing. "Nothing."

"Kat." Her brother rested the pitchfork against the side of the stall and walked over to her. "Come on."

She sighed. "I was thinking about the last time I went riding. With Ty."

"Ah." He took her elbow and turned her to face him. "Have you heard from him?"

"He's sent me a few texts asking how I'm doing, that's all."
Ty had come to see her in the hospital. Once. She'd been asleep,
so she only knew that he'd been there because her mom had told
her when Kathryn asked about the bouquet of flowers on the
table beside her bed. His texts were brief and always about her,
not how he was feeling about everything that had happened. He
hadn't asked if he could come around since she'd been home
from the hospital.

"Does he know?"

"About the baby?" Kathryn tugged a piece of straw from
Bonnie's mane and flicked it onto the floor. "I think so. I wanted
to tell him in person, or at least on the phone, but I called a few
times and he didn't answer. I finally left a message yesterday."

"And he didn't call back." The laughter was gone from
Aaron's voice now.

Kathryn leaned a shoulder against Bonnie's rounded side,
drawing comfort from the short bristly hairs and musky scent of
her. "No, but I don't blame him. This is a lot to deal with. He
needs time."

Aaron's jaw tightened. "He's had two months, Kat. You
went through a lot more than he did—you're still going through
it—and you're dealing with it."

She lifted a shoulder. "I know, but ..."

"Hello?"

Kathryn froze at the sound of someone calling from outside
the barn. Ty.

Aaron's eyes met hers. "Do you want to see him?"

All she'd wanted the last two months was for Ty to show up,
wrap his arms around her, and tell her that he still loved her. That
what had happened in that cabin hadn't changed how he felt
about her, and that everything was going to be okay. Now he was
here, and instead of the joy she thought she'd feel, a deep
apprehension gripped her. Obviously he was struggling to come
to terms with what had happened. What if he was here to tell her
that he couldn't? "I ... I don't know."

Aaron nodded. "I'll talk to him. If you decide you don't

want to, stay here and I'll tell him to go."

"Okay."

Her brother tugged gently on her ponytail before walking to the opening of the stall. "Aaron?"

One hand on the door post, he glanced at her. "Yep?"

"Be nice."

His eyes hardened a little. "No promises." Without another word, he strode across the barn floor. He'd left the double wooden doors open when they had come out to the barn after dinner, and Ty stepped into the opening. Kathryn's breath caught. In a gray T-shirt and black jeans, he was as cute as she remembered. A little thinner, maybe. And his hair was longer, as if he hadn't gotten it cut since the last time they'd been together. Kathryn ducked behind Bonnie's neck where he couldn't see her but she'd be able to hear what he and Aaron were saying.

"Hey, Ty." Aaron's greeting was uncharacteristically curt.

"Hi, Aaron." Ty's voice was equally tight. Kathryn pressed a hand to her stomach. Was he nervous about seeing her after waiting so long or because of what he'd come to say? "Is Kathryn around?"

"She is, but I'm not sure she wants to see you."

Ty scuffed at the gravel and loose hay around the door with the toe of his running shoe. "I get it. I should have come by a long time ago. I know that."

The misery on his face tugged at Kathryn's heart. *This is crazy. It's Ty. Listen to what he has to say.* She patted Bonnie's soft neck, drawing strength, then made her way to the opening of the stall. "I'll talk to him, Aaron."

He didn't move as she came up to stand beside him. "Are you sure?"

She wasn't sure. At all. "Yes. It's fine."

"All right. I'll be outside if you need me."

"Thanks."

Ty stepped aside as Aaron tromped through the door in his heavy work boots. Kathryn couldn't see the look her brother gave Ty, but his face blanched a little. He must have shot Ty some kind

of warning.

"Come inside." Without waiting for him to enter the barn, Kathryn spun around and strode over to the hay mow. A few bales were scattered on the barn floor at the base of the towering pile, and she sank onto one, not sure how much longer her weakened knees would hold her up.

Ty dropped onto a bale a couple of feet from her. "I'm sorry, Kath," he blurted out.

"For?"

"Not coming sooner. Or returning your calls. I've been a complete coward."

"It was a lot to process."

He shook his head. "Don't let me off the hook. I don't deserve that." One of his hands had curled into a fist on his thigh. The fingers of his other hand dug into the back of it, leaving trails of white across his skin. "How are you doing?"

Kathryn shoved her trembling fingers under her legs. The sharp tip of a piece of hay dug into her skin, but she was grateful for the distraction. "I'm not sure how to answer that. Some days are better than others. I still have a lot of nightmares. It's been tough. My family has been great—they've really been here for me."

He lifted eyes rimmed with dark shadows to meet hers. "And I haven't been."

"It's okay. You—"

"It's not okay." The words exploded from him.

Kathryn blinked. A movement by the door caught her eye. She shook her head slightly and Aaron moved away. Out of sight but not by much, she suspected.

Ty drove his fingers through his dark hair. "I'm sorry. I can't seem to forgive myself for what I did."

She jerked. "What *you* did?"

"Yes. Leaving you that night. I should have waited until you were in the car. If I had, none of this would have—"

Kathryn tugged a hand loose and bent forward to grasp his forearm. His muscles tensed rock hard beneath her fingers.

"None of this is your fault, Ty. I haven't blamed you. Not for a second."

He pulled his arm away. "I never was good enough for you."

Was? Why was he talking about them in the past tense? "Don't say that." All this time, waiting for him to show up, she'd told herself he only needed time to work through everything that had happened. That when he had, he'd return to her and the two of them could figure out a way to move forward together. Until this moment, she hadn't allowed herself to consider the possibility that they might not be able to. That *he* wouldn't be able to.

"It's true. You are better off without me, Kath."

"Ty, don't …"

"I'm sorry. I can't." He pushed to his feet. "I'm truly sorry."

For a moment, she couldn't move. She could only watch helplessly as he lurched toward the door. By the time she had willed her frozen legs to obey her and carry her across the barn floor, he was gone. Kathryn stumbled over a feed bucket, catching herself with both hands against the rough barn board next to the doorway. Through a crack between the boards, she could see Ty standing with his back to Aaron, his hands thrust into the pockets of his jeans, his shoulders slumped. Night had fallen while she and Aaron had been in the barn, and a single light dangling from a lamp post cast a dim glow over the yard.

"What are you doing, Ty? She loves you." When Ty didn't answer, Aaron grabbed his arm and forced him to turn around. "How can you walk away from—" He released his grip. Kathryn rested her forehead against the board. Ty's face was a mask of agony. His eyes, when he lifted them to Aaron's, were red and swollen.

Ty's jaw worked as though he was trying to form the words to reply. When he did, his voice was laced with grief. "I love her too. I'll always love her. But …" He lowered his gaze to his feet. "One of the things I loved most about her was that she was so trusting, so innocent."

Kathryn's knuckles scraped against wood as she tightened

her hands into fists.

"She hasn't done anything wrong," Aaron said hotly.

"I know. But that doesn't change the fact that she ..." He swallowed before continuing in a voice so raspy that Kathryn could barely catch the words. "That she's carrying another man's child."

She closed her eyes. White hot anger exploded in her chest and was pumped out to every cell in her body—not directed at Ty, but at the two strangers whose one night of brutal, senseless violence threatened to destroy all of their lives.

"Could you do it, Aaron?"

Her brother's shoulders had also slumped, as if they were both bowing beneath the weight of what had happened in that cabin. "Could I do what?"

"If this happened to the woman you loved. Could you still hold her? Love her? Marry her?" Ty's voice rose, shot through with a pain so deep that Kathryn was tempted to cover her ears.

Aaron didn't answer for a moment. When he did, the words were heavy with weary resignation. "I don't know. I hope I could."

Kathryn prayed to God that he'd never have to find out. Like Ty had.

"Until a few weeks ago, I would have said the same thing."

The quiet words pelted her like a handful of flung stones. As much as it tore the heart from her chest, she couldn't blame Ty for not knowing how to handle the situation. They were all feeling their way through this terrible time, hands stretched in front of them, groping through a darkness that only seemed to grow deeper as they went along.

"I've considered it a thousand different ways, and I ..." Ty withdrew his hands from his pockets and lifted them in the air. "I ... can't do it. I just can't." He started toward his car. After a few steps, he stopped and glanced over his shoulder. "Take care of her."

The pang that shot across Kathryn's chest made her gasp for air.

"I will." Aaron leaned a hip against the side of an empty hay wagon as though he needed the support.

Ty's headlights flashed through the crack before he swung his car around and drove out the lane, disappearing into the darkness.

Like they were all in danger of doing.

Kathryn slid along the boards to the ground, welcoming the pain as slivers dug into her arm and side. Bending her knees, she wrapped her arms around them and stared across the barn without really seeing anything. A shadow fell over the cement in front of the opening before her brother stepped inside.

"Kat?" He scanned the interior of the building. When he spotted her next to the door, he crouched in front of her. Kathryn didn't move, not even when he clasped her knees with both hands. "Are you all right?"

The words came to her muffled and distorted, as though he was talking to her from under the water. Her eyelids flickered as she attempted to focus on his face. The flash of alarm in his eyes should have stirred something in her—the desire to reassure him, somehow—but she couldn't summon the energy.

His lips moved as if in prayer, but all that came from his mouth was a low groan. It was that—the sound of his wordless suffering, a language she could understand—that finally got through to her, that drew her back.

"He says he can't be with me." The words were toneless, as though she was reciting the second law of thermodynamics.

Aaron grasped her hands and pulled them to his chest. "I know. I talked to him."

"I hate them."

He didn't ask who she was talking about.

"They've taken everything from me. Everything."

"Kat." He didn't say anything else. What was there to say? Words were meaningless.

Kathryn took a deep, ragged breath. "Do you know why I left the restaurant when I did that night?"

His forehead wrinkled as if he was trying to remember. "No."

"I was going home to get my Sunday school lesson ready." Dark shadows of rage flitted through her. "I was doing *God's* work, trying to serve Him the way I thought He wanted me to." She extricated her hands from his and pounded her knees with clenched fists. "I'm so angry with God, Aaron. I want to hate Him like I hate them." The anger evaporated as quickly as it came, and she dropped her face into her hands. "Except that I don't really want to hate Him. I only want Him to tell me why." The words ended in a cry, a plea for answers she knew might never come.

He rested his hand on her head. "You feel whatever you need to feel, Kat. God can handle it."

Kathryn lifted her head. "Do you know what I need to feel?"

Aaron shook his head.

"Nothing."

He shifted to sit on the floor, his back to the wall. Tugging her to his side, he wrapped his arm around her and drew her close. She rested her head on his shoulder. From her stall, Bonnie whinnied softly, as if sensing Kathryn's need for comfort. Numbness spread through her. Maybe she could find a way, if only for a few hours, to feel nothing.

Aaron rested his cheek on her head. Remembering the agony in his eyes as he tried to offer her at least a small measure of solace, she breathed a fervent prayer that he might be able to do the same.

Chapter Eighteen

Wednesday

Unfortunately for me, the memories of that dark time drove all thoughts of coffee from Kathryn's head. She turned away from the picture on the fridge and dropped onto her chair with a heavy sigh. I followed her, my sigh equally heavy. She had occasionally found a way over the years to feel nothing, but those times were rare and never lasted long. Her will to live, to be there for her daughter, to find me, was too strong.

I never said it was easy to do that, by the way. I go where I am directed, and for reasons I don't always understand myself I am usually instructed to stand at the end of a path lined with trials and pain.

Not everyone finds their way along the path, although I stand and silently cheer them on. I never know who will make it. I had watched Kathryn come a long way in her journey toward me over the years. Still, there had been moments, like the one at the ocean and the night Ty came to see her, when I wasn't at all sure she was going to be able to keep going. So far she had, but even I, with my limited foresight, could see that she had yet to face the biggest obstacles that stood between us.

I wasn't sure I could stand to watch. I hadn't had any vacation in what seemed like an eternity. This might be as good a time as any to put in for some.

My shoulders slumped. This was no time to take a holiday—not that such a thing was a possibility. I needed to be there for Kathryn. After all we had been through together, I wouldn't leave her now for all the coffee in Brazil.

Probably.

Clutching the mug she had eventually filled, Kathryn stared out the kitchen window, her thoughts returning to the one she'd made plans to go and see that day. Would she be able to do it? For a few minutes, contemplating the battle raging across her face, I wasn't sure. Then her chin lifted and she drained the last few drops of coffee. I'd seen that look in her eyes often enough over the years to know that she had decided.

Whether or not he was ready to see her, David Henley better prepare himself. Even with all the challenges he had faced over the years—most the result of his own poor choices—the most daunting one was about to show up on his doorstep unannounced.

August 2001

David wheeled the cart into the laundry room in the basement of the prison. Five industrial-sized machines lined the walls and he filled them all, threw in the soap, and slammed the doors.

He turned to go and stopped short. Somehow the six of them had crept into the room so quietly he'd had no warning of their approach. *Oh man.* This was not good. David had heard of this gang. Several inmates had warned him it would be a good idea to pay for their "protection"—namely, against themselves—but he'd refused to give them anything. Now, as they advanced toward him, he had second thoughts about that decision.

"Hey, guys." He lowered his head in a gesture of surrender. "Let's talk about this, okay?"

"Talk?" A tall, dark-haired guy with a thick Irish accent, obviously the leader of the group, laughed. "It's a little late for that, buddy."

"Yeah." A short man built like a tank who worked out in the gym for hours every day took a step toward him. "We've been trying to talk to you for a while now. We're done talking. We're more men of action anyway."

The others laughed.

"You should have taken us up on our offer while it was still good, man." The tall one raised his hands, palms upward, indicating that the matter was now out of his control. "You'd be surprised what a couple of packs of cigarettes will do for you around here."

David's heart sank. *Stay calm. You've been here before.* Okay, maybe not against six, but he'd learned a thing or two in this place—he should be able to take out a couple of them.

Lowering his head, he charged at the nearest man, a big linebacker type. A loud *oof* filled the air as his head connected with the guy's stomach. Adrenaline shot through him as the man sank to his knees. The feeling was short-lived, as the other five were on him in an instant.

David could do little to protect himself except to curl into the fetal position. Heavy boots pounded into the small of his back. He arched backward, gasping for breath. A foot connected with his head, and he cried out as pain exploded behind his eyes. Wrapping one arm around his knees, he circled his head with the other. Another kick connected with his face, below his right eye, and a blaze of fire ripped across his cheek. A dark fog swirled in front of his eyes.

The soft thud of boots on flesh, accompanied by frenzied laughter, were the last sounds David heard as he slipped into darkness.

He fought against consciousness when it came for him. Clinging to oblivion, David moaned when it slipped from his grasp. His body felt as if it had been dipped in a vat of oil and set on fire—like he would continue to burn but never be allowed the relief of death. Heavy eyelids pushed against the swelling to crack open.

A large black man sat on a chair beside his cot. He dipped a washcloth into cool water and wiped David's forehead. When he saw David was awake, a smile spread across his face. "Welcome back, brother." A perfect match for his intimidating size, the man's voice reverberated through David's pounding head. "We thought you were a goner there, for a bit."

"Is that still an option?" The words tore at his throat like shards of glass. He must have taken a hit there as well. Lucky for him, his windpipe hadn't been crushed. *Or maybe not so lucky.* The big man laughed and stuck a large, meaty hand toward him. For some reason, David's body didn't seem to be obeying anything his mind told it to do, and he couldn't raise his arm.

"Sorry, man." The stranger settled for slapping him on the shoulder.

A sharp intake of breath sent spasms of pain hurtling through David's chest and rattling along his ribs. *Don't scream. He's trying to help you.*

"Is he awake?"

As slightly as possible, David turned his head toward the door as two men walked into the room. The first was tall and wiry, and his head was shaved bald. Every exposed part of his body was covered with tattoos.

The other man was short with red hair. Freckles covered his grinning face. "Welcome to the land of the living, bro. We haven't met yet. I'm Pete, this guy is Tommy, and the big guy here goes by Tiny, for obvious reasons."

The three of them laughed, and David attempted a smile. A stab of pain reminded him that his face had taken at least one direct hit during the attack, and he dropped it quickly.

Tommy dragged a chair across the floor to his bed, then turned it around and sat on it, resting his arms on the back of it and rocking forward on two of the legs. "How are you feelin', buddy? They really did a number on ya, huh?"

David grimaced. "Given a choice between those guys and a Mack truck, I think I would have taken my chances with the truck."

Tommy tilted his head. "You must be wondering who we are. The guards brought you here to the infirmary after they found you pretty much dead in the basement. The doc did what he could for you then they asked us to come see you. They said you were one of us."

The three of them gazed at him as though he should know what they were talking about. David stared back in helpless confusion until Tiny came to the rescue. "You know, man, a believer?"

A light went off in his head. "Ahh." He sank onto his pillow. "One of you. Got it." The edges of his vision blurred. He wanted nothing more than to close his eyes and drift into nothingness again.

"It's all right, go to sleep. We'll be here when you wake up." Tiny dipped the cloth into the water. "It's good to have you around. We're kind of in short supply around here."

David nodded. Pain shot through his neck, and he winced. A sudden revelation pierced the thick mist swirling around in his mind. This was how she must have felt. Kathryn Ellison. Helpless. Outnumbered. Terrified. In so much pain that death seemed like the best of all possible options. He closed his eyes.

He deserved every hit he'd taken from those guys for doing that to her.

Chapter Nineteen

Kathryn was going to see David today. Absolutely, one hundred percent. She had charted her course and nothing would cause her to turn from it to one side or the other. What was yet to be decided, however, was *when* she was going.

When she strode from the kitchen, determination on her face, and headed up to her room, I assumed she was getting ready to leave. Too weary to follow, I sank onto the bottom step to wait for her return. The top step creaked, and I twisted to peer up at her as she descended. Instead of the formal outfit I'd expected, she'd dressed in running clothes. Ah. So we were going to work off a little steam before we went, were we? Was that an attempt to calm herself or to delay the inevitable? Regardless, I pushed off the steps and followed her to the door.

She shoved her feet into her running shoes. I pulled on a pair of my own—psychologically. I was most definitely not a runner. In times of uncertainty such as those I was currently experiencing along with Kathryn, I was, at best, a trudger. Not wanting to fall behind and miss out on anything, I was resolved to put my best foot forward. Or feet, in this case.

A flickering in the living room drew my attention. As Kathryn was tying her laces, I followed the well-worn ruts she'd carved between there and the kitchen in the hours since Nick's unexpected visit.

In the doorway, I stopped, bemused. Outside, the sun beamed from a cloudless sky. So why had dark shadows gathered along every wall of the living room, many of them slithering upward to glide like smoke along the white crown molding?

Lightning flashed outside the window. What in the world?

Then it struck me. The threatening weather was not, in fact, of this world. I shivered and wrapped my arms tightly around myself as a cold northern wind swept through the living room.

He was coming.

When Kevin Dylan had left the cabin that day, no voice had kept him from crossing over the border and disappearing, at least none that he was able—or willing—to hear. He'd headed straight to Florida, as far from British Columbia as he could get without risking another border, before starting to work his way west again. I'd watched him for a while, wanting to make sure he was really gone, that he was out of Kathryn's life for good. I'd watched until, sick with revulsion and disgust, I couldn't watch anymore.

April 2002

Kevin Dylan bent his leg and pressed the bottom of his shoe to the brick wall behind him. Even on this cool spring evening, the narrow alleyway between two businesses on a quiet side street in Wichita, Kansas stank of rotting garbage from dumpsters that hadn't been rinsed out in years.

Tugging a pack of cigarettes out of his shirt pocket, he tapped one onto his palm, worked the lighter out of the small box, and cupped his hand around the flame as he touched it to the end of the cigarette. After returning the lighter and the rest of the pack to his pocket, he took a long draw, letting the nicotine-laden smoke waft into his lungs, calming him.

Pressing a button on the side of his watch, he illuminated the face. Nine fifteen. He'd followed a redhead for a week now and knew she finished work at a record store a couple of streets over at nine. She should be coming by soon.

Dylan raised his head. Heels clicked against the sidewalk, heading in his direction. He shifted along the wall a little until he caught a glimpse of her passing beneath a streetlight half a block away.

His mouth twisted into a cold smile. She was alone. Good. Not that he couldn't handle the challenge. Another body meant things wouldn't be as tidy as he liked, however. And after what had happened with that woman in the cabin in Canada, he was determined to keep things tidy. His smile disappeared. Although he'd only been in Canada for twenty-four hours, in one night he'd left a trail as wide as the Sahara Desert. He'd been lucky to get away after that. He'd stayed in the States for a few years to let things cool off up there, but he was slowly making his way north again. In his mind he and Kathryn Ellison had unfinished business, and he didn't like to leave his business unfinished.

The memory of the cabin in British Columbia brought his mood crashing down. That whole situation had been a fiasco from start to finish. Sure, they'd been able to have a little fun, but even that fell flat somehow. Something about that woman's eyes still haunted him. And what had happened the next morning—Dylan went cold.

In every unguarded moment, her words echoed in his head. Talking to someone who wasn't there and then turning and gazing at him with those brown and green eyes and saying, "God help you."

And that light he'd seen, near the ceiling.

He'd really lost it at that point. He'd even started imagining things, started feeling like there really might be someone there watching everything that was going on. A chill passed through him and he shuddered. Next time he saw Kathryn Ellison he would put that light out for good.

Dylan's thumb and index finger tightened around the cigarette. The woman had nearly reached the alley. He reached for the knife strapped to his calf. Before he could lift the bottom of his jeans, the woman raised a hand and a smile broke across her face.

He bit back a foul word as she reached the person she'd greeted—some guy—at the opening to the alley. Abandoning the knife, Dylan shoved away from the wall and tugged the pistol from the back of his jeans. The man pulled the redhead into his arms. When she slid her hands under his suit jacket, the light from the lamppost glinted off something clipped to his waistband.

Dylan lowered the cigarette to his side to hide the red tip. A cop. Sliding a little deeper into the shadows, he pursed his lips.

Clearly the man's mind was on other things—it wouldn't require much to take him out. Dylan could exit the alleyway, use his weapon on the guy, and force the girl into his truck before either of them were able do anything to stop him. He grimaced. Gunning a cop down in the streets would draw far too much attention to himself. Even waiting for another night until the redhead was alone, as she had been the other evenings he'd followed her, was risky. Grabbing the wife or girlfriend or whatever she was of a police detective would bring the full force of the Wichita PD—maybe even the Feds, if they figured out what else he'd done since fleeing Canada—raining down on him.

After shoving the gun into his jeans, he forced himself not to move until the two of them strolled off, arm in arm.

Dylan dropped the cigarette onto the cement. It landed at his feet between a crushed beer can and a fast food takeout bag. He ground the butt with the toe of his boot, far longer and harder than necessary to extinguish the tiny glow. He could be patient. Another opportunity would present itself.

It always did.

Chapter Twenty

Wednesday

Thunder continued to rumble in the distance as I slipped out the screen door behind Kathryn. Thoughts and images of Kevin Dylan crawled all over me like bed bugs in a fleabag motel. I brushed off my arms and legs, knowing it wouldn't help. I couldn't worry about him. Not yet. If I was going to be any good to Kathryn, I needed to walk this journey with her one step at a time. At the moment, that meant doing my best to tamp down my desire to be on the road and away from here.

We'd leave the house and head to Maple Ridge at some point today. For now, I traipsed along behind her, relishing the last few moments of lounging on the lawn as she stretched, warming up. I zeroed in on her thoughts. Before she'd gone to the kitchen to make coffee that morning, she'd taken another trip to the living room. I'd hopped up onto the couch beside her. She had lifted the lid from the box and rummaged around for a few seconds before tugging loose an envelope that had been torn open across the top.

The first letter.

May 2002

"Come on, Tory, race ya to the mailbox." Excited squeals filled the air as Kathryn chased her daughter down the laneway. Blond braids bounced against the yellow and white checked dress Kathryn's mom had sewn for her first granddaughter.

Tory ran to the wooden post that held the mailbox, slapped her hand against it, and spun around to grin at her mother.

"You win." Kathryn hung her head in feigned defeat.

"Mail, Mommy, mail." The tiny hand reached up as far as it could toward the metal mailbox with sunflowers painted across both sides. Kathryn lifted her the rest of the way and Tory reached in with both hands to grab the pile. "Walk."

"Yes, ma'am." She lowered the girl to the ground and touched the side of her hand to her temple in mock salute.

With an imperious nod, Tory started for the house, clutching the stack of envelopes to her chest.

Kathryn suppressed a grin. Her daughter took her responsibility as official mail collector very seriously. It was probably the only time she wasn't running as fast as—

A brown and white rabbit bounded across the driveway in front of them, interrupting her thoughts. "Mommy, look!" Letters flew everywhere as Tory pointed a chubby finger in the direction of the bouncing white tail. Her eyes widened in dismay.

"It's all right, Tory." Kathryn rushed to help her. "We can gather them up again. Let's count them. One, two, three ..." She reached for another envelope. The return address ripped the breath from her body. Kent Institution, Agassiz, British Columbia. The letter had been sent to a law office in Vancouver and forwarded to her.

She bent forward, gasping for air.

"What's wrong, Mommy?"

"Nothing, honey." The words sounded strange to her and very far away. *Breathe.*

"What's going on here? Who made this big mess?" Gravel crunched beneath boots as Aaron approached them.

"Uncle Aaron." Laughter tumbled from Tory as her uncle scooped her up and swung her around. "Something's wrong with Mommy."

"I'm sure Mommy's fine." Aaron set his niece on the ground and glanced at Kathryn. "Maybe she wants the mail picked up. Should we help her?"

"Yes." Tory scrambled across the lane, gathering up the scattered envelopes and flyers.

Kathryn stared at the letter in her hand. *It can't be. He wouldn't ...*

"Kat?" Aaron's voice broke through her daze, and she

114

shifted her attention to him. When he saw her face, he left his niece and came to her side. "What is it? You look like you've seen a ghost." He studied the letter in her hand, his eyes narrowing. "Give it to me." Anger laced his words as he took hold of the envelope. "You don't have to read it. He has no right to send this to you."

Kathryn's fingers tightened around the letter with a rigor mortis-like grip.

Her brother contemplated her for a moment then released the envelope. "Come on, let's go in the house. You should sit down." He took her arm and led her up the lane, glancing over his shoulder as they went. "Come on, kiddo."

Tory picked up the last of the mail and skipped on ahead of them, her concern apparently forgotten.

Kathryn's mother was stirring a pot on the stove when the three of them entered the kitchen. Her father was grating cheese over a loaf of bread. The aroma of garlic, onions, and tomatoes wafted on the air. "Oh, there you are. I wondered—" Her mom tapped the spoon on the edge of the pot before setting it on the counter. "What is it, darling?" She wiped her hands on a towel and came around the counter to take her daughter's other arm.

"I'm okay." Bright sunlight poured through the window as Kathryn sank onto a kitchen chair, which didn't seem right somehow. She set the letter on the table in front of her and stared at it. *He wouldn't* ... No other thought would come to her.

"It's from him," Aaron said curtly.

Her father set down the grater, his face dark and stormy.

With a gasp, her mother pressed her fingers to her mouth. "Kathryn, throw it away." Her voice was tight. "He has no business writing you and dredging up painful memories."

The fury in her mother's voice, something Kathryn had rarely heard, penetrated the fog swirling in her head. Even now, from prison, David Henley was reaching out to hurt them.

"Yes, Kathryn." Her dad stopped next to the table. "Give it to me." He held out a work-worn hand. "I'll toss it into the stove."

She shook her head. "I can't. I'm sorry."

Her father waited a few seconds before lowering his arm and shoving his hand into the pocket of his work pants.

"Mommy? Why is everyone so sad?" Tory rested her arms on Kathryn's knees.

"Come on, Victoria." Her grandmother took her by the hand and led her out of the room. "Let's find a puzzle to do in the living room, okay?"

With a last, uncertain glance at Kathryn over his shoulder, her father followed them out of the room.

When they were gone, Aaron dragged another chair closer to her then perched on the edge of it. He took her ice-cold hand in his. "Hey." When she didn't move, he slid his fingers under her chin, forcing her to meet his eyes. "Listen to me, Kat. Get rid of this letter. Don't read it. You've been through so much the last few years, come so far."

Apprehension tightened her chest. Maybe they were right. Maybe she should throw it in the woodstove and forget it ever came. Something inside compelled her. "I can't. I have to read it."

"Why?" The anguish in his voice sent a wave of sadness washing over her. Sometimes she forgot how much her family had suffered since That Night.

"I'm not sure. But I have to."

Her brother took a deep breath. "Okay." The look on his face said this was anything but. "I'm staying here until you're done. You're not going to read it alone."

With a brief nod, Kathryn picked up the envelope. When her shaking fingers wouldn't cooperate, he took it from her, resting his hand over hers to still them. Without a word, he ripped open the envelope and handed it back.

Somehow she managed to withdraw a thin piece of white paper, folded in half. This would be a lot easier if she could breathe. Or swallow.

"Are you sure, Kat?"

116

Sure? That she wanted to be dragged back to That Night? No. But she had to do this. She nodded and scrutinized the piece of paper in her hand. Big, sweeping letters scrawled across the page. The date was written in the top right-hand corner. May 2, a week earlier. Olivia had told her that David Henley's trial had been postponed twice but was scheduled to start next month. Drawing in a shaky breath, she scanned the page.

Ms. Ellison,

I don't know how to begin. I've written this letter a hundred times, first in my head and then on paper. Each time I destroyed it, knowing it would cause you pain. Something pushed me to write you, so I'm making one more attempt.

I want to ask for your forgiveness. I know I don't deserve it and shouldn't even ask, but I need you to know that not one day has gone by that I don't regret everything that happened.

I had no intention of turning myself in after leaving the cabin. In fact, I'd driven to the border and was trying to cross over. Something kept telling me to turn around, so I did, very reluctantly. I checked into a motel room outside Vancouver where I spent the longest two days of my life. God was there, and even though I tried to push him away, he refused to let me go. After a long struggle, I finally gave my life to him.

I'm so sorry for the hurt and pain I caused you. I don't expect you to forgive me, but I had to tell you that.

David Henley

Wednesday

I shook out my arms and legs, as close to a warm-up as I ever indulged in, before easing into a jog alongside Kathryn. No dark shadows crept along the ground out here, and I lifted my face to allow the warm sunshine and cool breeze to drift over it.

Gravel crunched beneath Kathryn's running shoes as we ran, her thoughts racing faster than her feet. After she'd finished reading that first letter again, she'd set it on the coffee table and stared at it for a moment. Then she'd lowered her face into her hands, her shoulders shaking with sobs, the way they had the first time she had read it. That day, Aaron had wrapped his arms around her, holding her tightly until she calmed down. I glanced around, wishing he would show up now. He'd likely finished his chores and was having breakfast with Meg in the other house on the ranch property. Close by, but completely unaware of what was happening in the big house up the lane.

I'd give anything to have been able to tell him what was going on. If he knew, he'd have been here in a second, offering her the comfort and support he seemed to have a limitless supply of when it came to his sister. Kathryn could have called him, but apparently she had decided this was something she had to do herself.

All well and good, but she clearly wasn't thinking about me and how difficult all of this was to watch.

I'd fallen behind Kathryn, and I took a deep breath, hoping the infusion of oxygen would propel me forward. If she could handle what she was putting herself through in an attempt to ready herself to be in a relationship with Nick, so could I.

I only hoped we were both right about the limits of our endurance.

Chapter Twenty-One

"I told you to destroy it. Why would he write you? Hasn't he hurt you enough?"

Kathryn wiped the tears off her face with the back of her hands. "No, it's all right. I'm glad I read it. He—" Fresh tears welled in her eyes. Aaron reached behind him and grabbed a box of tissues off the kitchen counter and set it on the table in front of her.

Kathryn tugged one out and pressed it to the corners of her eyes. She studied his face. Concern wrinkled his forehead, but it was the anger that disturbed her. "Here." She nudged the letter closer to him. "You read it." He stared at the letter but didn't move. "Please, Aaron."

Exhaling loudly, he picked up the piece of paper by one corner as if even the act of touching it was distasteful to him.

"I know it's difficult, but please do it. It helped me and if it can help you at all …"

Her brother dropped his gaze to the paper. The same emotions Kathryn had felt reading the words—pain, anger, grief—crossed his face as he read.

But there was something else. He saw it, didn't he? Aaron set the letter on the table and gazed at her, a faint light in his eyes. In spite of all the hurt and sorrow, hope flickered—hope that God was somehow working her terrible experience for good. In the midst of the terror and violence in that cabin, tiny pinpricks of light had managed to force their way through the darkness.

That's something else that never fails to amaze me. It is a dark planet, has been since the day the first of your kind made the decision to turn away from the light. I can still feel it, that unfamiliar prick of pain that shot through me with that first bite of forbidden fruit. I thought then that the light was gone forever. A shadow fell over the planet in that moment—a heavy curtain drawn across the sky. We all felt it, that pain of separation, of ending, of innocence lost.

But we were shown then, and had it powerfully reinforced for us a few thousand years later, that light is stronger than darkness. I have seen it many times. Still, when the darkness hovers so thickly that I can no longer see my hand in front of my face, it is easy to forget.

David Henley just reminded me.

When Kathryn checked on her daughter that night, Tory's blond hair was spread across the pillow and her cheeks were flushed pink. One arm circled a soft white stuffed bunny that Kathryn's dad had given Tory on her first birthday. Moonlight streaming through the leaves of the maple tree outside the window cast a lacework of shadows across her face. *Sleep well, little one.*

Kathryn pushed away from the doorframe, descended the stairs, and tiptoed across the kitchen. The screen door creaked as she pushed it open. Settling into the porch swing, she tipped her head and closed her eyes, allowing the soft spring breeze to drift across her face.

"Mind if I join you?"

Without lifting her head, she smiled and patted the seat. Aaron sat beside her and they swung in silence, listening to the sound of crickets chirping in one loud chorus.

"Could you ever do it?"

Startled, Kathryn opened her eyes. "Do what?"

"Forgive him, like he asked?" Aaron stretched his arm along the swing, and Kathryn rested her head against it.

She sighed. "I don't know."

He nodded and ruffled her hair. They rocked in silence until

120

her eyelids grew heavy. Then she kissed her brother on the cheek and rose. "Good night, Aaron."

He appeared thoughtful but smiled at her. "'Night, Kat."

Drained and exhausted, Kathryn crawled beneath the covers. Her racing mind refused to allow her to sleep, and she tossed and turned. At last, she flopped onto her back and stared at the ceiling.

You're not going to let me ignore the question, are you? She blew out a breath. Forgive David Henley? That was something she'd never even considered. How could she? Tension stiffened every muscle in her body. So he sounded sincere in his letter— did that mean she had to forgive him?

Yes, because I have.

Clenched fists grasped the blanket at her sides. *No. I can't do it. It's too much to ask. You know what they did to me.*

A soft whisper in the dark brought tears dashing across Kathryn's face.

And you know what they did to me.

All the fight went out of her. Flinging an arm across her eyes, she lifted her free hand, palm up in a gesture of surrender. *I'll try. For you.*

The voice was unbearably tender. It's for you.

Where pain had burned in her chest a moment before, she sensed a lightening, as though a burden she didn't realize she'd been carrying had been lifted from her.

A cool breeze blew through the open window. The smell of newly mown hay trailed after it like the tail of a kite. Peace wrapped her in a cocoon, and Kathryn drifted to sleep.

Wednesday

Panting heavily, I sidled through the screen door a second before it slammed behind Kathryn. Thoughts of the letters had sent so much adrenaline coursing through her that it was nearly impossible for me to keep up. At one point I'd had to take a shortcut through the woods to come out a little ahead of her as she followed the road around a bend and started in the direction of home.

That adrenaline launched her through the kitchen and into the living room where she scooped up the letter she'd read that morning. Once again she grasped the handle of the woodstove and tugged it open. I was beginning to see the pattern. She would go through each item in the box, one by one, reliving the memories and closing the door on them forever by tossing them into the flames. It wasn't a bad plan, as plans went. In fact, I sensed that each clang of the woodstove door brought her closer to me. I only hoped the small steps she was making would bring her far enough, fast enough to reach me before it was too late.

I don't mean to be elusive, incidentally. I'm perfectly willing to be found, desperate even, but so much stands between me and my charges at times that I can only watch helplessly as they veer down a path that leads them anywhere but to me. I prayed that would not be the case this time.

Kathryn stood in front of the stove for a moment, staring at the ceiling as though she could see the shadows fluttering in the corners. Could she? Her expression didn't change, so I gathered she couldn't. Lucky her.

What would she do now? After her sleepless night, the couch likely called to her, but time was ticking away. We needed to hit the road before too long if we hoped to drive to Maple Ridge, confront David Henley, and return home before dark.

I yawned widely and slapped a hand over my mouth. I'd barely slept myself. Maybe a few minutes—thirty, tops—would help fortify us both for what lay ahead.

No such luck. Before I could make myself comfortable on my armchair, she had spun around and started for the door. My footsteps heavy and every bit of me aching from unaccustomed exercise, I followed her. Fear smirked at me as I stumbled past the spot where he lay curled in front of the stove. He swished his tail in my direction, swatting my legs as I passed by. Everything in me longed to grab hold of it and give it a good yank, but if I was going to be any kind of help to Kathryn this afternoon it would probably be good if all my limbs and digits remained attached.

By the time I managed to climb the last step—much like achieving the summit of Everest for me at the moment, only without the stunning view—water was running in the shower. I lowered myself to the floor, my back against the wall, waiting for her to wash and get dressed. The scent of citrus drifted out beneath the bathroom door and I inhaled it deeply, grateful for the boost of energy the aromas of orange, lemon, and grapefruit provided. Hopefully the shampoo was having the same effect on Kathryn.

Every little bit would help. When she did gather the courage to go and see David Henley, she would need all the strength she could summon from the resources that, until That Night, she had never even known she had.

Chapter Twenty-Two

Wednesday

I closed my eyes, hoping for a catnap, but even through the closed bathroom door, Kathryn's thoughts ping-ponged around in her mind. And mine. Thoughts of going to see David had stirred up memories like dust on moving day, leaving the air in the hallway murky and difficult to draw in without sneezing.

June 2002

Spending all day trying not to think about David Henley's trial had only resulted in Kathryn thinking about little else. She had stared at the ranch books for an hour, trying to work, but the numbers seemed to move around the page, arranging themselves in random, meaningless patterns. Finally, in exasperation, she grabbed her jacket and rubber boots and headed to the barn. Nothing like a little manual labor to get your mind off your problems, as her mom would say.

"Hey, girl," she said as she entered the building. "Mind if I take my frustrations out in here for a while?"

Bonnie lifted her head and whinnied softly. Accommodating as usual. Why couldn't people be more like horses? Kathryn grabbed a pitchfork and went to work.

Absorbed in the task, she didn't see the barn door opening and jumped at the tentative, "Hello?"

"Olivia!" She suppressed a grin at the sight of the officer who'd been assigned to her case picking her way across the barn floor, even though there was nothing on it but bits of hay and straw. "Do you want me to come outside?"

"No, no, that's okay," Olivia said. "I love animals and … all things barn-like."

When the officer reached the door of the stall and lifted a foot to inspect the bottom of her well-shined work shoe, Kathryn laughed. *City folk.*

Olivia's head shot up, and she glared at her. "Go ahead, girl, laugh all you want. One of these days I'll take you on a ride-along with me and we'll see how long you last in my world."

Her face turned serious, and Kathryn's chuckle died. *Uh-oh. What now?*

"Hey, did you hear about Aaron and Meg?" Hoping to lighten her friend's mood, Kathryn shared the big news. "They're engaged."

Olivia's smile appeared forced. "That's great, Kath. Really. Tell them I said congratulations."

"I will." She leaned the pitchfork against the wall of the stall. "What is it, Olivia?"

"David Henley's hearing is over."

"What?" Kathryn rested a hand on her horse's back. "I thought the trial only started today."

"That's the thing. There isn't going to be a trial. He pleaded guilty to the charges, so all they needed to do was have a hearing before the court handed down a sentence."

"That's good, right?" When Olivia hesitated, Kathryn's heart edged downward. *Please don't tell me I have to get involved.* She didn't want anything to do with this. She only wanted it to be over. "Isn't it?"

Olivia removed her blue cap and ran both hands around the rim. "I came straight here from a meeting with my friend Linda, the prosecutor for this case. Her team was counting on the fact that because Judge Karen Daley had been assigned to this hearing they wouldn't need to involve you at all."

Kathryn nodded. Exactly how she wanted it. So what was the problem?

Her friend cleared her throat. "Judge Daley is known for her zero tolerance. She routinely gives out the longest sentences of any active justices. Lawyers and cops love her for that. Linda was confident she'd give Henley the maximum sentence of fourteen years."

"And now they're worried she won't?"

"Something happened in that courtroom, Kathryn. Something that's difficult to explain. David Henley was open about what he'd done. The prosecution was hard on him, and it was clear he was guilty."

One shoe down. One to go.

"Something about him seemed to soften the judge and even the media. It was obvious he was broken up over what happened. Several prison guards even testified on his behalf. He appears to be a genuinely changed man."

"What does this have to do with me? I thought if he pleaded guilty I wouldn't have to testify."

"That's what I'm here to talk to you about. Linda would like you to come in and give a victim impact statement. She thinks that will go a long way toward getting him the maximum sentence."

Kathryn sank onto an overturned metal bucket, afraid her legs would give out if she didn't. "Can they force me to do that?"

"No, of course not. It's your right to make a statement if you wish, but you're free to waive that right. David Henley will still go to prison, and you can get on with your life, like you've been working so hard to do."

Stunned, Kathryn leaned against the stall. She couldn't make this decision alone. She needed to talk to her family. And pray. "When do I have to decide?"

Olivia winced. "Today. The prosecution waited until the last minute, hoping not to have to call you in, but the hearing is supposed to wrap up tomorrow." She tapped her hat against the stall boards a couple of times. "Take a few hours to consider it. I'll call you later, after you've had a chance to talk to your family. If you want my advice ..."

Kathryn glanced up as Olivia squared her shoulders.

"Linda wouldn't appreciate me saying this, but I don't think you should do it. You'd relive everything that happened to you that night and what you've gone through since. And you'd have to see David Henley. Do you think you should put yourself through that?"

Bonnie flicked her tail, shooing a pesky fly, and Kathryn stood and moved out of the way. She had no idea whether she should put herself through that, or if she even could. "I don't know. I need to think about it."

"I'll call you later. And Kathryn," Olivia studied her, as though weighing her next words, "I'll be praying for you."

Tears welled in Kathryn's eyes as she nodded. Olivia had been coming to church with her for a couple of years, off and on, but this was the first time she'd ever confessed to praying about anything. That promise meant more to Kathryn than she could say.

Her friend returned the dark blue hat to her head and turned to go.

"Olivia." Kathryn grasped her sleeve. "Would I have to tell them about Tory?"

Olivia shook her head. "The victim impact statement is for you. You can tell the court anything you want to about the way the crime has affected your life. You wouldn't have to tell them anything you didn't want them to know."

Kathryn dropped her hand and watched as her friend made her way across the barn floor.

One hand on the wooden doorknob, Olivia stopped and shot her a look. "You know I'm going to take days of flak from the guys for returning to work smelling like a horse, don't you?"

Kathryn laughed, but her smile faded as the barn door closed. Could she do it? Could she go over the details of that night again? A tremor passed through her. Most of all, could she be in the same room as David Henley, know that he was watching her and listening to every word she said? The thought made her stomach turn.

"I don't have to do it, do I?" She tipped her head to stare at the heavy wooden beams above her. "Please tell me this isn't something you're asking me to do."

"Kat?"

"In here." Too drained to move, she stayed where she was as

Aaron walked into the stall and stopped in front of her.

"What's up? I saw Olivia's car pulling out of the driveway. Is everything all right?"

"She was here about the trial."

"I thought there wasn't going to be one."

She blinked. They had all agreed it would be too difficult to be involved in the process unless absolutely necessary, so she hadn't known Aaron was following what was going on.

Aaron shrugged. "I read the paper earlier. It was on the front page, kind of hard to miss."

"Well, it is over, except for the sentencing and ... the victim impact statement." Kathryn ran her fingers through Bonnie's mane.

Her brother's shoulders sagged. "Kat, no. They can't ask you to go through that."

She didn't want to do it, but she was supposed to. Kathryn's fingers stilled. *Why? How can this possibly help me?*

It will help him.

A sudden affinity for the older brother of the prodigal son struck her, sparking a burning resentment that settled in her chest. Why should she help David Henley?

The words the father spoke to the older brother in the story flashed across her mind. *Because he's my son, and he was lost and is now found.* Her fingers tightened around the horse's mane. The Bible didn't record the brother's response to those words, but she was pretty sure that, like her, rejoicing was the last thing he'd felt like doing when he heard them.

"Kat?"

"Sorry. I'm trying to process all this."

"You're not thinking about doing it, are you?" Anger and concern gave his voice an edge that she understood completely.

"I don't know." Kathryn hesitated. "If I do, will you go with me to the courthouse tomorrow?"

Aaron rubbed a hand across his forehead. When he spoke, his tone was pleading. "Of course I'll go with you. But please think about what you're doing. The thought of you being in the same room with one of those men, going over everything you've been through, makes me crazy."

"Do you remember what you asked me after we read that letter?"

"About forgiving him?"

"Yes. I'm beginning to think it might be possible, and I believe this could help."

"How could you?"

"I can't. Not on my own."

A heavy silence hung in the air between them for a moment. "Even so, you don't have to go and see him again."

"I know. I need to pray about this. Olivia's going to call me in a couple of hours."

Aaron grasped the top of the stall, his knuckles white. Her heart went out to him as she patted Bonnie then brushed by her brother and left the stall. He was wondering the same thing she was, wasn't he? Whether or not the pain was ever going to end for any of them.

Kathryn hauled open the heavy barn door and headed across the lawn to the big stone farmhouse. Supporting herself on the railing, she climbed the stairs to her room and dropped onto her knees by the side of her bed. She'd never really thought about it before, but maybe the hard part for the big brother wasn't so much that the father threw the feast for his brother, but that he was asked to attend, probably even to give the welcome back toast. Did he do it? If he did, would the father have appreciated the enormity of the act and how much it cost his elder son? What exactly was in it for the brother who'd been so faithful?

The burning in her chest was doused by the answer. The reason the big brother probably did go to the feast and even picked up his goblet of wine at some point and raised it to the safe return of the prodigal.

Her face dropped into her hands. And it was the reason she would go to the courthouse tomorrow. Not to try and get David

Henley's sentence extended, but to speak on his behalf.

He would have felt the pleasure of his father. Is there any greater compensation than that?

There isn't, of course. It happens to me, occasionally, and it makes everything I've gone through worthwhile. Still, it was one thing to make the decision to go and face David Henley and quite another to find herself in the same room as him. I woke up the next morning feeling extremely ill and would have given anything to stay in bed for the day. Instead, I rose and, weak and trembling, forced myself to accompany her.

For an immortal being, I have a very strong awareness of my own mortality. I have expired many times in the line of duty, although I always find myself living again somewhere else. Even so, death is painful and the threat of it debilitating. I stumbled and nearly fell to my knees several times as I followed Kathryn up the wide cement steps of the courthouse the next day.

As it turned out, on my knees would likely have been the best place for me anyway.

Chapter Twenty-Three

June 2002

He's here. In this building. Kathryn sat in the hallway outside the courtroom, twisting her hands in her lap and praying for calm. The realization that David Henley was on the other side of the heavy oak door behind her threatened to suck all the air out of her chest.

The door opened and a young man with dark, curly hair stuck his head around the corner. "Ms. Ellison? They're ready for you."

Aaron stood and reached for her hand. When she rose, he wrapped his arms around her. "It'll be fine, Kat. Meg and I are here, and we'll be praying the whole time."

A weak smile was all she could muster as she turned and entered the courtroom. The walk to the front of the room seemed to go on forever. She saw Henley as soon as she sat in the chair the clerk directed her to, and the memory of that night slammed her against the back of the seat.

I can't do this.

Panic rose in her throat, and she gripped the arms of the chair, struggling to breathe. *I'm not alone.*

Look into his eyes.

Kathryn shook her head. *I can't.*

Look. He's not lost anymore. Rejoice with me.

Her gaze locked with David Henley's. Olivia was right. Something about him was different. Searching his eyes, she realized what it was. He wasn't alone, either. An almost indiscernible emotion sparked deep inside her. Not rejoicing. But something.

Judge Karen Daley peered at her over the top of her horn-rimmed glasses. "Ms. Ellison, because of the guilty plea in this case, you were not required to testify. Before the defendant is sentenced, however, it is your right to make a victim impact statement. Anything you say will be taken into account when sentencing is handed down. Do you wish to make a statement?"

"Yes, Your Honour." The judge nodded at her to continue. Kathryn cleared her throat. "You've already heard what happened to me, so if it's all right, I'd rather not go over the details again." She glanced at Henley. The eyes that met hers were filled with pain, but he didn't glance away.

Kathryn described everything she had been through since That Night, and how her life had been affected. A hush fell over the courtroom. As weak and weary as I felt, I forced myself to pay attention, to see if she would actually go through with her plan. I wasn't sure whether I would feel better or worse if she did.

When she finished, she gazed directly at the accused. "David Henley wrote me recently to ask for my forgiveness."

A collective gasp from those gathered in the courtroom greeted that announcement.

"I believe he's sincerely remorseful over what happened. In fact," Kathryn pressed her lips together to stop the trembling, "I'd like to ask the court to show leniency to him when handing down its sentence."

As I had predicted, a shocked silence swept across the room. Henley's eyes glistened, but he smiled at her faintly. She nodded. Warmth spread through her body, as though she'd been shivering outside in the cold and had been brought in to stand, hands outstretched, in front of a blazing fire.

You were right. There is no greater compensation than this.

The exchange between her and David Henley had not gone unnoticed. Conversation erupted in the courtroom. Reporters who had scribbled away while she was speaking shot out of their seats and left the room, cell phones pressed to their ears. Olivia's friend, Linda Carmichael, shoved a strand of hair behind one ear, the prosecution bench in chaos around her.

Judge Daley held up a hand, calling for quiet for several seconds before the buzzing room came to order. When it was calm again, she shifted her gaze to Kathryn and studied her for a moment before speaking. "Thank you for coming in today, Ms.

Ellison. I assure you I will take your statement into account when I render my decision." With a swish of her robes, she stood and exited through the door behind the bench.

Olivia strode to the witness stand and grasped her elbow, escorting her through the room and out the door. Aaron and Meg pushed their way through the humming crowd behind them.

"In here, guys," Olivia said. She ushered them into an empty room down the hallway and closed the door. Kathryn sank onto the nearest chair, her heart pounding.

Aaron slid an arm around her shoulders and held her until her heartbeat returned to normal. Then he let her go and stood. "Let's go home."

She nodded. The only thing she wanted at that moment was to see Tory and throw her arms around her daughter. A quiet knock at the door squelched that idea. Aaron glanced at Kathryn. When she shrugged, Olivia pulled open the door. A tall man with light brown hair stood in the hallway, appearing slightly uncomfortable in a suit and tie, his hand on the back of the dark-eyed woman beside him.

"Sorry to bother you, Ms. Ellison. We wondered if we could speak to you for a minute."

Kathryn rose. "Of course, Mr.—"

"Lawson, Nick Lawson. This is my sister, Halyna."

Kathryn studied the woman. Halyna Lawson's face, framed by long, dark hair, was pale, but she lifted her chin and stepped forward. Kathryn took the hand she held out, shocked at how cold it was. Almost as cold as her own.

"I don't know if you recognize my name or not. I was the one those men were after that night."

Kathryn's knees weakened, and she pressed a palm to the table to support herself. "I'm sorry, I didn't know. We haven't been following the proceedings until now. It was too painful."

Halyna nodded. "I understand. Nick and I have been keeping up with them, as I've never been able to let go of the thought that I should have been the one who was taken that night. My ex-boyfriend, Jeff Walker, hired those men to bring me to him. He told them I had long dark hair and described my car to him which, unfortunately, was the same make and color as yours. He was extremely unstable—which is why I broke up with him— and somehow he'd convinced himself he could win me back if he got me alone in that cabin."

Kathryn touched the woman's arm. "You aren't responsible for what those men did. They made their own choices."

Tears welled in Halyna's eyes. "Thank you for saying that. I appreciate it." She slipped her hand through the crook of her brother's arm.

He covered her fingers with his and faced Kathryn. "We won't keep you. I know it's been a difficult day."

She nodded, her throat too tight to speak. Nick Lawson's dark brown eyes met hers and held them. Surprise and confusion rose in her, tightening her stomach muscles. The same conflicting emotions flickered in the gaze still fixed on hers. Neither of them moved for a moment, until Aaron cleared his throat and she blinked.

An uncertain smile played around Nick's mouth. Kathryn managed a small smile in return, and he nodded before following his sister out of the room.

When the door closed behind them, Aaron rested his hands on her shoulders. "Are you all right?"

Kathryn took a deep breath. "I will be, once we're home."

"Okay. Let's go."

Olivia opened the door. The four of them started along the hallway of the old courthouse, their footsteps echoing off the cold marble floors. Up ahead, Kathryn caught a glimpse of two uniformed officers. A current of shock jolted through her. They were escorting David Henley between them.

Beside her, Aaron stiffened, his hands closing into fists. Kathryn gripped his sleeve and they stopped. The men led Henley into a room and shut the door.

Talk to him.

No. You cannot ask me to do that. In spite of her protests,

Kathryn's feet grew heavier as they approached the door. She closed her eyes in surrender. *You're going to have to explain this to Aaron.* Because she couldn't, and he would be beside himself. She stopped. "I need to see him."

"What? No way, Kat." Aaron grasped her elbow as if he would drag her from the building if he could. "You did what you had to do for him. That's enough."

Kathryn turned to Olivia as though he hadn't spoken. "Is it possible? Can I talk to him?"

Her friend hesitated. "You should go through official channels and apply for victim-offender mediation."

"Please, Olivia, that could take months. I need to talk to him now."

"You can't be serious!" Aaron's voice rose. "Don't you think you've been through enough for one day?"

"Aaron." Meg touched his back. "If Kathryn feels strongly about speaking to him face to face, it might not be a bad idea."

Aaron whirled on her. Meg didn't flinch under his hard gaze but held her ground until his shoulders slumped in defeat.

"I'll see what I can do." Olivia strode toward the room where David Henley had disappeared and knocked. One of the cops came out of the room to speak to her, closing the door behind him. The two of them exchanged words, and Olivia gestured toward Kathryn. After shooting a glance at the three of them, he shook his head.

"Good." Aaron's hand tightened on Kathryn's elbow. "Let's get out—"

The two officers walked toward them as Olivia pleaded her case. "Come on, Decker, she's been through a lot. She only needs to see him for a few minutes."

"Then she should go through mediation."

"You know how long that takes. Please. I'll owe you one."

Decker studied Kathryn. She held her breath, not sure which way she wanted him to go. She tugged her arm free from Aaron's desperate grip. At least she'd tried.

"Okay, fine. Five minutes, but if I hear about this it's on

your head. And you owe me big."

"Sure. Donuts on me for the next year." Olivia started toward Kathryn.

"Hey, we get our donuts for free," he called after her.

"I know." She smiled sweetly over her shoulder but sobered when she reached the group. "Okay, Kathryn, you have five minutes. Are you sure you want to do this?"

"No." Cold shivers prickled across her skin and Kathryn suppressed a shudder. "But I need to."

Decker called the second cop out of the room, and the two of them stood scrutinizing her as she approached. They didn't seem too sure about what was going on. She knew exactly how they felt. Still, neither made a move to stop her as she approached the door.

"Kat."

She bit her lip at the anguish in Aaron's voice.

"Let me come with you at least."

Her heart ached for him, but she shook her head. "I have to do this alone." She refused to look back, knowing she'd change her mind if she saw how much pain this was causing him.

"I'll be right outside." Olivia opened the door and held it for her.

Kathryn stepped into the room.

David Henley sat on the far side of a table, hands cuffed in front of him. The color drained from his face when he saw her.

Kathryn tried to swallow, but her throat had gone dry. She pulled out the chair across from him and sat down before her trembling legs could give out. *You better give me the words to say, because I have no idea where to begin.* When she looked at him, his eyes reflected the trepidation that she felt, but he met her gaze without wavering. A jagged scar that hadn't been there the last time she'd seen him ran below his right eye. What had happened to him?

"I have five minutes," she said.

He nodded.

Kathryn hesitated then lifted her chin. "Why didn't you stop him?"

Henley bent forward slightly, as though her words had knocked the air out of him.

She continued, not waiting for an answer. "I saw you hesitate and I thought ... I hoped you'd help me. Instead, you went along with it." Her voice broke, and she twisted her fingers together to stop them from shaking. "How could you have done that?"

"I don't know." A tremor ran through Henley's words. "I've asked myself that question a thousand times." He took a quivering breath. "I wish I had stopped him. I've wished that every day since it happened. If he had killed you—"

"Where is he now?"

"I have no idea." He lifted his shoulders. "We weren't close. We'd only done a few jobs together. After what happened in that cabin, he'd never want to see me again. Although ..." His blue eyes connected with hers. "I don't want to scare you, but Dylan will be humiliated by what happened that day. He's not the type to let that go."

A cold chill passed through Kathryn's body. She ignored it, determined to stay focused. She had so many questions for him but no time to ask them, so she went to the one that weighed most on her heart. "Did you mean what you said in your letter?"

This time Henley spoke without hesitation. "Yes, every word."

"Because it's pretty easy to write words on a page when you don't have to look the other person in the eye."

A wry grin crossed his face. "Believe me, there was nothing easy about writing that letter. But you're right. You deserve more than a written apology." He swallowed hard. "I am sorry for what happened that night, sorrier than I can say." He lifted his cuffed hands and rested them on the table, his fingers spread in supplication. "I know God has forgiven me, but I'll regret what I did to you for the rest of my life."

I watched the battle play out across Kathryn's face. Believing him would put the burden on her to forgive him or to refuse and carry the weight of hatred and bitterness for the rest of her life. Neither was an easy choice. I hadn't noticed Truth in the corner, but he stepped forward now and placed a hand on her shoulder. Another one who was cut a lot of slack, but I supposed that was fair. It is hard for humans, not being able to read minds, to sense when another is attempting to deceive them and when they are not.

Kathryn straightened as though she felt Truth's firm touch and nodded slightly. She could let go. "I … forgive you."

For a moment he only stared at her, as though unable to process the words she had said. Finally, he nodded. "Thank you." His voice broke. "You don't know what that means."

Neither moved for a moment, until a knock on the door broke the spell.

"I'm sorry, Kathryn. It's time to go."

She rose and walked to the door Olivia held open. When she reached it, she stopped and glanced back. Henley was watching her and, in spite of the sheen in his eyes, a hint of a smile crossed his face.

Olivia pulled the door shut behind her. Darkness swept across Kathryn's vision as a loud, rushing sound filled her ears. Aaron reached her in time to catch her as she collapsed into his arms.

Forgiveness is a wonderful being, but she is high maintenance. That is not an accusation or petty gossip, only a statement of fact. She would be the first one to admit to being very demanding.

Still, I admire her greatly, and being around her is incredibly empowering to me. In fact, once I realized Kathryn was going to be all right, I literally—and at great risk to the professionalism I work hard to maintain—skipped down the hallway behind them.

I had no idea at the time how long that reprieve would last. What I did know, although I hadn't been sure as recently as that morning, was that I would live to see another day.

And, to give credit where credit was due, I had Forgiveness to thank for that.

Chapter Twenty-Four

Wednesday

I fidgeted as I sat on the gleaming hardwood floor. As hard as I tried, I couldn't muster an ounce of the elation I'd felt after Kathryn spoke to David at the courthouse that day. Likely because Fear had padded out of the living room to take up a post at the bottom of the stairs. When I glanced down, his dark gaze was riveted on mine. He knew as well as I did what Kathryn was determined to do today. And clearly he planned to exploit that knowledge to his advantage. Possibly to even prevent her from being able to carry out her plan. I shifted again, trying to find a comfortable position. The effort was fruitless.

I was being summoned.

I argued against moving, although I don't know why I bothered. As far back as my memory goes, a few millennia at least, arguing has never worked—why do I keep trying? I only do it when I'm feeling especially tired and grumpy. Like now.

Don't worry, I'm still more than capable of doing my job. Too capable, apparently, or they'd leave me alone and let me rest and recover from the trauma I've gone through over the last twenty-four hours. Again.

I exhaled loudly, as close to expressing displeasure with the dispatch orders as I dared to approach. Then I uncurled my legs and stood, forcing my aching limbs to move me in the direction of another kitchen in another farmhouse several miles away.

Nick poured himself a cup of coffee, his fifth or sixth today. With a deep groan, he sank onto the wooden kitchen chair and shoved a hand through his already disheveled hair. Even tired and rumpled, the man was incredibly attractive. I guess if I had to rouse myself from my station outside Kathryn's door to go traipsing out into the world, this wasn't the worst place to end up. I slid onto the chair across from him and waved a hand over his coffee, directing the rich aroma toward me as I leaned in to inhale deeply.

Of all things human, coffee is the thing I crave the most. I've never tasted it, of course, but the smell alone is enough to curl my toes in equal parts delight and envy.

Nick did not appear to be similarly delighted. In fact, the dark circles under his eyes and the deep lines furrowing his forehead suggested much darker emotions. Frustration, likely.

And longing, definitely. Attempted patience where patience had long since worn thin—the sign of an exceptionally good man. Anger at the circumstances, beyond either his or Kathryn's control, that had conspired to keep them apart for so long. And love, maybe? Could anything but love have waited this long, wanted so much, given up everything?

The next few days would tell for sure. I had no doubt they were both about to be stretched like elastic bands in the hands of forces outside of themselves, pulled to the absolute limits to see if they would snap or somehow manage to hold up under the intense pressure. Like I said, I'm not God, so I have no way of knowing which way it would go. Only time would tell.

And, unfortunately, time was something the two of them, although they didn't know it yet, had very little of.

I studied the weary face across the table from me. Dropping my gaze to the steaming mug in front of him, I narrowed my eyes. Why was Nick Lawson trying so hard to keep himself awake, when there was clearly nothing that could be done for a few days, and he needed sleep as badly as I did? More so, maybe, as I had grabbed a quick nap in front of the fire earlier, and wasn't suffering through quite the degree of angst that he was at the moment. I pursed my lips. Maybe he did know, or suspect, deep down, that time was running out for the two of them.

I wasn't sure how he could, except that Love is, in my opinion, given a lot of leeway sometimes. With his help, I have seen people do extraordinary things, even break through the invisible boundaries that normally hem them in for their own protection. I hadn't seen it often, but then, I had rarely seen two people go through as much as Nick and Kathryn had. Maybe the book I went strictly by—more or less—would have to be rewritten for them. Or thrown out entirely.

The thought unnerved me. And delighted me at the same time, nearly as much as the delectable aroma of the coffee.

Ignoring the mug in front of him, Nick stared into space, somewhere over my shoulder. Fearing another long interval of silence and inactivity, I started to lean in toward the mug again. Then the force of his thoughts hit me, a wave so powerful it nearly sent me tumbling from my chair. He'd gone back, to the second time he and Kathryn had met. In the cereal aisle, of all places. Not my first choice for a romantic encounter. Sadly, I am never able to arrange those as I would like to, since any hint of interference on my part in human affairs is met with a sharp rebuke.

I comforted myself with the fact that it rarely mattered, that the surroundings—even boxes of sugar cereal and wheat flakes—faded into nonexistence when the eyes of certain people met.

Like they had that day.

March 2007

Nick drew in a sharp breath. It was her. Kathryn Ellison. He hadn't seen her for almost five years, but her face was burned into his mind. He'd thought of her more times than he could recall since that day and wondered how she was. He wheeled his grocery cart closer. "Ms. Ellison?"

She'd been studying the wall of cereal boxes and discussing the options with the older lady next to her. Nick guessed it was her mother. Other than the short, silver hair, the profile was the same. Kathryn turned to him with a friendly smile that faded as recognition flickered in her brown eyes. "Mr. ... Lawson, isn't it?"

His heart sank. He shouldn't have bothered her. All it could do was stir up painful memories. He forced a smile, desperate to set her at ease. "It's Nick. Good to see you again."

Their eyes locked, and he worked to draw in a breath. She'd had the same effect on him that day in the courthouse.

"And it's Kathryn." Her voice had gone hoarse. She cleared her throat. "How is your sister?"

He appreciated what it cost her to continue the conversation, to ask about the woman who, inadvertently, had been the cause of so much pain in her life. His smile faltered. "Actually, she was recently diagnosed with cancer. She's in treatment now."

Her shoulders slumped. "I'm so sorry."

Nick nodded. "Thank you." He tried to tear his eyes from hers, but he was drawn to them against his will, his heart refusing to take orders from his brain like it had since the first time he'd seen her.

"Kathryn?" The woman with her rested a hand on her arm.

"I'm sorry." She introduced him to her mother and he shook her hand.

"I … we should go," Kathryn said, both hands tightly grasping the handle of the cart.

Nick stayed where he was, watching her walk away from him. When she turned at the end of the row and disappeared from view, he sagged against the metal shelves. What was it about that woman that sent conjoined feelings of pain and desire coursing through him? Even now he fought the urge to go after her and manufacture an excuse to keep talking. Anything to spend a little more time in her presence.

Straightening, he glanced around, warmth flooding his face as though the people pushing past him might have overheard what he was thinking.

He needn't have worried about that. Humans have yet to figure out how to read each other's thoughts, and I pray they never do. While it comes in handy in my line of work, it's certainly not something I would wish on anyone.

All of the Beings observing them were capable of it, but if I could have, I would have assured Nick that none of us was laughing at him. We had, in fact, all taken a collective breath—existentially speaking—anxious to see if the two of them would let the moment slip through their fingers. Sadly, they did. Or maybe it wasn't sad at all. In the big picture of things—which is what we all are charged to be mindful of—it may prove to have been the right thing to do, the only way that, in the end, they could finally be together.

Not able to see that far down the road, all I could do was hope.

Nick maneuvered the cart toward the check-out, hoping to see her and praying he wouldn't. Kathryn was nowhere in sight, and he breathed a sigh of relief. That was it then. They lived forty minutes apart and he hadn't run into her in five years. It could be years before he'd see her again. The ache in his chest at the thought took him by surprise.

Nick paid for the groceries and strode to his truck. Once inside, he sat for a few minutes, fingers wrapped around the steering wheel as he willed his heart to slow its rapid beating. *What is going on here? Is this from you?* He let go of the wheel and rubbed his face with both palms. Could these feelings come from God and still cause him—and her—this much pain and confusion?

He leaned forward to turn the key. It didn't matter much. Clearly she wasn't ready to see him and may not be for a long time, if ever. Which was for the best. He had enough to think about with Halyna's illness. The wisest thing would be to put Kathryn Ellison out of his mind once and for all.

Somehow Nick knew, even as he turned onto the highway and pressed on the accelerator to increase the distance between them, his brain didn't stand any more of a chance against his heart in this battle than it had in any of the others he'd fought with himself over her. Her face flashed across his memory and his face twisted in a grimace.

Maybe even less.

Wednesday

The force of his thoughts dwindled to an occasional burst of power, like an electrical wire with a short in the circuit. I knew exactly how he felt. He propped one elbow on the table and rested his head on his hand. As I slipped out of the room, I glanced over my shoulder and shot up a prayer that he would be able to get some rest soon.

And while I was at it, I tacked on that I wouldn't mind a little of that for myself, if it wasn't too much trouble.

Chapter Twenty-Five

Wednesday

Love was up to his old tricks again. When I returned to the hallway outside her bedroom, Kathryn's thoughts had drifted to the same memory as Nick's, of that meeting in the grocery store.

Although it sometimes bothered me how much freedom Love had to become involved in the situation, this time I didn't mind. I was intensely aware of the inexorable march of the hands around the clock. If his interference moved us along faster, I certainly was not about to object. I was a little concerned about Kathryn. Living through her experiences had been overwhelming the first time, and it didn't appear as though it was much easier this time around.

So I was glad that Love had been sent in to help us both through this. Not that his presence guaranteed anything.

At this point, though, it certainly couldn't hurt.

March 2007

The barn door creaked open. "Kat?"

Kathryn didn't answer her brother. Of course he'd found her. This was where she always came to hide out when life became too much for her. Since the night she'd been attacked, she had lost track of how many times Aaron had come searching for her out here with the horses. The stables were his retreat of choice as well. The horses never asked questions, only gave and received love day or night. In a perfect world, people would be the same. She winced. If anyone knew this wasn't a perfect world, it was her and her family.

His boots crunched through the brittle straw lining the cement floor as he made his way along the stalls. She sighed, resigned. If she really hadn't wanted him to discover where she was, she'd have found a better hiding place than this. Gripping the brush firmly, she worked it through Bonnie's coarse mane.

"Kat." Aaron stepped into the last stall. She continued to brush the horse feverishly. He reached her in three strides and grasped the hand clutching the brush.

"Hey." She stopped brushing, but her eyes remained fixed on the horse's gleaming sides. "Mom said you saw Nick Lawson at the grocery store today."

"Yes." She tried to tug the brush from his hand, but he didn't let go.

"She said you seemed pretty shaken up after you talked to him."

Kathryn shot him a sideways glance. "That's a bit of an overstatement."

"So you're okay?"

"I'm fine. We ran into him. We talked for two minutes and we left. That was it."

"Must have been an intense two minutes for you to get so worked up."

Kathryn withdrew her hand, conceding the brush. "I'm not worked up."

Aaron set the brush on the shelf behind her and contemplated her in silence.

"Fine. I'm a little worked up."

"Do you want to talk about it?"

"There's nothing to talk about. I can handle this myself." She ran a hand down Bonnie's soft neck.

Aaron slid two fingers under her chin and lifted her face. "I know you *can*, Kat. I came out here to tell you that you don't have to."

Her long, drawn-in breath sent a shudder through her whole

body.

Aaron let go of her and grasped her elbow. "Come on."

Kathryn followed him over to a bale of hay in the corner. He sat and tugged on her arm, pulling her down beside him. "What upset you so much?"

She slumped against the wooden boards behind them. "It's hard for me, seeing him or anyone connected with what happened. It brings back too many memories." A tear slid down one cheek, but she swiped it away, impatient with herself. No matter how many tears had been shed, by all of them, over what had happened in that cabin, there always seemed to be more hovering near the surface, waiting to be drawn out at the slightest provocation. Not that seeing Nick Lawson was a slight provocation.

Aaron studied her. "Is that all it is?"

"Isn't that enough?"

"Yes, actually. More than enough. But ..." Aaron squeezed her cold fingers. "It seems as though there's more going on here."

"If you mean, did I feel anything around him besides the fear and pain I've been dealing with for years, then no."

"You were afraid of him?"

"Not of him, no, of remembering." Kathryn brushed a few pieces of straw off her jeans. "That was it."

"You're sure?"

"What else could it be? It can't be anything more than that."

"Why not?"

"Because I ..." She leaned her head against the wall. "I couldn't. It's too soon."

"It's been eight years, Kat. You deserve to find someone amazing who will love you the way you deserve."

She blinked. That thought was one she hadn't considered since Ty had walked out of her life. "Maybe. Someday. But Nick Lawson can't be that person."

"He does seem to have a powerful effect on you."

"Only because he—"

"Reminds you of the past, I know. But I think it's more than that."

Kathryn shook her head.

Aaron slid his arm around her shoulders. She rested her head against his flannel jacket. "Keep your mind open. And your heart, okay? If you shut those down, they will have won."

When she didn't answer, Aaron tightened his grip. Another deep sigh shuddered through her. Was her brother right? Did Nick Lawson stir up more in her than she was willing to admit, even to herself?

He did, of course. Love hovered in the periphery of Nick and Kathryn's vision even then. Mind you, it's not always hearts and flowers and happy endings when he's around. Life is not a fairy tale, as I'm sure you know, and Love is rarely nice and simple. In fact, he can be messy and difficult and painful. I very often find myself picking up after him in an attempt to maintain some semblance of order. Still, the effort is almost always worth it.

And he is tenacious. I thought I detected his presence even back in the courthouse that day, although it was faint and barely perceptible, like heat shimmering above the sidewalk on a hot July afternoon. Not where I would have expected to find him, but he knew his business better than I did. He showed up to be there for them, ready and waiting, like I was. And as often and as hard as they have pushed him—and each other—away, he has retreated, but he has never left them entirely.

Which means that Hope is here as well. Goodness, it's getting crowded in the old farmhouse. Almost claustrophobic. Not that I'm complaining. I have a feeling it will take every one of us, working collectively, to bring all of them through this in one piece.

Chapter Twenty-Six

Wednesday

Kathryn spun away from the living room. When she withdrew a pair of heels from the front closet, I didn't attempt to mimic her action of sliding them onto her feet. Not my type of footwear. Although I always preened a little in front of the mirror before attending one of our parties—because really, you never knew—I was smart enough not to attempt to totter anywhere on anything resembling stilts. I had enough trouble avoiding calamity on the balls of my own two feet.

Kathryn flung open the door and stepped onto the porch, her low heels clacking on the wooden boards. I trotted beside her as she headed to her car, yanked open the door, and slid behind the wheel. Fear nipped at my heels all the way from the porch to the car, and I resigned myself to the fact that he would accompany us to see David. I jumped into the passenger seat. Fear crouched to leap in after me.

Suddenly, something bolted past him in a blur, knocking him off balance enough that he stumbled a little to the right. By the time he'd regained his stance, it was too late. The blur somersaulted past me to score a two-footed, Olympic-gold-medal-gymnast-style landing on the console. I clapped, thrilled to behold the last-minute stowaway. Definitely a trade-up from Fear. Determination took a sweeping bow. He held out a fist, and I bumped it before he dove into the back seat.

My knuckles where they'd touched his were coated in a thin layer of grit. Determination was perpetually covered in the stuff, and he tossed it over his charges as freely as the mythical Tinker Bell sprinkled fairy dust. I started to brush it away then stopped. What was I doing? I could use an extra dose of grit today as much as Kathryn could. I shook a little off onto the rest of me for good measure then glanced out the window.

Emboldened by the glass between us, I waggled my fingers

at Fear, still crouched on the gravel. He sent me a scorching glare as Kathryn accelerated onto the gravel driveway. I'd pay for my insolence next time I saw him, but for now he'd been left in our dust and I could breathe a little easier.

I caught a glimpse of Determination in the rear-view mirror and smiled. I'd spent a lot of time with that guy since being assigned to Kathryn. Except for her worst days, when Discouragement or Despair wrapped themselves around her as tightly as a wet suit and kept him at bay, he was one of her closest companions. He and Faith had each grasped a hand and led her through more dark days than I could remember, guiding her closer to me one tiny step at a time.

With him in the car, I was confident that nothing would stop us from getting to David Henley now. I felt a little sorry for the man but, after all, it was his own decision to keep reaching out to Kathryn that was leading us to his door today.

August 2007

David sat at a table in the corner of the prison lounge, trying to block out the sound of the game blaring on the TV. A growing pile of crumpled papers beside the blank notebook in front of him mirrored his increasing agitation.

What was he doing? She didn't want to hear from him. He sighed and picked up the pen he'd thrown on the table in frustration. Why did he feel the need to do this? It was crazy. *I hope they don't figure out they're letting a crazy man go free tomorrow.* Large, scrawling lines of text swallowed up the blank page.

"Hey, man. Can I join you?"

David lifted his head and smiled at Tiny, his closest friend in prison, then pulled his feet off the chair across from him and dropped them to the floor so the big man could sit down. His arm slid across the page as his friend settled onto the seat.

"Writer's block?" Tiny nodded toward the pile of paper.

"Something like that."

Tiny's eyes narrowed.

David held his breath, hoping his friend wouldn't ask him what he was doing. He was sure Tiny wouldn't understand what he himself couldn't begin to comprehend.

Tiny crossed his arms over his massive chest. "So you're leaving us tomorrow."

"Yeah. Apparently The Powers That Be have decided, no doubt wrongly, that it's safe to let me back on the streets."

Tiny grinned. "What time do you go?"

"Three in the afternoon. I have a flight booked to Toronto at six."

"Gonna follow your dream, eh?"

David snorted. "Believe me, it's not my dream. My dream would involve someplace a lot warmer. With a beach. And a drink with a little umbrella in it."

Tiny laughed, but his expression sobered when his eyes connected with David's. "Seriously, man. I'll be praying for you. And if you think about it, say a prayer for your old friend stuck here trying to fulfill his own calling."

David studied him. "How much longer have you got?"

"Oh, it'll be quite a while before I hit any beaches, that's for sure." He paused then waved his hand at the pad of paper in front of David. "You wanna talk about it?"

"Not really." His gaze dropped to the page he'd been writing on. "I mean, I don't know how to explain what I'm doing. It won't make any sense to you because it doesn't make any sense to me. And I'm pretty sure it won't make any sense to her, either." He bit his lip, realizing he'd said more than he meant to.

"Her?"

"Kathryn Ellison." He braced himself for a negative reaction. Although maybe it wouldn't be terrible if Tiny talked him out of this ridiculous thing he was considering doing.

"David." Tiny reached over and gripped his shoulder, waiting until David met his eyes. "If you're feeling compelled to do something, even though it doesn't make sense and"—a grin spread across his face as he glanced at the pile of rejected attempts—"even though it's difficult, that sounds like something God's putting on your heart to do."

His shoulders sagged. "I thought you'd tell me I was crazy and I should leave her alone."

"God works in mysterious ways, my friend. You of all people should know that."

"You're right, I do know that." The long, incredible nights spent at the dingy motel in Vancouver played through his mind. David held out his hand. "Thanks, Tiny. I'll never forget you. You're the one responsible for the fact that I'm heading to Toronto tomorrow instead of some tropical island. Come to think of it," he started to pull his hand back in feigned anger, "I may never forgive you, either."

Laughing, the big man grasped his hand. "You take care, brother. And keep listening to that voice, no matter how crazy the words may sound. Remember the big picture. You gotta know that somehow things do work together for good, even though we don't always see it happen."

With a final squeeze of David's shoulder, Tiny stood to go. David nodded and watched his friend until he disappeared from sight down the hallway. Shaking his head, he picked up his pen for one last try.

❧

For the first time in years, the sound of metal gates sliding shut and locking didn't cause David's heart to sink. This time he was on the right side of the fence, a free man. *I know I've been free for eight years now, but this feels pretty good too.* He threw his duffle bag into the back seat of the waiting cab and climbed into the passenger seat.

Inside the airport terminal, he spotted a row of mailboxes. He wrangled an envelope from the back pocket of his jeans and dropped it in the first box. The sound of the door slamming shut was an emphatic period at the end of the long debate he'd had with himself. It was done now. Too late to change his mind. Fighting the urge to wrestle with the box to retrieve the letter, he whirled around and walked away.

The screen was filled with flight numbers and destinations. David searched to find Toronto. What was he doing? He didn't want to go to Toronto. In fact—he scanned the screen—what was in the opposite direction? Oh. Japan, if his memory of tenth grade geography was correct. Not exactly what he'd had in mind, but at least he'd be free to do what he wanted there. He turned away from the screen with a sigh. Time to trust the big picture.

David headed in the direction of his gate, only slowing slightly when he passed a line of people waiting to board a flight to Hawaii.

If all things really did work together for good, would it be too much to ask for God to show him how on earth that was going to happen? Because frankly, he couldn't see it. He dropped onto a window seat and adjusted the headphones over his ears, hoping to lose himself in a movie so he wouldn't have to think about what lay ahead. Five minutes later, he yanked the headphones off and dropped them into the seat pocket in front of him, his mind racing in too many directions to concentrate. David rooted through his bag and withdrew the information the school had mailed to him a few weeks before. With a grimace, he settled back in his seat to read it.

That didn't last long, either. He tossed the papers onto the empty seat beside him and groaned as he banged his head against the headrest. A minister? He appreciated the humor but not the fact that he was the butt of this particular joke. Grinding his elbows into the armrests, he pressed the tips of his fingers together. There were a thousand places he'd rather be going at the moment, a thousand things he'd rather be doing. A familiar feeling worked its way up from the pit of his stomach, trailing a burning acid after it that settled in his chest.

Defiance.

Although it tightened every muscle in his body, he welcomed it with relief, like an old friend who'd shown up at a party where he didn't know anybody.

The words spewing out of his former companion were

poison, and David knew it. He leaned in to listen anyway. *Why are you doing this? You're a free man. You don't owe anybody any—*

His head shot up. What was he talking about? He didn't owe anybody? He could work his tail off for the rest of his life and still not give back a fraction of what he'd been given. He dropped his head into one hand and squeezed his eyes shut. *I'm sorry. I don't know why you bother with me. For some reason you've chosen me to do this thing, and I've done nothing but complain.* When he opened his eyes, dusk was creeping across the prairies that stretched out below him as far as he could see.

No more. God had a plan, and whether or not David ever saw the big picture didn't matter. He'd shut up, do whatever he was given to do, and be thankful that God kept not giving up on him.

David rested his temple against the window and felt something he hadn't felt strongly since he'd asked God what He wanted him to do with his life. Peace settled over him like a blanket. The burning tension drained from him as he relaxed under the comforting weight.

Tendrils of red and orange spread across the sky outside his window, and his eyelids grew heavy. The lighting on the plane dimmed as passengers flicked the switches above their heads. David reached for his then stopped. A small smile crossed his face as his arm dropped. Leaning his head against the seat, he closed his eyes and, for the first time in years, went to sleep in the light.

Now there's another metaphor I like. Against all odds, David Henley had found his way into the light, where his chances of bumping into me increased dramatically. After he did, the two of us settled, for the most part, into a relatively comfortable relationship. Unfortunately, I have never quite been able to shake a feeling of uneasiness, as though the foundation of our relationship lies across a huge fault line and could be shaken to pieces without warning at any point.

And, as I have come to know and like David pretty well over the years, I can't help hoping that he has a strong shelter nearby to retreat to.

If my hunch is correct, that point is going to be reached sometime in the next few hours.

Chapter Twenty-Seven

Wednesday

Kathryn usually used a heavy foot on the accelerator, but today the speedometer needle hovered a little under the limit. While she was not deviating from her course, clearly she wasn't in a tremendous hurry to reach her destination either.

What a strange relationship she and David had. Every point of contact between them was like a brand lifted from the fire and pressed against tender skin. Still, neither had been able to break it off. At least, not until they did. Or he did, anyway.

And now she was grabbing the bricks off the pile they'd built up between them and using them to lay down the road she could drive on to get to him again. The effort cost her. Every brick scratched at her skin and tore at her nails, but she kept at it. Nothing had ever been able to stop her once she'd made up her mind about something. Not even the idea of facing the man who had caused her and everyone she loved so much pain.

Or the way she felt every time she received a letter from him. The day the second one arrived, eight years after That Night and five years after she'd confronted Henley at the courthouse, she'd clutched it in her hand, agonizing over whether to return it without opening it. Her story would have been much different, I'm sure, if she had.

I say *different*, not necessarily *better*. It's extremely difficult to tell these things with a finite mind, which, like you, I possess. She wouldn't be about to head to Maple Ridge to see him, that's for sure. And we would find out some time in the next hour or two whether or not that would have been for the best.

August 2007

Kathryn set the pile of mail on the table, still holding one envelope in her hand. The only sound in the house was the loud drumming of her heartbeat in her ears. Aaron had taken Meg, who was expecting their second child, to a doctor's appointment, and her parents were out running errands. The school bus wouldn't drop Tory off for another hour. She was alone.

Kathryn sank onto a wooden chair at the kitchen table and stared at the envelope. If Aaron was here, he'd tell her to get rid of it. *That's exactly what I should do. Destroy it.* She grasped the envelope with shaking fingers.

"Go ahead. Rip it up." The desperation in her voice bounced off the walls in the empty kitchen. "End this thing once and for all." It was sound advice, but she couldn't bring herself to take it.

In spite of everything that had happened, a bond had formed between her and David Henley. Their encounters had been intense and emotional and infused with a supernatural power neither of them could comprehend. Without her realizing it was happening, a connection had formed between them that was almost palpable.

Kathryn glanced out the window. No one had come home while she was lost in contemplation. She had to do this now or not at all.

She tore open the envelope.

Ms. Ellison,

I'm sure you've heard by now that I've been released from prison. I wanted to write to let you know I've moved to Toronto. You won't believe what I'm doing here, as I can hardly believe it myself. I've come to attend Bible college.

A friend of mine on the inside, Tiny, once told me he thought God had chosen me to do something special. I was skeptical, as I'm sure you must be, but somehow I couldn't let go of the idea. For several days I prayed to know what God wanted of me. And then, not knowing what else to do, I shut up and listened.

One night it hit me that I was supposed to be a minister. I know that must be hard for you to swallow, but for me it's a hundred times more so. I grew up as the son of a preacher and had turned my back on him and everything he represented a long time ago. I'm sure God is enjoying the irony of my situation but, believe me, I've been dragged here kicking and screaming. I know it's what I'm supposed to do, but part of me hopes they'll turn me away at the door, which, of course, they'd have every right to do.

I'm telling you this so you won't worry about running into me. I also wanted you to know that you're a big reason I'm here. I truly believe that you forgiving me changed the course of my life.

If I don't get a response to this letter, then I'll know and completely understand that you want to end any connection with me.

I hope you're doing well and have been able to move on with your life.

David Henley

For a long time after reading the letter, Kathryn sat at the table and stared out the window. When Aaron's truck wheeled up the driveway, for reasons she didn't fully understand she stuffed the sheet into the envelope, carried it to her room, and hid it in a drawer in her desk.

For days she tried not to think about it, but the words David Henley had written had burned themselves into her mind. A week later she went into her room, locked the door, and sat at her desk. She opened the drawer and withdrew the envelope.

After reading the words again, she opened another drawer and took out a box of stationery. Her hands shook as she set it on the desk, and she clasped her hands in her lap, bending forward to ease the pain in her stomach.

What was she doing? She couldn't do this to herself, to her family. She rubbed her sweating palms on her shorts. Somehow, she couldn't not do it. Kathryn stared at the blank sheet of paper for a minute until, with a sigh, she picked up her pen and began to write.

Wednesday

I couldn't imagine what was going through Kathryn's mind as the tires ate up mile after mile beneath us. Fortunately, I didn't have to. Even above the hum of the engine, I could catch snatches of her frenetic mental activity, enough to know that she couldn't settle on any one thought long enough to work it through rationally. It was too much to deal with, really, and I was surprised, as I always am, by the human capacity to cope.

Of the many strategies you have developed to do this, shutting off the flow of thoughts is a pretty effective one. Given the sudden dead air around me, Kathryn had evidently chosen to go with that. I didn't blame her, but it did make it more difficult for me to know what she was going through. I'd have to keep my eyes and ears open and try to figure it out as we went along.

Her foot pressed down on the gas pedal. As impatient as I had been the last twenty-four hours, I now reversed that position and wished she would slow down a little. Mentally—the only way I could, unfortunately—I fastened my seatbelt. Apparently now that she had decided to do this, Kathryn was determined to get there as quickly as possible. I didn't have to read her thoughts to figure that out.

I only had to grip the door handle—figuratively—as hard as I could and pray that we would reach our destination in one piece.

Chapter Twenty-Eight

Wednesday

An endless line of fence streamed past the window in ribbons of white. The sight was hypnotic, and I'd nearly fallen into a trance-like state when I was yanked into reality. The dam holding in Kathryn's thoughts had clearly been breached, as they gushed through her mind now with near-destructive force. I straightened. What had caused the dam to burst?

I studied the property behind the fence line. Ah. Nick Lawson's ranch. That would do it. The black pickup was parked in front of the garage. I glanced over at my charge. Her fingers grasped the steering wheel as tightly as I continued to grip the door handle. Although she clearly tried to keep her eyes on the road ahead, her gaze did shift to the right a little, more than once. Had she seen the truck? If so, she—

He's there rang through my mind, loud enough that I jerked and nearly banged my head against the glass. Which answered my question. Of course she would know he was there. Even if she hadn't seen the truck, Kathryn had always been keenly aware of Nick's presence when he was anywhere nearby. For years she'd been careful not to take this road, but her mind was so frazzled today that she must have turned onto it without thinking about it, or him.

Well, she was thinking about him now. Not about his visit of a few days ago, as I might have expected, but about another day, years ago, and a surprise encounter with Nick. The one that had led to him eventually showing up on her porch on Tuesday afternoon. The one that had given me—and him—hope that maybe the two of them might find a way to be together.

The aroma of thick, rich coffee drifted through my mind, and I loosened my death grip on the door handle a little and closed my eyes, remembering.

June 2011

At the sound of the woman's voice ordering a medium coffee with double cream, Nick glanced up from his book. His chest muscles clenched. Kathryn. Not bothering to mark his spot, he closed the book and set it on the table next to his own mug of black coffee. She stood with her back to him, her long, dark hair cascading over a peach-colored blouse. Her arm circled the shoulders of a young girl beside her, blond hair hanging in two braids. *Who is that?*

Nick drew in a breath, the mocha aroma hanging in the air steadying his nerves, a little. His mind struggled to process the fact that the woman so often on his mind had materialized in front of him. He still didn't fully understand the powerful hold she had on him. In an attempt to forget her, he'd dated a few other women over the years. Actually, a lot of other women. More than enough for him to know that it was no use. Every time, gazing at one of them across the table in a restaurant, or holding her hand as they walked along the shore of the ocean, the only one he could see—or feel anything for—was Kathryn Ellison.

It was completely illogical. He didn't need anyone to tell him that, although a lot of his friends had over the years. How could he be so invested in her when they'd only met a couple of times? What was he, some sort of love-struck teen in a Shakespearean tragedy?

Nick hadn't even been sure he believed in the concept of soul mates or *the one* before the day he met her. He still didn't know if such a thing was a universal truth or if it was only true for him. All he knew with absolute certainty was that Kathryn was the only woman in the world for him. And if she couldn't be with him because of his connection to what had happened to her in the past, well then, he would have to be alone. He couldn't marry another woman when his heart had belonged to the one standing in front of him now since the day he had heard her speak on behalf of her attacker in that courtroom. It wouldn't be fair.

162

Kathryn accepted the paper cup the woman behind the counter handed her. "Thank you." Coins clinked in the tip jar before she turned to survey the room, clearly searching for an empty table. The place was small, and the handful of tables all had people sitting at them, students mostly, laptops open, obviously settled in. When their eyes met, she froze, staring at him for a few seconds. Nick smiled and held up his hand. Her shoulders relaxed and she lifted a hand in response.

Kathryn rested her fingers between the girl's shoulder blades as they made their way around tables, stopping beside his. "Nick, hi."

"Hi, Kathryn." Who was the young girl? Had Kathryn gotten married? His gaze swept over the fingers clutching the paper mug. No ring. "Busy place, isn't it?"

She surveyed the room, a smile warming her eyes. "It certainly is."

"You're welcome to join me." He nodded to the empty seat across from him. "I can grab another chair."

Her cheeks paled slightly. "Oh no. I don't want to disturb you. We should get back to the farm."

"I need to use the restroom before we go, Mom." The girl tilted her head to gaze up at her, one blond braid swishing across her arm.

Mom? Nick swallowed. When had that happened? Who was the girl's father? A tight knot formed in his stomach. Even knowing the jealousy was ridiculous when he had absolutely no claim on her affections or faithfulness to him, he had to work to shove it away. His eyes met hers again. She was watching him, as though she could read the thoughts spinning through his head. "I'm sorry. Nick, this is my daughter, Tory. Tory, say hi to my friend Mr. Lawson."

Her friend. Better than nothing, anyway. Nick held out his hand to the girl. "Nice to meet you, Tory."

Her cheeks held a tinge of pink as she shook it. "You too." She let go of him and craned her neck again. "Can I go, Mom?"

"Do you want me to come with you?"

Her daughter rolled her eyes and released a long-suffering sigh. "I'm eleven. I can go by myself."

"Hey." Kathryn tapped the girl's head lightly with one finger. "Attitude."

"Sorry." When the girl grinned, her freckled face lit up like a Christmas tree.

Nick couldn't help smiling in response as Kathryn nodded. "All right then. I'll wait here."

Tory flounced to the restrooms at the back of the coffee shop. Kathryn watched her a moment. When she shifted her attention to him, Nick gestured to the empty chair. Kathryn set her coffee on the table and pulled it out. For a moment after she sat, she stared at the paper cup clutched in her fingers, as if trying to figure out what to say. Nick gave her time. Finally, she lifted her head. "I guess you're wondering about her."

Yes, I definitely am. Nick lifted his shoulders. "Do you have a husband I don't know about?" He tried to say the words lightly, teasingly even, but wasn't sure he succeeded in hiding the way the thought of her committing her life to another man grated across his chest like sandpaper.

Kathryn played with the plastic tab on the lid of the cup, her smile sad. "No. No husband."

It took a few seconds for the truth to hit him. *Ah.* Tory had said she was eleven. That meant she was most likely a product of what had happened in the cabin that night, twelve years ago. Nick reached across the table and covered her hand with his. "I'm sorry, Kathryn. I had no idea."

She shook her head. "I didn't say anything during the trial because I didn't want him to know." Her face brightened as she glanced in the direction her daughter had disappeared. "But don't be sorry. Not for her. If it hadn't been for Tory, I'm not sure I would have been able to keep going after what happened to me. She's the greatest joy of my life."

The memory of what she had gone through—the recounting of events that he and Halyna had sat through during the trial—

twisted his insides. Even then, before he'd met her, the details he'd heard had sickened him, broken his heart. And terrified him, knowing how easily it could have been his little sister in the cabin that night. "I can see that, the way you look at her." The hand beneath his was soft. Everything in Nick wanted to close his fingers around it, pull it to his chest, refuse to let go. He released her.

She flipped the tab on the cup again. "How is your sister?"

"She's doing well. The cancer's in remission for the second time. In fact, she's getting married in a couple of weeks."

Kathryn's face lit like her daughter's had. Whoever her father was, Tory was all Kathryn. "That's amazing news. I'm so happy for her, for all of you."

"Thank you. It was definitely rough for a while, but James, her fiancé, hung in there with her every step of the way. He's a great guy."

"Good. I'm glad to hear that. Please congratulate her for me."

Nick rested his hand on top of the book he'd been reading. "Or you could tell her yourself."

She blinked. Before she could object—or he could lose his nerve—he rushed to add, "I could really use a plus one at this thing. And Hally would love to see you again. You wouldn't be interested in coming, would you?" He was pretty sure he hadn't been any more successful at making the question sound casual than he'd been at asking if she had a husband—as though it didn't really matter to him one way or the other. Could she tell how badly he wanted her to say yes?

She contemplated him, biting her lower lip.

"You'd be doing me a huge favor. If I don't bring someone, my Aunt Doris will spend the entire day trying to match me up with every single woman there."

The corners of her mouth twitched. "So it would purely be to keep your aunt off your back?"

"One hundred percent." With her eyes on him, he couldn't bring himself to deceive her. "Well, maybe seventy-five percent."

Kathryn laughed. Any knots that had formed in his stomach loosened at the sound. He could definitely get used to ... Nick shifted on the hard plastic seat. No. No getting used to anything. If he was lucky, she'd agree to be his date for the wedding, as much or more to see his sister as to spend time with him. He couldn't set his heart out on the chopping block in front of her any more than he already had. Not when the past still threatened any possibility that they could ever be together. Inviting her to the wedding was likely a huge mistake, but he couldn't bring himself to rescind the offer. Or to hope that she would refuse it.

"All right then. To save you from Aunt Doris, I'll come. I would love to see your sister again. And watch her get married."

As he'd thought. She was doing this to see Halyna. He'd need to remind himself of that often over the next couple of weeks to keep his hopes from rising too high.

"That's great. She'll be thrilled to see you. It's Saturday, June 20th at four in the afternoon, Covenant Church."

Kathryn nodded. "I know it. I'll be there." She slid to the front of the seat.

Before he gave himself time to think it through, he reached for her hand again. She stilled, her fingers warm in his. Prickles of electricity spread up his arm. "It was great to see you, Kathryn. And to meet your daughter. She's lovely. Not surprisingly."

Pink tinged her cheeks the same way it had Tory's. "Thank you. It was good to—" Her gaze flicked to the rear of the coffee shop, and she withdrew her hand from his seconds before her daughter reached the table. "I'll see you in two weeks."

He didn't bother trying to keep the anticipation out of his voice. "I'm looking forward to it."

"Me too." She picked up her coffee cup.

Clearly oblivious to her mother's desire for a quick getaway, Tory folded her arms on the table. "So, Mr. Lawson, how do you know my mom?"

Nick's gaze slid to Kathryn's. The trapped animal panic that flickered across her face suggested she hadn't planned what she would tell her daughter if that question came up. He focused on Tory, meeting the blue eyes that were watching him expectantly. "My family doesn't live too far from yours, so I've run into your mom occasionally in town." A bit of an exaggeration since his family's ranch was twenty minutes east of Surrey and the Ellison place was a good twenty minutes west. It was a big province though, so *not far* was relative. "The last time was at the grocery store when she was there picking out cereal with your grandma. And my sister Halyna is a friend of your mom's too. In fact, Halyna is getting married in a couple of weeks, and your mom is coming to the wedding."

The last bit was a little low—an attempt on Nick's part to ensure that Kathryn didn't renege on her promise to accompany him. Tory's question would no doubt get her thinking about all the reasons she should, and now she'd have to try to explain them to her daughter if she changed her mind about being his date. Manipulative, maybe, but he wasn't sorry. Not if it meant he'd get to see her again, and for a whole day this time.

"Cool." Tory pushed off from the table, clearly done with the conversation.

When Kathryn's hazel eyes met his, the panic on her face was gone, replaced by a *well-played* smirk. He dipped his head slightly, acknowledging that he understood she knew very well what he had done.

"Goodbye, Nick."

"'Bye, Kathryn. See you later, Tory."

Her daughter waved. "See you."

Nick waited for them to maneuver around the few tables in the place and disappear out the door before he slumped in his seat. They were going on a date. Well, at least twenty-five percent of their time together could be counted as a date. Could he keep up the pretense that seventy-five percent was merely her doing him a favor? Somehow he doubted it. Her laugh had suggested she was as aware as he was that one hundred percent of him wanted her there, with him, and had nothing to do with preventing Aunt Doris from trying to match him up with another guest.

I guess I don't need to tell you where I was that day, or how I felt. I was in my favorite place, nestled on the counter with my back pressed to the industrial-sized coffee maker, surrounded by the aromas of coffee and fresh-baked cinnamon buns and cookies. After witnessing the exchange between Kathryn and Nick, I was even more content. So they were going to a wedding together. I'd have to dig my best gown out of storage for the occasion. Even if my human charges couldn't see me, I still preferred to dress appropriately for any event to which I accompanied them.

So had Nick and Kathryn turned a corner? Not being able to see along the road in front of them, I couldn't say for sure. Still, I had a very good feeling about those two. So much so that warmth spread all through my body. Of course, I did have the hot metal of the coffee maker pressed along the length of me.

Even if I hadn't, the looks the two of them had exchanged would have warmed me as effectively as that blessed machine had.

Chapter Twenty-Nine

June 2011

The bride floated up the aisle on the arm of an older man, her father, no doubt. Nick's father. Smiles wreathed the faces of those standing around Kathryn, but her own smile was shaky, tempered by the knife-like shock slashing through her at the sight of the woman who was meant to have been taken to the cabin That Night instead of her. Tingles shot across her skin. She hadn't seen Halyna since that day in the courthouse. The glimpse she caught of her now between the rapid blinking of her eyes and the glancing at the program clutched in her trembling fingers was unexpectedly rocking her to her core. For a few, wild seconds she swayed on her feet. Was she going to pass out and ruin the most important day of Halyna's life? *Breathe.*

She concentrated on inhaling and exhaling deeply. The light scent of flowers, the sunlight streaming through the stained-glass windows that lined both sides of the small church, and the soft classical music accompanying the bride to the front where her groom waited for her managed to calm her and she loosened her grip on the program. The minister prayed and then asked those gathered to sit. Kathryn sank onto the wooden pew, relieved to have made it through the first unsettling moments in Halyna's presence.

Throughout the ceremony, Kathryn's thoughts whirled like sticks caught in an eddy of water. She should be watching the bride and groom. Although she'd technically only met Halyna once, she felt deeply connected to the woman and was genuinely happy for her and her family. Although seeing her sent a pang hurtling through Kathryn like a bolt of lightning, what had happened to her—the choices Halyna's ex-boyfriend and the two men he had hired had made—were not Halyna's fault. Kathryn certainly didn't wish her any harm. She had no idea what Nick's sister had been through the last few years, but it had to have been incredibly difficult.

Halyna's hair was short now, a pixie cut around her face, but she looked radiant in her silk gown and veil. And the way her husband-to-be gazed adoringly at her suggested that the two of them had a promising future together. That stilled the angst that had been rippling through Kathryn.

Still, she couldn't help wondering how different things might have been if the men who had abducted her hadn't made the mistake they had. Would Halyna have survived the encounter with the two men or with her ex? If she had, would she have been as traumatized as Kathryn? Would she still be marrying the great love of her life today? Maybe Kathryn would have been married by now, to Ty, and her path might never have crossed with Halyna's.

Or Nick's.

The ache that thought caused startled her, and she shifted her attention from the bride and groom to the best man. Nick looked extremely handsome in his tux and crisp, white shirt. He'd gotten a haircut since she saw him at the coffee shop, but the odd wayward curl still wound its way around his ear. He was watching her, and when she glanced over, he smiled.

Kathryn couldn't sort out everything she felt when her gaze melded with his. From the moment they had first met, she had been drawn to him. Except that she couldn't be drawn to him. Like Halyna, he reminded her too much of a past she would give anything to forget. Tory's innocent question in the coffee shop two weeks ago had driven that point home for her, in case she'd been tempted to forget. Which she had been, when he'd reached for her hand and held it in his, his warm brown eyes searching hers. For a few, brief seconds, she'd longed to toss away every protest, shove away every bit of reluctance she had to get involved with him. But she couldn't.

Not for the long term, anyway. For today, she was determined to set everything standing between them aside and be all in. Anything less wouldn't be fair to him. Or to herself.

Kathryn tore her gaze from his and concentrated on the

couple in front of the altar. When the minister pronounced them husband and wife, James took Halyna's face in his hands and kissed her with an unreserved joy and enthusiasm that could only be the result of having overcome tremendous odds to be together. *The kind that you and Nick would experience if you could let go of the past.*

He was watching her again. Kathryn could feel it, but she kept her gaze steadily on the newlyweds as they started down the aisle. Even when Nick passed her, exiting the church behind the happy couple, she faced forward, clutching the top of the pew in front of her for support. Should she stay? She had promised she would, to speak to Halyna and to shield Nick from anyone who might try to pair him with someone else. Although maybe it wouldn't be such a terrible thing if they did.

Nick was waiting for her. Somehow she knew that, although she didn't fully understand it. It was wrong of her to keep him waiting. It was certainly wrong of her to hope, even for one second, that he wouldn't find happiness in the arms of another woman before she was ready to commit to him. Because what if she was never ready? She had to free him, even if that meant losing him forever to someone else. As much as that thought might send pain pulsing through her, if she cared about him at all, she needed to do it. Today, if they had a moment alone. Which she had to make sure they did.

Swallowing hard, Kathryn followed the other guests to the exit. The bridal party stood on the sidewalk in front of the church, greeting guests as they came out the door. Kathryn waited in line until she reached the bride.

"Kathryn." Halyna reached for both her hands. "Thank you so much for coming."

"It's my pleasure." Kathryn squeezed the slender fingers clutching hers. "I'm so happy for you and James. And the wedding was beautiful."

"Thank you." Halyna let go of her and slid her hand through the crook of her new husband's elbow. He'd been talking to one of his ushers, but he swung around at her touch. "James, I want you to meet someone. This is Nick's friend, Kathryn Ellison."

"Ah." James held out his hand. "Kathryn. It's good to meet you finally. I've heard a lot about you."

He had? Warmth that had nothing to do with the bright sun shining in a brilliant blue sky crept up Kathryn's neck as she grasped his hand. "It's good to meet you too." She contemplated Halyna's introduction. Nick's friend? Was that what she was? Did she want to be his friend? Was the designation too much to describe their relationship or too little? Giving her head a small shake, Kathryn released James's hand and smiled at him and Halyna. "I wish both of you the very best in your marriage."

Halyna grasped her elbow. "You're staying, aren't you?"

Was she? Even now, she couldn't bring herself to make the decision one way or the other. What would she do to put in time until the reception, other than drive herself crazy thinking about the conversation she and Nick needed to have?

"We took our pictures earlier, so dinner will start in a few minutes, around the back of the church."

Ah. So no time to brood. Or panic. Before she could respond, Halyna stepped behind her husband and grasped her brother's arm. "Nick, come talk to Kathryn. Convince her she needs to stay for dinner."

Kathryn's chest tightened as Nick allowed his sister to drag him over to stand in front of her. He grasped her fingers and held them in his strong warm ones. "Kathryn. You aren't going to bail on me, are you?" He leaned closer and lowered his voice. "Aunt Doris has already introduced me to three different women. I'm counting on you to save me."

In spite of the intensity in his eyes, his voice was light and the knots in her shoulders loosened a little. "I suppose I did promise."

"Yes, you did."

Halyna rested a hand on her brother's back. "You two go find your seats. We'll be there shortly."

Nick smiled and held out his arm toward the rear of the

building, his other hand still clutching hers. "Shall we?"

The decision made—for her as much as by her—Kathryn nodded slightly and followed Nick as he led her along the side of the old wooden church. A huge white tent dominated the lawn behind the building. This late in the afternoon, the heat wasn't unbearable, but still, Kathryn welcomed the coolness and shade when they stepped inside.

She drew in a breath as she scanned the room. Round tables with white linen cloths dotted the interior. Huge bouquets of wild flowers in blue bottles sat in the middle of the tables, and white mini lights had been strung everywhere, giving the space a fairytale feel. Appropriate, given the journey Halyna and James had been on the last few years.

An older couple stood to the right of the entrance. Nick inclined his head in their direction. "My parents. Can I introduce you?"

Was she ready for that huge step? *All in.* She could do that. For one day. "Of course."

He let go of her but rested his hand on the small of her back as he guided her over to them. "Mom, Dad, I want you to meet Kathryn Ellison."

It was clear where Nick got his looks. Even in his sixties, the man who had accompanied Halyna up the aisle was an extremely handsome man. The glimpse into Nick's future threw her a little, but she smiled when his father greeted her with a strong handshake. "Welcome, Kathryn."

His mother wrapped her arms around Kathryn and hugged her. Her dark eyes glowed when she stepped back, her hands warm on Kathryn's arms. "It's lovely to meet you."

"You too."

Her eyes searched Kathryn's, and she appeared about to say more. Then a cluster of people entered the tent and she let her go. "Please excuse us—we need to perform our hosting duties. We'll talk again."

Would they? Kathryn nodded, watching for a moment as they greeted other guests. "They're lovely, Nick."

"Yes, they are." His voice, close to her ear, was husky, as though the sight of her with his parents had moved him. "I'm glad you got to meet them."

"Me too."

Nick directed Kathryn to the far corner of the tent, away from the few guests already seeking shelter inside. When he pulled out a chair at one of the tables and held it for her, she glanced around the space. "No seating plan?"

He grinned. "Nope. Hally and James are too laid back for that kind of thing. No head table, either, so I'm free to sit with my ..." he cleared his throat, "with you."

Kathryn sat and hung her purse on the chair as Nick settled on the one beside her. Was this the time to talk to him? The start of the reception might not be the ideal moment, but what if they didn't have another one? Her pulse pounding in her throat, she turned a little in her chair to face him. "Nick."

For a few seconds he didn't respond, only searched her face as though he knew what she was about to say and wanted to put it off as long as possible. Then he straightened his shoulders and took her hands in his. "Yes?"

"It's been so good to see you—in the coffee shop and now, today."

"It's been incredibly good to see you as well."

His thumbs rubbed gently over hers, and for a moment she lost her train of thought. "The thing is ..." She bit her lip. Was she prepared to close the door completely to whatever it was that had sparked between them the moment they had met?

A small smile crossed his lips, but the eyes that met hers were sad. He knew. "What is the thing?"

"I don't know if you have even been thinking about a future for the two of us—"

Nick lifted her hand and pressed his lips to the back of it. "I think you do know. From the moment I saw you, there's never been anyone else for me. No one serious."

Her heart thudded against her ribs so hard he had to be able to hear it. "Maybe there should be."

He furrowed his brow as he lowered their clasped hands to his knee. "What does that mean?"

"It means that I'm not ready." Her voice shook a little, and he tightened his grip. "I don't know if I will ever be ready, and it's not fair of me to ask you to wait."

"I don't recall you asking." Nick leaned against the white folding chair. "But if you're not ready, I'm not going to push you. I am, however, going to hold you to your commitment."

"And what commitment is that?"

"To spend today with me. I'm calling an *as if* day."

Kathryn's lips twitched. "And what, exactly, is an *as if* day?"

"It's a game Hally and I used to play. Whenever one of us called it, he or she came up with an identity that we would take on for that day. Sometimes we were movie stars, or people who spoke with a British accent, or fugitives on the run from the law. And we had to be those people all day long."

"So you want us to spend the day as if ..."

"We are a real couple, with absolutely nothing standing in our way and a bright future together."

The light, breezy scent of the camomile daisies in the blue bottles on the table drifted on the air. Kathryn breathed in the fragrance. The muscles that had tightened in her abdomen when she'd slipped into her yellow dress earlier that afternoon—getting ready for her date with Nick—eased a little. "That sounds like an extremely dangerous game. Do you really want to go to all that trouble to fool Aunt Doris?"

"Oh, it's no trouble, believe me. Not for me. And I'll let you in on a little secret." He bent forward and lowered his voice to a conspiratorial whisper. "Today was never about Aunt Doris."

Kathryn tugged one hand from his and fingered the coarse embroidered edge of the white linen tablecloth. So they were finally being honest with each other. The two of them had never had a conversation like this one, laying everything out on the table between them. Would accepting his challenge make it easier or harder to walk away from him at the end of the day? *Don't do it.* Playing that game was playing with fire. Except that she couldn't say no, not when he was regarding her with such a hopeful look in his eyes. And not when she desperately wanted to take this one chance to spend time with him. Before she could over-analyze the situation, she lifted her chin. "All right."

The smile that went deep into his eyes, driving away the sadness, eased her anxiety further, and she let go of the tablecloth.

"All right?"

"Yes. I mean, it isn't even a day, right? It's already dinnertime, so it's more like five hours."

"The five-hour boyfriend." Nick grinned. "Sounds like a great idea for a reality show."

Kathryn chuckled. "Sadly, that is about how long some of the relationships on those shows last."

"We're on then. And remember, the rules state we both have to be completely in. We aren't pretending to be in a relationship this evening—we *are* in one."

"Got it."

Nick squeezed her fingers gently before letting her go. "First order of business. Let me get you a glass of punch."

Kathryn nodded. Chewing on her thumbnail, she watched as he made his way to the far side of the tent, to a table that held three crystal punch bowls. What was she doing? This was going to seriously complicate an already deeply complicated situation. She lowered her hand to her lap.

Right now, in this moment, she couldn't bring herself to care.

Chapter Thirty

June 2011

Punch splashed over the side of the crystal glass, and Nick set it on the table. Pressing both hands to the linen tablecloth—now dotted with splotches of red—he took a long, deep breath. *Relax. It isn't real.* The problem was, the whole thing was far too real. Having Kathryn here with him, spending the evening with him as though the two of them were together, was likely the worst idea he'd ever had.

He swiped a bead of sweat off his temple with his fingers. Why had he suggested that crazy game? The thought hadn't even occurred to him until he opened his mouth and blurted it out. Even as he spoke the words, he figured she would never go for the idea. But she had. Nick reached for the ladle. Why had she? Was she more ready than she thought she was? Hope flickered as he poured punch into a second glass.

Or maybe it was a game to her, a way to kill time until she had fulfilled any obligation she might have to keep him company today. The ladle clattered into the punch bowl. An elderly gentleman in a gold shirt and brown tie standing at the end of the table shot him a reproachful glare. "Sorry." Nick handed him the ladle before picking up both of the glasses he'd somehow managed to fill.

This wasn't a game. Not to either of them. The battle that had raged in her eyes before she'd surprised him—and herself, no doubt—by picking up the gauntlet he'd thrown down, had shown him how seriously she took this. Whatever *this* was.

Nick reached their seats and set the cups carefully on the table. His tuxedo jacket weighed on him heavily and he shrugged it off and hung it over the back of the folding chair. That was exactly the problem. Neither of them truly knew what it was. Or what it could be. And that was why he had made that ridiculous proposal. He wanted to know, even if only for a few hours, what this might look like, might feel like, if they actually gave themselves over to it. And he wanted her to know. Maybe it would help, somehow. Give her a window into what she was fighting so hard against and reveal to her that she didn't have to keep fighting. That nothing frightening waited for her on the other side of her fear and trauma. Only him and quite possibly the greatest love either of them had ever known.

The weight that dropped onto his shoulders at the thought of trying to prove that to her buckled his knees a little, and he sank onto the folding chair. "Nick." Kathryn rested a hand on his knee, and he resisted the urge to glance at it. "Your Aunt Doris and I were having a nice chat about you." She flashed him a smile and tilted her head almost imperceptibly in the direction of his aunt, who'd taken a seat across the table from them.

Nick shifted his attention from her to his aunt, her usual resplendent self in a purple dress and a hat tilted to one side over short, bottle-red curls. "Aunt Doris. Lovely to see you, as always."

"Thank you, Nicholas George."

He didn't have to glance over at Kathryn to know she was smirking at that. "So you've met my girlfriend, Kathryn?" Nick slid his arm around Kathryn's shoulders. He'd have a lot of explaining to do when this day was over, but having her warm fingers tighten over his kneecap was worth every bit of what would come when he had to face the inquisition of his family and friends.

His aunt's false eyelashes fluttered several times across the top of her cheek bones, at the spot where she had liberally applied two perfect circles of rouge. "Girlfriend? I had no idea." She regarded Kathryn with new interest. "How long has this been going on?"

Good question. Nine years? Five minutes? Probably should have thought out a few answers to the inevitable questions they would face during dinner.

"Not long." Kathryn's voice, smooth and even—how did she do that?—saved him from fumbling his response. "Tell me,

Mrs. Lawson, where did you find that wonderful fascinator?"

Fascinator?

Aunt Doris waved a hand through the air. "Call me Aunt Doris, dear. You're family now."

Nick gulped, half-expecting Kathryn to bolt at that. His arm tightened slightly around her, but she didn't attempt to move.

Aunt Doris's face was animated as she launched into a lengthy description of her favorite stores within a two-hour radius of Surrey. Nick gave up trying to follow what she was saying and concentrated on the woman beside him as she chatted easily with his aunt. Aunt Doris's daughters, his cousins Esther and Paige, joined them at the table and peppered Kathryn with questions all throughout dinner. She answered them but managed to deflect the focus onto them over and over, so deftly he was sure none of them noticed. Of course, they were a family who enjoyed talking about themselves and their interests, which helped.

His thumb brushed across her arm, beneath the short sleeve of the dress she wore. The one that appeared to have been woven from sunshine. Her gaze slid to his, and a small smile curved up the corners of her mouth. That smile, the warmth in her brown and green eyes, and the silky feel of the dark hair flowing down her back was robbing him of any ability to think clearly, let alone form a coherent sentence. Fortunately, the women sitting across from them didn't seem to notice.

Nick was fairly certain his struggles were quite apparent to Kathryn, as she jumped in often to help him answer one of the myriad questions about their relationship he was unable to form a response to. Every time she did, the eyes that met his danced with amusement. Her hand still rested on his knee, the only thing keeping him grounded in this space and at all aware of what was happening around him. The desire for all these people surrounding them to disappear and for the two of them to be alone grew stronger and stronger—a pressure that increased in his chest until he could barely draw a breath.

They couldn't go anywhere. Not before he'd given the toast as best man and the speech portion of the event was over, at least.

When someone called his name, inviting him to come to the microphone, Nick removed his arm from her shoulders, reluctantly, and her fingers slid from his knee. She offered him an encouraging smile as he slid his jacket on and made his way to the makeshift podium. Gripping both sides of it, he managed to deliver the speech he'd been working on for the last few weeks.

He hoped he did, anyway. Like the rest of the evening, his toast passed by in a blur. He seemed to get through it okay. Lots of people laughed—whether at his jokes or at him he wasn't sure and didn't particularly care. When he finished and raised his glass to Hally and James, everyone followed suit. Relief flowed through him as he walked back to his seat. He'd performed the last of his duties and was now free to spend what might be his final couple of hours in a relationship with the incredible woman sitting beside him.

When she didn't return her hand to his knee, Nick reached for it and clasped it in his, resting them both on his leg. Her thumb brushed over his as she continued to chat with the other people at the table, which didn't lessen his desire to be alone with her one bit. Music started, and Nick forced himself to watch as Hally and James danced the first number in each other's arms. He'd heard about brides glowing but hadn't understood what that meant until he witnessed the phenomenon on his sister's face as she gazed up at her new husband. His chest tightened. It was impossible for him to put into words how happy he was for her. She'd been through so much and had born it all—the brutal chemo treatments, the loss of hair, the agonizing wait for test results—with a sweet grace and patience he couldn't begin to fathom.

If she'd faced an enemy he could have battled with his bare hands, he'd have gladly done it, even at the cost of his own life. Unfortunately, there was little Nick could do to fight the enemy of cancer, other than to be at her side every moment. With James at her other side, and her strong faith in God, she'd come through to this place of victory. What none of them would put into words was that the enemy would always hover on the periphery now, casting a shadow over any future plans they might try to make. So they lived for each day and gave thanks for every good thing that came their way. Like this wedding.

Other couples streamed around tables to join the newlyweds, and Nick stood and held out a hand to Kathryn. "Care to dance?"

"Of course." Kathryn excused herself from the conversation with his aunt and cousins, took his hand, and followed him to the wooden floor they'd erected in the center of the tent.

The soft, slow strains of "Unchained Melody" drifted on the air as Nick wrapped an arm around her waist and pulled her to him. For a minute or two neither of them spoke. The soft scent drifting from her hair reminded him of his mother's rose garden on a warm summer day. He closed his eyes and breathed in, trying to capture every detail of this moment in his memory to hold on to in the weeks and years ahead when his arms might be empty again.

Kathryn lifted her head and smiled at him. "Did you specifically request this song?"

Nick hadn't been paying much attention to the words. He listened now, their plaintive yearning such a strong reflection of the longing in his heart the lyrics might have been written for him, for this moment. "No. But I could have." The last line, a plea for God to speed the love of the lost one to the one who ached for her, sent a pang through his chest as he tightened his arms around her. Kathryn rested her head on his chest and he leaned his cheek against her hair, willing the song to go on forever.

When it ended and she made no move to leave his arms, he held her through three more songs, the two of them swaying slowly to the music. After a while they took a break for punch. Kathryn didn't object when they finished, and he took both their glasses and set them on the table before leading her to the dance floor again. Through a thick haze, he grew aware that the crowd on the floor was thinning and that most of the tables were empty. The event was winding down.

James and Halyna left in a flurry of well wishes and hugs. After they'd gone, Kathryn lifted her purse from the back of her chair and said goodbye to Aunt Doris and his cousins. Then she slid a hand through the crook of Nick's elbow. "Walk me out?"

His throat tight, he nodded and led her to the exit and across the lawn to the parking lot. He checked his watch. Almost ten. His dress shoes felt full of cement as he trudged across the lot. She stopped next to a blue Sonata and her hand slid from his arm. He wished desperately he could take it and hold on, refuse to let her go, but he couldn't. She was leaving and he had no idea whether he would ever see her again.

"I had a wonderful time today, Nick."

"So did I."

"It was fun pretending for a while."

The wistfulness in her voice threw kindling on the tiny flame of hope he'd been attempting to bank all evening, and he rested his hands on the roof of her car on either side of her. "It doesn't have to be pretend."

Kathryn bit her lip, studying him. "Except that it does. For now."

That wasn't shutting the door completely. The flame flickered brighter. "All right then." The face of his watch glowed in the dark parking lot and he glanced at it. "But we have seven minutes left of our *as if* day, which means we're still together. And there's only one way two people in a relationship would end a day like this."

She tilted her head back a little. An invitation. "I know."

Nick slid his hands from the roof of the car to her face, reveling in the feel of her soft skin beneath his. He leaned in slowly and pressed his lips to hers. The sensation was everything he had dreamed it would be and more. He moved closer, deepening their connection. Knowing he might never have another chance, he poured everything he had felt since the moment they'd met into the kiss, praying that she would understand what he couldn't put into words. When he finally pulled back, he studied her face. Had that changed anything? The sadness in her eyes was not encouraging, and he lowered his hands.

"I should go."

Nick took a steadying breath, his head spinning a little. "You're the only woman for me, Kathryn. So I'll wait for you. As long as it takes. But I'll be praying about us, and I hope you will be too. When I believe that God is telling me the time is right, I will come for you."

"And if I'm still not ready?"

He reached for her hand and clasped it to his chest. "Then I'll hold the memory of today in my heart as the best day of my life and always be grateful for it."

Kathryn glanced at the silver watch clasped around her slender wrist. "You know, we do have one minute left."

Nick managed a grin. "Use it wisely."

She slid her free hand into the hair at the back of his head and tugged him closer. When her soft, warm lips touched his, he gave himself fully to the feel and taste of her. If this was goodbye, he'd make it one neither of them would ever forget.

The slightly glazed look in her eyes when she ended the kiss suggested he might have been successful. That fact offered him scant comfort when her hand slid from his head and she gently extricated her fingers from his. "Goodbye, Nick."

Summoning every bit of strength left in him, he managed to open the door of the Sonata and hold it for her as she lowered herself onto the driver's seat. "Goodbye, Kathryn." He closed the door.

She started the engine then hit the button to lower the window. Nick gripped the frame as she gazed up at him, moonlight glimmering in her eyes. "The day Tory was born was the best day of my life."

"Of course it was."

She reached over and covered his hand with hers. "But today was a very, very close second."

Before he could answer, she let go of him and slid the

transmission into drive. Nick stepped back. He kept his eyes on the red and white glow of her taillights until she had driven the car out of the lot and turned onto the street. A small smile crossed his face as he started across the nearly-empty lot to help with the clean-up.

The second-best day of her life. It might not be exactly what he hoped to hear at the end of their day together, but it was something.

The door had definitely not been closed.

No, Kathryn had left that door cracked open slightly. While sometimes what slipped through those tiny openings was malevolent and led to heartache, or worse, occasionally those openings left room for Hope to wriggle through. Which, as I watched, she did.

I slipped through the small crack after her. As long as Hope was around, so was I.

Chapter Thirty-One

Wednesday

With the Lawson ranch miles behind us, Kathryn's mind turned to the man she was going to see. The memory of the *as if* day she'd spent with Nick at Halyna's wedding still lingering in the background, it was only natural that thoughts of another wedding would gradually take over. Thankfully, her pressure on the gas pedal had eased a little, and I uncurled my fingers from the handle, opening and closing my hand a few times to get the circulation going again.

Kathryn hadn't been there, of course, with David, but I was. Having taken up his company again after those agonizing days in the motel room, I was still with him, years later, when the journey toward his own wedding began. A journey that at times appeared it might be another possible ending for him and me.

Only time would tell.

March 2012

David sat across the table from Laura Hamilton, content to watch her as she spoke. Soft music played in the background of the café. Ceramic cups tinkled as patrons swirled spoons through lattes and cappuccinos. *I could gaze at you all night.* Soft blond hair brushed Laura's shoulder as she tilted her head to one side, something she did often when looking at him. Her blue eyes sparkled and danced as she spoke about her family and her life growing up.

"David, you're staring at me."

"Sorry, I can't help myself." He reached across the table, grabbed her hand, and brought it to his lips. A soft pink flush spread across her cheeks. David laughed and released her, then lifted his mug of café mocha and took a sip.

"Once again you've let me go on and on about my life, and

you haven't told me anything about yours."

David's smile dimmed. "There's not much to tell. I'm the only child of a preacher and his wife, and I pretty much grew up in church. Not very interesting. I'd rather hear about the big family you grew up in. That way I can live vicariously through you and pretend my life has been a lot more fun than it has."

"I find it hard to believe you've had no adventure in your life." Laura stirred her hot cocoa and licked the whip cream off the spoon before setting it on her napkin. "Be honest. Didn't you ever get tired of being the good little preacher's kid and rebel a bit?"

His smile froze. This conversation was heading into dangerous territory. He had to get her off this subject. Maybe if he told her part of the truth. "My dad and I did butt heads quite a few times during high school, but I got straightened around. Obviously, or I wouldn't be here." He grabbed her hand. "Hey, do you want to get out of this place? Go for a walk?"

"Sure, I'd love to."

David breathed a sigh of relief as Laura jumped to her feet. That had been too close. He held the door for her then followed her out into the cool spring evening. The two of them headed for their favorite spot—a boardwalk that wound its way around the shores of Lake Ontario.

It was a beautiful evening. A full moon shone down from a starlit sky, sending trails of sparkling light dancing along the surface of the lake. David glanced at the beautiful woman by his side as they strolled along, hand in hand. He couldn't believe she was interested in him, but it had been months, and she still seemed to want to be with him as much as he wanted to be with her.

Tell her.

No way. He shook his head. *It's too late. I love her and she says she loves me. Revealing my past to her now would only hurt her.*

Tell her.

David refused to be swayed. *There's no way I'm going to*

dredge up something that happened years ago—something that I have not only served my time for, but for which, may I remind you, you have forgiven me. The voice faded, but the disquiet remained. He stopped under a big maple tree near the shore and drew Laura into his arms.

She smiled at him, her face innocent and trusting. He wouldn't do anything to tear that trust from her eyes. What purpose would it serve? Uneasiness churned in his stomach. David lowered his head and brushed his lips against Laura's. The spark that rippled through his body took his mind off the conflict raging within him. He stroked her soft, blond hair, feeling a moment of complete happiness.

After a moment, he sighed. "I better take you home."

"I suppose." Laura reached for his hand. "Do you remember the first time we met?"

"Sure. I was at the library, cramming for an exam."

"And I was going over my defense for the thesis I was presenting the next day, trying not to panic."

"We ended up at the last free computer at the exact same second and, if I remember correctly, neither of us ended up doing any work that evening. Instead, we sat and talked and talked." He smiled at the memory.

"As I recall, I was the one doing the talking and you were listening, as usual. That was the first of many, many evenings where you turned out to be a major distraction for me. It's a wonder I managed to wrap up my thesis at all."

"*I've* been a distraction for *you*? I think you are equally to blame in that department, Laura Hamilton." When the corners of her eyes crinkled with laughter, the tightness in his chest finally eased.

Alone in his room, doubts assailed him. David fell to his knees, determined to convince God he knew what he was doing. "Maybe you're right. Maybe I should tell her, but the price of that confession could be a lot higher than I'm willing to pay. You've brought her to me, God. Why would you want me to drive her away? It doesn't make any sense."

His head dropped into his hands. Words from his last conversation with Tiny flashed through his mind. *If you're feeling compelled to do something, even if it doesn't make sense and even if it's difficult, that sounds like something God's putting on your heart to do.* David raked his fingers through his hair.

"No. It was one thing to write to Kathryn. That was difficult enough. You can't want me to do this, to put Laura's and my happiness on the line. We could do so much for you—serve together at the church you give us." David winced. Even as he said the words, he knew they were a desperate and futile attempt to bargain with God.

"I can't," he whispered, his voice thick with misery.

He felt it immediately. The peace that had covered him like a blanket was gone. God hadn't removed it—he'd kicked it off himself. He crawled into bed and huddled under the sheets. "I can have this. I can have Laura and I can have you too. You'll see."

David lay in the dark, eyes open and unfocused, until the promise of clear skies the night before was broken by a gray drizzle pounding against his window.

"I'll think about it." He turned on his side, drew what meager warmth he could from the half-hearted vow, and drifted into a restless sleep.

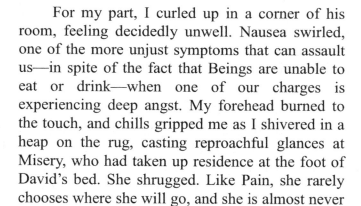

For my part, I curled up in a corner of his room, feeling decidedly unwell. Nausea swirled, one of the more unjust symptoms that can assault us—in spite of the fact that Beings are unable to eat or drink—when one of our charges is experiencing deep angst. My forehead burned to the touch, and chills gripped me as I shivered in a heap on the rug, casting reproachful glances at Misery, who had taken up residence at the foot of David's bed. She shrugged. Like Pain, she rarely chooses where she will go, and she is almost never

sent by the Creator. More often than not, she is sucked into the presence of a human as a result of his or her questionable decisions.

I eased into a new position, hoping it would help, and inclined my head slightly in her direction, acknowledging that truth. She sent me a sympathetic glance before flopping onto her other side, her back to me. Good. She wasn't terribly comfortable either. Hopefully that meant that she wasn't settling in, that before long David would reverse course and do the right thing.

If he did, Misery would be free to scuttle away, and I would be able to stop longing for the sweet release of death that would carry me from his presence forever.

Chapter Thirty-Two

April 2012

"So? What do you think?" Laura grinned as she reached over and brushed a crumb from the corner of his mouth. They sat on a blanket in the park, eating a picnic lunch she'd packed for them. "Do you want to come home with me for Easter? Will your parents mind?"

David almost laughed. "No, I'm sure they won't mind." *I can't put this off any longer.* He took a deep breath. "In fact, I've been wanting to talk to you about that and a few other things that happened in my past that I haven't been honest with you about."

Laura set her cookie on a paper plate, her forehead wrinkling.

His throat tightened. *You better help me. I can't do this alone.* "The thing is," he reached for her hand and clung to it, "one of the reasons I don't talk about my family very much is that I don't have a good relationship with them ... at all."

She nodded. "I figured you were holding back from me. That's why I've pressed you so often to tell me about your life."

"Remember when I told you that I did rebel a bit as a teenager?" She nodded again but didn't speak. David was glad, not sure he'd be able to get out what he had to say if she interrupted him. "It was more than a little rebellion. My father was a strong, conservative minister who ruled our home with an iron fist. My mother's a saint, but she was never able to stand up to him, no matter what he said or did, or how he treated me."

Laura squeezed his hand.

"Sometimes he made me so angry I had to do something to lash out at him. The best way I found was stealing things. Since the point was to humiliate my father, I didn't even make much of an attempt not to get caught. At sixteen, I was sent to a detention center for six months. When I came back, my dad—"

His voice broke. Her eyes filled with tears, but the thin

smile she managed encouraged him to keep going. "My dad stood in the doorway. He told me to leave and never come back, that this was no longer my home. The worst part was glancing at the upstairs window and seeing my mother watching what was going on and letting it happen, letting him send me away."

"Oh, David." Laura reached out and wiped a tear off his cheek. "What did you do? Where did you go?"

"I had a friend, Mark, whose parents agreed to let me stay with them. If they hadn't, I don't know where I would have ended up. On the street, I guess. With them, I was able to finish high school. I even did a couple of years of college before—" His stomach clenched. He'd said more than he'd intended.

"Before what?"

David's heart pounded.

"David?"

"I ..." The words caught in his throat.

Tell her.

He tried to swallow, but his throat had gone dry. "I couldn't forget about the stealing—the thrill of easy money and the power of a weapon in my hands." David raised his eyes to meet hers. "I returned to it for a few years, gas stations mostly, until I got caught and did some real time. That scared me. I never wanted to be in that place again."

Laura's fingers brushed across his face, tracing the line of the scar that ran beneath his right eye. "Is that where you got this? In prison?"

"Yes," he answered honestly. "Six guys jumped me when I was down in the basement doing laundry one day."

"That place ..." Laura's voice shook. "That's pretty far from where you are now. What happened to bring you back to God?"

The torment etched across her face sent pain darting through his chest. *I can't do it. I can't tell her everything. Look at her. How can you ask me to hurt her more than I already have?*

A cold chill ran down his spine. David shuddered. He'd settle for a half-truth. "The whole time I was doing that stuff, God was after me. He refused to let me go. I finally realized I

191

couldn't fight him anymore."

Laura stared at the blanket for a moment. When she raised her head, tears had left tracks on both her cheeks. "I appreciate you being honest with me. Only, I wasn't expecting ..." She drew in a deep, quivering breath. "I need to think about what you've said."

"I understand. I'll wait for you, Laura. I'll wait as long as you need me to."

She scrambled to her feet and gathered up the remnants of their picnic. David helped stuff everything into the backpack, his heart aching at the grief in her eyes. When she turned to go, he lifted a hand to touch her then let it drop to his side.

"I'll call you." Laura didn't meet his gaze.

He watched her go. When she was out of sight, he plodded along the shore of the lake. His inner voice was silent, and he felt completely and utterly alone. He'd done the best he could. He'd told Laura the truth, a big part of it anyway. It might take her a while to come to terms with what he had told her, but at least now there was a chance she'd return to him.

David stopped and picked up a rock from beside the path, flinging it with all his might into the water. If only he could find strength in defiance—stand tall with the conviction that he'd done the right thing no matter Who tried to convince him otherwise. He couldn't, though. Not when the only thing he wanted to do was crumple to the ground and admit he'd failed. Failed God. Failed Laura. Failed himself. Again.

He hurled another rock into the water. Even if that was true, he wasn't sure he could have done anything differently. His gaze traveled to the cloudless sky, shimmering above the surface of the lake. *Please try to understand. If I'd told her everything, told her about Kathryn, I would have lost her forever. That's a sacrifice I can't make.*

Absolute silence.

David did crumple then, dropping to his knees beside the water, ignoring the curious glances of passersby. His face dropped into his hands, and he groaned as the truth hit him. Until he was put to the test, he hadn't realized how much he *was* capable of sacrificing.

Don't leave me. Clenched fists dug into his forehead.

Never.

He nearly collapsed with relief when he felt it. The power of the universe in a single word. Peace draped around his shoulders. Still, it wasn't the same, and David knew it.

What he had willingly given up today was now gone, and he wasn't sure he would ever get it back.

Chapter Thirty-Three

Wednesday

Loud music pulsed through the car, jerking me into the present. Kathryn's new plan appeared to be to deafen us both, thereby drowning out the thoughts echoing through our minds. Her plan was working. She'd managed to stick a thumb, figuratively speaking, in the dam in her mind and close off any further thoughts of Halyna, Nick, or David.

It wasn't as simple as that for me. A threatening storm front that, of the two of us, only I could see swirled above the horizon. I peered through the front windshield. Definitely rolling closer. The thick, dark cumulonimbus clouds portended a severe thunderstorm at best, an F-5 category tornado that destroyed everything in its path at worst.

My imaginary grip on the door handle tightened, but this time my apprehension had nothing to do with the speed at which we were traveling.

October 2012

It wasn't often that I was caught completely off-guard, but because I hadn't been able to stomach Kevin Dylan any longer, I didn't see it coming when Olivia showed up at the door one day, thirteen years after Dylan had fled the country. It would cost me on my next evaluation, but I figured it was worth it. Apparently, we would all be receiving low scores on that report, as no one else warned me, either. Other than a few sordid types who only hung around the shadowy fringes of our world, all of the others must have abandoned Dylan as well.

And it turned out all right, as the news she brought was good, at least as far as those of us who were involved with Kathryn were concerned. Those Beings who had a charge in the Wyoming State Penitentiary in Rawlins, however, and there were a few, might not have been as pleased.

❦

"Hi, Kathryn."

A warm smile creased Kathryn's face as she pushed open the screen door. "Olivia. This is a nice surprise."

"Sorry to drop by without warning. I have news I didn't want to give you over the phone."

"Come on in. I'll get us a drink."

The officer sat at the kitchen table, setting her blue cap on the seat beside her. "Thanks." Olivia smiled as Kathryn handed her a glass of iced tea and sank onto the chair across from her.

Kathryn took a deep breath, trying to relax muscles that had tensed at the sight of her friend. "Is it good news or bad news?" *Please be good news.* She could really use some of that right about now.

"Both, actually." Olivia rested a hand on hers. "The good news first. We got him."

Shock froze her, and for a moment Kathryn couldn't speak. When she did, it was nearly in a whisper. "Kevin Dylan?"

"Yes. Last night. Apparently there's been a massive manhunt going on for him in the States the last few days because he's been linked to several other assaults."

She clasped her hands in her lap. "He's hurt other women?"

"Unfortunately, yes. But the last time he got sloppy, and a witness saw him leave the scene. He was able to give the police a good description, and they released a composite sketch two days ago. One of Dylan's neighbors recognized him and called 911. They arrested him at his apartment last night."

"Why did it take so long to track him down? Were none of these women able to give the police a description?"

"No." Her friend hesitated. "That's the bad news. None of them survived. You're the only woman that we know of who had an encounter with Kevin Dylan and lived to tell about it."

A cold weight settled in Kathryn's stomach.

Olivia squeezed her hand. "Are you all right?"

"I guess so. But I feel terrible for those poor women. I know what kind of terror Dylan must have put them through. And their families—" Her voice cracked. "They must be devastated." She straightened the salt and pepper shakers in the middle of the table, trying to push away thoughts of what those women had experienced. "I do feel better knowing he's behind bars tonight. As much as I've tried not to think about it, David Henley's warning in the courthouse that day brought back a lot of the fear I thought I had put behind me."

"Of course it did. I have to admit I was concerned as well. I did a lot of research on Kevin Dylan, and the thing that kept coming up was how thorough he was. It worried me that he would consider his failure to kill you an incomplete job and that he'd come back to finish it. In fact ..."

"What?" Kathryn wasn't sure she wanted to know.

"After a woman in Florida, where he must have gone right after he left you, the other attacks were in Tennessee, Kansas, Nebraska, and Wyoming. In that order."

She thought for a minute and then drew in a sharp breath. "He was coming back."

"Seems like it. He was taking his time, and he may have had another reason for heading this way, but—"

"He could have been coming for me."

"We'll never know that for sure. But it doesn't matter anymore. You don't have to worry about him again. And I'll sleep better at night now too."

Kathryn managed a smile. "I appreciate your concern, Olivia. I guess a lot of people will rest easier now."

"Yes, and for a long time. Kevin Dylan will get the death sentence for sure for everything he's done."

"Has he actually confessed to any of these crimes?"

"Well, it wasn't so much confessing as bragging, from what I hear. The man has shown absolutely no remorse for anything he's done. Seems almost proud."

A shudder of disgust rippled through her. "What could have happened to turn him into such a monster?"

"I've been investigating that as well. He had a horrific childhood. His father was severely abusive. When he was five, Dylan hid behind the couch in their living room and watched him beat his mother to death."

Another cold chill shook her, and Kathryn wrapped her arms around her waist. "It doesn't justify the kind of man he's become, but it does help to understand, a little, what drove him."

"I guess." Olivia sipped her iced tea. "I won't have to testify, will I?"

"No. Because of his confessions, there won't be a trial. You don't ever have to have anything to do with him."

"I hope not. I never want to hear that man's name, let alone see him."

Olivia picked up her cap, smoothed her short hair back, and set it on her head. "You won't. He'll never breathe fresh air again or hurt another woman." She drained the last of her iced tea. "I guess I should get to work."

Kathryn nodded as she rose. Her friend touched her arm. "You sure you're okay?"

"I think so. It's a lot to take in, but I really appreciate you coming out to tell me all this. As sad as what he did is, I'm glad to know he's finally been stopped."

"So am I. This case has been my number one priority for years. I'll be happy to move on. Not that any of them are easy to deal with."

"I'm sure they aren't. I can't imagine what you have to see every day."

"It's not usually pretty. But once in a while something good does come out of all the bad." She gave Kathryn a quick hug. "Like our friendship."

"You're right." Kathryn smiled. "Thanks again for coming. And I didn't even make you tromp through horse manure this time."

"I appreciate that. I had horseshoes and air fresheners on my desk for a month the last time."

Kathryn laughed and held the door open. She followed Olivia out and gripped the porch railing with both hands as her friend headed across the lawn toward her cruiser. She was still standing there a few minutes later when Aaron parked his truck at the end of the walkway. Kathryn didn't move as he strolled toward her.

"Hey, Kat." He stopped at the bottom of the stairs. "Everything okay?"

She released her tight grasp on the railing and shook out her hands. "I think so."

His eyes narrowed as he came up the steps. "Has something happened?"

"They caught Kevin Dylan."

Her brother's eyes widened. "Finally. That's great news." He studied her face. "Isn't it?"

"Of course it is. Olivia was here a few minutes ago telling me about it."

"You don't seem as happy as I would have thought."

Kathryn sighed, and Aaron rested his hands on her shoulders. "What is it?"

"There were other women. At least five of them. And he killed them all."

His face paled. "Kat. That's terrible."

"I know. I *am* happy that he's finally behind bars, but my heart is breaking for those women and all the people who loved them."

Aaron tugged her to him. "At least it's over now. He can't hurt anyone else, ever again."

Tears welled in her eyes. "I know." She pressed her cheek to the soft flannel of his shirt. "It's over."

And in her head, she almost did believe that, especially when her brother's arms were around her. Even so, a nagging fear made it difficult for her to breathe—the suspicion that, in spite of the fact that Kevin Dylan was behind bars and out of her life forever, somehow it wasn't over after all.

I couldn't shake the feeling either. I had felt the cold, rank breath of Fear whispering across my neck that day even before I saw him creeping across the porch. I tried swatting him away when he got too close. As with most bullies, it sometimes worked to stand up to him. Not this time. He bared his teeth and snapped at me, almost catching my fingers in his sharp incisors before I yanked my hand out of his reach. His growl was low and warning, and I took an involuntary step backwards as he turned toward Kathryn.

When he exhaled, sour air swirled around her and Aaron and she shivered. Her brother tightened his arms around her as if he felt the invisible presence and was trying to protect her from it.

Fear, I was inordinately happy to see, took a step back himself. I didn't allow myself a smile, knowing if he spun around and caught me watching him it would be wise not to have a smug look on my face.

When he did turn around, it was to throw me a glance that suggested he could—and given the slightest provocation would—truss me and have me for breakfast. Then he slunk off to a dark corner of the porch and settled himself there to wait.

And while he sometimes crept as far away as the edges of the ranch, out of sight and almost out of scent, never in all the years since the night in the cabin had he left Kathryn's presence completely.

And given those storm clouds on the horizon, I'd wager that it would be a while before he did.

Chapter Thirty-Four

Wednesday

"I'm done." Kevin Dylan threw his cards onto the table.

"Me, too." Matt McGregor tossed in his hand and stood to go. As he and Dylan walked down the hall, McGregor brushed against his shoulder. "It's on. Tomorrow morning. 4 am."

His heart rate accelerated, but Dylan's face remained impassive. His chin dipped slightly toward his chest.

"You got the money?" McGregor asked.

Another nod.

"Good."

In his cell, Dylan dropped onto his bunk. One more night and then, if all went well, he'd be a free man. He rolled over and grabbed the paper from under his mattress.

"Won't be long now, sweetheart." He glanced at the newspaper clipping before shoving it into his pocket and settling onto his back again. "I have a big surprise planned for you."

Darkness fell over his cell as the lights were turned off. A smile twisted across Dylan's face. He folded his arms behind his head. Everything was coming together now.

A few more days and then the light would finally go out for good.

Chapter Thirty-Five

Wednesday

I shoved the growing threat to the back of my mind, determined to enjoy this road trip with Kathryn. More than she was, at least, which wouldn't be difficult. This was no pleasure trip for her. She stabbed at the button for the radio with her thumb, plunging the vehicle into silence. The fingers that continued to grip the steering wheel were white with tension. Still, I turned my face toward the cracked-open window, loving the feel of wind rushing over me. I couldn't do anything to make this easier for her, so I might as well make the best of the situation.

She hadn't seen David Henley in person in seventeen years, although they'd written back and forth for fourteen of them. Her fingers tapped the wheel, and I tore my concentration away from the scenery rushing past the window in a blur to listen in on the thoughts trickling through her mind. The letters. She'd opened another one after finally pouring herself a second cup of coffee that morning.

May 2013

Kathryn,

Work at the church here in Toronto is going well. The minister is a great man who really cares about the people. Unlike my father, he's not watching for what they're doing wrong all the time so he can correct them.

Laura and I are going to be married next June. I wrote my mother to tell her, even though I know they won't come. I still had to let them know. My mother loves me and maybe my father does too, although he has no idea how to show it. If I ever have a child of my own, I pray I won't make the same mistakes.

It's strange to think about that happening. I've experienced more than my share of miracles in life, but to have a child has to

*be one of the greatest miracles of all. It would prove once again
what a God of grace we have.*
   I hope you're doing well.
   David

Kathryn stared out her window at the big maple tree in the
front yard, the letter lying in front of her on the desk. David had
spoken of Laura before, and Kathryn wasn't surprised to hear
they were getting married. The news stirred up conflicting
emotions—resentment, mostly. She wasn't sure if that was
toward David or God. Both, maybe. How was it fair that she was
alone when he had found someone who could accept him for who
he was, in spite of his past? She narrowed her eyes. Did Laura
even know about her? Could any woman get past that and be
willing to marry a man who'd been capable of doing what he had
done?

Self-pity began to compete with the resentment for
prominence in her mind. Kathryn shook her head to clear it of
both. Deep down she supposed she was happy for him, that he'd
found someone to share his life with. That in itself was a miracle,
for anyone.

The sight of Tory with Rachel and Josh, Aaron and Meg's
kids, wandering out of the barn after finishing their chores,
interrupted her troubled thoughts. Four black and white kittens
nipped at their heels. In spite of her emotional turmoil, she had to
smile. The three of them were growing up so fast. In a few short
years, they'd be heading out into the world. For now, their lives
were fun and uncomplicated. Hers had been too, at their age.
Unfortunately, she hadn't appreciated that until she grew up and
life unexpectedly became very complicated.

Her smile faded. *Father, protect them from going through
anything like I did, please.* The thought sickened her and she
shoved it away.

Kathryn reached for the letter and sighed. David. She
couldn't even remember when they'd started to call each other by

their first names. It still frightened her a little, as if one of the walls that protected her fragile heart had been torn down.

As for finding someone to spend her life with, she still believed that she'd been right to tell Nick she wasn't ready for a relationship. Since he hadn't contacted her since Halyna's wedding, God must be telling him the same thing. Days like today, reading David's letter, it could be a struggle to rest in that knowledge.

Kathryn propped her chin on her hand. This was why Aaron and her parents would have told her to end her connection with David a long time ago. They would never understand how she could maintain contact with the man who had wreaked such havoc in her life.

She couldn't understand either why she was so drawn to stay in touch with him, to know what he was thinking and feeling and going through in his life. David would, no doubt, be equally at a loss to explain why he continued to write to her and to read her letters. The memories they invoked must be as painful for him as for her, given how hard they'd worked to put the past behind them.

Somehow, as implausible as it sounded, the letters were a part of that process. Kathryn wasn't sure that Meg or any other counselor would agree, but reading the words, confronting the feelings and the memories they stirred up, contributed to the ongoing healing in her life and in her heart. She and David were like the ragged edges of a torn garment. Every word that they exchanged was like a needle pushing through torn cloth, painful yet drawing them closer together and restoring them both to wholeness.

Kathryn read the part where he contemplated having children. Her chest constricted. She'd never told him about Tory. That was the one part of her life that she protected from him and refused to share.

"Kath?"

Meg stood in the doorway of her room. Kathryn shoved the

letter under a notebook and shifted to face her. Although Aaron's family joined them for dinner two or three times a week, Kathryn hadn't realized they were coming tonight, or she wouldn't have taken the letter out of her drawer.

"Sorry to startle you. I wanted to let you know that supper will be ready soon." Her sister-in-law paused for a moment. "Is everything all right?"

Kathryn's throat tightened at the confusion on Meg's face. She needed to share this with her. She'd kept this secret to herself for years, and she couldn't do it anymore. She stood and crossed the room, taking Meg's hand to draw her inside before shutting the door.

"I want to show you something, but you can't let anyone else know about it, even Aaron. Especially Aaron. Can you do that?"

"I don't know if I can promise that, Kath. Why don't you tell me about whatever it is you're hiding, and we can discuss what to do after that, okay?"

She nodded. *I have to do this. I trust her. She won't do anything to hurt Aaron or me.*

Meg perched on the edge of the bed and waited.

Kathryn removed the piece of paper from beneath the notebook and handed it to her sister-in-law. She watched Meg's face, trying to gauge her feelings. Suddenly she had trouble drawing a breath. This was a mistake. She had no idea how Meg would react to the letter. She should have thought it through first. Kathryn clenched sweaty fists in her lap.

Meg's eyes widened as she read, but no other emotion crossed her face until she finished and looked up. "Oh, Kath. Why? I don't understand. How long has he been writing you?"

"After that first letter, I didn't hear from him for over three years, until he was released. Then he wrote to tell me he was going to Toronto so I wouldn't worry about running into him."

"That makes sense, I guess. But then you wrote him?"

Kathryn exhaled. "I know it wasn't the best idea. For some reason I felt compelled. What we went through together in that cabin, and in the courthouse ..." As usual, she was at a loss for words to explain the relationship.

Meg set the letter on the desk. "Do you want to hear what I think as a friend or as a counselor?"

"Both, I guess, although I'd rather not hear that I'm losing my mind."

"You're not losing your mind. Actually, as a counselor, it makes sense. You went through several intense experiences together. He was there when you thought you were going to die, and you both felt the presence of God in that cabin. I can't imagine the exchange in the courthouse that day, but it's understandable that there's a bond between you that you can't explain."

Kathryn opened her mouth to respond, but Meg stopped her with a hand in the air. "Having said that, as your friend, it worries me that not only are you keeping in touch with this man, but you're hiding it from your family. Aaron would be devastated if he found out."

Tears pricked Kathryn's eyes. "I know. He deserves better than that. But I can't tell him, Meg. Not yet." She bit her lip to keep it from trembling. "Are you going to?"

Meg sighed. "Secrets have a way of coming out, Kath. And when they do, there's almost always more pain than there would have been if you'd been honest in the first place."

Kathryn held her breath.

"I don't like it," Meg said, "and I encourage you to end this relationship. But no, I'm not going to tell Aaron. This is your secret. You'll tell your brother when you're ready."

Relief surged through her. "Thank you. I need to think about what I'm going to do. I appreciate you giving me time to do that."

Meg smiled and squeezed her hand. "Anyway," she said in mock exaggeration, "as I was saying, supper is almost ready. Are you coming?"

"I'll be right down." The tantalizing aroma of roasting chicken floated up from the kitchen and she was suddenly ravenous.

You see? I know my charge. She eats when she's relieved or happy, and not when fear and worry weigh on her like a load tied across the back of a pack mule. In the last twenty years, she has skipped a lot of meals, which has been very hard on me, quite frankly. I can only consume food and beverages vicariously through humans. I breathe in the tantalizing aromas and then tap into the sensations of enjoyment and satiation my charge experiences. An empty plate or, worse, food that is allowed to grow cold and then thrown into the garbage, does absolutely nothing for me. If I actually needed the food to subsist on, I would have dwindled to nothing by now.

Sigh. Life as a metaphysical being can be such a challenge. So much responsibility for what happens rests on our shoulders, and yet we have so little control over how events will transpire. That control has been given to the most fallible creatures in the universe, a decision that initially raised a lot of eyebrows. Even after it all went horribly wrong, we did understand it, to a degree, knowing as we did the character of the One who made the decision. And since then we'd all experienced the joy and victory that came when one of you managed to choose the right path, which also helped to clear up a little of the mystery.

Still, even though we know there is always enough light to show you the way if you ask for it, it doesn't make watching you stumble along in the near-dark, tripping over the stones in your path as you try to make your way along, any easier to watch.

Chapter Thirty-Six

Wednesday

Remembering Kathryn's anxiety over sharing her secret with Meg tempered the rush of warmth I felt as I recalled the letter in which David had told her he was getting married. Still, I smiled to myself, seeing vividly in my mind the event that he had written her about and recalling how close he and I were that day.

June 2013

David lifted up the veil and smiled at Laura. Blue eyes sparkled at him as he leaned in and kissed her soft red lips. He couldn't believe she was his wife. What he really couldn't believe was that, after everything he'd done, God would allow him so much happiness.

They walked down the aisle hand in hand. Good thing they hadn't gone with the traditional bride's family and friends on one side and groom's on the other. His side of the church would have been pretty empty. If only he could have had Tiny and the guys here. Now *that* would have been a celebration.

David stiffened at the sight of two familiar faces in the crowd.

Laura's grip on his hand tightened. "What is it?"

"My parents. I can't believe they came."

She craned her neck. "Where? Which ones are they?"

"I'll introduce you when they come out." David's mind raced at the thought of seeing his father again. His mother had come to visit him several times while he was at Kent, but he hadn't seen his father since the morning he returned home to tell her about what had happened to him in that seedy motel.

His heart pounded. What if his father said something to Laura, told her about his past? His marriage could be over before it began. He wouldn't be able to leave Laura's side all day.

The thumping in his chest subsided. That wouldn't be a hardship. He'd be happy to never leave her side again, in fact.

David and Laura greeted the guests as they came out of the church, which seemed to him to take an interminable length of time. As his new wife introduced one family member after another, he struggled to stay focused.

"David." She laughed and elbowed him in the side more than once in an attempt to keep his attention.

His parents finally came through the door. When they reached him, he took both his mother's hands in his and kissed her on the cheek. "Mom. I didn't think you'd come. I mean, it's so far. I never expected ..."

"David." His mother squeezed his hands. "Of course we came. You're our only son. We couldn't miss seeing you marry this beautiful girl."

He let go of her and slid his arm around Laura's shoulders. "This is Laura." And this was so surreal. He had never thought he would introduce his wife to his parents.

His mother placed both hands on Laura's cheeks. "Hello, Laura. It's a pleasure to meet you. Welcome to our family."

His chest tightened. David turned to his father and stopped short. His father's eyes were full of tears. Never in his entire life had he seen his father cry.

What was going on here?

Something else gleamed in his father's eyes, besides the tears, that he couldn't remember ever seeing.

"Hello, son." His father thrust a hand toward him.

It was pride. His father was proud of him. David hesitated then grasped his father's hand. "Hi, Dad."

Remembering his wife, David drew her closer. "Dad, this is Laura, my wife."

Smiling, Laura held out a hand. "It's good to meet you, Mr. Henley."

David's father took her hand. "Please, call me Jack. We're family now."

When they had moved on, Laura rested a hand on David's back. "He seems great. I take it he's changed since the last time you saw him?"

"More than you'll ever know." David shook his head. "Of course, he wasn't the only one who needed to change. It seems God's been working overtime with the Henley family."

She wiped a tear off his cheek with her finger. "Grace," she murmured as the next people in line moved toward them.

"Absolutely."

At the reception, he continued to be drawn to the table where his parents were eating. Every few minutes, one or two of Laura's family members would go over and introduce themselves to his mother and father. David's father stood to greet each one as they stopped by. His parents' laughter floated toward him several times during the evening.

When he wasn't watching them, David's eyes strayed to Laura as they sat and listened to the speeches and the toasts. She glanced at him often as well, and once she winked. *Oh lady, you better watch that, or I'll be grabbing your hand and taking you some place considerably less crowded.*

When the guests began to filter out of the room, his parents came over to talk to them. Reaching for his mother's hand, David held it between both of his. "How long are you staying?"

"We fly out tomorrow afternoon at four."

Laura rested a hand on his mother's arm. "Why don't we take you to the airport?"

David swiveled to stare at his wife. He'd wanted to make the same offer but didn't think he should when they were supposed to be on their honeymoon.

His mother pressed a hand to her chest. "Oh no, we couldn't let you do that."

"Please," Laura insisted. "I've just met you and now you're leaving. I'd love more time to get to know the people who raised my wonderful husband."

His father nodded. "We'd like that."

"Great." Laura smiled. "Why don't we come by your hotel

around one?"

"That sounds wonderful. We'll look forward to spending a couple more hours with you."

David stared at the door that closed behind his parents.

"Happy?" Laura's warm hand slipped into his.

He contemplated her. "Let's see. The woman I love vowed to spend the rest of her life with me. The father I haven't spoken to in years gazed at me, with tears in his eyes mind you, as if he was proud of me for the first time ever. Yeah, I'd say it's been a pretty great day."

Laura laughed, the sound like music in his ears. "Why don't we get out of here?"

At the end of a long, incredible day, the most incredible words of all.

⌖

It was a wonderful and difficult night. Being with Laura, holding her in his arms, was like coming home after a long, arduous journey. Even so, dark memories assaulted him, of another night, another bed, another woman—

David shuddered and pulled his wife close, burying his face in her soft white shoulder, able, for a few hours at least, to let go of the past.

Chapter Thirty-Seven

"Come and sit with me." David's mother slid her arm through Laura's and led her to a bank of seats in the waiting area at the airport.

Sensing his dad had something he wanted to say, David walked through the busy terminal with him. Neither spoke until his dad grabbed his shoulder and turned David to face him.

"I wanted to let you know that I've resigned as pastor of our church."

David blinked. He never thought his father would give up his pulpit.

His dad took a deep breath. "I've come to realize that the way I led my church and my family may not have been the way God intended when he called me to the ministry."

David couldn't believe what he was hearing. He was having an increasingly difficult time reconciling this man with the overbearing, demanding father he'd resented his whole life.

"I need to tell you how sorry I am."

The weight of the anger and bitterness he'd carried for so long pressed in on David. *It's time to let it go.* He knew what it was like to need forgiveness. He could not withhold from his father what God—and the woman whose life he'd almost destroyed—had given to him.

"I'm sorry too, Dad." When their eyes met, a crack appeared in the wall they'd spent years constructing between them.

The two of them strolled to the waiting area side by side. Laura and his mother were talking as though they'd known each other for years. The two women who meant the most to him, together. David swallowed the lump in his throat and glanced up. *You did this, didn't you? In spite of everything, you've never broken your promise not to leave me.*

The announcement that their flight was boarding crackled

over the public address system. His father wrapped arms around him, holding him for a moment before slapping him on the back. "Goodbye, son. You and Laura are always welcome at home." David nodded, not trusting himself to speak.

His dad kissed Laura on the cheek and picked up their carry-on luggage.

David grasped his mother's arms lightly. "Mom. Thanks for coming. It's meant more to me than I can say."

"Goodbye, son. Please come and see us soon." She hugged him, then turned to Laura and pulled her daughter-in-law to her. "Take care of him."

"I will."

"We'll take care of each other." David draped his arm around Laura's shoulders. When his parents had disappeared down the ramp, he tugged his wife closer. "Well, Mrs. Henley, you heard my mom. I believe you were told to take care of me?" He leaned in to whisper in her ear.

A pink flush spread across her cheeks. "Somehow, I don't think that's what your *mother* had in mind. And besides, you said we'd take care of each other. It works both ways, you know."

Laughing, David guided her toward the parking lot and their hotel. "Oh, don't worry. I know what I said. Believe me, that is one promise I fully intend to keep."

Wednesday

Both of the letters she had opened that morning went into the woodstove after Kathryn's pitiful attempt at breakfast. The fire had dwindled to ashes by then, so she had lit the corners with a match and held the envelopes between two fingers until they were mostly consumed by flames before tossing them inside and shutting the door. The clang of metal on metal had become comforting and familiar—the sound of headway being made, if slowly and painfully. I reminded myself not to get too comfortable. There were still memories to be exhumed from the little shoebox she had tucked under the coffee table before leaving the house.

As we pulled into the church parking lot in Maple Ridge, it occurred to me that, as many miles as we had come together, the hardest part of the journey still lay ahead.

Chapter Thirty-Eight

Wednesday

The smile on David's face as he studied the young couple across the desk from him helped to relax me a little. Pre-marital counseling was one of his favorite aspects of the job, and since he'd spent the morning doing it, he was in a really good mood. The best—or worst—time to send someone's life crashing around him, depending on how you measured that sort of thing.

Seeing two people so in love, so full of hope for the future, always brought David joy. Every time it reminded him what a gift it was to find the person God intended for you to spend the rest of your life with. After six years of marriage, when he looked at Laura, he still felt the same thrill that he had the day of their wedding.

While he listened to the prospective bride and groom in front of him, his thoughts drifted occasionally to that day. And to the two days their sons had been born. As he had told Kathryn he would be if such an event occurred, David was overwhelmed every time he thought about those particular miracles. His throat tightened now at the memory of his oldest son Cody's birth five years earlier. He could still feel the soft skin of his newborn son as he held him in his hands for the first time. Wonder had driven all words from him—something she is particularly fond of doing—and he could only gaze at Cody, at the tiny fingers and toes and the little mouth and nose.

I studied the couple in front of him as he swung his attention to their discussion. So full of hope. In fact, Hope was the one responsible for the continuing popularity of the institution of marriage, in spite of the high failure rate. It was only when she was lost, or forced to go, that everything fell apart completely.

"What do you think is the most important characteristic of a strong, healthy marriage?" David asked.

The groom didn't hesitate. "Honesty."

A pang shot through David as he nodded. As happy as he

was with Laura, he had struggled for years with the fact that he kept his past hidden from her. It was a heavy burden to bear. For better or worse, I had a feeling the load was about to be lifted from his shoulders, whether he wanted it to be or not.

The door shut behind the couple and I braced myself, knowing that the next time it opened David's life would change forever. With no idea of the weight of these last few seconds of relative peace in his life, he picked up the picture of his sons from the desk and studied it intently.

What would they say if they knew? Would they ever be able to forgive him? Would Laura? With a heavy sigh, he reached out to set the picture in its usual spot.

As he did, the intercom on his phone buzzed.

Time for David to head to that shelter I referred to earlier. I didn't have to see the future to know that the ground was about to give way beneath his feet. I felt for him, I really did. I know he brought all of this on himself, but still, if I couldn't find compassion for a person suffering through the consequences of his own actions, I wouldn't find myself in the presence of Compassion at all, as every one of you finds yourself in that state on a fairly regular basis.

And that would be too bad as, quite frankly, I enjoy Compassion's company almost more than any other's. Although we don't suffer through, er, *experience* the same base emotions as humans do— attraction, desire, romantic love—if we did … well, let's say that I admire his heart and kind nature considerably.

So I welcome him when he comes into a room and lucky for you I do. When one of you has fallen— yet again—if Compassion didn't come along in some form or another, it would be that much easier for me to be driven away and irretrievably lost.

"Yes, Janet?"

"Reverend Henley, there's a Kathryn Ellison here to see you."

His heart began to beat erratically. If I wasn't worried about his health and well-being, I might have smiled at the way his receptionist spoke the words, so calmly, as if they weren't causing the room to spin around him. He couldn't breathe or speak or think what to do. Several seconds passed before Janet spoke again, more hesitant this time. "Reverend?"

"Send her in."

David forced himself to stand on trembling legs and stumble around the desk as the door opened. A wave of shock passed through his entire body. She'd hardly changed at all. Even after all these years. Her hair was still long and dark, and her eyes, when they met his, still seemed to probe into the secret, hidden places deep inside of him. The memory of that night in the cabin crashed through David's mind, as clearly as if it had happened yesterday, and he swallowed hard.

I tensed, ready to … well, I didn't know what I would do, exactly, if he went down, but it seemed prudent to be ready, regardless.

Kathryn stepped into the room, shut the door, and leaned against it. He didn't blame her. His own legs threatened to give out under him any moment.

"Reverend."

"No, Kathryn." He shook his head at the title.

She nodded. David waited, fists clenched, as her eyes scanned the walls of books. Her gaze lingered at the south-facing window where soft sunlight filtered in, giving the room a warm, comforting feeling he'd always loved. It was a beautiful space. I'd spent a fair amount of time here in the last few years, and I felt right at home. I sought out my favorite spot to relax, a leather armchair in front of the window. Sunlight fell across it all afternoon, making it ideal for napping—not that I'd be doing any of that today. I hopped up into the chair and settled in to see what would happen.

Kathryn's eyes focused on the wooden cross hanging on the

wall behind him. The sight of it seemed to give her strength as she shifted her gaze to him.

David held his hand out toward one of the leather chairs in front of his desk. When she sank onto it, he took the other one, clasping his hands in front of him.

I struggled to keep up with the questions racing through his mind. *Why is she here? What could have brought her to see me now, after so much time?* I cupped a hand behind my ear. A loud, thundering noise nearly blocked out the sound of his thoughts. If she did get up the nerve to speak, his heart pounded so violently in his ears that I wasn't sure he'd even hear her.

"I'm sorry to come without an appointment."

Waving his hand through the air, David dismissed her apology. "I meant it when I told you my door would always be open to you."

Kathryn lifted her chin in a gesture he remembered well. It was a summons to courage she needed to make before she could face him. He often imagined her doing it before opening his latest letter or picking up a pen to write him back.

"How have you been, David?"

"Good. Laura and I are very happy. We have two boys now."

She contemplated the picture he turned toward her, smiling faintly. "Does Laura ..." she paused, as though uncertain how to continue. "Does she know?"

"About you? No." David took a deep breath, trying to calm the beating in his chest. "I've wrestled for years with keeping my past a secret, but I've never been able to bring myself to tell her everything."

Kathryn crossed her legs and clasped her hands on her knee. "Sometimes telling the truth seems like it will do nothing but cause pain to the ones we love."

Another long pause. David studied her. What was she working so hard to say?

"There's something I've never told you." Her eyes darted around the room and settled on the door. It occurred to him that she might bolt from the room without finishing. He wasn't sure he'd try to stop her.

Instead, she faced him. "I have a daughter."

His brow wrinkled in confusion. "But I thought you never married."

"I didn't." The eyes searching his said a lot more than her words.

The truth swept over him. Speaking, even forcing himself to keep breathing, took a monumental effort.

"Is she ... mine?"

"I don't know." She stared at her clasped hands, giving him a minute to digest the news before lifting her head. "She's wonderful, David." Kathryn's eyes glowed as she spoke of her only child. "Beautiful. Smart. Funny. She's been a joy to me her whole life."

"Does she know?"

"No. I've never been able to bring myself to tell her the truth either. She was raised to believe that God was the only father she needed. When she was little that was enough for her, but that has changed."

David gripped the arms of his chair, giving her time to find words to express the inexpressible. Years of sorrow—more even than he had known she'd had to bear—heavily weighted her words.

"She's angry. Angry with me. Angry with the father she's never known. Angry at God. Even so, I wouldn't have come to you, thrown your life into upheaval, except that ..."

His stomach clenched as she struggled to finish. "She's become driven to find out who her father is. I've tried to persuade her that some truths are better left uncovered, but she is determined to seek them out."

David's heart sank. His closely guarded secret may not be a secret much longer. Truth really did have a way of coming out, usually in the most explosive way.

Which was true. Although it's almost always better when Truth shows up, he is a bit of a showman. I often wonder if it's as necessary as he seems to think to burst onto the scene like Liza Minnelli sweeping onto the stage, arms spread and singing at the top of her lungs.

"When she confronted me, I knew it was time to find out the truth, to help her discover answers to a past that has always been filled with questions for her. I wanted to be the one to come to you, to ask you ..." Again she stopped, as though uncertain how to frame the request.

"What can I do, Kathryn? I'll do whatever you need."

"There's a doctor at Ridge Meadows Hospital who does the test that will tell us what we need to know. Here's his number." She unclasped her hands and fumbled in her purse before tugging out a crumpled piece of paper. A weak smile quirked the corners of her mouth. "I'm sorry. I wasn't sure I would actually come here. This piece of paper has been in my garbage can more than once. But I decided I had to see you before she found out the truth on her own."

David grasped the paper in trembling fingers. "It's okay. I'm glad you came. I'll go right away." The paper crinkled as he clutched it tighter. "Do you ever question God? Ask Him why He allowed a case of mistaken identity to cause so much pain in your life?"

I cocked my head, interested to hear her response to the question she had wept and screamed into her pillow for years. Kathryn lifted a hand, palm up. "I question God all the time. I've yelled at Him, and tried to turn away from Him, more times than I can say."

"Why haven't you?" A spark of anger flared in his chest. "I think I might have if—"

She shook her head. "No, you wouldn't have. Once you're His you know that, no matter what happens, you can't leave Him. And somehow, He used what happened for good. It brought you to Him and my daughter to me. And she's made everything I've gone through worth it." She rose and slid the strap of her purse

219

over her shoulder.

I smiled in satisfaction. Kathryn sounded pretty sure of herself, but I knew from personal experience that hadn't always been the case. On more than one occasion she had grabbed some breakable object without warning and hurled it across the room, and I'd instinctively ducked, forgetting that it couldn't hurt me. No, it had taken a long time—and many, many hours on her knees—to arrive at the conclusion that good had come out of everything that she had gone through.

"Kathryn."

One hand on the doorknob, she peered over her shoulder at him.

David hesitated. He had no right to ask, but he was desperate to know. "Would you tell me her name?"

The silence stretched between them. He was asking for something he didn't deserve, and clearly she was struggling with that. Then her face softened. "Her name is Victoria. We call her Tory."

David nodded, grateful for the gift.

Kathryn left then, pulling the door shut behind her.

I'd have to run to catch up, but I couldn't resist watching him through the glass window in the door for a few seconds, waiting to see what he would do. So far the ground hadn't opened up, but the news was fresh, so there was time yet for that. And, for that matter, for all kinds of fallout to occur.

David picked up the phone, dialed the number Kathryn had given him, and made an appointment for that afternoon. His hands shook so badly that he had to fumble to find the cradle. Then he sat, staring at the doorway where only moments before she had stood. So many seconds ticked by that I finally gave up and took a step away from the door.

When I heard the sound, I glanced back. His face had dropped into his hands and he was weeping. Not, I knew, for what was to come as much as for all that his past had taken from them both.

Chapter Thirty-Nine

Thursday

The creaking of the porch swing nearly lulled me to sleep in my old rocking chair tucked in the shadows of the porch. After our emotionally draining adventure in Maple Ridge the day before, and a considerably slower—thankfully—drive home, Kathryn and I were dragging our feet by the time we reached the farm.

His duties dispensed for the day, Determination had given me a wave and set off on foot in the opposite direction as I climbed out of Kathryn's car. That left me to face Fear on my own. I braced myself as I jumped out of the vehicle after her. As expected, my old nemesis waited on the porch, his eyes glowing yellow in the dim moonlight as I followed Kathryn up the stairs, sticking as close to her as I possibly could as we entered the house.

Fear shoved past us both, snapping and growling in my face. With so much still undecided, he didn't have the power to rip me apart, as much as the drool flicking from his lips suggested he would like to. Not yet, anyway. Even so, his hot breath and menacing fangs turned my knees to water as I staggered over to the couch.

Somehow he managed to turn in circles without taking those beady eyes off me. Kathryn dropped onto the couch, close enough that I had to shuffle sideways to avoid being sat upon. She bent forward and rummaged through the box for a moment before wrestling out yet another letter. The wave of sadness that washed over her and splashed onto me told me which one it was without me having to commit any ethical violations by reading the words myself.

Fear, having found a comfortable spot in which to lie, stopped circling and dropped in a heap in front of the fire.

Waiting, like me, to see which of us would survive.

August 2015

Kathryn tugged on the metal tab at the top of the mailbox door. Reaching inside, she withdrew the pile of mail and snapped the door shut. With Tory working at an ice cream parlor for the summer before her sophomore year of high school, and their parents retired and living in a condo in Surrey, the house was quiet. A little too quiet.

The woods at the edge of the lawn caught her eye. Kathryn stepped off the driveway and meandered along the path, thick with needles that cushioned her footsteps. The day was warm, and although shafts of light worked their way through the branches to fall to the ground around her, beneath the spreading branches of the trees it was cool and still. Only the tapping of a woodpecker somewhere overhead broke the near silence.

Kathryn took a deep breath infused with the heavy scent of pine. Peace flowed in with the air, and she smiled as a chipmunk scurried across the path in front of her. A patch of white trilliums growing beneath a tree that had fallen a few feet away captured her attention, and Kathryn wandered over and sat on the log, in no hurry to return to her office in the farmhouse to work on the books for the ranch.

She flipped idly through the stack of mail. Bills, mostly, and flyers. One envelope, her name and address scrawled across the front in large, looping handwriting, caught her eye. Glancing at the return address in the top left corner, she drew in a quick breath. N. Lawson. Nick had written her a letter? Why would he? It had been four years since Halyna and James's wedding, and she hadn't heard anything from him. Most days she was grateful for that. She'd made it clear she wasn't ready, and he had promised to wait until he felt strongly that the timing was right. When he didn't contact her, she'd mostly been content to trust that he hadn't felt that yet. Other days she missed him so terribly that her chest ached with it. He lived less than an hour away, but he might as well inhabit another world for all she saw him.

Although she tried not to, she did keep her eyes open

whenever she was in town. Several times tiny electrical shocks had tingled through her when she'd seen someone she thought might be him, but it always turned out to be someone else. The disappointment she felt keenly every time told her a lot, but still she made no attempt to reach out to him.

And now he had written to her. What could he possibly have to say? She set the rest of the mail on the log and flipped the envelope over. After sliding her fingertip beneath the flap and ripping it open, she tugged the piece of folded paper out. It rattled a little in her fingers as she unfolded it and read the few, handwritten lines.

Dear Kathryn,

This is such a hard letter to write. I considered coming to see you, to tell you in person, but I told you I wouldn't before God made it clear the time was right. Regardless of the circumstances, I want to honor that.

I know you don't know Halyna well, but somehow the past has connected the two of you in ways none of us can truly understand. Because of that, I was sure you would want to know that her cancer has returned. The prognosis is not good this time. While we hope and pray, we are also preparing ourselves for a difficult road ahead.

As always, James is her rock. His faith is strong, like hers is, and they are doing a better job than I am at leaving all of their fears in God's hands and believing that God knows what is best for them.

Please pray for Hally and James and for my parents and me. I'm not sure what the future holds but, short of a miracle, it is not going to be easy.

I hope you are well. You remain in my heart and are so often in my thoughts. Although watching you drive away after Hally and James's wedding was one of the hardest things I have ever done, looking back I believe it was for the best. The timing was not right for us. I don't know if or when it will be, but I'm trying to trust God with that as well.

Yours always,
Nick

A tear slid down Kathryn's cheek as she read the words again then tucked the letter into the envelope and set it on the pile of mail on the log. She'd known such a thing was a possibility, but Halyna and James were so deeply in love, on some level she'd thought that that would be enough to defeat this insidious threat to Halyna's life.

Propping her elbows on her knees, she rested her forehead on the palms of her hands. Poor Halyna and James. Her heart broke for them. And for Nick. Pain stabbed through her as tears dropped onto her denim shorts. He'd sounded so sad in his letter. And more than that, he had seemed discouraged. Not only because of the battle his sister faced, but because he was struggling to see God at work in their lives.

They'd never discussed their faith, but Kathryn knew from the way he spoke that he was a believer, although she had no idea how or when that had happened. What was clear was that his faith was being severely tested by Halyna's illness, which she could understand better than most people. After That Night in the cabin, she'd railed at God. She'd been so angry with Him, so incapable of understanding why He hadn't protected her. Wasn't He supposed to be her refuge and fortress? The place she could run to for shelter from her enemies?

If rapists and deadly diseases didn't count as enemies, Kathryn wasn't sure what did. The cabin flashed through her mind. Kevin Dylan, slowly advancing toward her, knife gripped in his hand like he did over and over in her dreams. Those eyes that she had never been able to erase from her memories—that dead, cold stare of a remorseless killer. She knew, when she saw it, that she was going to die. That nothing could stop it.

But then … Kathryn lifted her head. Something had. What had Dylan seen when he glanced up and terror had crossed his face? An angel? Kathryn hadn't seen anything, but whatever was there had saved her. Whatever God had sent there. God *had* been

her protector and shelter that day. Shock rippled through her. Had she been so consumed with the trauma and horror that she had never fully acknowledged that? Had she ever really thanked Him? Yes, He had allowed those men to hurt her—on a fallen planet, people suffered when others used their free will to commit atrocious acts—but He had stopped Dylan from killing her. And she had known, even in the midst of what was happening, that He was there with her.

With a groan, Kathryn lowered her head to her hands again. "Forgive me, Father, if I have never thanked you for that. For sparing my life and for restoring joy to it through Tory. You are my shelter and my safe place. Help me not to forget that."

Even when she had, her anger had dissipated over the years as God had proven to her over and over that He was with her. That while she would never fully understand His ways, she could trust that He would never leave her.

"God, help them." The words, although whispered, were filled with anguish and shattered the stillness of the woods around her. "I don't know why you are allowing Halyna to go through this, but help me to trust that you are still in control and that you are still good." Straightening, she wiped the moisture from her cheeks with her fingers.

Kathryn tipped her head to gaze at the sky. Through the branches, the patches of blue and white were divided and framed like the stained-glass windows in a church. "Help Halyna and James and Nick and their parents and everyone who loves them to understand that. Give them the strength and courage to walk this road again. And help them to feel you with them every step of the way."

For a long time she sat on the log, staring into the trees without really seeing them. The high-pitched squeal of a mosquito near her ear finally drew her out of her sorrowful reverie. It must be getting late. Aaron would wonder why she wasn't helping with the chores. She didn't help out in the barn very often when their kids were home—her job was keeping the books and any administration work—but when someone was away, like Tory was this evening, she was happy to jump in and assist.

Her heart heavy, Kathryn pushed off the log, careful not to step on any of the trilliums as she stumbled to the path. The dainty flower was a symbol of peace and hope. Because it was so fragile and easy to kill, in many places it was also a protected species.

Kathryn contemplated that as she made her way through the trees to the house. Peace and hope were fragile as well and so easily destroyed. The peace she'd felt when she first entered the woods had been destroyed by a few strokes of a pen. How much more had the peace and hope Nick and his family had enjoyed for a few years been obliterated by the phone call of a doctor giving them the results of Halyna's test?

Should she write to Nick? He hadn't asked for anything in his letter except that she pray. And she would, every day. While that was the most powerful thing she could do for him, for all of them, she wanted to offer more. What could she do that would help in any meaningful way?

She would pray for an answer to that question. Nick had taught her that—to pray and then wait for God to show her what to do and when. And if he could listen and be patient, so could she.

Chapter Forty

Thursday

After burning Nick's letter the night before, Kathryn had spent another restless night on the couch. Forget about working through everything she needed to work through before Nick returned. My primary concern was starting to be whether or not he would be able to wake her when he did get here. At some point—and I doubted it would happen before too many more days passed by—exhaustion would catch up to her and pull her into such a deep sleep that only love's true kiss would be able to wake her.

Not that Nick wouldn't be more than willing to offer that. I grinned wryly.

In spite of her lack of sleep, Kathryn seemed remarkably serene this morning. My brow furrowed as I shifted my gaze to the swing beside her.

Ah. Peace had been sent in.

———

I love that guy. Of course, Peace hadn't completely left. He never does fully leave the presence of any of you humans who have embraced Faith. The two of them are inseparable. Still, while he doesn't die a slow, mournful death like I occasionally do, he can be shattered. Usually into a million pieces, like glass. A gut punch will do it, like the one he took from Terror when he and Horror jumped into Kathryn's car that night along with Kevin Dylan.

Thankfully, the creator restored him to wholeness—the way He can with any of His created beings. Then He sent him into the cabin where he was able, even in the midst of the attack, to pry Fear's deplorable cousins off of Kathryn, kick them to the foot of the bed, and take their place next to her.

So yeah, I am particularly fond of Peace, who inevitably helps my cause when he draws close to a charge of mine.

Although the raucous level of our parties plummets whenever he meanders onto the scene, it is literally impossible to be angry with him—or anything else—when he is around.

Especially since a lot of the more unsavory types among us, the ones not sent by the Creator— Discouragement, Jealousy, Discontent, and even Fear and his relatives, much to my delight—tend to slither out the back door when Peace comes in the front.

Which explained why the rug by the woodstove had been empty this morning when I'd glanced into the living room before accompanying Kathryn out onto the porch.

When he caught me watching him, that trademark slow, easy, lying-in-a-hammock-on-a-summer-afternoon grin of his slid across his face. The one I was pretty sure he knew made the hearts of us female Beings skip a beat or two. I returned the smile. Minor cardiopulmonary events aside, I was extremely glad to see him here today. Both Kathryn and I could use a little Peace, given what we'd been through the last couple of days and the gathering storm that continued to loom on the horizon.

As I often did when he was around, I closed my eyes. The calm that drifted on the air like the scent of peppermint rising from the cup of tea Kathryn clutched in both hands as she swung gently back and forth settled over me.

The steam wafting through the air carried her thoughts to me as well. The letter from Nick she'd withdrawn from the shoebox and read the night before was still on her mind, although the sorrow had eased a little. Unlike those unsavory beings,

Sorrow could stay in the room when Peace entered. Even so, if a charge of Sorrow's had been drowning in a storm of grief when Peace arrived—as was often the case—he almost always waded in to help. Every time he gathered that human in his strong arms and carried him or her to shore, using his own body to protect them from the gusting winds and battering waves around them as he did.

Exactly what I hoped for on Kathryn's behalf today as she relived the hours she'd spent on another porch, swaying on a different swing, a few days after receiving the letter from Nick with Halyna's sad news.

August 2015

Katherine turned into the long farm lane and drove toward the house. Wooden planks rumbled beneath her tires as she crossed a bridge over a stream running along the front of the property. Huge willow trees, garlands of green draping over the water, lined the meandering creek. The deep croaking of frogs rose from the long grasses at the edge of the water and drifted through her half-open car window as she approached the house.

In the twilight, lights gleamed from the windows of the barn. Nick was likely out there, finishing up chores or stacking hay bales from a second cutting of the fields, like Aaron was doing tonight. Kathryn—along with Aaron, Rachel, and Josh—had helped bring in the bales today, but Kathryn had excused herself after dinner.

For days the letter Nick had written her had weighed on her mind. Her heart ached for Halyna and James. They'd only had five years. Kathryn had prayed for her many times since the wedding, asking God to keep her healthy and to give them the long life together that a love like theirs deserved.

Her prayers had shifted in recent days. To a request for healing or, if that was not God's plan, for strength and comfort and mercy for all of them. Tonight, Nick was on her heart and in her thoughts. After hours on her knees, she'd felt called to go to him, to let him hear from her own lips that she was there for him and praying for them all.

She parked the car under a towering maple tree in the front yard and switched off the engine. Breathing a prayer that she would find the words to say, she stepped out of the vehicle and made her way on slightly unsteady legs to the front porch. No shadows moved behind the well-lit windows. Should she knock? The last thing she wanted to do was disturb them, especially Halyna. She shot another look at the barn. It was getting late. Likely whoever was out there would come to the house soon. Probably best for her to wait for them out here.

Kathryn wandered over to the porch swing at the far end of the veranda. As it was half-hidden in shadows and surrounded by potted plants, she felt, when she sank onto it, almost as though she had returned to that log in the woods. In contrast to the hard, wooden slats of the swing on her porch, this one was wicker and the back of it stretched a couple of feet above her head before curving forward to create a cocoon-like feel. The floral cushion that lined the bottom and the soft throw pillows in the corners made the swing as comfortable as any piece of furniture in her living room.

In the gathering darkness, the farmyard was peaceful and still. The hum of cicadas blended with the song of the frogs, and Kathryn pushed off the porch slats with her sandaled foot. The swing rocked gently, and she rested her head against the back. The tromping of boots on the porch steps roused her and she straightened.

Nick and James reached the top of the stairs. Deep in conversation about the weather predictions for the next few days, neither glanced in her direction. Kathryn stood and took a couple of tentative steps forward. "Hi."

Nick stopped mid-sentence as both men halted and swung their gazes in her direction. "Kathryn."

He sounded surprised, but nothing in his tone hinted that her visit was unwelcome or an intrusion. All she could detect was … joy. Her tense muscles relaxed as she peered past him to his brother-in-law. "James, I was so sorry to hear Halyna's news."

In the dim light of the sconce next to the door, a shadow passed over his face. "Thank you, Kathryn."

"Please tell her I'm thinking about her and praying for all of you."

"I will. We appreciate it." He inclined his head toward the door. "I'm going in to check on her. Good to see you again."

"You too." She waited until the screen door had creaked open and James had disappeared inside before turning to Nick. "I hope you don't mind that I came by uninvited."

"Mind?" His voice cracked a little. "I've never been so happy to see anyone in my life." He closed the distance between them and gathered her into his arms. Kathryn rested her cheek on his chest. His heart thudded against her ear, the rhythmic sound soothing the turmoil that had swirled through her since reading his letter. For a long time they stood there, swaying gently to the accompaniment of crickets on the front lawn.

Nick's navy T-shirt smelled of earth and hay and hard work and something light and sweet, like clover, and Kathryn inhaled deeply. For the first time she could remember, the sight of him did not stir up the horror of that long ago night. All she experienced was peace mixed with grief over what he was facing. And overwhelmingly, a deep longing to stay here in his arms forever.

When he finally stepped away, he took her face in his hands. "I can't believe you're here."

"Neither can I." She managed an uncertain smile. "When I got your letter, I had to come. I needed to see you."

"Here." He took her hand and led her to the porch swing. They settled on it and she shifted to face him. A piece of hay had caught in his hair and she plucked it out and held it up to show him. "You've been working hard."

His grin was more restrained than usual. "It helps."

Her smile faded. "I'm sure it does." She rested a hand on his leg. "So the doctor didn't give you any hope?"

He covered her hand with his, twining their fingers together. "Very little. It's spread this time. She could do more chemo, but

...." He lifted his shoulders. "Hally doesn't want to go through that again. Not when the most it would do is offer her a few extra weeks, possibly months. I don't blame her for that."

"How long did they give her?"

"Barring a miracle?" He drove his fingers through his hair with his free hand and blew out a breath. "Six months. Maybe less."

Tears pricked her eyes, but Kathryn blinked them away. Tonight wasn't about her or her heartache. It was about Nick and being here for him. "I'm so sorry."

"Thank you." He ran a finger down the side of her face. "Can you stay?"

"For a little while. Tory's at camp, so no one's at home to miss me."

His eyes locked with hers. "*I've* missed you."

Her throat tightened. "I've missed you too."

Nick slid an arm around her shoulders and pulled her to his side. For a few minutes they rocked in silence, until she tipped her head to contemplate him. "Have you eaten?"

"Yeah. We had dinner before we went out. I'm good, unless you want me to go in and take a shower."

"You're fine. I love the smell of hay. Makes me think of Aaron."

"Great. I remind you of your brother—exactly what I was going for."

Kathryn laughed. "Only the smell on your clothes. Not in any other way. Believe me." That was about as bold as she'd been with him. But studying his face, the lines of sadness and weariness extending from the corners of his eyes, she wanted to reach out to him. To be as honest as she could be and hope that somehow that brought him a little comfort.

For a moment he only gazed at her. Then a small smile crossed his face. "Thank you for that."

She rested her head on his shoulder. "You look tired."

He pushed against the floor of the porch with his boots, setting them rocking again as his arm tightened around her. "I haven't been sleeping well since we got the call. Not sure when the last time was that I had a full night's rest."

"Then rest now. I'm not going anywhere."

He pressed a kiss to the top of her head. The full moon cast a soft glow over the ranch, trickling through the branches of the maple to shimmer along the ground. Kathryn closed her eyes, the far-off howl of a wolf and the orchestra of insects humming lulling her again. After a few minutes, Nick's breathing grew deep and even. Kathryn smiled and breathed a prayer for a dreamless sleep for him.

An hour or so later, the screen door creaked open and James peered through the opening. *Everything okay?* he mouthed.

Kathryn smiled and nodded. He offered her a thumbs up before disappearing inside and closing both doors. She and Nick were alone.

Chapter Forty-One

August 2015

The chirping of birds in the maple tree in the front yard woke Kathryn. She blinked several times, trying to orient herself. A cool morning breeze brushed over her face, carrying the scents of freshly cut fields and the sweet, slightly citrusy aroma of peonies from the heavily laden bushes that lined the front of the veranda. Nick's veranda.

She shifted her gaze to the man beside her. Nick's eyes were closed, his long, golden lashes resting against his cheek bones. The tranquility on his face tore at her chest. If only he didn't have to wake up and recall everything that was going on in his life. She remembered that from the days and weeks following her attack. Sleep—when it wasn't rife with disturbing dreams—was a refuge. Then she awoke into the living nightmare that was her life as she dealt with the trauma of what had happened to her.

The screen door creaked open slowly. James emerged, holding the door with an elbow and clutching a steaming mug in each hand. A smile broke across his face when his eyes met hers, and he jutted his chin at Nick. "That's the most sleep he's had in weeks," he whispered as he stopped in front of the swing and handed her one of the mugs. "Are you doing okay?"

She nodded. "I'm fine." Bending over the cup, she inhaled deeply. "Thank you for this."

"You're welcome." James studied his brother-in-law. "Maybe I should take this inside and keep it hot."

"Don't even think about it." Nick's hand shot out, although he didn't open his eyes.

James chuckled and handed him the mug. "Bacon and eggs are in the pan. I'll let you know when they're ready."

"Thanks." Eyes still closed, Nick lifted the mug a little into the air.

When James had gone inside, Nick opened one eye and glanced at her then straightened on the swing. "I was worried you might have been a dream."

She grinned. "Nope. I'm here. In the flesh."

Nick trailed his fingers along her bare arm. "I can see that."

Her cheeks warmed, and she ducked her head and took a sip of the hot coffee. Given the amusement in his eyes, she hadn't hidden her reaction to his words—or his touch—very well. "How did you sleep?"

"Amazingly well. Like James said, better than I have in weeks. Thanks to you."

"I didn't do anything."

"You were here. That was all I needed." He sipped from his own cup before reaching over and setting the mug on the porch railing. "I had no intention of making you sleep out here all night. Sorry about that."

"It was fine. Kind of fun, like camping."

He cocked his head. "Do you enjoy camping?"

"I love it. Our dad used to take Aaron and me all the time. It's been a while, but I'd like to do it again sometime."

"Me too. Maybe someday we ..."

Her fingers tightened around the mug. What had he been about to say? And why had he stopped?

Exhaling, Nick leaned forward and rested his forearms on his legs, clasping his hands between his knees. "I want you to know that nothing has changed for me. If anything, my feelings for you—and the belief that we are meant to be together—have only grown stronger. But ..."

He stopped again. When he sat up and met her gaze, Kathryn offered him a small smile. "Always a *but* with us, isn't there?"

"Seems like it." The sadness she'd seen in his eyes the night before was back. "The thing is, I have no idea what the next few months are going to be like. I need to be fully here for Hally."

Kathryn reached for one of his hands. "I get it. I really do.

Of course you have to be here for your sister. If it were Aaron or Meg or Tory I would feel the same way."

"If things were different, if this wasn't happening to Hally…"

She squeezed his fingers. "I know." Reluctantly, she released his hand and stood. "I should go."

"You don't have to. The least I can do is make you breakfast." A sheepish look crossed his face. "Actually, that's not true. The least I can do is offer you the breakfast that James made."

She smiled. "As generous as that is of you, I better not. With Tory away, I need to cover for her in the barn this morning. Aaron will be worried if I don't show up soon." After setting the mug on a small table between two wooden Muskoka chairs, she made her way to the steps. The floorboards squeaked behind her as Nick followed.

At the top of the stairs, he stopped her with a hand on her arm. She faced him, leaning against the porch railing for support. Nick slid his fingers into her hair on either side of her face. The thumbs that stroked her cheeks were strong and warm and calloused from hard work. "I don't know how to thank you for coming last night."

"You don't have to. I wanted to be here."

"I feel stronger now. Not only physically after getting some rest but mentally and emotionally. Better able to face what's coming. So thank you."

"You're welcome." She took a quivering breath. "I'll be thinking about you, Nick, all of you. And praying."

"I'd appreciate it." He rested his forehead on hers. When he lifted his head, he searched her face. For a moment it appeared as though he wanted to say more, then he lowered his hands. "Goodbye, Kathryn."

The word pierced her chest. How often had they said it to each other? "Goodbye." She stumbled down the steps and over to her car.

When she opened the door and glanced at him, Nick stood

236

where she had left him, watching her. He smiled and lifted his hand. Kathryn nodded before sliding behind the wheel.

The morning sun cast a golden glow over fields of wheat and corn as she drove home. What had happened to her last night? Something had definitely shifted inside. For the first time, being in Nick's presence had brought comfort, not pain. If he hadn't been the one to pull away, she might have ...

Kathryn rubbed the side of her hand across her forehead. It didn't help, thinking that way. Nick was right. This wasn't the right time for them. Like he'd asked her to do at the wedding, she'd continue to pray that they would know when it was. If it ever was.

Still, leaving him had hurt, far more than she'd thought it would. But if her being there last night had helped him to face what lay ahead, even a little, then it was worth every bit of what it cost her to get in her car and drive away.

Chapter Forty-Two

Thursday

"Where you headed, Dylan?"

"None of your business." Kevin Dylan straddled the Harley he'd spent most of the rest of his savings on and fastened the buttons on his jean jacket.

"Fine." McGregor threw his hands in the air. "I'm only making conversation."

Dylan's eyes narrowed. "If I were you, I'd be pretty careful who I *make conversation* with from now on. Anybody comes after me and I'm coming after you."

"Don't worry. I'm not talking to anybody. I have as much to lose as you do."

"Don't forget it. That money I paid you wasn't only for getting out. It was to keep your mouth shut too. And preferably to get you out of my life."

"Well, I didn't think it was going to make us best friends."

Dylan snorted. "You got that right."

"No problem. I don't want to see you again any more than you want to see me." McGregor spun around and stalked away, a dark silhouette against a backdrop of pink and gray sky. "Have a nice life."

Dylan kicked the stand up on the bike and turned the key in the ignition. "Why start now?" he muttered before revving the engine and spinning through the gravel and onto the road. He kept his eyes open for cops. He was desperate to get across the border into Canada before his face got plastered all over the Internet, but he couldn't afford to get pulled over. A speeding ticket now would be the equivalent of a tax evasion charge for Al Capone—a relatively minor infraction that would cut short the freedom he'd managed to purchase. The wind whipped past him as he maneuvered the bike along the highway. Dylan breathed deeply. It had been a while since he'd inhaled air that didn't carry the acrid smell of cigarette smoke and too many bodies crammed into a small space. It had cost him to be out here, but it was worth every penny.

And when he saw *her* again, ran his hands over her creamy white skin and saw the terror in those eyes of hers, the return on his investment would skyrocket. White-hot adrenaline coursed through his chest, and he pressed on the gas, anxious to close the miles between them.

I shuddered, an involuntary reaction I always had when I saw Kevin Dylan. I wasn't the only one—that seemed to be the general response, particularly among those who had spent more than five minutes in his presence. And riding with Kathryn was wild enough—no way I was hopping on that bike. Definitely not my kind of ride. Not a door handle in sight.

Not to mention that I didn't trust the driver half as far as I could fling him and his Fat Boy, or whatever it was.

In any case, I'd seen enough. Dylan was on his way, and while I refused to travel with him, I would be there at the other end, with Kathryn, to face him when he arrived.

I allowed myself one more shudder as I turned away, for good measure.

Chapter Forty-Three

Thursday

David wrestled with God all night long. His pillow was a rock beneath his head as he tossed and turned, trying to get comfortable. Finally, he abandoned all thoughts of sleep and rolled onto his side. Laura was beautiful in the soft moonlight streaming through the window, her long blond hair spread across the pillow. She looked so peaceful. The ache in his chest was unbearable.

I followed him when he got up and crept down the stairs. He went into his study and switched on the little desk lamp then dropped into his big black leather chair. Too worked up to settle, I paced his office, listening in on the thoughts that bounced and tumbled through his tortured brain like rocks down the side of a mountain. The quiet words he'd shoved into a shadowy recess in his mind for so many years now echoed in his head again.

Tell her.

Truth stood behind him, a heavy hand on his shoulder. Resting his head on his folded arms, David moaned. I could see his dilemma. The results wouldn't be back for a day or two. If he wasn't the father, Laura would never have to know. But Truth would not be served that way, and from the grim set of his features his patience had about run out.

Not my decision, although my relationship with David did hinge on the direction he chose to go tonight. Reason enough, in my opinion, for me to listen in on this particular prayer. Not that I took any enjoyment from the eavesdropping. It was as agonized and painful a conversation as any I had overheard. Still, I needed to know what he was thinking, enough that I stopped pacing and bent over the desk, clasping both hands behind my back to keep from wringing them in my angst.

If I tell her now, it will destroy her. It will destroy us. I could lose her.

Yes, you could. And if you did, would I be enough for you?
There it was, the question David had grappled with—or avoided grappling with—since the day he had met Laura. Apparently he was not going to be allowed that luxury any longer.

David lifted his head as the question resonated through him. *Could* he lose everything and everyone he loved and not lose the peace that came from knowing God would never leave him?

I held my breath, well aware that the moment was a second turning point in his life. After a while, I realized he was not going to answer this one quickly, and I exhaled. I shouldn't have been surprised. Over the years, David had shown a remarkable ability to stand up under the weight of that heavy hand on his shoulder. He had stronger nerves than I did, let me tell you, to withstand the pressure. Even so, tonight was different, and we both knew it. If he shut the door on Truth this time, I think even David realized that the knock may never come again.

He spun his chair around and stared into the cold, empty fireplace until a soft, gray light began to lift the darkness outside his window. A deep anguish ripped through his body. "Yes." He closed his eyes against the pain the word cost him. "You are enough. But I don't want to hurt her. I don't want to let her go."

Deep in his soul he felt the words, a gentle whisper he wasn't even sure was the voice or only the jasmine-scented breeze that ruffled the curtains as it drifted through his window. Still, the words calmed him.

Trust me. Trust her.

David nodded in surrender. He would trust them both. There was nothing else he could do.

Chapter Forty-Four

Thursday

Kathryn carried the teapot and her mug in from the porch and stood at the sink to wash both. When she dried her fingers on the towel hanging on the handle of the stove, she glimpsed the phone sitting next to the oven, and she pressed both palms to the countertop and drew in a deep breath.

She'd been standing in this same spot three years earlier, trying to decide what to make for dinner when the phone rang. I held my breath, knowing who was on the other end of the line. Unaware that the simple act would cause upheaval in her life once again, Kathryn had calmly reached for her cell.

January 2016

"Hello?"

"Kathryn?"

She froze. Even through the device, the sound of his voice sent such strong shockwaves through her that she nearly dropped the phone. "Nick."

"I have a favor to ask. Halyna is really sick. The doctors say she doesn't have a lot of time left."

Her hand tightened around the receiver, a sharp pain jabbing her chest at the sadness in his voice. "I'm so sorry to hear that."

"The thing is, she's been asking for you, and I wondered if there was any way you might be able to stop by and see her for a few minutes today."

Kathryn made her way to the kitchen table and sank onto a chair, dropping her head onto one hand.

"I know it's a lot to ask, but—"

"No, it's okay. Of course I'll come. Where is she?"

Nick gave her the information. "Thank you for doing this. I really appreciate it. I wouldn't ask if she wasn't …" His voice

broke, and she pressed her eyes shut, waves of his unbearable sorrow washing over her. "I'm sorry."

She shook her head. "Please don't be. I understand. I'll get there as soon as I can."

"Thank you."

Kathryn pressed the off button on the phone and sat at the table for several minutes, staring out the window. Two cardinals flitted through the oak tree outside, the red wings of the male startling against a white dusting of snow on the branches. It always seemed wrong to her that the sun continued to shine and birds still sang when such suffering and grief were happening in the world. Sorrow should be reflected in gray, drizzly rain streaming against the window and all animals and birds huddling beneath the trees in silence.

With a heavy sigh, Kathryn pushed to her feet. Abandoning the recipe book on the counter, she headed for the stairs to get ready. Halyna was practically a stranger. Still, the events of that night in the cabin did wind through both their lives and bind them tightly together—as Nick had said in his letter.

And the thought of seeing Nick again, when clearly the timing between them was still wildly off—she'd never wanted anything more or less in her life. *Go, Kathryn. Be there for him.*

The rest would have to figure itself out.

Chapter Forty-Five

January 2016

Nick sat on a bench outside his sister's room, elbows on his knees, his head resting on both hands. A dull ache settled in behind her breastbone as Kathryn walked along the hallway toward him. His shoulders sagged under the weight of the burden he bore. He sighed as she approached, and tears pricked the back of her eyelids. She blinked them away. "Nick?"

He raised his head slowly. The ache in her chest intensified. Rings of exhaustion and sadness circled his eyes, but he managed a small smile. "Kathryn." He rose and held out both hands.

She placed hers in his, drawing strength from him.

"Thank you for coming."

"Of course. How is she?"

Nick let go of her and scrubbed his face with both hands. "Not well. I don't think she has much longer." He swallowed hard. "She's been asking for you. She really wants to see you. But the doctor said to keep visits short."

"I won't stay long."

Nick opened the hospital room door and took her elbow. Kathryn's chest constricted. Halyna appeared so small and frail lying on the bed. Fluid, likely morphine, dripped from the bag hanging from a stand through a tube and into her hand. Soft music played in the background. In spite of the circumstances an aura of serenity filled the room. James sat in the chair beside the bed, holding her hand. He let her go when they came in the door and rose to his feet.

His face bore the same marks of weariness as Nick's, but the warm smile that curved his lips and the lines at the corners of his eyes told her that Halyna's last years had been filled with love and laughter. The thought comforted her and a little of the heaviness lifted.

"Thank you for coming, Kathryn."

Nick touched Kathryn's back lightly. "Do you mind if she speaks with Halyna for a few minutes?"

"Not at all. She's been asking for you." James moved out of the way as Kathryn walked to the side of the bed.

She gripped the raised bedrails to stop her hands from shaking.

On the other side of the bed, Nick leaned over his sister. She appeared to be sleeping, and he brushed his fingers across her cheek. "Hally?"

She stirred and opened her eyes. They were as dark as Nick's and shone with a soft light as she turned toward Kathryn.

"It's Kathryn Ellison. Do you think you can talk to her?"

Halyna nodded and reached out a hand. Kathryn grasped it. The shadow of a smile played at the corners of Halyna's pale lips. "Could we have a few minutes alone?"

Nick met Kathryn's gaze across the bed. She nodded, and he and James left the room. When the door had closed behind them, she shifted her attention to Halyna.

"Thank you for coming, Kathryn. I've wanted to talk to you for a long time." Her voice was clear but very quiet.

Kathryn bent forward to hear her better. "I'm so glad Nick called me."

Halyna laughed softly. "That's the one good thing about dying—you tend to get whatever you ask for."

Kathryn joined in, amazed at this woman's ability to make her laugh under these circumstances. She studied the drawn face. Even with death casting a pall across her thin cheeks, Halyna was still a beautiful woman, and her eyes were filled with fun and warmth. Regret stabbed through Kathryn. If only she'd reached out over the years, taken the opportunity to get to know Nick's sister better. They could have been close friends, although the same unease that seeing Nick had caused her might have always been a faint shadow in the background of their relationship.

"I wanted to tell you again how sorry I am for what happened to you that night. I've never been able to get over the feeling that I was responsible. If I had never met Jeff—"

Kathryn pressed her fingers lightly against Halyna's hand. "None of it was your fault. I've never blamed you for anything that happened."

"Then you forgive me?"

"I don't believe there's anything to forgive, but if there is, then yes, I do."

Halyna closed her eyes and let out a breath as though she'd been holding it, waiting for Kathryn's answer. "Thank you."

When she opened her eyes again, they were filled with an earnestness that tightened Kathryn's stomach muscles.

"There's something between you and Nick, isn't there? I felt it that day in the courthouse, and I know Nick did too. And it's only grown stronger for him over the years. I think that's why, although he has dated occasionally, he's never had a serious relationship with anyone since then." The thin fingers gripped Kathryn's tighter, as though willing her to listen. "I know it might be hard for you, for both of you, but I hope and pray you won't let the past keep you from finding each other."

"Halyna, I—"

Halyna raised the hand with the intravenous needle off the blanket. "You don't have to say anything. Only promise me you'll think about it, please." She lowered her hand as though it was too heavy to hold in the air for long. "He's such a good man and he's going to need ..." She turned her head and coughed. When she stopped, her eyelids dropped again.

"I will think about it, I promise." Kathryn's voice lowered to a whisper. "I should go now and let you rest."

Halyna's eyes opened. "Wait. There's one other thing I wanted to tell you. We started going to church after David Henley's hearing—Nick and my parents and I. Over the next few months we all became believers. I wanted you to know that, so you could see that something good came out of what you went through."

Tears welled in her eyes. "Thank you. That means so much to me."

"Good, I'm glad." The woman's dark eyes searched Kathryn's intently before the corners of her mouth turned up. "Goodbye, Kathryn. God bless you."

"Goodbye, Halyna."

Kathryn laid the hand on the blanket reverently and stumbled to the door on legs that had gone weak. Nick and James stood in the hallway. James came over immediately and touched her shoulder. "Thank you for talking to her." He opened the door and returned to his wife's side.

When she raised her eyes to meet Nick's across the hallway, the tears that had threatened slid down both her cheeks. He came to her and took her in his arms, the strength of his hold flowing through her. After a few moments, Kathryn drew in a deep breath and wiped the tears off her cheeks with her fingers.

He grasped her upper arms and searched her face. "Are you okay?"

She nodded. "I'm so sorry, Nick."

"Thank you for seeing her. I know that couldn't have been easy for you."

"I'm glad I came. Your sister is a wonderful woman. I wish I could have gotten to know her better."

"So do I." The intensity of his gaze tore the air from her lungs.

"I better go."

"I'll walk you out." He slid an arm around her shoulders as they made their way along the hallway. The heavy warmth of it soothed her.

"Do you remember the *as if* game?"

She managed a smile, recalling Halyna's wedding. "Yes I do, Nicholas George. Vividly."

He rolled his eyes. "I knew you'd pull that out at some point."

"Is George ...?"

"My dad." They reached the elevators, and Nick dropped his arm and stabbed the button with his thumb. "You just missed him and my mom. They went home to get a few hours of rest."

"That's good."

The car was empty when they stepped in, and he propped a shoulder against the wall and faced her. "Anyway, we had a lot of fun with that game, but once in a while it got us into trouble. One time in particular, when I was maybe twelve and Halyna was ten, I made the ill-advised decree that we would be astronomers and spend the entire day gazing at the sky."

"Oh dear."

"Yeah. Not too smart. The thing was, once we committed to the *as if*, we were really stubborn about it and wouldn't quit, no matter what. I think we both ended up with detention that day because our teachers weren't very impressed."

Kathryn let out a short laugh at the thought of the two of them staring out the windows of their classrooms, refusing to face the front. She pressed her lips together. "Sorry."

"It's okay. It is funny now. Not so much that night when my parents also got upset with us. My dad ended up sending us to our rooms. After a while he came up to talk to us. He went to Hally's room first, which was across the hall from mine. When he finished talking to her and opened the door, I could hear her crying. Since she was normally pretty tough, that really got to me, especially since it was all my fault." He pushed away from the wall. "It's always destroyed me, seeing her hurting." He clenched a fist and ground it against his chest. "Gets me right here, you know?"

Kathryn's throat tightened. "I know."

He unclenched his fist and framed her face with his hands. "And I feel the same way about you."

The look in his eyes was almost more than she could bear. He ran his thumb under her eye, wiping away the moisture that had gathered there. Kathryn summoned a tremulous smile. "So I remind you of your sister? Not exactly what I was going for."

Nick grinned, the sorrow clearing from his eyes. "Only in that. Nothing else. Believe me." He pressed a kiss to her forehead before lowering his hands. "When my dad talked to me that night, he had a lot to say about respecting others and listening to authority. Then he told me that a good man doesn't lead other people into trouble. He leads them out of it. That struck me hard and I've never forgotten him saying that. I've tried to live my life that way ever since. Only now my sister is in trouble, and there's nothing I ..." His voice broke.

Kathryn wrapped her arms around his waist. He pulled her close, his hand cupping the back of her head.

"Your dad sounds like an amazing father."

"He is. That part's killing me too, seeing my parents go through this. Thankfully, their faith is strong, and so are they. Halyna comes by it honestly." The elevator stopped moving and the doors slid open. Nick let Kathryn go and waited for her to step out. Clasping her hand tightly, he walked her to the main doors, stopping when they reached the sliding glass doors. "I should get back."

"Of course."

Nick squeezed her fingers. "It meant a lot, you coming here today." The sadness in his voice rooted her feet in place.

"I'm glad I was able to. You and your family are in my prayers every day."

"That helps more than I can tell you."

Walking away from him required monumental effort, but Kathryn placed one foot in front of the other and somehow made it across the parking lot to her car. She felt his eyes on her until she opened the door and slid behind the wheel. For a few seconds she stared out the front window, cold shivers shaking her from head to foot.

Bright sunlight reflected off the snow on the hood of her car and she grabbed her sunglasses from above the visor and slid them on. Tears blurred the view on the other side of the glass. Were those for Halyna, Nick, or herself? All of them, she guessed. There was more than enough pain to go around, and more than enough tears shed and still to fall.

A memory of the soft glow in Halyna's eyes brought a thoughtful smile to her face. Blinking away the tears, Kathryn tugged off the sunglasses and lifted her face to the light streaming through the window. She could still feel the soft warmth of Nick's wine-colored T-shirt against her skin, hear the faint pounding of his heart beneath her cheek. As helpless as he felt to relieve his sister's suffering, she felt equally helpless to relieve his.

Only God could do that. And like she had promised Nick, she would be praying for him every time he came to mind in the coming days. Which—she touched her fingers to her cheek where his had rested only minutes before—would likely be very often.

Chapter Forty-Six

Thursday

The sound of rattling paper brought me back to Kathryn. She'd wandered into the living room and settled herself on the couch. Bending forward, she picked up the folded program she'd set on the coffee table the day before. For several long moments she sat, gripping it in both hands and staring at the photo of Halyna on the front of it. I folded my arms on the back of the couch.

Apparently, we are to move through this process at a snail's pace. If I were a petty being, this would annoy me. Instead, what I feel is concern. If and when Nick Lawson showed up at her door again, it would be desirable for Kathryn to have worked out all the issues, opened and closed all the doors she needed to, or else he could drive away for good this time.

Unfortunately, there is nothing I can do to speed up the pace. There never has been. She has always had to work through what happened to her the best way she knows how, leaning heavily on her family and friends.

Aaron has helped her the most. I honestly don't think she would have made it through everything without him. Meg, not only her sister-in-law but her best friend since kindergarten, has also been instrumental in her recovery.

And my friend, that wonderful Being, Grace, of course. It goes without saying that Kathryn could never have come as far as she has without her. And she has come a long way since That Night. And since the day that wrenched her heart open again.

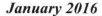

January 2016

Nick saw her as soon as he rose and turned to follow his sister's casket out of the church. Kathryn sat halfway down, on the aisle. Through his haze of tears, her face was the only one he could clearly see. A smile flitted across her face, but the eyes that met his were dark with sorrow.

Nick inclined his head as he passed by, grateful she was there. Even if she wasn't his and might never be, he drew strength from her presence and straightened his shoulders as he exited the church into the cool spring air. He nodded and pressed the many hands that reached for his as friends and family moved past, murmuring words of comfort and shared grief. The faces and words blurred together as he waited for the one he needed to see the most.

And then she was there, standing in front of him, her hand held firmly between both of his. "Kathryn."

All the tenderness he felt came out in his voice and her eyes watered. "Nick, I'm so sorry. I only met Halyna a few times, but somehow it feels like I knew her forever. She was a very special person."

"Yes, she was." His voice had thickened, and he cleared his throat. "Thank you for seeing that. Your visit meant a lot to her. It seemed to give her peace her last few days."

"I'm glad. It meant a lot to me too."

Nick was vaguely aware that the line was growing behind her, but he couldn't bring himself to let go of her hand, knowing that when he did, she would walk out of his life and he might never see her again. "Can you stay for coffee?"

Uncertainty flickered in her eyes.

Please stay. His chest tightened as he waited for her answer. He needed her today, needed to be able to glance over and see her, even if they didn't speak again. Without that he didn't know if he had the strength to get through the darkest day he had ever known.

The tension in her shoulders relaxed as she squeezed his hand. "Yes, I can stay."

He managed a small smile. "Good."

Kathryn nodded and slowly withdrew her hand from his. Nick clenched his fists to avoid grabbing it again and refusing to let go. His eyes were less compliant—they followed her as she moved through the rest of the line, speaking softly to his family and hugging James. Not until the next person in line spoke to him did he break the magnetic pull and focus on the face in front of him.

When he had finally talked to everyone, he followed his family along the hallway of the old church and into a room where sandwiches and cookies were laid out on large trays. The comforting smell of coffee and warm fruit pies floated through the air. Nick scanned the crowds of people. Disappointment slashed at his barely-maintained composure when he didn't see her. She was gone. He could hardly blame her. She didn't know anyone here but him and James, and she barely knew them although, as she had said about Halyna, he felt as though he had known her forever.

Nick accepted the cup of coffee someone held out for him and mumbled his thanks. Grabbing a plate, he filled it from the various trays, not caring what he took. It would all taste like sawdust anyway. His only interest in eating was to give him the strength to get through the next few hours and days, a task that felt like carving out a path through a wall of mud with his bare hands. He sank onto a chair in a quiet corner. James followed him and took a seat across the table. His brother-in-law sat staring at his plate of food with as much enthusiasm on his face as Nick felt. The weight of the day pressed in on him and Nick closed his eyes.

"Is it all right if I join you?"

He blinked. Kathryn stood at the end of the table, a cup of tea in her hand. The thrill of joy that shot through him scared him badly, but he didn't have the strength to repress it or begin to sort it out. Not today. He tugged out the chair beside him, and she set down her cup and slid onto it.

"I thought you'd left."

Her smile was gentle and flowed over his hurting spirit like a warm spring rain. "No, I was at the back of the sanctuary talking to your mom. She's very sweet."

"Yes, she is. Halyna is ... was a lot like her." He hated that, talking about his sister in the past tense. It seemed so final, as if she no longer existed. Which she didn't—not on earth anyway. The idea of her in heaven with Jesus and their grandparents and other people they had loved and lost, her suffering over forever, comforted him a little. Kathryn covered his hand with hers for a few seconds before withdrawing it and wrapping her fingers around her cup. Still, it helped—that brief contact sent warmth coursing up his arm. Nick took a sip from his own cup. James was watching him closely, and Nick lifted his shoulders slightly. A small smile toyed at the corner of his brother-in-law's mouth.

"So James, how did you and Halyna meet?"

James shifted his attention to Kathryn. "We met at church, when she was pretty sick and doing chemo. I was blown away by her faith and her strength through everything that was happening. I would have married her sooner, but she insisted on waiting until she was better, so as soon as she went into remission I proposed." Grief and joy mingled in his eyes.

Nick understood that. It hurt to talk about his sister, but it was cathartic at the same time, remembering her and everything they had done together.

"And you married her knowing ...?"

"That I would likely lose her? Yes, I knew it, and I didn't make the decision lightly. Still, I figured that every relationship is a risk, and the possibility of being hurt or going through loss is always there. It's worth it—when it's right, when you're with the person you're meant to share your life with. I don't regret a single moment I had with Halyna, even though the pain of losing her is almost unbearable. In fact, I'd do it again in a minute."

Kathryn nodded, a thoughtful expression on her face. Nick studied her from the corner of his eye. Having her here sent the same conflicting emotions flooding through him as talking about his sister did—joy that she was so close he could reach out and touch her and pain at the thought that she would soon be gone. Again. James's words echoed in his head. He and Kathryn had obstacles to surmount—more than most people. Even so, his belief that they were meant to be together had never wavered, not from the moment they'd met.

God had a plan for them. Although now wasn't the time— not when his heart had been shattered over the past few weeks and months. He needed time and a lot of healing before he would be ready. He only prayed that when he was—when God had healed them both to the point where they could fully give their hearts to each other—that she would be ready. If not, he'd continue to wait. Nick straightened in his seat, his resolve steeled. Somehow, someday he would show her that they were worth taking a risk on, no matter what they had to work through to be together.

But not today. The grief of losing Halyna was too strong. Once again, the timing was off for them.

When Kathryn rose to leave, he walked her out the front door of the church and across the slightly icy surface of the parking lot to her car.

She held out her hand to him and he took it, clasping it tightly. "Goodbye, Nick." The depth of emotion that flowed between them when their eyes locked forged a connection he could almost reach out and touch.

The timing might be wrong, but he couldn't stop himself. He pulled her to him. For a moment he rested his head against hers, the feel of her against him so right he wasn't sure he could release her. Then he took a deep breath and lowered his arms to his sides. "Goodbye, Kathryn." As he said the word that always slashed across his chest like a dagger, he prayed he would never have to say it again.

Not to her, anyway. Summoning every bit of the strength that seeing Kathryn had given him, he opened the door of the church. Time to say goodbye one final time to his sister before he and his family had to let her go.

Chapter Forty-Seven

Thursday

The program crinkled as Kathryn clasped it under her chin. Stretching out on the couch, she rested her head on the armrest and closed her eyes. Good. The storm clouds I'd been watching gather on the horizon—the ones Kathryn couldn't see—had deepened to black and an ominous thunder rumbled in the distance. We both needed sleep before the first drops of rain began to fall.

I glanced out the window. Although it was only mid-morning, a thick, otherworldly darkness pressed against the glass. I closed my eyes, as much to block out the sight as to rest. Peace was still hanging around, and I took advantage of his presence to start for the armchair by the fire, hoping for a decent nap.

Halfway across the room I slammed to a stop, as though I'd walked into a wall I couldn't see. I tipped my head to stare at the ceiling? Now? Really? *I was hoping for a few minutes to ...*

It was no use. The Creator was sending me somewhere else, so I would go.

The nap would have to wait.

Thursday

I had to be here. It was my job, my assignment. More than that, I wanted to be there for David in case he needed me. On the off chance. It was killing me, though. Literally. It hurt to draw breath, and the rattle in my chest when I did alarmed me greatly. Walking away would be a lot easier—maybe spending the day deep in a rainforest somewhere or on top of a mountain, as far from the nearest human as I could get. You humans are very hard on me, you know. Whenever I start to think everything may be all right between us, something or someone comes along to wrench us apart. Like what has happened with David this week.

Having said that, if he and I do make it through this—and it's still a very big if—it will all be worth it.

Which was why, in spite of the imminent threat to my existence, I would be here today instead of lost in the Andes somewhere. It's partly obedience and loyalty, and partly the same morbid fascination that prevented Kathryn from tearing her gaze from the knife in Dylan's hand as he walked toward her. There's something about death. While terrifying, it is also awesome and powerful for those of us—and you—who believe, knowing as we do that death is merely a portal to another, better world. Until the very last breath, there is also the hope, which we all cling to, that death may be averted and life will continue. And hope is right and good, given that life is one of the Creator's greatest gifts.

So when Laura left this morning to run a few errands, I sank onto a kitchen chair and rested my sleep-deprived brain on my folded arms as David took a box of cereal out of the cupboard and poured his boys a bowl. He sat at the table and watched as they dug in.

Overwhelming sadness had trenched deep lines across his forehead, and his eyes glistened. Would they ever have a morning like this again?

"Hey, boys." His voice caught. "How would you like to go to Aunt Beth's today to play with Jonathan and Sasha?"

"Yeah!" Cody and Simon jumped off their chairs and ran circles around the kitchen table. In spite of my weariness, I had to smile. Kids were great. So many—although not nearly enough, in my opinion—are blessed with obliviousness to the depths of darkness that exist in the world. For my part, I did what I could to stretch that innocence out as long as possible. I hadn't been able to do it with David, certainly not as long as I would have liked. Depending on what transpired in this little house today, perhaps I would fare better with his sons. I listened in on his tortured thoughts as he contemplated them.

No secrets with you guys, nothing hidden. David always knew what they were thinking and feeling. He tapped a clenched fist against his mouth. *Stay that way, boys.* The last thing he wanted was for his sons to grow up to have terrible secrets that weighed on them and threatened to destroy everything and everyone they loved. Nothing was worth that, as he well knew.

I added a hearty, if silent, amen to that.

Laura's sister and brother-in-law, Beth and Peter, had moved to Maple Ridge a year after David and Laura had, much to Laura's delight. Beth loved having the boys, and David knew they'd be welcome to stay as long as it took for him and Laura to talk. He buckled the wriggling boys into their car seats and drove the ten minutes to Beth's house. After the intense quiet of Kathryn's ranch, I welcomed the noise and confusion. For about three of those minutes.

When he wheeled into the driveway, they were greeted by two large dogs and one four-year-old boy, all jumping on them as David and his sons piled out of the car. Not being a big fan of dogs, who seem to have an uncanny ability to detect my presence and sniff me out—usually when I am attempting to be my most discreet or, like today, when I am feeling extremely vulnerable—I did not venture outside.

David's chest clenched as his sons disappeared around the corner of the house behind their cousin. "Goodbye, boys."

"David?" Beth walked toward the car, two-year-old Sasha balanced on one hip. "Is everything okay?"

"Not really." He rubbed a hand against his forehead. "Would it be all right for the boys to stay for a while? Maybe overnight?"

"Of course. They can stay as long as you need."

He squared his shoulders, bracing himself for questions we both knew he wouldn't be able to answer.

"Is there anything else I can do?"

David let out his breath before leaning in and kissing little Sasha on the forehead. "You can pray. I have to talk to Laura today about something in my past I've never told her. It's going to be difficult for her, for us, but it's something I have to do. I should have done it a long time ago."

Beth nodded. David's sister-in-law had a quiet spirit. While

I couldn't quite relate, I did appreciate it, and David did too. Never more than today. The tears that had glistened in his eyes at breakfast, hovering below the surface ever since Kathryn had walked into his office the day before, would no doubt spill over if he tried to explain any further.

Lamp posts and stores and houses streaked by the window as we drove home. It wasn't until the car slowed almost to a crawl that I glanced out David's side and realized that we were almost at the church. He wanted to go in. I felt the desire emanate from him so strongly that if I had reached out a hand I think I might have felt it pulsing in the air. He would have given anything to sequester himself in that brick building—pretend his life wasn't about to get turned upside down.

Both hands clutched the steering wheel as tightly as they had in the border crossing line that day so many years ago. I studied David's face. Would he turn in and escape to the peaceful silence of his office—his own personal rainforest? We sat for so long that I started casting furtive glances into the rear-view mirror, worried that we might be plowed into from behind, but no other vehicles appeared on the quiet street. The only sounds were the clicking of the turn signal and the pounding of his heart.

"God, help me!" The tormented cry was ripped from him. He switched off his blinker and drove toward home. I wasn't sure whether to be relieved or sorry. It was a moot point. Either way there would be consequences, and all I could do was stick with him to find out what the ramifications for him—and for me— would be.

Laura was in the kitchen unloading the dishwasher. Every step David took required sheer willpower. He stopped in the doorway and leaned against the wooden frame for support, watching his wife as she worked. The sun shone through the window above the sink, shimmering off her long blond hair. Singing loudly, she hadn't heard him come in. He could still change his mind and slip out.

Help me.

"Laura."

She flashed him a quick smile as she strode toward the cupboard, her hands filled with clean plates.

"I need to talk to you." He had to work to push each word out.

She didn't seem to notice how difficult this was for him. David froze as she called out, "Does this have anything to do with that beautiful woman who came to see you yesterday? You know, you can't get away with anything in a ..."

I managed a wry grin. You had to love a small church.

The smile on her face faded when she faced him. "David?"

"Laura, I ..." His voice broke, and he gazed at her helplessly.

Laura set down the pile of plates and walked toward him. She took him by the arm and directed him into the living room. When she sat on the couch, he sank onto the cushion beside her.

I propped a shoulder against a wall, both knees shaky. Too afraid to watch, I covered my face with both hands. I did, however, position myself close enough that I wouldn't miss a word.

"Where are the boys?"

"They're fine. They're at Beth's. I asked her to keep them while we talked. There's something I need to tell you." How he was going to be able to get out the words, to make any sense to her at all with his mind racing in a hundred different directions and his mouth refusing to cooperate, he had no idea.

"David, you're scaring me. Whatever it is, tell me. Please."

He dragged a breath into a throat that had gone bone dry.

I parted two fingers so I could peek out and see how he was doing.

"I have to tell you about something I've done. It does involve the woman who came to see me yesterday."

The color drained from his wife's face. "Did you and she ... did you have an affair?"

David shook his head. He almost wished he could tell her that *was* what had happened. Somehow that would be a lot easier. "I need you to listen and not say anything, or I'll never get this out."

Laura nodded. He took her hands in his. They were cold as ice but his were the same and there was nothing he could do to warm them up. "I told you before we were married that I was in prison for robbery. That was partly true. I did time for that. But the really hard time, the experience that brought me back to God, was for something else."

Are you sure this is the right thing to do? Because if it is, I have to know you're here. I can't do this alone.

I glanced around. Standing room only, it was so crowded. It wasn't any of us that David wanted at the moment, though—only the One who had sent us all here. Fair enough.

He was here too, as always.

Trust me. Trust her.

Squaring his shoulders, David squeezed Laura's hands, hoping to bear at least part of the brunt of what she was about to hear. "Twenty years ago, I was involved in a scheme to abduct a woman. Her ex-boyfriend paid another guy and me to bring her to a cabin." The room spun around him, and David forced himself to take another breath. "We got her there and started drinking, waiting for the boyfriend to show up. Sometime during the night the other guy suggested we have some fun with her."

Horror filled Laura's eyes. He desperately wanted to turn away, but he couldn't. He needed to see what she was going through—to feel the pain that every word, like a physical blow, caused her—so he kept his gaze fixed on her face. He owed her that much and more.

"We ..." David didn't know if he could say it, the word was too terrible, too ugly, but he owed it to Kathryn as well. He would say it, if it ripped his heart out of his chest as it came out of his mouth. "I raped her."

Shock and pain registered in her eyes before she closed them, shutting him out. Tears slipped from beneath her eyelids. Laura yanked her hands from his and wrapped her arms around her body as though trying to protect herself from him—from the pain of the words that still hung in the room. He waited for several minutes as she sat, rocking back and forth in silent misery.

At last he could stand it no longer. He reached out a tentative hand and touched her arm. "Laura."

"No." Her eyes opened but didn't meet his. She stumbled to her feet and staggered from the room. David stayed on the couch, the slapping of her sandals on each step a powerful rebuke. When their bedroom door slammed, he winced. For several minutes, he didn't move. He barely breathed.

Then he heard it—a strange, almost inhuman keening that rent the air. He had only heard that sound once before and it had haunted him for twenty years. It was the sound of pain and suffering so deep, so incomprehensible, that neither words nor weeping could begin to express it. Pressing his face into his hands, he began to sob.

Pain is an interesting Being. I never know for sure, when she shows up, whether she will bring my charges to me or drive them farther away. I don't really know how much control she has over it, but her presence can send them in either direction. Quite often it helps. In fact, at times I have almost wished she would show up, so I could catch someone's attention and spur them to move one way or the other.

Pain was most definitely in David Henley's living room this morning, perched on the arm of the couch, close enough to touch him. I was tempted to sidle between them, to try to somehow protect him with my body, but unfortunately it doesn't work that way. I know. I've tried it before, and it only resulted in my charge rejecting me for good.

So again, I waited. For someone who detests stillness and quiet, I am subjected to both on a regular basis. Someone's idea of humor, I guess. Well, if whoever does it is laughing now, they're the only one, because no one else around here is. They rarely are when Pain is in the room.

I sat cross-legged in a patch of sunlight falling across the taupe carpet and propped my chin on my hand to watch them both. Pain doesn't particularly enjoy her job. She has told me herself that she is happiest when she is walking away from an assignment after her part is done. Even now, her gaze, locked on David's face, is full of compassion.

Of course, she's known him almost as long as I have, and the two of them have spent a lot of time together over the years. She was with him when he left his parents' house and drove to the police station to turn himself in. Actually, a lot of us were. And he'd needed every single one of us to get through that experience.

Today would be no different.

Chapter Forty-Eight

Thursday

The late afternoon sun crept across the living room floor. I made a game out of guessing how long it would take to reach the landmarks along its path. Ten minutes to the footstool, seven more to the edge of the area rug, twelve to the coffee table. It didn't help. The line of light finally inched across to the far side of the room. From my thousands of years of watching the sun rise and set each day I knew the journey couldn't actually have taken weeks, although it felt that way. The light fell across David's face as he lay with his head on the arm of the couch, staring at the ceiling.

The warmth was a rousing caress on his cheek, and David struggled to sit up. He wanted to give Laura time and space, but he needed to see her, to know she was all right. The stairs creaked under his shoes as he trudged up. I pushed to my feet with a deep sigh—not quite as free of self-pity as it should have been—and followed him.

Laura sat in the armchair by the window. Both arms were wrapped around knees clutched to her chest. She stared out the window and didn't move when he entered and crossed the room. He dropped to his knees in front of her. More than anything he wanted to reach out and take her in his arms, but he didn't dare touch her.

His wife gave no sign that she was aware he was there. In shock, probably. Or denial. Finally she turned her face toward him. Her red, swollen eyes made his heart ache. They were dull, as though the light had fizzled and gone out when he'd told her what he'd done.

"Why didn't you tell me before?"

"I didn't want to hurt you. It was in the past. I didn't think you ever needed to know."

I winced. Not that he had anything better to offer, but as

excuses went, those were exceptionally weak.

"You were afraid," she said flatly.

David swallowed. "Yes."

"Was that her? Yesterday?" When he nodded, Laura scrutinized him, her forehead wrinkled. "Why?"

He gazed at her miserably. My fingers went back over my eyes, leaving only a tiny slit for me to peer through.

"There's more, isn't there?"

"Yes."

"Tell me." Her shoulders slumped under the weight that was already too heavy to bear.

"She had a baby. A little girl. I didn't know about her until yesterday. Now her daughter is nineteen and she wants to know about her father."

Laura's face took on a gray pallor, as though life was seeping out of her in front of his eyes. Her lips moved, but he could barely make out the word. "You?"

"I don't know. I had the test yesterday to find out."

Her face dropped into her hands. Not knowing what else to do, he stayed on his knees in front of her until she lifted her head. "Before yesterday, had you seen her since it happened?"

"Only briefly, at my sentencing. But ..." David didn't want to tell her, but he couldn't keep anything from her, not anymore. He took a deep breath. "We have kept in touch, written letters."

"Since we've been married?" Her voice was incredulous.

"Yes. Until three years ago, when I broke off contact with her."

Laura's eyes narrowed as though she was trying to comprehend what he was saying. "Why would she want to stay in touch with you?"

"I'm not sure. I don't think either of us could explain it. Something happened when we were in that cabin. Kathryn started talking to God, and all three of us could feel him right there. I've never experienced anything like it."

"And she was able to forgive you just like that?"

"No, not for three years. I had written to tell her how sorry I was for everything that had happened. I didn't hear from her, but the day I was sentenced she came to the courthouse to give a victim impact statement. While I was waiting for the judge's ruling, she came into the room and confronted me. She asked whether or not I meant what I had written." David pressed his fingers to his temples, overwhelmed by the memory of that day—the pain and joy of the conversation in that little room.

"I said yes. She must have known I was telling the truth, because she told me then that she forgave me. I didn't write again until I was released and wanted to let her know that I was going to Toronto so she wouldn't worry about running into me. She wrote back, and we kept writing until you and I made plans to come to British Columbia and I stopped."

Laura wrung her fingers in her lap. "I need time to think about all of this. Can you give me that?"

"Of course. Take as much time as you need. I'll bring you something to eat. I asked Beth if the boys could spend the night."

She nodded and gazed out the window again.

David sighed and rose to his feet. Grateful to have something to do, he went downstairs to put the last of the dishes away. I trailed along after him, more or less resigned to the fact that there was nothing to do but wait. Again.

He made Laura a sandwich and heated water for tea. It helped him a bit to do those things for her, although I could read the thought loud and clear that driving his fist through a wall would help a lot more.

"I told you I shouldn't tell her," he hissed once, glancing at the ceiling.

Trust her. Trust me.

The tension left his shoulders for the first time since Kathryn had walked through the door of his office the day before.

When we ventured up to the bedroom, Laura hadn't moved from her position by the window. David set the tray on the table beside her. She didn't acknowledge his presence. A stab of agony pierced him, but he left without speaking, determined to honor her request.

At nine o'clock, David was sitting at the desk in his study when Laura descended the stairs. I had almost nodded off in the leather chair by the window, but I rubbed my eyes and focused on her when she stopped in the doorway.

"I'm going for a walk."

His fists clenched under the desk. The idea of her going out in the dark and walking around alone terrified him, especially after everything that had happened. He wasn't in a position to question anything she decided to do at this point, though. Resting his elbows on the desk, he lowered his head into his hands as the front door closed.

David tried to pray, but his heart was too heavy to utter the words. The promise that there was one who would speak for him at a time like this, when grief and fear and sorrow weighed so heavily that no words could be formed, was the only faint light in the darkest night he'd known in twenty years.

Laura returned an hour later. He could only watch as she walked past his door without glancing in and went upstairs. Moving numbly, David built a fire, then twisted his chair around and sat, staring at the flickering flames until they burned down to glowing embers.

I've rarely met a human who didn't agree that physical pain is preferable to heart pain. My male charges in particular seem to find some sort of redemptive value in being plowed between the eyes or socked in the jaw. It's both cleansing and releasing, apparently, and I believe this to be true. I have often observed Guilt slinking away from the scene after the human he has been plaguing has been punched in the nose.

Plaguing is Guilt's special gift, by the way, and not a very nice one. He isn't a favorite among any of us, although we have been forced to put up with his presence ever since the day he and his close buddy Shame laughingly pointed out to the first man and woman that, in case they hadn't noticed, their ... uh, wares were on display for the fallen world to see.

Shame is not a particularly popular guy either, but at least he is generally acknowledged to be productive at times, which helps his reputation somewhat. And he was the one sent to get David Henley's attention in that motel room in Vancouver, which he did, in a big way. He also holds the honor of being the starting point in a sort of spiritual connect-the-dots. You know, shame to remorse to repentance to grace to forgiveness to redemption and, to complete the puzzle, to restoration. This position does earn him a few more invitations to our parties than Guilt receives. To be honest, neither of them gets many of those, since the two of them tend to be regarded as, well, to borrow a rather crude human term, poopers.

But I digress. Waiting inevitably does that to me. Back to the redemptive power of physical pain. David had experienced it that day in prison when he was beaten half to death by the gang he'd refused to pay. A deeply distressing experience and yet, somehow, redemptive.

In most humans, because they are a reflection of their Creator, the sense of justice is strong. And when that justice is meted out, even in an extremely unpleasant way, something deep inside senses it was right, that it was well-deserved. A distant, echoing reminder that one day justice will be perfectly measured out and served. All will be put to right.

Justice is an intimidating Being. He doesn't say much, but when he does, all the Beings tend to stop what they are doing and listen. Frankly, I am more than a little in awe of him. At our parties, he generally stands in one place, arms crossed, looking for all the world like something Michelangelo might have carved out of marble. Only with clothes on, of course.

If he does enter the room, my go-to move is to seek out another Being, someone I can peer around to admire him from a safe distance. Mercy is my first choice, if she's in attendance. And if it isn't a party with dancing. If it is, she's usually only available for a few minutes before he strides across the room and holds out his hand to her. The two of them are always dancing partners and breathtaking to watch. They glide across the floor in flawless synchronicity, the perfect counterpoint to one another. Although he is huge and rippling with muscles and she is more ethereal—like a sheath of fine silk fluttering in the breeze—she never shrinks before him like a lot of us do. The two of them move together in a stunning display of perfectly balanced teamwork that typically results in all of us setting down our drinks, abandoning our conversations, and watching, mouths slightly agape.

The chiming of the clock on the wall above the mantel reined in my rambling thoughts. David raised his head and swung a weary, red-rimmed gaze over his shoulder. Midnight. He needed to see his wife. Joints creaked as he rose and forced his unwilling body to move toward the stairs. A pang of sympathy shot through me when a memory from eleventh grade English class flitted through his mind. If he glanced in a mirror right now, would he find, like Mr. Wilde's Dorian Gray, that overnight he had withered and aged, the consequences of every failing and vice etched across his face for all to see?

David pushed open the bedroom door and stepped into the room. The tray was untouched on the table by the window. Not a great sign, but not surprising. Laura lay curled up on her side of the bed, asleep.

His heart broke at the sight of her tear-stained face. He reached for the blanket folded at the foot of the bed and laid it over her. Then he backed up until he felt the armchair behind him and sank onto it. David sat there for hours, watching his wife. His one fervent thought, repeated over and over, echoed so loudly in my head that, although I had stretched out on the blanket beside her, I knew I wouldn't be going to sleep any time soon.

Please don't let this be the last night we spend in this room together.

Chapter Forty-Nine

Thursday

Thick fog swirled through the bedroom. David fell asleep in the armchair, one head resting on his hand, pain and weariness grooved deeply across his face. *This is all a little much, don't you think?* I shot a glance toward the heavens. *They're only human, you know. How are they supposed to make it through this all alone?*

Alone?

I'm sure He would have laughed at that, except that He never laughed when Pain has wrapped herself so tightly around any of you.

They're never alone.

I scanned the room. It *was* crowded, even here. The load pressing on my shoulders lightened a bit. An idea occurred to me, but I hesitated, pretty sure what the answer would be. Still, it wouldn't hurt to ask, so I lifted my hands in a pleading gesture.

Couldn't you send Deliverance?

I bit my lip and waited through several agonizing seconds of silence. I'd made the request before, although never with as much desire for a positive response. For reasons of his own, the Creator rarely sent Deliverance in. When He did, it was because, presumably, He had decided that pulling one of you out of your trials would be more beneficial, big picture-wise, than allowing you to wade through. Like I said, it didn't hurt to ask. When the answer did come, it was soft and gentle, taking a little of the sting out of the words.

Not this time.

I nodded. I had hoped … But I would have to trust that the Beings that had been sent would be able to bring my charges through to the other side. I took a mental roll call of everyone present, drawing comfort from the results. Unfortunately, it would be harder for David, Laura, and Kathryn to feel that comfort. It always is for human beings—your vision is so limited. You tend to only want to believe what you can see with your eyes, or better yet, reach out and touch with your hands. Unfortunately for you, as it says in the sacred Word, Faith is the evidence of things *not* seen. Of course, that only refers to what can be detected by the human eye, and there are plenty of other ways to see.

Even then, it is possible to choose, even embrace, the blindness.

I sighed and shifted to get more comfortable in my chair. Voluntary blindness. You all choose it, at times. To be fair, we do too, on occasion. It tends to be easier, in the short term. The problem is that easier is rarely better. If David had chosen to see Truth standing in front of him years ago, on the shore of that lake, and agreed to bring him home to meet Laura, I wouldn't be here right now, wondering if he was about to lose everything in his life that was important to him.

Which was entirely possible.

Truth had shown up anyway, even without an invitation. He is a much more patient Being than I am, but he will stand outside and wait only so long. Inevitably there will come a point when he will put a shoulder to the door and shove his way in.

All that remained to be seen now was whether his presence meant that I could stay in this home or be driven away.

Chapter Fifty

Thursday

Nick stabbed his pitchfork into the pile of straw and tossed the load onto the floor of the cattle stall. The bedding already lay thick on the cement floor, and his T-shirt had been clinging to his soaking torso for half an hour, but he refused to quit. He jabbed at the pile again, grunting as he heaved the next forkful into the far corner.

"Is it working?"

He whirled around. James stood next to the stall's open doorway, arms folded on top of the wooden wall.

"What?" Nick stuck the pitchfork into the straw and leaned one arm on the end of it, swiping the other across his forehead.

"Killing yourself to keep from thinking about whatever—or whoever—you're trying not to think about."

Nick shook his head. His brother-in-law knew him well. Too well. He'd come out here often over the years to try and drive thoughts of Kathryn from his head through sheer physical exertion. Clearly he hadn't been as discreet about that as he'd thought. It hadn't worked any of those times either, but it was better than sitting around doing nothing. He jerked the fork loose, ready to stab another load. "I don't know what you're talking about."

"Hey." James walked through the doorway and took the implement from his hands, shoving it into the pile. "Time for a break."

"I don't need a break."

James disappeared through the stall doors. Knowing it was useless to argue, Nick followed him out of the barn. A light summer breeze carried the scents of rain and damp earth, and some of the tension leached from his shoulders as they crossed the yard and climbed the stairs to the wide veranda.

"Sit." James tapped the top of a pale blue Muskoka chair.

"I'll get us something to drink."

Nick stood for a moment, staring at the door that had closed behind his brother-in-law and contemplating fleeing. The last thing he felt like doing at the moment was making conversation, especially since the topic was almost definitely going to come around to the woman he was desperately trying to evict from his mind. *Coward.* He heaved a sigh and dropped onto the chair. His eyes scratched from the dust and dirt hanging thick in the air of the barn, and he closed his eyelids and rubbed them with his fingers.

"Here."

Nick jumped when a cool glass touched the back of his hand. He reached for the bottle of cola James held out to him. "Thanks."

"No problem." His brother-in-law settled on the rocking chair beside him and took a sip from his own bottle. Neither of them spoke for a few minutes. The loud chirping of the crickets swelled as the sun dipped low in the sky, draping the farmyard in an orange glow.

Nick relaxed in his chair. It did feel good to get off his feet. He lifted the bottle and downed half its contents. The cold liquid dampened his dry throat, and he sighed with contentment. He set the bottle between his knees and eyed the last of the sunset through the maple trees in the front yard. Maybe they could sit in silence and enjoy the peace and quiet for a while.

"So?" James prompted.

He should have known James wouldn't let him off that easily. Nick kept his gaze focused on the western sky. "So what?"

"You wanna talk about it?"

"Do I have a choice?"

"No."

Nick let out a short laugh and took another sip before facing his friend. Worry lines were etched into the contours of his face, but they didn't dim the laughter in the depths of his bright blue eyes. Nick frowned. Even when James and Halyna had been going through their darkest valley, the laughter was still there at the end. How had he managed that? How had he not let his life end when hers did?

"It's Kathryn." Nick set the bottle on the wide arm of the chair.

"I figured that."

"I went to see her a few days ago."

"And it didn't go well, I take it?"

Nick mulled the question over in his mind. "I wouldn't say that. In fact, for a few brief moments I thought we might finally work things out."

"What happened?"

"What always happens. She pulled away. I don't know why I even bother."

James didn't answer.

Nick held out as long as he could before letting out a heavy breath. "What?"

"Do you really not know why you bother?"

"I don't suppose there's any chance I can get out of you telling me."

A slow grin crossed his friend's face. "Nope. Not that you need me to."

Nick started to rise. "You're right, I don't. Good night." And he didn't. He knew exactly why he bothered. And he also knew he had no right to be so frustrated. Kathryn's request had been reasonable—she only wanted a few days to make sure she'd let go of the past once and for all. He definitely did want her to do that.

A strong hand clapped over his arm, and he sank onto the chair.

"You love her."

He thought about it but decided against arguing. He'd lost that same argument with himself a dozen times—it wasn't likely he'd fare any better against his brother-in-law. "Maybe. But I'm not sure that's enough."

"It's enough."

His head jerked at the quiet words. James sounded so confident. How could he know for sure?

The grip on his arm tightened. "It's not always enough, I know. But I've watched this thing with you and Kathryn play out for years. I know you've faced more challenges than most people ever have to, but you've weathered each one. There's no question in my mind that the two of you are meant to be together, and in spite of your feeble arguments—" He raised a hand when Nick started to protest. "I know there's no question in your mind either. It's always been a matter of time with the two of you, and I have a very strong feeling that the time is now."

Nick winced. He hated when James was right, although he should be used to it by now. And maybe, in this case, he didn't want him to be wrong. "I thought so too."

His mother loved to tell the story—usually in a mildly accusatory tone—of how long Nick had taken to decide he wanted to come out and see the world. Her due date had approached and then passed by, and she didn't go into labor for another two weeks. According to her, the two weeks after she had reached what she'd thought was the finish line seemed longer than the previous nine months combined.

He now understood what she meant. After waiting so long to go to Kathryn and finally coming to a place where he believed their time of waiting had come to an end, each additional day felt at least a year long. Still, it wasn't fair to take out his impatience on her. Especially since he had been the one to ask for more time the last couple of times they had seen each other.

"When are you going to get her?"

"She said she needed a few days."

"Ah, a light at the end of the tunnel this time. You didn't mention that."

Nick's eyes narrowed. "Don't be smug. It's not pretty on you."

James laughed. "Too bad. I've always wanted to be pretty. So when are you going back?"

Nick let out a hiss of exasperation. "Like a dog with a bone, aren't you? I don't know for sure."

James stared into his soda for a minute. "Remember when Halyna and I first met?"

Her name still stung, but a little less with every passing year. "Sure."

"She pushed me away with everything she had in her." James chuckled. "Stubborn as a mule, that one."

"I remember." Nick rubbed a patch of condensation off the neck of the cola bottle with his thumb. "I sat on this porch with her a hundred times while she went over the long list of reasons why the two of you couldn't be together."

"She gave me the same list every time I came to see her. She was determined that she was going to work through everything that stood between us, mostly the cancer, on her own."

"What did you do?"

"I listened. And when she ordered me to go, I left. And then I gave her a few days to miss me and come to her senses." James shot him a grin before taking a swig from his bottle. When he lowered it, he looked thoughtful. "I always picked a day when I'd come here again. Helped me stay away. And stay sane, for that matter."

"Did you ever wish you'd listened to her and not come back?"

James didn't hesitate. "Never."

"Good to know."

"It might help with all this pent-up tension if you had a day to work toward."

"What pent-up—" Nick exhaled loudly when James's eyebrows rose. "Okay, fine." He threw a hand in the air. "Sunday."

His brother-in-law nodded but didn't speak. After a few moments, he raised his bottle and tipped it toward Nick. "To Sunday, then."

He lifted his drink and clinked it against the one James held out. "To Sunday."

In spite of losing yet another argument to his brother-in-law, a smile twitched at the corners of Nick's lips as he tilted the bottle and drained the last of his drink.

Chapter Fifty-One

Friday

Sometime around dawn, David's thoughts finally stilled long enough for me to doze off. Light pouring into the room and the loud chirping of a blue jay outside the window woke us both a few hours later. *She's gone.* David jumped to his feet and made his way downstairs, searching in every room. Even as he did, he knew he wouldn't find her. The house was too quiet, too empty.

I clambered onto the kitchen counter to watch him as he held the kettle under the tap in the kitchen sink and tried, with shaking fingers, to plug it into the wall. I was feeling a little better today, stronger, because I knew something he didn't yet, although I wasn't entirely sure what it meant. A flash of pink in the backyard caught his eye as he trudged past the window above the sink. The mug he'd been holding slipped from his hands and fell to the floor with a crash.

David stepped over the mess and strode to the back door. I leapt from the counter and followed him, eager to find out which way the wind was blowing this morning. The soft breeze, with its familiar scent of jasmine, brushed past us as I followed him to the deck chair Laura sat in on the back patio. I studied her face as I licked a finger and held it in the air. Ah, definitely blowing in from the south. Not quite a Zephyr—too much of a bite to it— more of an unexpected but very welcome Chinook. The type of wind that, while it did tend to melt the snows after a long, cold winter, more often than not brought with it a great deal of rain. Fitting, as David and Laura were likely to face a bit of weather yet before all of this was over.

"Laura." Tremendous relief washed over David. If nothing else, she was still there.

He dragged a chair over and sat in front of her, arms resting on his knees as he met her eyes. They were still red and swollen and fresh tears sparkled on her cheeks, but something else shimmered in their depths—a peace that hadn't been there the night before.

"I won't stay. But I haven't told you yet that I'm sorry. I'm so sorry for what I did, and even more sorry that I kept the truth from you for so long. I didn't trust you enough, and I didn't trust God enough. I don't even know how to ask you to forgive me."

Laura held up her hand. "What you told me yesterday, I never would have believed it if you hadn't told me yourself. I feel numb right now, like I'm in shock. It's going to take time for me to think this through."

"I understand. I'm willing to wait as long as it takes." David hesitated. "Do you want me to go? Move out for a while?"

Laura shook her head. "I keep thinking about that woman, Kathryn. If she could forgive you and God could forgive you, I don't see how I couldn't. In time. Right now the only thing I know is that I'm not going anywhere, and I don't want you to either."

His chest squeezed. There was nothing he wanted more than to reach out and touch his wife, wipe the tears from her face, but he clasped his hands together. He had no right—not now. But Laura had given him more than he had dared to dream of. She had given him hope. And for now that was more than enough.

I shook my head in amazement. I wouldn't have predicted this the day before, but apparently Hope and I were going to be allowed to stay. The road ahead of David and Laura wouldn't be easy, but if we hadn't been kicked out yet, there was a strong chance that we could finally settle in and get comfortable here.

Good, because at the moment, my attention was desperately needed somewhere else.

Chapter Fifty-Two

Friday

Kathryn bolted upright in bed. Nightmares had kept her from any kind of sleep that actually might strengthen her for the day ahead. The abrupt movement jolted me from my semi-conscious state, and I straightened in my chair. Although her eyes were red and her cheeks stained with tears, the sheets around Kathryn lay flat against the mattress. Terror and Pain and Horror, who had climbed onto the mattress next to her sometime in the night, were gone. Faith was curled up at the foot of the bed, her head resting on one arm as she watched Kathryn. She hadn't left then. Deep inside I'd known she wouldn't, but in the thick black of night it's sometimes a lot easier to listen to Doubt—another one who rarely gets invited to our parties—and start to wonder.

My hands trembled, but when I lifted them slowly to my face I could make out every line and wrinkle. Bright light streamed through the branches of the oak tree to fall across my feet. The cold mist dissipated under its gentle touch, and I wiggled my toes in relief.

Like David, Kathryn and I had survived another night.

Kathryn flung away the covers and swung her legs off the side of the bed. I dropped my hands as she stalked across the room and grabbed the silk housecoat from its hook on the back of her bedroom door. I gripped the arms of the chair and pushed to my feet. Now what?

Leaning heavily on the railing, I descended the stairs stiffly and wandered through the empty kitchen. The sound of crumpling paper drew me to the living room. The shoebox was lying upside-down on the couch, the letters scattered across the cushions and the floor. Kathryn struck a match and tossed it on a pile of newspapers she had shoved into the stove. Whirling away from the flames, she strode to the couch and dropped to her knees. She gathered up all the envelopes, leaving a single, folded sheet of paper on the couch, and dug her elbow into the cushion to push herself up.

Before the flickering fire could die, she started tossing letters into the stove. The flames flared as the envelopes caught and began to shrivel and turn brown. I wasn't sure why—her thoughts were too scattered and incoherent for me to follow them—but she glanced at each letter before throwing it in with the others. Twice she tugged one loose from the pile and dropped it on the floor. When they were the only two left of the ones she'd carried to the stove, she shut the woodstove door with a loud clang, snatched the envelopes, and staggered to the couch.

Fear padded across the room, yellow eyes gleaming and tail swishing. Which meant that, while Faith had stayed, sometime in the night Peace had retreated. Too bad. Although I'd suspected it wouldn't last, the short reprieve yesterday had been nice.

Bumps rose on Kathryn's flesh as Fear passed by. Sinking to the floor with her back to the couch, Kathryn drew both knees to her chest and, clutching the letters tightly, rested her head on her folded arms. And suddenly I understood exactly where she was planning to go now. When she shut off her thoughts completely— trying to calm herself, no doubt—I filled in the blank space by going over a conversation that she had not been privy to, but which had set in motion the chain of events that had brought her to this moment.

February 2016

"Well, son, I'm sure you can imagine our most serious concern with your application."

"Yes, sir." David wiped his damp hands on the front of his navy pants then clasped them in his lap. Although the dream of becoming a minister hadn't been his to begin with, in taking the steps to follow the calling he'd received in prison, that's exactly what it had become. The huge question of whether or not a church, aware of his past, would actually take him on in this position remained—a question that would be answered in the next few minutes. If not, David would be driven to his knees in an attempt to find out where he was expected to go from here. He took a deep breath, trying to slow the rapid beating of his heart.

"Your training and experience are well in line with what we're searching for in the leadership of this church. However ..." The head of the board of elders, Ed Schaeffer, blue eyes sparkling beneath thick white eyebrows that rose now as he shuffled through the pile of papers in front of him, glanced over at him. "Your past offences, particularly the latest charge and the years spent in prison, are a grave consideration for us, of course."

David nodded. "I understand that. I have no defence for my past actions except to say that, after giving my life to God, I'm not the same man I was."

The head elder nodded. David noticed the others around the table—four men and three women—all with their eyes fixed on him, also nodded.

One of the women spoke up. "We've talked to a number of people about you. Their testimonies appear to confirm that, indeed, you are a changed man. For example, the warden at Kent Institution speaks very highly of you."

"Warden Peters has been incredibly supportive. It was his recommendation that got me into Bible school in the first place."

"Which says a great deal about your conduct at Kent." Ed Schaeffer fixed his gaze on him. "We have spoken to several of the professors you studied under as well as the dean of your college. The pastor you worked with in Toronto commended your work, your character, and your dedication." He rested a gnarled hand on top of the papers. "We are all sinners, David, every one of us. And all saved by grace, thank the Lord, or none of us would be here around this table. Even the apostle Paul zealously murdered believers before his experience on the Damascus Road. Chief of sinners, he called himself. Yet he was personally responsible for building up the early church and the spread of the gospel around the world."

David winced. "Chief of sinners. I would certainly put myself in that category—until I had my own Damascus Road experience in a cheap motel outside Vancouver seventeen years ago."

Ed chuckled. "That's a story I'd like to hear one day." He sobered as he met David's gaze again.

His stomach muscles tightened. *Here we go.*

"We are all in agreement that you are the man we'd like to have lead our congregation. That being said, we are responsible for the care and safety of this congregation. The position comes with the stipulation that at no time will you meet alone with any female member of the church. That is the policy of many male pastors anyway, and it's generally a good principle to follow."

The muscles in his stomach began to unwind. Were they really offering him a church of his own? "I understand completely."

"As well, after much discussion, we have determined that what you have told us, and the research we have done into your past on our own, will remain between the nine of us. Your transformation appears to be real and complete, and no one here will hold your past against you. In fact, I see no reason it ever needs to come up again."

Good, because my wife doesn't even know. Guilt wormed through him, but he worked to keep his face steady as the head elder continued.

"At New Hope Church, we believe very strongly—as our name indicates—that people can change. In fact, we believe it's impossible to have an encounter like the one in the motel you mentioned without being completely transformed. We hope that you will accept our offer to fill the position of head pastor at New Hope. We'd be happy to welcome you on board."

More grace. There never seemed to be a limit to the amount extended to him, and David couldn't be more thankful for that, being in need of so much of it. He stood and held out his hand to Ed, who grasped it firmly in his own. "I'm honored by your offer, sir. And humbled. I do need to ask for a few days to discuss this with my wife and one or two other people, but I'll let you know as soon as I can."

"Of course. Take all the time you need. This is a big decision, so we'll wait to hear from you." The other board members in the room all shook his hand as well. David studied their faces but found no trace of judgment or uncertainty on any of them. He was overwhelmed. His own church and now the opportunity to come home. Both of those prospects filled him with equal parts excitement and fear.

No decision could be made, however, until he had contacted the one who would be the most affected by his return to British Columbia. He had no idea how she would react to the possibility of him being so close again, but he was determined to abide by her wishes on this. David had done everything he could to follow the plan laid out for him to this point in his life. The rest was up to God.

And Kathryn Ellison.

Chapter Fifty-Three

Friday

I contemplated the envelopes in Kathryn's hand—the last two David Henley had ever sent her. Would she be able to throw them in the fire with the rest? They had been written to shut a door, but by keeping them Kathryn had wedged a foot in the opening and not allowed that to happen. Closing doors always seemed so much harder than opening them. So many things could get in the way, could keep them propped open, if only a little. I'd seen it often enough over the millennia to know that sometimes what slipped through was good, as with the door she'd left cracked open with Nick.

Other times, it was the deadliest of Beings that squeezed through the smallest of openings.

March 2016

"Go, Stars!" Kathryn slid to the edge of her seat. The Surrey Stars, Tory's high school basketball team, were involved in a nail-biter, fighting it out with Richmond. *Come on. Come on.*

With less than a minute on the clock, Surrey was behind by four points. They started out of their own end. Tory's best friend, Carly, a tall, slender redhead and captain of the team, had control of the ball. The team jogged down the court. Carly passed the ball to her teammate Jamey, who returned it. Carly jumped into the air and slammed the ball into the net.

"Yes!" Kathryn leapt to her feet along with the rest of the cheering, screaming fans. Twenty-nine seconds on the clock. The Richmond team started back. Jamey jumped in front of the player with the ball and knocked it out from under her hand. Suddenly Surrey had control again. The seconds ticked down. Kathryn clasped her hands in front of her face, afraid to watch.

Jamey passed the ball to Tory, who maneuvered around an

opposing player. Three seconds on the clock. Two seconds. Tory slammed the ball against the floor. It rebounded into Carly's hands. From outside the zone, the team captain launched the ball. Everyone in the gym drew in a collective breath and held it. The basketball arced through the air. At the sound of the buzzer, it dropped with a swish into the net. The gymnasium erupted.

"Yes! Way to go, Tory!" Kathryn scrambled down the bleacher stairs and crossed the gym floor. She gave her daughter a quick hug before Tory was pulled into the circle of exuberant teammates.

Kathryn stepped back. *I know, I know, you want to celebrate with your friends. Believe it or not, I remember what that was like.*

She waited outside the dressing room for Tory and her teammates to emerge. Jamey had invited three of them to her place for a sleepover after the game, and Kathryn had offered to drive them.

"You know, Mom, I could drive myself," Tory had responded when she made the offer.

"I know. But—"

"But you don't want to see me growing up and doing things on my own." Her smile took a little of the sting out of the words, but there was a lot of truth to them.

It was hard for Kathryn to see her little girl growing up. It was Tory's first day of kindergarten all over again. Her independent daughter was ready to leave her behind and strike out on her own, and there was nothing she could do to stop her. Not that she really wanted to. She was proud of Tory and loved her feistiness and self-assurance. Still, it was hard to let go when it had been the two of them for so long.

When she stopped the car in front of Jamey's place, Kathryn glanced at the house.

"Jamey's parents are here." Tory intercepted her look. "Thanks for the ride, Mom. I'll be home around noon tomorrow, okay?"

"Okay." Loaded down with boxes of pizza, the girls poured

out of the vehicle and surged toward the house. "Have fun and be good," Kathryn added when she was sure they were out of earshot. She shifted the car into gear and reversed out of the driveway. Groaning, she rubbed her neck to work out a kink.

All she wanted was to go home and relax in front of the fire with a cup of tea. "Kathryn, you're getting old." These days she felt much older than her thirty-nine years. "Maybe because a lot of women my age are still having babies and my baby is growing up way too fast." She wrinkled her nose when she realized she was talking to herself in the empty car. Definitely getting old.

Meg and Aaron had turned on several of the house lights for her before heading to their smaller home on the property. Her parents were in Arizona where they spent winters now that she and Aaron had taken over running the ranch, so Kathryn had the place to herself. The house was really too large for her and Tory. Kathryn had offered to switch with Aaron and Meg since there were four of them, but they loved their cozy log house on the property and didn't want to move.

With a sigh, Kathryn slipped off her shoes and padded across the kitchen floor. The house seemed so big and empty all of a sudden. Who would she talk to when Tory moved out in a couple of years?

Nick.

She froze halfway across the kitchen floor and pressed a hand to her stomach. Halyna's funeral had only taken place a couple of months ago. Nick wouldn't be ready to move on from that loss any time soon.

Still, she could call him. Even if it wasn't the right time, he would come.

But it wouldn't be fair of her. Kathryn closed her eyes, picturing him there in her kitchen. The feel of his arms around her was so strong that for a moment he was as real as the whistle of the kettle on the stove.

Kathryn's eyes flew open. "Stop it. I don't want to think about that tonight." She felt alone enough in the quiet house without thoughts of Nick making the place—and her life—seem even emptier than it was.

Inhaling the soothing aroma of chamomile tea, she carried her steaming cup to the kitchen table. Aaron or Meg had obviously gotten the mail, as a pile sat in the middle of the table. Kathryn took a sip of tea as she flipped idly through the pile. David's familiar handwriting scrawled across the front of one of the envelopes stole her breath. Had Aaron seen this? Not likely, or he'd have been waiting in the house when she arrived, demanding answers.

Her chest tight, she set the mug on the table and picked up the envelope. A few weeks earlier she'd received another note from David. Like always, she had opened it with a mix of trepidation and anticipation.

Kathryn,

I'm writing to let you know that I've been offered a church, New Hope Community, in Maple Ridge, B.C. I asked for time to think about it, because I needed to know how you'd feel about me coming back. Please be honest. The last thing I want is for you to be worried about running into me in a grocery store or on the street one day.

I know you've worked hard to put the past behind you, and I'd never want to do anything to stir up painful memories. I'll wait to hear from you before I give them my answer.

David

When she had finished reading that letter, Kathryn had sat at her desk for a long time. David had served his time and had every right to come home. Still, her stomach had clenched at the thought that she might run into him somewhere. What if Tory was with her?

The words had caught in her throat when she'd tried to pray. What was she so afraid of? Maple Ridge was an hour away, and she knew which church he'd be at. The chances of running into him were small. Even so, the thought of him being that close …

She'd closed her eyes and whispered, "Tell me what to do." Only then had she been able to write and give him her answer.

The fingers that grasped the envelope were trembling. He was writing to let her know his decision. A shudder passed through her and she dropped the piece of mail on the table and took another sip of tea, hoping the hot liquid would help. It didn't. Somehow she knew that, whatever David said in this letter, nothing would be the same between them again.

Forcing herself to let go of the warm mug, Kathryn removed the letter from the envelope and scanned the words.

Kathryn,

Thank you for your letter encouraging me to come home. I don't think I could have come back to B.C. before now, but I'm sure that, outside of Vancouver anyway, no one will remember ever hearing my name, let alone the details of something that happened seventeen years ago in a different town.

New Hope is a small church, and I feel it's where I'm supposed to be. Now that I have your blessing, I'm more convinced than ever that God is leading me home. Although I understand if you'd rather not see me again, I want you to know that if there's ever anything you need, my door at New Hope will be open to you.

David

Kathryn bit her lip. What was it about this letter that caused such a stab of pain in her heart? The tone was friendly and kind, but she sensed a pulling back, a distancing of himself from her that she'd never felt before.

Reading the letter over again, she understood. The revelation should have relieved her, but instead she felt the deep, dull ache of unexpected loss. Tears welled in her eyes and fell onto the paper, smearing a few of the words. As apprehensive as she'd been about him returning to British Columbia, she hadn't been prepared for this, either.

After seventeen years and all they had been through together, David Henley was saying goodbye.

Friday

Kathryn lifted her head. Another tear had tracked its way down her cheek, and she swiped it away with the back of her hand. She had always been impatient with tears. From our long association, I knew she had rarely shed any before That Night. But afterwards, well, I never knew a human being could drain so much liquid from her body without shriveling up and blowing away in the wind. And not only her—Aaron, her mother, her father, her friends. Combined, they'd shed more tears than anyone could count in a lifetime.

Except for the Creator, of course. They say He collects each one and, knowing His heart, I believe that is true, although I've never seen it. I do hope that the bottle reserved for the tears of this family is a big one, because I have a feeling that, as full as it must be by now, if there isn't a lot of room left at the top, sometime in the next few days it could very well overflow.

Chapter Fifty-Four

Friday

David sat behind the big oak desk in his office at the church, trying to work. He grabbed a reference book from one of the shelves that lined the walls and flipped through it aimlessly. Exhaling in frustration, he slammed it shut.

I jumped and threw him a reproachful glare, for all the good it would do me. I took a deep breath, trying to calm down. The fact that my last nerve was being stomped on this week was not his fault. Not entirely, anyway. And if I was jumpy, I could hardly blame him for practically climbing the bookshelves that lined the walls of his office. There was little chance he would be able to concentrate on anything this morning but the phone call that could come any minute—the call that could change his life.

David swung his chair around and stared out the window, resting his chin on his clasped hands. *A daughter. I could have a daughter.* The thought moved him more than he cared to admit. Not that he would have any rights whatsoever where she was concerned, but still … What was she like? Hopefully she took after her mother, no matter who her father turned out to be.

I tried to keep up with his thoughts. He jumped from one to the next as though they were stepping stones in the creek he used to play in when he was a little boy. His next leap took him to Kathryn—what he knew of her, her faith, her character. In spite of the questionable genes on her father's side, Victoria Ellison had likely turned out to be a wonderful woman. He shoved to his feet and walked around the room, shaking his hands in an attempt to burn off excess nervous energy. I sincerely hoped it would work, as the frantic pace of his movements and his thoughts was wearing me out, especially since he hadn't visited the coffee machine down the hall yet, something he usually did as soon as he entered the building.

He jumped to another stepping stone. If he was her father,

would Kathryn be willing to share anything about their daughter—her interests, her talents, her plans for the future? He let out a short laugh. If Tory was as determined as her mother said—and she had to be to force Kathryn to come to him in person—then maybe he'd get a chance to meet her in person. Once, anyway.

David slipped from that last rock and landed hard, both feet in the water. All of this was useless speculation until he got the results of the test. He dropped his gaze to the phone on his desk and willed it to ring, then changed his mind and prayed that it wouldn't. He needed more time. So much had happened in the last forty-eight hours that his mind couldn't process the information it had already received.

And Laura. David sank onto his chair. What must she be going through right now? He thought back on that morning. After he'd come in from the backyard, he'd gone upstairs to get ready for work. The last thing he wanted to do was leave her, but he'd given the doctor his office number because he didn't want to get the call with the results at home, so he needed to go to the church. When he came downstairs, his wife had been sitting at the kitchen table with a cup of coffee. The mug he'd used every morning of their married life had been swept into the garbage. Like the proverbial straw, that small loss sent a pang through him out of all proportion. He grabbed another mug out of the cupboard and filled a cup for himself before sliding onto a chair across from her.

Neither of them spoke for a few minutes, until she glanced up. "It's amazing how you never see them coming."

"What?"

"The days that change your life forever." She smiled to ease the pain of her words, but David felt the sting anyway. "I mean, you can be out running errands, or emptying the dishwasher, or…" she took a deep breath. "… racing for a computer like the day we met, things you've done a thousand times." Laura rubbed her thumb over the mug clutched between her fingers. "Then, in a minute, in seconds, everything changes."

David stared into his own mug, not sure what to say to her, how to ease the suffering she was going through. Then he felt her hand on his and glanced up. Immediately, she withdrew it and wrapped her fingers around her blue "World's Greatest Mom" mug again, but that brief touch, the few seconds of contact between them, filled his heart with hope.

"You have to go."

Not sure if he could speak around the lump that had formed in his throat, he nodded.

"It's okay." Her voice shook a little. "Come home when you know."

David had waited another few seconds, until she'd smiled weakly, before he had swallowed the last of his coffee and left her sitting at the table.

He swung his chair around, picked up a pen, and tapped it on the wooden desk. When the clock on the wall behind him began to chime, he counted the low, echoing bongs. Eight, nine, ten and then silence. In disbelief, he swiveled his head around to check. It seemed impossible that only an hour had passed since he'd arrived at the office.

This was crazy. It could be hours yet, maybe even tomorrow, before he found out anything. *I need coffee.* The pent-up energy that propelled him to his feet told him more caffeine was probably the last thing he needed. Unwilling to sit at his desk another minute, however, he headed for the door.

The phone on the desk rang.

I clenched my fists in frustration. So close.

David froze, his heart pounding. After three rings, he forced himself to let go of the door knob and shuffle across the room. A second before the answering machine clicked on, he leaned across the desk and grabbed the receiver, nearly dropping it in his haste.

"Hello?" He turned his head and cleared his throat. I strained to hear the voice on the other end of the line. "Yes, hi. I've been waiting for your call." He listened in silence for a moment. "Thank you. I appreciate you letting me know." Not sure the person had finished speaking, David replaced the receiver. He'd heard everything he needed to know, and so had I. He rounded his desk and sank onto the chair, his knees nearly buckling beneath him. Resting both elbows on the wooden surface, he dropped his face into his hands.

The minutes ticked by as he sat, not moving. I clasped my hands in my lap to keep them still. The man had been given momentous news—I could allow him a few minutes to absorb it. Not that I had any alternative. When the clock chimed again, eleven times, he finally raised his head. *Kathryn. I need to see her.* For the second time that morning, he picked up the receiver with trembling hands. He dialed the cell number Kathryn had given him. It rang two, three, four times. She wasn't going to answer. He was almost relieved.

Not wanting to leave a message, he was about to set the receiver on the cradle when he heard her voice.

"Hello?"

He quickly pressed the phone to his ear. "Kathryn, it's David."

Silence greeted his words. They'd never talked on the phone before. That fact alone, without the added weight of the news he was calling to tell her, had to be causing her to reel somewhat. David waited patiently.

"I've been expecting your call." Her voice was thin and strained.

"I have the results. Could we meet somewhere?"

Silence again as Kathryn contemplated his question. When she sighed, I knew she had waged a momentous battle with herself. "Where?"

"There's a rest stop on Highway 99 with a gazebo that looks out over Boundary Bay. Do you know it?"

A brief pause. "Yes, I know it."

"Can you meet me there? In half an hour?"

"I'll be there."

David didn't move until a loud, insistent beeping reminded

him that he still clutched the receiver in his hand. He managed—barely—to set it in the holder, then grabbed his jacket off the coat rack by the door and headed to his car. Maybe he should have called Laura first, but he wanted to give his wife the news in person. And he needed for his conversation with Kathryn to be over when he did, so he didn't have to leave Laura after telling her what he'd learned.

I followed David across the parking lot, shaking slightly myself from a combination of heightened apprehension and lowered coffee inhalation. Frankly, I couldn't help thinking that I'd have a much better chance of surviving the next couple of hours if only those two things were reversed.

Chapter Fifty-Five

Friday

The gazebo sat overlooking the ocean, along a pathway that wound behind a patch of trees. I couldn't see if Kathryn had arrived yet, although there was one other car in the parking lot. The hands that gripped the steering wheel were damp and David wiped them on his jeans, taking several deep breaths in an attempt to slow the rapid beating of his heart.

He grasped hold of the door handle, pushed it open with his shoulder, and climbed out of the car. The heaviness in his feet was familiar, but I'm sure that didn't make the walk along the winding path any easier. The roar of the surf against the shore pounded in his ears and he tasted the salt that hung in the air at the edge of the ocean.

When the gazebo came into view he stopped, his breath swept from him. A hillside, dotted with rocks and tufts of grass, sloped downward until it gave way to green, frothy water lapping against the sand. Seagulls dipped and rose above waves that broke white beneath them. Kathryn faced the water, her long dark hair blowing in the wind that swept in from the ocean.

His chest ached. She had suffered so much anguish—much of it at his hands. David took another step toward the gazebo. Several small stones gave way under his feet and skittered across the path.

Kathryn turned.

Neither moved as a look passed between them. Then she smiled, faintly. David forced himself to smile in return, hoping to ease the trepidation on her face. The ground seemed to shift beneath his feet, and he clung to the railing as he climbed the stairs to where she waited, her face pale against the backdrop of sea and sky. If only there was something he could say or do to make this easier for her.

Well aware of the intensity of the situation, I climbed onto the white wooden gazebo railing and wrapped both arms around a post, figuring the most productive thing I could do was stay out of the way.

As though trying to read the answer to the question that was creasing lines of worry across her forehead, she searched his eyes.

David stopped in front of her, wanting to see her face when he told her. "Kathryn."

She nodded. He laid his hand, palm up, on the gazebo railing. Her gaze dropped to it, then sought out his face again.

He hadn't touched her since that night in the cabin—had never touched her except in anger and violence—so he couldn't imagine the struggle she faced now in spite of the forgiveness and healing that had taken place in the last twenty years. "It's all right," he said softly. "You don't have to—"

The movement stopped him.

Her eyes never left his face as she slowly raised her hand and set it on his.

A tremor passed through him at her touch, and he blinked away tears, overwhelmed at the gift she offered. "Thank you for meeting me. I needed to see you, to tell you the results face to face." His voice caught and he closed his fingers over hers. "I'm not the father, Kathryn. Victoria is not my daughter."

The words appeared to crash over her and she swayed on her feet. David squeezed her hand, afraid she might collapse, but she drew in a deep breath and stilled. "I was hoping ..." She stopped and closed her eyes. When she opened them again, his stomach clenched at the agony there. "How can I tell her?"

A bench lined the interior wall of the gazebo and he led her to it. Still holding tightly to her hand, he gave her a moment to take in the news.

A faint light shone in her eyes when they met his. "At least now Laura won't have to know."

She must have seen the shadow cross his face. Her shoulders slumped. "You told her."

David nodded. "She was devastated, but I think we're going to be able to work through it." He contemplated her, as always unable to understand the force of their connection. A wave of sadness wracked his body. *I have to let her go.* In spite of the realization, he couldn't bring himself to release the hand that had been given to him with such trust.

A look of understanding passed between them, and his grip on her hand tightened. "Goodbye, Kathryn."

She nodded. He forced himself to release her and stumble down the gazebo stairs and up the pathway. Before he rounded the curve that would take her out of sight, he took one last look.

Kathryn stood, framed against the ocean, one hand holding back the hair that blew around her face and shoulders. David closed his eyes and froze the picture in his mind, knowing that was how he would remember her as he turned and walked away.

Being immortal, and omnipresent, I have never been able to fully grasp the depth of emotion that can be felt by two human beings who know they are saying goodbye to each other for the last time, on earth anyway. I have had to walk away from humans and have watched many die, but always in the back of my mind is the sure knowledge that I could see them again whenever I chose. And I have been able to find and be found by other Beings at any time and place since the creation of Eden. Never have I left any of them knowing there was a possibility that I might never see them again.

Frankly, there are more than a few for whom the degree of sadness I'd feel over that would be very small.

Watching David and Kathryn today—and allowing myself to tap into her pain sensors and think and feel everything she did as he walked away from her—gave me a new appreciation for the heartache and grief that accompanies all endings.

And that understanding lent a new fervor to my prayers that there would be no more endings like that in her life.

Or, at the very least, not in the next few days.

Chapter Fifty-Six

Friday

Kathryn sat at her desk, trying to work on the books. Knowing her as well as I did, I understood why she had decided she needed to work right now, after seeing David that morning and in the midst of everything that was going on. She was in desperate need of a distraction. I understood the feeling, although my desperate need at the moment was for sleep. I had stretched out on her bed, hoping for a short nap, but the thoughts whirling through her head buzzed through mine like the sound of heavy traffic outside the window, making rest impossible.

Kathryn tried to add numbers, but over and over again they refused to come out right. Maybe because she had no idea what she was typing into the computer.

A cold tremor snaked up her spine. I raised myself on my elbows as she rubbed her hands over her arms, trying to dispel the chill that shook her body in spite of the warm day. I didn't have to read her mind to know that she was thinking about Nick and how much she'd give to feel his arms around her right now. Her gaze dropped to the cell phone on her desk and her arm shifted toward it. Would she give in and call him?

I shifted on the bed, trying to get more comfortable. The timing still wasn't right, but that hadn't stopped a lot of people from charging ahead into a relationship. It would be easy, but she'd regret it. They'd waited so long—it would be too bad if they gave in now, when they were so close. I held my breath, but she pulled her knees to her chest and tightened her arms around them. Her thoughts weren't whirring now, they had stopped abruptly, as though all that traffic humming in her brain had been brought to a screeching halt by a sickening crash of a thought that left it in one crumpled, smoking heap.

Kevin Dylan, cold-blooded killer on death row, was the father of her little girl.

Horror coursed through her. I grimaced. I could never indulge in the enticing tastes of coffee or fresh bread or dark, rich chocolate, but I could taste that emotion like a bitter poison on my tongue.

A gentle breeze blew through the bedroom window, and Kathryn closed her eyes. Warm fingers trailed across her face and arms, drawing the icy horror from her. The sweet scent in the air washed away the bitter taste in my mouth, and I flopped onto the pillow and crossed my arms behind my head. A calm settled over my charge that she hadn't felt since she'd talked with David in the gazebo—since their conversation had stirred up dark memories of Kevin Dylan once again.

Forgive him.

Kathryn raised her head. The curtains that had rippled in the wind settled against the window pane.

Forgive him.

"No. You cannot ask me to do that. It's too much."

But He could ask. And so could Forgiveness. She might be high-maintenance and demanding, but never without a reason. She and Compassion are often linked together—something that, since I am not petty, does not bother me at all—and I am well aware of her endgame. She knows the weight of unforgiveness is staggering and desperately wants to see every one of you give it up. Only then can Peace move in and take up permanent residence.

You have to appreciate her motives, even if what she asks of you seems more than you can hope to accomplish on your own.

Which, of course, it is.

Kathryn stared out the window at the darkening sky. Long tendrils of cloud, tinged rose and orange by the sun that had sunk below the top of the barn, stretched across the horizon. "He's not even sorry," she whispered.

The sound of chirping crickets, swelling as dusk settled over the ranch, soothed her roiling thoughts as it had done every summer evening since she was a child. With a soft sigh, Kathryn rested her cheek on her folded arms.

"I'll try."

Chapter Fifty-Seven

Friday

Kathryn stretched and groaned before pushing back her chair. She'd be wanting tea.

Weariness clung to me like wisps of cobweb as I followed her into the kitchen. Holding the kettle under the tap, she filled it to the top. A sharp knock sounded on the screen door. Kathryn froze, the box of teabags in her hand. She wasn't ready. Not yet.

"Kath?"

The tension and anticipation that had tightened her shoulders dissipated, and she set down the box and hurried across the room. "Meg. Come in." She held the door wide for her sister-in-law, who brushed past her and into the kitchen. "I'm making tea. Do you want a cup?"

Meg hesitated. She had something to say, I could tell. She was practically quivering with it. Few people had as much patience and self-control as she did, however, and she managed to bite it back and nod. "Sure, thanks."

Kathryn's gaze lingered on her friend's face for a few seconds, but she headed for the tea pot without speaking. Apparently that was one door she was willing to leave closed, at least as long as possible.

I almost grinned at the slow, deliberate way she went about getting the milk out of the fridge, pouring it into the little jug, and lifting the sugar bowl from the cupboard. Her unhurried movements were driving her sister-in-law crazy. I had never seen Meg so worked up. It was like gazing into a mirror, watching her bounce impatiently on the balls of her feet.

Finally everything was on the table, and Kathryn had no more reason to delay. "Come. Sit." She waved a hand across the table. Not meeting Meg's eyes, she poured the tea. The hot liquid swirled into the cup, and I breathed in the light scent of raspberries. Not quite as intoxicating as coffee, but not bad. I heaved myself onto the island, pressed my palms against the cool marble, and crossed my legs, intensely interested in how this conversation would play out.

"Milk?" Kathryn raised the jug and Meg shook her head. "Sugar?" When she reached for the bowl, Meg's grasp on her self-control finally slipped.

"Kathryn Anne Ellison. You've been serving me tea for years. You know I don't take milk or sugar. Now stop putting me off and tell me what is going on with you."

Kathryn blinked. Slowly, she lowered the sugar bowl and pulled both hands into her lap. To hide the trembling, no doubt. Meg's eyes narrowed. She didn't miss much.

"What are you talking about?"

With an exasperated exhalation of breath, Meg leaned forward. "I was on my way over here to see you the other day when a man drove in and got out of his truck. Twenty minutes later, he drove away again, and since then no one has heard a thing from you. I've seen you on the porch a few times, so I knew you were okay, but that's all I was sure about. I've tried to wait it out, assuming you would come to me if you wanted to talk. I've practically had to restrain Aaron from roaring over. When he went out to a meeting tonight, I decided I couldn't wait any longer. It's been three days, Kath. Three days."

Kathryn studied the hands clasped in her lap. "I know. I'm sorry."

"You don't have to be sorry. Only tell me what's going on." Meg rested a hand on her arm. "Are you all right?"

The expression on her face must have answered that question.

"Oh, Kath." Meg slid around the table to the chair beside her and wrapped her arms around her.

Resting her forehead on Meg's shoulder, Kathryn let herself really cry for the first time since Nick had driven away.

Which was for the best, as far as I was concerned. Self-control was all well and good, but sometimes nothing washed away hurt and fear like a good weeping session.

After a few moments, Kathryn lifted her head. Meg tugged a couple of tissues out of the box on the table and handed them to her. "Do you want to talk about it?"

"I don't even know where to begin."

"How about with the man who came by? Was it Nick? I'm guessing that's what started all this. Whatever this is."

Kathryn nodded. "It was. And yes, it was Nick."

"What did he want?"

Kathryn let out a shaky laugh. "Me, apparently." She pressed a tissue to the corner of her eye. "He says the past has kept us apart long enough."

"I can't argue with that. So where is he now?"

"I sent him away."

Meg's famous self-control had clicked back in. She barely blinked at that. "Why?"

Kathryn twisted the tissue in her hands. "I had a few things I needed to work through before I could be with him."

"And have you?"

"Partly. I went to see David Henley."

The blue eyes studying her widened. "When? Why?"

"Wednesday. I talked to Tory on the phone after Nick was here, and she told me she was determined to find out who her father is. I went to see David so I could finally give her the answer she's searching for."

"Did you get it?"

Kathryn played with the tea bag string hanging along the side of the china teapot. "Yes. He got tested and I met with him again today so he could give me the results."

"And?"

"He's not her father."

Meg's cheeks paled. "Oh, Kath. I'm sorry."

"So am I. Now I have to figure out how to tell my daughter that her father is a serial killer and rapist about to be put to death for everything he's done."

The words ended in a sob and I thought she might break

down again, but she only reached for her tea and took a sip.

Meg ran a finger around the rim of her china cup. "When is she coming home?"

"Sunday, she said."

"What about Nick? How long will he wait?"

"He said he would give me a few days. We left it at that."

"Oh, honey. You should have called me. You didn't have to go through all this alone."

"Yes, I did. Although, to be honest, I haven't really felt alone."

I nodded in satisfaction and tipped my head to shoot a look toward the white-spackled ceiling. Hopefully this affirmation that I was doing a competent job hadn't gone unnoticed. Not that anything I did, competent or otherwise, ever went unnoticed. Still, the acknowledgement was nice.

Meg squeezed her arm. "Do you want me to stay?"

"Thanks for offering, but no, I'm okay. I still have a couple of things to do before I see Nick again. I've been going through everything in that old shoebox."

"Really? What are you doing with it?"

"Burning it." Kathryn let out a short laugh. "It's been very cathartic. An old picture of Ty, David's letters, and everything else I've been holding onto, tossed into the woodstove."

"So everything is gone?"

"Pretty much. I have a couple more to go through tonight and then I'll throw them in the stove and the box after them." She covered Meg's hand with her own. "I feel as though it might almost be over, Meg. Like I'm finally going to be able to move on with my life."

"I'm so glad. That's all I've ever wanted for you."

"I know. Now I have to help Tory get through this."

"Aaron and I want to be there for her. Will you call us when you're going to tell her?"

"I will. I'd like for you to be here. So would Tory, I'm sure."

Meg finished her tea and rose. "I'll try to keep Aaron away

until then, although it hasn't been easy. I've had to use every possible means to distract him." She rinsed her mug out at the sink and set it on the dish rack.

Kathryn grinned. "Knowing how he still looks at you, after fifteen years of marriage, I'm guessing it wasn't that hard."

Meg leaned against the counter, her cheeks flushed. "Yeah, other than the two teenagers running around and the fact that I catch him glancing in the direction of this house every two minutes, it's kind of been a second honeymoon."

"You're welcome."

Meg laughed and crossed the room to wrap her in a hug. "We'll come on Sunday. But call me any time, day or night, if you need me before then, okay?"

"I will. Thanks, Meg."

A sharp twinge in my bones kept me from joining in their laughter. I doubted that telling Tory the news about her father would be the only thing—or even the worst thing—that Kathryn would face between now and the end of the day on Sunday.

But I was not in control of any of that. All I could do was trust the One who was.

Chapter Fifty-Eight

Friday

Kathryn's footsteps were lighter as she carried the teapot and her mug to the sink. Meg's visit had reminded her that people who loved her were close by if she needed them. The faint glow of headlights a ways down the road brought a smile twitching across my lips. Another person who loved her was nearby, although Kathryn didn't know it. My friends and I hadn't been the only ones watching her today.

And not only today, for that matter.

Nick reached for the gearshift. He had to leave now or he'd give in and pull into her driveway. And then what? Bang on her door? Force her to see him before she was ready, before she had done whatever it was she needed to do to close the door on the past? There was no way that would go well. His hand gripped the cool plastic, but he didn't shift into drive. *What am I doing?* He did know. Like the other times, he had to see her. Had to know that she was all right. He shook his head. He couldn't keep watching her like this—it was borderline stalking, for goodness sake.

He'd lost track of the number of times he'd driven to Kathryn's home over the years, wanting to stop in and see her. Somehow, he could never bring himself to do it. Not when the timing wasn't right, and it would do nothing but stoke pain in both of them when he had to leave again.

He watched as Meg climbed the stairs to the porch. He was glad Kathryn had someone to turn to, but more than anything he wished he could be the one to comfort her, to hold her, to help her through whatever she was going through this week.

After her sister-in-law left, he watched for a few more minutes, until the lights went out in the kitchen and the soft glow of a lamp flooded the living room as she moved in there.

Taking a deep breath, Nick shoved the truck into gear. He

performed a three-point turn and headed in the direction he'd come, not even allowing himself a quick glance in the rear-view mirror. She was okay. He hoped. And prayed. That was all he could do for now, and he knew from personal experience that it was a lot. If his aching arms tried to tell him it wasn't enough, that was his problem and he'd have to deal with it. He'd spent a lot of time on his knees over this and it appeared as though he was heading there again.

One word repeating over and over in his head like a mantra, like a prayer, kept him driving away from the one place in the world he wanted to be at the moment.

Sunday.

Chapter Fifty-Nine

Friday

Kevin Dylan's chest heaved. Ten yards from the top of the hill, he collapsed. His sweat-soaked shirt clung to his body. Gasping for breath, he flung an arm over his eyes. If he removed his arm, he was terrified he would see it following him, narrowing the distance between them once again.

His heart rate slowed. *I have to get up.* He needed to get home. Even there, he knew it would find him. Dylan lifted his arm a few inches. He held his breath as he peered around. Nothing penetrated the thick darkness that covered him like a shroud.

Relief washed over him. He started to struggle to his feet. And froze. His stomach clenched. Pinpricks of light broke over the horizon. The rays penetrated the darkness like beams from a lighthouse.

Dylan scrambled up. He lost his balance and fell backwards, barely managing to break his fall with his hands. Gaining his feet, he began to run. As he crested the hill, he risked one glance back. His heart felt as though it stopped beating. The luminous cloud behind him was growing, stretching across the sky. It reached out toward the hill he had climbed.

On either side the darkness fell back, not strong enough to stand in its path. Dylan tried to run but couldn't move. When he glanced down, he'd sunk into mud up to his knees. Cold terror snaked through his body, paralyzing him inch by inch. When it reached his neck, the fear clasped around it like a noose. All the breath was squeezed from his body. He clawed at his throat in a frantic attempt to draw in air.

The light rose behind him, creeping up the hill like a panther stalking its prey. Dylan grabbed one leg and pulled with all his might. Nothing. Bending forward, he dug his hands into the dirt. Handful after handful of sludge flew through the air as he scooped it out. Thick, wet mud oozed around his legs. The hole filled in as quickly as he could dig it. The ground was soon shot through with streaks of red as his fingernails scraped and broke on stones and gravel.

It reached him then, a soft, glowing mist that swirled around him like the gauzy veils of an exotic dancer. In spite of himself, Dylan was awed by the cloud, shimmering with millions of sparkling shards of glass, reflecting the light until it danced on the air.

He let out a choking sob and sank to the ground. The mist enveloped him. His only defense was to cover his eyes, but the cloud undulated around him like a living thing. The shards of glass tinkled together, creating beautiful, terrible music. He slid his hands from his eyes to his ears, desperate to block out the melody that drew him, against his will, toward the dancing light.

He threw back his head and howled, yanking on handfuls of hair in his anguish. The haunting music faded away, replaced by a louder, more insistent thumping. Dylan opened his eyes. The light receded as the smoke-yellowed ceiling of the motel room came into focus in the flickering blue light of the television he'd fallen asleep in front of an hour earlier.

"All right!" he shouted, and the thumping from the other side of the wall stopped.

Shaking his head to clear it of the nightmare, he sat up and swung his legs over the side of the bed. The light again. A tremor shook him. Asleep or awake, he felt it behind him, pursuing him like a baying dog that had caught scent of its quarry. Nothing made it go away entirely, although sometimes he was able to push it far enough into the distance to wrap the darkness around him like a protective cloak.

It was almost time. He was so close now, closer than he had been in twenty years to the place where the nightmares had begun. Dylan's knuckles whitened as his fingers closed around an imaginary throat. When he saw her again—when he snuffed out the light in those eyes that haunted his dreams every night—it would finally be over. He was glad it had been so long. As much as he longed to end his own agony, Dylan wanted to draw hers out even more. Let her think she was safe, that he wasn't coming for her after all this time. It would only increase her shock and terror when he did show up at her door. A cruel smile twisted his face. He had been patient. And it would be worth it.

Dylan grabbed for the remote and stabbed at the buttons. *Come on. Come on.* There had to be something on that could take his mind off everything.

After flipping a couple of times through the few channels the motel offered, he gave up and whipped the remote at the TV. Dropping his head into his hands, he ran his fingers through his hair. Remnants of the dream swirled around his sleep-deprived mind. Unseen eyes seemed to follow every move he made. His skin crawled.

Where was it? Dylan grabbed his backpack and dumped the contents onto the floor. He dropped to his hands and knees and felt under the bed. His fingers closed around a pistol and he pulled it out, relaxing at the feel of the cold steel in his hands.

Ah, my friend. The only one that never let him down. A smirk twisted his features. The light dimmed and receded. Dylan stuck the gun into the back of his jeans, grabbed his faded denim jacket off the back of a chair, and headed out the door.

Fear had seen what was happening in that motel room too. I could tell by the sneer that contorted his face when our eyes met across the living room. My eyes narrowed. He was stronger tonight, even bolder than usual. That happened whenever he was with Kevin Dylan. The two of them fed off each other, gave each other a twisted sort of increased strength and confidence.

Unfortunately, being in either of their company had the opposite effect on me.

I really do try to see the good in everyone, and I know that Fear can sometimes save people from harm. Still, I would have given anything for him to have found someone—and somewhere—else to hang around tonight. I didn't need his presence to tell me I should sleep with one eye open. In fact, two would be better—one on Kathryn and one on the door.

I didn't expect Dylan to arrive in the vicinity until the next day, but if he didn't bother trying to get any more sleep between now and then and pushed himself to get across the border, it could be sooner. Either way I was staying awake.

Not that I had any real option. Fear's loathsome presence always made sleep difficult, and from the way Kathryn was tossing on the couch, she hadn't exactly sunk into a deep, restful slumber either. Might be just as well. If something did happen in the night, I preferred to have her alert and able to dial the phone. If she couldn't, unless he could hear her screams all the way to the other house on the property where he slept, this time Aaron wouldn't be there to drive Fear—or anyone else—away.

Chapter Sixty

Saturday

Kevin Dylan drove through the night. After he cut and dyed his hair dark brown in some seedy motel room in Washington State and picked up a fake passport from an ex-con buddy there, no one had given him a hard time at the border. He arrived within a few miles of the ranch as streaks of light stretched across the sky in front of him.

Sneaking on to her property would be easiest in the dark, and he was in no hurry. The anticipation of seeing her again, of completing the only job he had left undone over the years, had grown slowly as the miles passed beneath his tires. He preferred to court the feeling for a while, woo it until the excitement built to the point where it would explode when he walked through the door and terror flared in her eyes. After waiting twenty years, he wouldn't rush it now.

Squeezing the brakes, he slowed the bike and veered onto the shoulder, stopping in front of a stand of trees that lined the quiet road. With a grunt, he maneuvered the motorcycle across the ditch and into the bush. Once he was confident he was far enough from the road that he couldn't be seen by any passing vehicles, he propped the bike against a tree and sank to the ground. Stretching out on a patch of grass, he folded his arms behind his head and closed his eyes. He'd wait out the daylight, and when it faded away he would make his way the last few miles toward his destination.

To her. And to the light. And to the end of both.

I turned away, repulsed. I'd been peeking through the trees, not wanting to get too close but needing to make sure that we still had a few hours before he would show up. A lot could happen in a few hours, and maybe something would occur to change the course of events as they appeared to be playing out now.

It was becoming increasingly unlikely, but I reached for my friend's hand and grasped it tightly.

At the moment, all I could do was cling to Hope.

Chapter Sixty-One

Saturday

Late-afternoon shadows stretched across the yard as Tory strode into the kitchen. The house was quiet, but she wasn't surprised no one was there to greet her. After talking to her mother on the phone, she'd worried for a couple of days until deciding that nothing would ease her mind except coming home from university a day earlier than she'd planned and seeing for herself if her mom was okay.

I followed her up the stairs and into her room, willing Kathryn to hear her moving around and wake up. Unfortunately, she'd had another rough night, and after doing her chores that morning and cleaning the house when she came in, preparing for her daughter's homecoming, she'd stretched out on the couch again.

Tory's bags landed with a soft thud on the floor as she sank onto the bed and tossed her car keys onto the desk with a clatter. It was so good to be home. She was glad she hadn't waited until tomorrow.

She pursed her lips. She knew her mom was a little freaked out by her insistence on finding out about her father. Of course, the idea freaked her out as well. The thought of discovering who he was, maybe even meeting him ... A small shudder rippled through her. As often as she'd thought about it over the years, she was smart enough to know it might not be the joyful reunion she'd always pictured.

And then there was Nick Lawson. What could be important enough to keep her mom from running into his arms? Tory had only met the man once, but she'd seen her mother after she had been with him and he clearly had a strong effect on her. Maybe now that she was home, her mom would be willing to explain it to her. Tory glanced at her watch. 4:30. Her mom's car had been parked in the driveway, but she didn't appear to be home.

Maybe she was out in the barn with the horses. Brushing aside the curtain, Tory bent over her desk to peer out the window. The barn doors were closed and she couldn't tell if anyone was inside. Spinning around, she crossed the hall to her mom's room and pushed open the door.

"Mom?" The room was empty. A light breeze ruffled the frilly, floral curtains. Tory smiled. She loved this room. It reminded her of Saturday mornings when she was a kid and would crawl into bed with her mom to watch cartoons. As a teenager, she'd head straight here after being out with friends and throw herself onto the great pile of fluffy pillows to tell her mother every detail of her evening. She sighed.

I never realize how much I miss this place until I come home.

In spite of my uneasiness, I had to smile as well. Those evenings had been as much fun for me as for them. Tory's enthusiasm was contagious, and both Kathryn and I usually ended up laughing until our faces ached as she shared everything that had happened with her friends.

My smile faded at the worry on Tory's face now. Something clearly didn't feel right. She left the room and loped down the stairs. I raced ahead of her, hoping to see Kathryn up and brewing tea for the two of them, all evidence of letters and papers and shoeboxes gone. My heart sank.

The light acrid smell of a wood fire hung in the air as Tory crossed the kitchen, which was odd for this time of year. From the living room doorway, she could see her mom lying on the couch. That was extremely unusual for the middle of the day. She tiptoed over to the coffee table and reached out, thinking she would wake her, but stopped mid-air. Fatigue had painted dark circles under her mother's eyes. Tory withdrew her hand, suddenly not wanting to disturb her.

She studied the weary face. Her mother appeared as though she hadn't slept in days. What was going on? A piece of paper lay on the floor beside the couch, and Tory crouched to pick it up. Halyna Lawson's funeral program. All of this must have

something to do with Nick Lawson's visit the other day then—
and the things her mom said she had to work through before she
could be with him, whatever those might be. She'd have to wait
until her mom woke up to ask her.

I swiped at the two envelopes on the coffee table, hoping to
knock them to the floor where I could shove them under the rug
with my foot. Unfortunately, my powers, while considerable, do
not extend to being able to move physical objects. Several
thousand years of trying had not altered this immutable fact, but I
refused to give up. Especially when a desperate need existed.
Like now.

Tory pushed to her feet and started for the kitchen, but the
envelopes, still lying out in the open despite my best efforts,
caught her attention. Her eyes narrowing, she picked them up—
unnecessarily flaunting, in my opinion, the ease with which she
accomplished the maneuver. The return address was somewhere
in Toronto, but there was no name on the envelope. That was
weird. Something else she'd have to ask her mom about when she
woke up.

She started to drop the letters onto the table, but something
stopped her. I glanced around. Curiosity. Darn her. She had a real
knack for showing up in places and at times when she was most
certainly not wanted, causing no end of trouble whenever she did.
After checking to make sure her mom was still asleep, Tory
backed up slowly to the armchair by the woodstove and sat,
pulling both feet up beneath her to sit cross-legged. For a few
moments she stared at the large scrawling writing on the front of
the envelopes, contemplating the possible contents.

Curiosity, as she is wont to do, began to get the better of her.

Tory stole another glance toward the couch. She'd hear if
her mom stirred. She held the envelope up to the wan sunlight
filtering in through the window—Curiosity clearly playing her
like her own personal cello—but she couldn't see anything.

*What are you doing? Reading other people's mail? Pretty
low.* She bit her lip, struggling with her conscience. Her mom
didn't keep secrets from her. And if these letters did contain

private information, she wouldn't have left them lying around like that, would she? Of course, she hadn't been expecting anyone to drop in at the farmhouse today.

She should wait until her mom woke up to ask her about them. But what if she refused to tell her what was inside? Tory sighed. Then she should respect that and let it go.

I grimaced. This debate with herself was getting Tory nowhere. And it was getting me a crick in the neck from swiveling my head as she lobbed arguments back and forth like tennis balls over a net.

Tory scanned the front of the envelopes again. According to the postmark, they'd been sent three years ago. Surely her mom wouldn't mind her reading a couple of old letters. They shared everything. At least she thought they did. Curiosity sent me a smug look as Tory widened the slitted-open top of the envelope with two fingers. I returned it with a fierce glare that, as usual, didn't faze her in the slightest.

Tory shifted in her chair so the letters would be hidden from sight if her mom woke up. Her mother's voice in her head reminded her that if she felt the need to hide what she was doing, she probably shouldn't be doing it. Which was true. She hesitated another second, then took a deep breath and slid the thin piece of paper out of the envelope. There wasn't much on it, only a couple of paragraphs, and she scanned those, her heart beating faster as she read.

Kathryn,

I'm writing to let you know that I've been offered a church, New Hope Community, in Maple Ridge, B.C. I asked for time to think about it, because I needed to know how you'd feel about me coming back. Please be honest. The last thing I want is for you to be worried about running into me in a grocery store or on the street one day.

I know you've worked hard to put the past behind you, and I'd never want to do anything to stir up painful memories. I'll wait to hear from you before I give them my answer.

David

Painful memories? What painful memories? Tory read the letter twice more before stuffing it into the envelope. The sides ripped slightly as she worked the paper in, and she winced. Now her mom would know she'd found a letter that was obviously deeply personal. She held a hand in front of her face, surprised to see that it was shaking.

Why did she feel so nervous? Her mom would understand. Even as the thought passed through her mind, Tory wasn't so sure. Respect for other people's property and privacy had been drilled into her since she was a kid. She didn't know what it was about that letter, but she felt as if she had seriously breached both of those rules. She needed to return it to the coffee table. Now. She straightened one leg and the other envelope fell onto the floor.

Tory stared at it. Since she'd already poked her nose in where it didn't belong, was it much worse to read the other one? Not giving herself time to think about it this time, she snatched the envelope off the floor and pulled out the paper.

Kathryn,

Thank you for your letter encouraging me to come home. I don't think I could have come back to B.C. before now, but I'm sure that, outside of Vancouver anyway, no one will remember ever hearing my name, let alone the details of something that happened seventeen years ago in a different town.

New Hope is a small church, and I feel it's where I'm supposed to be. Now that I have your blessing, I'm more convinced than ever that God is leading me home. Although I understand if you'd rather not see me again, I want you to know that if there's ever anything you need, my door at New Hope will be open to you.

David

Tory set the letter on one leg. Tugging the other one out of the envelope again, she laid the two of them side by side and stared at them, trying to make sense of their contents. Some of the words had smeared, and she rubbed her thumb over the spot. Had her mom been crying when she read this letter? Who was this David anyway, and what could have happened between them that was so painful he'd stayed away from home for seventeen years?

I held my breath, waiting for her to put the pieces together. It didn't take long.

Eyes widening, she drew in a sharp breath. If David Henley was worried that her mother wouldn't want to see him, the only possible explanation was that they'd had an affair.

Tory calculated the numbers in her head. He'd mentioned something that had happened seventeen years earlier, and the letters were three years old. Whatever it was, it had occurred twenty years ago. The more she thought about it, the more convinced she was that she was staring at the handwriting of the man she'd wondered about her whole life.

I waved a hand in front of my face. Smelling salts would be better, but I didn't happen to have any of those on hand. None of my charges did either—at least, they hadn't for the last hundred years or so.

I drew in a steadying breath. This might turn out all right yet. Now that Tory had jumped to a conclusion, even a faulty one, Curiosity might actually come in handy. If she could use her evil powers for good for a change and direct Tory to wake up her mother and confront her with her theory, Kathryn would be able to calm her down before she did anything rash. I searched wildly around the room, but now that her chaos-inducing work was done, Curiosity—the little minx—had slipped out the door and disappeared. Frustrated, I returned my attention to Tory, her thoughts so loud and angry that I almost covered my ears in a futile attempt to block them out.

A minister? How could her mother have had an affair with a minister? It didn't make sense, although it did explain why no one in the family would talk about it. Tory's head came up sharply. What about him? How could someone who called himself a man of God refuse to own up to his responsibility and acknowledge her as his daughter?

Rage welled in her, knotting every muscle. Did his congregation know about his past? Tory gritted her teeth. If she had anything to say about it, they would.

She jumped to her feet, both letters falling onto the brightly colored area rug. Tory stepped over them, not caring anymore if her mother knew she'd read them. She raced up the stairs to her room and grabbed the backpack with her wallet and cell phone off the floor.

I gulped and threw another glance at Kathryn. The woman had barely slept for days—keeping me up in the process to the point of sheer exhaustion—and she picked this particular hour to finally slip into a deep sleep. That was just great.

After tiptoeing down the stairs, Tory crossed the kitchen and carefully opened the screen door, holding her breath at the soft creak. I gritted my teeth and, resigned, headed after her. No sound came from the living room—naturally—and the door shut behind us. Tory skidded to a halt in the driveway. Her keys. She'd left them on the desk. Should she risk going upstairs again after them?

The old farm truck in front of the barn caught her eye and she hurried over. As usual, the keys hung from the ignition. It took three attempts, but the engine finally turned over and roared to life as I dove into the cab beside her. Tory threw the truck into reverse and backed into the driveway, then pulled forward, spinning her tires on the gravel.

The ancient Chevy had never been driven so hard. If it was possible for years to be taken off my life, a good dozen or so would have been shaved from the end, I'm sure, as she tore recklessly along the highway. In any case, we arrived in the parking lot of New Hope Community Church in a little under fifty minutes. She hit the brakes and the truck screeched, mercifully, to a stop.

Tory scanned the sign in front of the church, searching for his name. Her eyes narrowed when she found it. David Henley.

One lone car sat in the parking lot. She slammed her shoulder against the truck door to fling it open before jumping out. "That better be your car, *Reverend* Henley." Tory slammed the door so hard that the windows—and my teeth—rattled. "Otherwise, you and your family will have an unexpected guest for dinner tonight."

I try not to let my limitations bother me. I always have what I need when I need it, but sometimes it's hard not to wish I had what I needed even before I needed it, if you know what I mean. Normally I am quite happy to be unable to see into the future. Today, so much is going on, so many things could happen to change everything, that a little bit of insight would be a great comfort. Except that it likely wouldn't be. Which is probably why the Creator designed things the way He did. Still, I can't help but worry about David. And Kathryn. And Nick. And Tory.

I slipped through the church door a second before Tory allowed it to swing closed behind her. After crossing the threshold, I nearly stumbled under the enormous weight of anxiety I suddenly realized I was carrying on my shoulders. Not my job, by the way. All worries and concerns that come our way are to be immediately forwarded upstairs. Sometimes, in the thick of everything that is going on, I forget. Breathing a fervent apology, I transferred them over. Immediately, my steps lightened.

I refused to stop and wonder how long that would last.

Chapter Sixty-Two

Saturday

If I thought the burden I carried had been heavy, the glimpse I caught over Tory's shoulder through the window of the office door revealed a man bowed low under the weight of everything that had happened to him the last few days. Or—to be more accurate—over the last twenty years. And maybe, if we're being entirely accurate, I should say the things he had done to himself. And to others.

Still, he didn't have to bear that weight alone. In fact, he knew as well as I did that he wasn't supposed to be carrying it around. He'd have to remember that on his own, and I prayed he would before he broke under the strain. Especially since I suspected a few more bricks were about to be added to the pile.

"I have no idea what to say." David stared at the blank computer screen. "You'd think this would get easier." But it was never easy—uncovering secrets, shattering trust and, worse, faith. He still wasn't sure he could do it. David glanced at his watch. He was anxious to get home and see Laura, to find out if she was all right.

Footsteps sounded outside his door. David winced. *I hope that isn't anything that's going to keep me from getting home. Not tonight.*

A sharp rap sounded. He reached for the off button on the computer, but his hand froze midway when the door flew open and he caught a glimpse of her, framed in the doorway. It was Kathryn, only younger and with long blond hair. David's chest constricted. He could be looking at his daughter. Except that she wasn't his daughter—she was the daughter of a convicted murderer. Had her mother told her that yet?

Tory stood in the doorway, both fists planted on her hips, her feet apart. Attack stance. I slipped around her and into the room, heading straight for my favorite chair by the window. If shots were going to be exchanged here—and knowing Tory I suspected they would be—I was quite happy to find a spot outside of the line of fire to watch.

"I see you know who I am." The shards of ice in her voice pierced his chest. "And I'll bet you're not happy to see me."

David's shoulders sagged. Kathryn was right about the anger. Her daughter was giving him a look that made it clear that even if she didn't know all the details, she held him personally responsible for the years she'd spent growing up without a father. And she wasn't wrong, as far as that went. A fist of grief tightened around his heart as he peered past her anger and saw the pain that had driven her to his doorstep.

David rose and started to come around the desk. He stopped when she took a step backward. "Victoria," he said gently. "I *am* happy to see you. Please come in." He pointed to one of the leather chairs facing his desk. When she hesitated, he returned to his desk chair. "Please."

Tory lifted her chin and marched across the room. She perched on the edge of one of the chairs, spine rigid as though daring him to deny whatever she had come to accuse him of.

David almost smiled. She was her mother's daughter, all right.

He waited a minute, trying to give her time to say what was on her mind, but she remained silent, twisting her hands in her lap.

David guessed Kathryn hadn't told her anything yet, but she had figured out about him somehow. She must have come straight to the church without stopping to form any plan of attack. He decided to help her out. "You're obviously angry with me. Do you want to tell me what that's about?"

Tory drew herself up even straighter. "I believe you know my mother, Kathryn Ellison."

"Yes, I know her." The fist clenched tighter.

"The thing is, I've never been told who my father is, but

I've come across letters in my mother's possession that suggest maybe you and she ..." She shifted on the chair. I tilted my head. Was she starting to second-guess her decision to confront him? Her features hardened slightly. If she was, she clearly planned to push through. "Did the two of you have an affair?"

My gaze shifted to David. What would he do with that volley? A movement behind him captured my attention. After being ordered from David's presence for twenty years, Truth now appeared to have taken up permanent residence in his shadow. I doubted David would be able to resist the pressure of that hand on his shoulder or if he would even choose to. Living with a dark, painful secret for so long had cost him dearly, and I was pretty sure he no longer had a taste for it.

Still, his heart sank. Victoria only knew part of what had happened, and not the worst part. Should he tell her? If he didn't, she would go home and confront Kathryn. David was pretty sure that, to protect her daughter and maybe him as well, Kathryn would struggle with telling her everything. Knowing he didn't have a choice, David sighed. He owed it to both of them to confess what he had done and to ask Kathryn's daughter for forgiveness as well.

He swallowed hard, knowing his words were going to devastate her as much as they had his wife. "No, your mother and I didn't have an affair. The truth is ..." He lowered his gaze to his desk, hoping the confession would come easier if he didn't have to meet those piercing blue eyes. "The truth is I raped her."

Silence greeted his words. There was no sound, no movement across the desk. David raised his eyes then wished he hadn't as the horror on her face plunged like a dagger into his chest.

"Victoria," he said heavily. "I was a different man then. Both God and your mother have forgiven me, and as you can see," he waved his arm around the room. "I've spent the last twenty years trying to make up for what I did."

Her eyes blinked as though she was trying to comprehend what he was saying. "Then you *are* my father?"

The dagger in his chest twisted. How much more could she take? And how much was it even his place to reveal?

"No. I'm not. Your mother came to see me last week to tell me about you. Before that, I had no idea she even had a child. She knew you might track me down, and she wanted to be the one to tell me about you." David pressed his palms to the top of his desk. "The thing you don't know is that I wasn't the only one there that night. There was another man. Your mother asked me to take a paternity test so she'd have an answer to give you. The results showed that I am not your father."

Sheet-white, Tory collapsed against the chair. David started to rise, alarmed, but she held up a hand to stop him and he sank onto the seat. After a moment, she raised her head. Tears streaked her face as she lifted a trembling chin. "Then who ...?"

"I don't think I should be the one to tell you that. If your mother wants you to know who your father is, she'll tell you. But Victoria," his voice was pleading, "please be kind. Kathryn went through a terrible time, and if she hadn't had you and God I don't know if she would have survived."

"God!" Tory gripped both arms of the chair as she spat the word out at him. "Do *not* talk to me about God. Where was he when my mother was being raped? Where was he when she was alone and pregnant and when I was growing up without a father?"

The words struck him like arrows shot from a bow. For a moment, David couldn't speak. Then he met her gaze. "You have every right to ask those questions. I know it seems like God abandoned you and your mother, but talk to her. She'll tell you that's not what happened." He drew in a deep breath, praying for the right words to say. "I'm here today because, at the worst moment of her life, God was there with her. He didn't stop what was happening. You'll have to ask Him if you want to know why not, but He was there. He was so real that every person in that place felt him and none of us has been the same since."

Her anger deflated in front of his eyes, a balloon pricked by a pin. She slumped as the fury that had energized her seeped away.

I wiped a hand across my forehead. It appeared as though no fatal shots were going to be fired. Not here, anyway. The night was young. I lowered my hand.

"I've given her a hard time for years for not telling me anything about my father. I thought she was ashamed of something she had done," Tory whispered, staring at her hands.

Oh, Kathryn. His heart ached for her. "Your mother will understand. No one knows better than I do how capable of forgiveness she is."

Using the chair arms to brace herself, Tory stood. "I better go talk to her."

"Does anyone know you're here?"

"No. My mom was asleep when I found the letters, and I left right away."

"Do you want to call her? Ask her to come and get you?"

She shook her head. "I'm all right to drive. I need time to think. I'll call her on my cell."

David stood and came around the desk. "Victoria." His voice broke. "I'm so sorry." She bit her lip and studied him for a moment before nodding. "For the record, even though the past may have made it difficult for us to have a relationship, I would have been proud if you had been my daughter."

Tory's eyes filled with tears. She offered him a faint smile before she turned and walked out the door. I shot a glance over my shoulder as I followed her. Yep. Definitely a man about to break. Knowing what he was planning to do the next day, my stomach knotted. If he went through with it, one of two things would happen—he'd remember there was someone waiting to take the weight from him and he'd let go of the tight grasp he had on it, or one more pebble would be added to the load and he would crash to his knees.

I clenched my fists, wishing I could lift it off for him. Sadly, I didn't have the power. People could stand in line to add their grievances to the load, but only One could take them all away. And He never did so without being asked.

David propped his elbows on the desk. He couldn't remember any week in prison more difficult than the one he was going through. Not even the time he got beat up. At least that kind of wound healed eventually. Blowing out a long breath, he scrubbed his face with both hands. Two painful confessions and he still had one more to make. He pushed away from the desk, switched off his computer and lamp, and grabbed his jacket.

No matter what things might be like at home, David desperately needed his wife.

Knowing there was nothing more I could do for David at the moment, I hurried out the door of the church, once again narrowly missing having my hind end clipped. Slamming doors is a favorite pastime for you humans, especially in times of duress. I can see how it might be stress-relieving. Even so, it makes life quite hazardous for those of us who follow in your wake. Just FYI.

I hustled into the passenger seat of the truck and imagined myself fastening my seatbelt. Although I couldn't actually do it, picturing the action in my mind did offer a small measure of security, something I needed as I suspected the ride home might be as wild as the ride to the church. And after that the ride was likely to get bumpier. With that thought, I did the only thing I could do under the circumstances. I grabbed hold of the door handle and held on tight.

Chapter Sixty-Three

Saturday

From my perch on the window seat, I watched Kathryn sleep. She appeared at peace, if still fatigued. I ached for her, knowing that her tentative respite was about to come to an abrupt conclusion. I drew in a long, deep breath as she stirred on the couch, wanting to be calm and collected when she woke up and realized what had happened. She struggled to raise eyelids weighed down by an exhaustion that hadn't been relieved by an hour or two of sleep, as painfully—for me—deep as it had been.

With a low moan, she forced herself to sit up. *I need coffee.* The thought of the reviving liquid gave her the strength to move. Pressing both palms to the cool glass of the coffee table in front of her, she pushed to her feet. Once she had a shower she'd feel—

I knew the second her eyes fell on the letters still lying on the floor. Every muscle in her body went rigid, as though an electric current was being pumped through her. Who had dropped those there? The breath jammed in her throat. *Tory.* Her daughter must have come home early and ... She couldn't finish the thought. In a daze, Kathryn rounded the coffee table and dropped to her knees, snatching up the letters and staring at them. "What have I done?"

I tried to keep up as her mind raced.

Tory must have found them and gone ... A tremor shook her. She'd gone to see him.

Clutching both letters to her chest, she clambered to her feet and lunged for the phone she had turned off the night before so she wouldn't be disturbed. It took three tries to get through to her voicemail, her fingers trembled so violently. Four messages. She stabbed at the numbers to play them. The first three were from friends—light, mundane messages about everyday happenings that had no place or meaning in her world at the moment.

Desperately she skipped over them, praying for the one message she needed to hear.

"Mom?" She closed her eyes at the distress in Tory's voice. Carrying the phone into the kitchen, she sank onto a chair, still clutching the letters in one hand.

"I'm all right. I went to see David Henley."

A sob caught in Kathryn's throat. *Please help her, Father. Help us all.*

"He told me what happened, Mom. I need to talk to you. I'll be home soon."

Kathryn pushed the off button. *Oh Tory, I'm so sorry.* Kathryn should have told her herself. Even as she thought it, she wondered if she would have been able to tell her everything about David. Maybe it was better that she had heard the truth from him. She would have seen the kind of person he was now and that might help her, somehow, to forgive him.

The screen door creaked open. "Kat? Do you know where the truck—" Aaron's question broke off when he saw her. Meg followed him into the kitchen.

I pressed a fist to my mouth. I had been so busy following Tory and David and Kathryn and Dylan today, I'd lost track of Aaron. This was becoming a veritable perfect storm, with fronts moving in from all directions.

Kathryn glanced over. The color drained from her sister-in-law's face when she caught a glimpse of the letters in her hand.

"What is it? What's wrong?" Aaron sounded alarmed.

Kathryn rubbed her temple with the tips of her fingers. "Tory knows."

"Tory knows what? Kat, what are you talking about?" When she didn't respond, Aaron strode over and took hold of the letters, tugging them out of her unresisting fingers. I backed slowly away from him, cowering—I'm not ashamed to admit—on the far side of the table. As I said earlier, I am not as hardy as some of the others, like Faith. I don't always survive storms, and this was shaping up to be one of those that witnesses would be quick to hang the tag "of the century" after.

Kathryn's eyes met Meg's.

"Oh, Kath," Meg said softly. "I thought you burned them."

"I did, all except these last two. I was going to get rid of them today, but Tory must have come home early, while I was asleep. I—"

Aaron raised his head and stared at her. The words died on her lips. She'd never seen him look at her that way.

I shrank even farther into the shadows.

"Kathryn." The cold fury in his voice reached into her chest and settled there. "You've been *writing* him?"

She nodded, unable to push the confession past the grief and guilt blocking her throat.

Aaron turned to Meg. "And you *knew* about this?"

"Aaron." Kathryn stood, steadying herself with one hand on the table. "Please don't blame Meg. She wanted me to tell you."

Aaron ignored her.

"How long?" The question was spat out at both of them. Neither responded. Aaron fixed his eyes on Meg. "How ... long?"

Meg's shoulders sagged. "Years."

Aaron crumpled up the letters and flung them on the floor. "Where is Tory now?"

How could she tell him? He was already beside himself. If he found out where Tory had gone, Kathryn didn't know what he'd do.

A movement next to the table caught my eye. Truth had barged his way in here as well.

With his presence, the weight of everything she'd kept from her brother for years overwhelmed her. *I'm tired of keeping secrets. I can't do it anymore.* "She went to see him."

"She what?" Anger and disbelief hurtled the words toward her like weapons. "Where is he?" He was already heading for the door.

"Aaron, she's okay."

Her brother spun around and stalked toward her. Kathryn

resisted the urge to move out of his path. He stopped inches from her.

I covered my face with my hands, peering out between my fingers so as to not miss anything.

"*Okay*? How can you say that?" His eyes were wild, and she had to force herself not to turn away. "She's gone to see a convicted rapist alone. Who knows what he'll do to her, even if he does suspect that she's his daughter."

"He won't hurt her. He's not that man anymore. And he's not her father." The words slipped out before she could stop them. She bit her lip, her heart sinking at the look that crossed his face.

"How on earth could you know that?"

Kathryn couldn't answer. Aaron's gaze bored into her. "You've been to see him too."

She nodded miserably.

"Tell me where to find him."

"She's not there anymore." The words came out in a hoarse whisper.

"Then where the hell is she?"

Stunned, Kathryn could only gape at him. She'd never heard her brother utter a swear word in his life. Aaron grabbed her arms. She gasped as a dart of fear shot through her.

"Aaron!" Meg cried out from across the room, but her husband didn't seem to hear. Something, rage or fear, had taken over. I checked between my fingers. Both. He shook her. "Answer me, Kathryn. Where is Tory?"

"I'm right here." All three of them turned. Aaron abruptly let go of Kathryn's arms. Tory stood in the doorway, her face streaked with tears. She uttered a plaintive wail. "Mom."

Kathryn skirted around Aaron and crossed the room. She gathered her weeping daughter into her arms. She held her until sobs no longer wracked her body then smoothed the hair back from her face. "Come." She took her by the hand and led her into the living room. I scuttled after them, pressing my back to the wall to avoid walking too close to Aaron. Fear had slunk to his place in front of the woodstove, but Rage still hovered around him like the white-hot thermosphere around the earth. I knew from past experience he was more than capable of singeing me if I invaded what he considered his personal space.

"Kath, we'll go." Meg sounded uncertain. She and Aaron had followed them into the living room, stopping inside the door.

"No, please stay." Tory sniffed. "I'm sure you know everything anyway. I'd like you to be here."

I curled up on the armchair by the woodstove as Kathryn sat on the couch beside Tory. Aaron and Meg took the leather chairs across from them. Kathryn grasped her daughter's hand. "Honey, I'm so sorry you had to find out this way."

Tory shook her head. "No, it was my fault. When I found those letters ..." Kathryn couldn't look at Aaron as her daughter drew in a deep, quivering breath. "He told me he wasn't my father. He said there was another man there that night. Who was it, Mom? Who is my father?"

Blood pounded in her ears. Kathryn willed herself to be calm so she could think.

Father, help us all.

"Tory." She squeezed her daughter's fingers. "What David Henley told you must have been hard to hear. But the truth about your father will be even harder. Are you sure you really want to know?"

"No." Tory clutched her hand. "But I *need* to know."

Kathryn nodded, her heart aching for her little girl. Except that she wasn't a little girl anymore. She was a woman, and it was time to tell her the truth.

"The name of the other man is Kevin Dylan. After he left the cabin that night, he went on hurting people. He killed at least five women. He's in prison now, in Wyoming." Kathryn grasped Tory's arm with her free hand, trying to give her strength. "He's on death row, and he's been given an execution date."

Her daughter moaned. "When?"

"Two weeks."

A blur from the corner of my eye caught my attention.

Determination back-flipped across the room, hip-checked Horror out of the way, and vaulted onto the arm of the chair next to Tory, flinging an arm around her shoulders. A cloud of grit drifted over her neck and back.

She straightened. "Mom, I have to see him once before it's too late. I can't ask you to come with me, but will you try to understand if I go?"

Kathryn sighed in resignation. "I've already booked the tickets to Wyoming. Our flight leaves Monday afternoon."

I gulped a little. When had she done that? Must have been while I was visiting David. Or maybe Nick. That would be fun— defending myself for that bit of negligence on my next evaluation.

Tory tugged her hand from her mother's and threw her arms around her. "Thank you."

Kathryn's gaze met Aaron's over Tory's shoulder. The wildness was gone, but what remained frightened her even more. She had always been able to read him. Not now. *He's shutting me out completely.* A cold chill passed through her. Closing her eyes, she tightened her hold on Tory.

When she released her, Tory managed a weak smile. "I think I need to go to bed. Would you come up with me?"

"Sure, honey." She was grateful for the reprieve, although she'd have to face Aaron eventually. Tonight, she couldn't handle one more difficult conversation.

I was grateful too. I felt along the length of my arms and legs and exhaled in relief. The worst seemed to have passed—for now—and so far I appeared to be relatively unscathed.

Tory stood. "'Night, Uncle Aaron." Leaning down, she gave him a quick hug.

"Good night, Tory."

"'Night, Aunt Meg." Tory walked to the bottom of the stairs and stood there, waiting for Kathryn.

"Good night, Meg." Kathryn forced a small smile and kissed her sister-in-law on the cheek. "Thanks for being here."

Meg nodded. Her smile didn't quite reach her eyes.

Kathryn felt for her. *She's dreading having to face Aaron and it's all my fault.*

"Good night, Aaron," she said softly.

Aaron caught her hand as she walked by. "Hey." His tone was grim. "We'll talk tomorrow, okay?"

Kathryn nodded.

I jumped off the chair and headed after them, thinking that might be the safest place to be tonight. A glance over my shoulder confirmed the decision. Meg bit her lip as she shot a wary look at her husband. I didn't envy her. The set of his shoulders and his clenched jaw indicated that it was going to be a long night over at the smaller ranch house. I wasn't too worried about them. I had established a firm relationship with them years ago, and it would take more than this—although this was a lot— to threaten it.

Chapter Sixty-Four

Saturday

The palms of Kevin Dylan's hands scraped against stone as he crept along the side of the old farmhouse. A few feet ahead of him, loud voices burst out of an open window, and he pressed his back to the wall. When the sound subsided to unintelligible murmuring, he released his breath and moved forward. A shaft of light fell through the glass and pooled at his boots. Dylan ducked into the shadows.

The place was crawling with people. He bit back the foul word that rose in his throat. It wouldn't be tonight. Fine. He'd waited twenty years—a few more hours wouldn't kill him. Or her, apparently. Tomorrow, then.

Sliding one boot at a time through the grass, he inched closer to the wooden frame, trying to catch a glimpse inside. A figure passed in front of the window and he froze. It was her. Desperate to see her, he pushed up on the toes of his boots, risking a peek through the glass. A small smile played across Kathryn Ellison's lips as she said goodnight and leaned in to kiss someone on the cheek. Dylan lowered his heels and stumbled against the cold stone, his ragged breaths sending puffs of smoke spurting out from between clenched teeth.

For years he had waited to see her again, hoping to find her as tormented by their encounter as he had been. With a single glance, that hope dissipated into the cool night air.

Obviously she had forgotten everything they had gone through together. Dylan reached behind him until his fingers brushed against the cold metal of the .38-calibre pistol stuck in his jeans. Well, that's what he was here for—to remind her.

He'd find a place to hide out for the night. By morning her guests would be gone, but he would still be there. Watching. And waiting for her to be alone so he could have her to himself. If prison had taught him anything, it was patience.

Dylan edged away from the circle of light. In the dim glow

emitted by the sliver of a moon, he scouted out a small shed next to the barn. A dirt-speckled window faced the farmhouse. *Perfect.* The door creaked on its hinges, and he held his breath. When no one came out of the house, his lungs emptied. He felt along the wall for something soft to lie on. His fingers brushed against several feed sacks hooked on a nail, and he grabbed them and tossed them into a corner. With a heavy sigh, he dropped to his knees. Thick dust billowed up from the bags and coated his skin and throat. He buried his face in the crook of his arm to stifle a cough. Not exactly the Beverly-Wiltshire Hotel, but slightly better than sleeping on the damp, dirt-packed floor.

Dylan shoved his hand beneath his denim jacket and grasped hold of the gun before sinking onto the makeshift bed. Bending one knee, he jerked up the leg of his jeans. The knife slid out of the sheath strapped to his calf with a soft swish. He settled onto the sacks, clutching a weapon in each hand. They both fit so perfectly in his palms—he wasn't sure which one he liked more. And as often as he'd thought about this meeting over the years, he had never been able to choose which one would be the instrument of her death and his freedom.

He lifted and lowered his hands slowly, weighing his options. He'd had this debate with himself before, the last time he and Kathryn Ellison had met. It hadn't mattered then. The light had driven him away before he could use either weapon. Cold chills skittered across his skin, and he shook his head to clear it of the memory. Nothing would stop him from extinguishing the light this time—he'd been haunted by it long enough.

Dylan set the weapons on the ground beside him with reverent care and folded his arms behind his head. It didn't matter which one he chose this time either. Both would draw out the fear in her eyes and end his nightmare once and for all.

He would wait then. Wait and see what the morning light would bring. And then he would decide.

Chapter Sixty-Five

Tory tugged a pair of shorts and a T-shirt—her usual night time attire—out of a drawer. "What was going on when I walked into the kitchen tonight? I've never seen Uncle Aaron so angry."

"Neither have I." The weight in Kathryn's chest pressed down hard. "He's pretty upset with me right now."

"Why?" Tory headed into the small bathroom off her room, leaving the door open. "None of this is your fault."

"Oh, Tory." Kathryn sank onto the edge of her daughter's bed. "It has to do with those letters you found. I never told Uncle Aaron I was keeping in touch with David Henley because I knew he'd want me to stop. When he found out tonight, he was furious." She shuddered, remembering the rage on her brother's face. "And he was worried about you, especially when I told him where you'd gone. If you hadn't come home when you did, he would have come after you."

Her daughter poked her head out of the bathroom, a toothbrush clutched in one hand. "I'm sorry. I'm the one who read those letters when I shouldn't have. I didn't mean to cause so much trouble." She disappeared again. Water ran in the sink. Kathryn waited until it stopped and Tory flicked off the bathroom light.

"This isn't your fault, Tory. I should never have kept those letters from your uncle. Aunt Meg warned me something like this would happen, and she was right. And as much as I've hoped you'd never have to find out about your father, it was time for you to know the truth. Nothing good ever comes from keeping secrets from the people you love." She shifted toward the foot of the bed so her daughter could turn back the covers. "Something I learned the hard way tonight."

Tory sat beside her. "There's so much I still don't understand. Why did you write those letters? How could you have kept in touch with a man who ... did what he did to you?"

I hopped onto her desk and propped my chin on my hand. It

was a good question, I'd give her that. I was extremely interested in the answer myself, although I knew that Kathryn wouldn't be able to adequately put it into words. Still, it was always kind of interesting to watch her try, and I was in desperate need of a distraction after the emotional strain of the last few days.

"I can't really explain it. What we went through together created a strong connection between us. It was difficult for both of us to let it go."

"But you have?"

"Yes." She couldn't keep the sadness out of her voice at the memory of their last meeting.

Tory crawled into bed. "Mom," her voice was thick with exhaustion, "will you stay until I fall asleep?"

"Of course." Kathryn stretched out beside her. Too worked up to settle, she turned on her side and watched Tory as sleep slowly smoothed away the troubled lines from her face. Tears had left tracks on her daughter's cheeks, and Kathryn traced them with her fingertips. Resting her head on one arm, she closed her eyes.

Father, I've made a mess of things. Forgive me, please. Help Aaron to forgive Meg. I should never have gotten her involved in this. She doesn't deserve his anger. And help him somehow to be able to forgive me.

When she was sure her daughter had settled into a deep sleep, Kathryn leaned over and kissed her on the forehead, then got up and crossed the hall to her room. With a sigh, I slipped off the bed and traipsed after her, absorbing the waves of sadness and fatigue that radiated from her as she lowered herself to her desk chair and dropped her face into her hands.

Father, help us all.

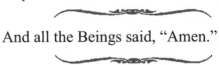

And all the Beings said, "Amen."

Chapter Sixty-Six

Saturday

The haunting call of an owl startled me awake an hour later. Kathryn still sat at her desk. My heart sank. Why hadn't she gone to bed? She would need all her strength to face the day ahead, and sleep was the best way for her to get it. If she sat up all night doing goodness knows what, I wasn't sure she would be able to make it through. I was quite sure I wouldn't.

I forced myself to listen to what was going through her mind. Oh. She was praying again. Or still. Maybe sleep wasn't the best way for her to fortify herself for whatever lay ahead. In the hour I had been sleeping, she had come to terms with what had happened between Tory and David and between her and Aaron. Peace had slipped into the room.

I glanced across the room at Faith, sitting on the window seat in front of Kathryn. When our eyes met, her expression was a gentle chastisement. I nodded in acknowledgement, my cheeks warm. As close as Faith and I were, I had a tendency to lose sight of her when one of my charges was going through a crisis. For the next twenty-four hours, I would need to keep my eyes on her at all times. When she smiled at me, the tension left my shoulders and I turned back to Kathryn.

Soft moonlight streamed through the leaves of the oak tree outside her window and flitted across her face and arms. Here, in the home where she had grown up, her family all around her, she was once again surrounded by warmth and light. However, as she had finally come to understand, those things were ethereal. Like moonlight, they were mere reflections of a much greater source. When she had felt them slipping through her fingers, she'd tried to hold on to them, but that had been like clinging to a shadow rather than the object casting it.

She raised her face to the light. *I've groped my way through a darkness so deep, and been shaken by a cold so bitter, that I've sometimes forgotten that, even in the middle of the night, the sun is still in the sky. I've doubted that it will ever shine again. But you've always been there, haven't you?*

Always.

She gazed out the window at the moon, full and glowing above the roof of the barn. *And Monday, when Tory and I step out of the warmth and light and into the dark and cold?*

I will be there.

Kathryn smiled. That was all she needed to know.

My smile faded as hers grew. My eyes met Faith's. Her face had also grown serious. Because what both of us knew, and Kathryn did not, was that cold and dark were about to blow in and surround her, doing their best to choke out the warmth and light long before Monday ever came.

Chapter Sixty-Seven

Sunday

Tory slept late the next morning. Kathryn woke when the sun filtered through the leaves of the big maple outside her window. The rays made their way across her bed until they lay warm and comforting on her cheek. Then she threw back her covers, pulled on jeans and a T-shirt, and padded down the stairs to the kitchen. Within minutes, the rich aroma of dark, French vanilla-flavored coffee filled the kitchen. She breathed deeply. I stood beside her and inhaled equally deeply, the invigorating effects of the aroma spreading through me. Mmm. Faith and coffee. I think I could survive pretty much anything if I only had a limitless supply of both. Kathryn poured herself a cup and sloshed in a little cream before heading out to the porch swing.

I climbed onto the railing where Faith had sat swinging her legs the day Nick Lawson had come by. So much had happened since then—it seemed a lifetime ago. I studied Kathryn's face as she swung gently. Yesterday deep lines of worry and exhaustion had spoked out from her eyes. The grooves were still there, but not as deep. Clearly the company she had kept in the night, as I had wandered in and out of sleep, had renewed her inner strength. Nothing could have made me happier. I rested my head on a post and said a prayer of my own, letting go of the worry that had plagued me all night.

Mourning doves circled and dipped around the silo, cooing to each other. A new day. Somehow, in the light of morning, it was easier to believe that everything would be all right.

Please let everything be all right.

Kathryn set her empty mug on the railing next to me and tipped her head, breathing in the smell of newly mown hay in the field. Peace rested a hand on her head and she closed her eyes, nearly lulled to sleep by the gentle rocking of the swing.

Aaron's boots tromping across the yard from the barn

roused her, and she straightened. Kathryn reached out to grasp Peace, but he had slipped from her side to come and lean against the railing next to me. A twinge of apprehension wriggled through her as her brother swung himself onto the veranda.

"Hey," he said quietly.

"Hey."

Aaron joined her on the swing. They rocked in silence for a minute, until he bent forward and rested his arms on his knees, clasping his hands together. "Kat."

Relief flooded through her, nudging out the apprehension. She couldn't remember him ever calling her Kathryn before last night, and she prayed he'd never do it again.

Aaron took a deep breath. When his eyes met hers, she was startled to see they were filled with tears. I was less startled, having been there with him more times over the years than I could recall as he shed tears that he refused to let her see.

"I will never, for the rest of my life, forget walking into that hospital room after you were attacked and seeing you ..." He shook his head.

Her heart ached at the pain in his voice.

"I swore then that I would never let anyone hurt you again. And when Tory was born, I made the same promise to her."

Aaron pressed his thumb and forefinger to the corners of his eyes. Kathryn blinked away tears of her own. "When you got that first letter, years ago, I felt as though I was breaking that promise, like he was coming back into your life, and I was desperate to stop him. I didn't want you to get hurt again."

Kathryn rested a hand on his arm. Her brother sat up and took it in his. "I was hurt and upset when I found out you'd been writing him for years and didn't tell me. But even more than that, I was afraid. I could see you and Tory heading for more pain, and I felt powerless to stop it. That's why I got so angry. I'm sorry."

She squeezed his hand. "Don't apologize, Aaron. You had every right to be angry. I'm the one who's sorry. I should never have kept those letters from you."

"So you've been to see him?"

"Yes."

"How many times?"

"Twice—both in the last week."

Aaron blew out a breath. "Are you *trying* to kill me, Kat?"

Her laugh was shaky. "No. But I had to know who Tory's father is. She was so determined to find out, and I wanted to tell her before she stumbled across the truth. Which of course she ended up doing anyway."

"I trust you, so I have to believe you were doing what you felt you had to do. But I will never, no matter how hard my wife tries to explain it to me, understand this connection that you and he have."

Kathryn smiled faintly. "Neither will I."

"Are you going to see him again? Or hear from him?"

"No. It's over."

Aaron nodded. "Meg and I want to go to Wyoming with you."

"I was hoping you'd say that. I bought tickets for you when I got ours."

He laughed. "Pretty sure of yourself, weren't you?"

"No," she said softly. "Pretty sure of you."

He gazed at her for a moment. "Meg said Nick Lawson came by to see you."

His name sent a pang through her she couldn't quite identify. Pain? Longing? Hope? All three, maybe.

Glancing around the porch, I confirmed those suspicions to be true.

"Yes. He wants us to be together, Aaron."

"And what do you want?"

"I want that too. But I told him I had a few things to work through first."

"So that's what all this has been about, with the letters and the visits to David Henley?"

"Yes. I also needed to let go of Ty and Halyna and, most of all, everything I've been afraid of for so long."

"Do you think you have?"

"Pretty much." She squeezed his hand. "I'm still a little afraid, but I want to be with Nick. I want to move on with my life more than I want to avoid facing the past."

Aaron's eyes probed hers. "It's been a long journey, hasn't it?"

"Yes, it has. And you're a big reason I've come as far as I have."

"I want you to be happy, Kat, and safe. That's all I've ever wanted."

She let out a breath on a soft sigh. "I guess neither of those things is ever guaranteed. I'd settle for finding peace and being loved right now."

"Well, I guess the peace part is up to you. But you are loved, probably more than you'll ever know."

Kathryn smiled as he leaned over and kissed her on the cheek. When he drew back, he ruffled her hair, and she punched him lightly in the arm. "You can't help yourself, can you?"

His eyes danced as he grinned. "Nope." He stopped the swing with his feet and stood. "Better get the chores done before church. Are you coming?"

"I think so, if I can drag Tory out of bed in time. I want to make sure she's okay first, after last night."

The dancing stilled. "Yeah, I guess that news must have really thrown her. Still, it's good to finally have it out in the open, isn't it? No more secrets."

She met his gaze. "No more secrets."

Aaron bounded down the stairs. Kathryn watched him as he crossed the yard and headed for the barn. *Thank you, Father.* She picked up her empty mug and rose from the swing. Time to check on her daughter and get ready for church.

And she still had one more fire to go.

Yes, she did, although it wasn't the one she was thinking of. A few drops of rain splattered onto my head. Last night was the first hint of bad weather for Kathryn, and she had weathered it well enough. Beside me, Peace had grown wan and shimmery. The calm that had fallen over the ranch today wasn't coming from him—it was an illusion, the eye of the storm. And I had a feeling—I shot a dark glance toward the shed out by the barn and shuddered—that the winds and rain were going to become considerably more intense, deadly even, before Peace would fully return to this place again.

Chapter Sixty-Eight

Sunday

David stood in front of the mirror in his bedroom, struggling to put on his tie. If my heart hadn't been so heavy on his behalf, I might have smiled. I'd watched him trying to master that skill his entire life, but he was rarely able to accomplish the maneuver successfully. He caught Laura's reflection as she came into the room and sat on the bed behind him. Abandoning his efforts, he turned around and leaned against the dresser.

Lines creased her forehead that hadn't been there a week ago, but she was still the most beautiful woman he'd ever seen. He fought the urge to cross the distance between them and take her in his arms. His throat constricted. Would he ever be free to do that again?

"I'm going to tell them this morning."

"I'm coming with you."

David contemplated her. He wanted nothing more than to have his wife there with him, but it was too much to ask. "You don't have to."

She rose and walked over to him, taking his tie in both hands and crossing one end over the other. It was a Sunday morning ritual for them, and the normalcy of her actions—in contrast to the craziness of the past few days—caused an unbearable ache in his chest.

"For better or for worse," she whispered.

David touched her hands then lowered his arms to his sides. "It doesn't get any worse than this, does it?"

"Oooh boy, I hope not." A wry grin crossed her face. "We better head out. The boys are waiting in the car."

"Laura." David caught her hand as she turned to leave. "Thank you."

She squeezed his fingers. Then, not letting go, she walked toward the door. As they descended the stairs, he kept his eyes on their clasped hands in amazement.

This was the miracle of marriage, I reflected, as I followed them. Not having a frame of reference, except vicariously, I am constantly amazed by the fact that, although many walk away at the slightest provocation, many more hang on no matter what. They steadfastly refuse to let go, even when hanging on means following the other person through dark valleys of their own making to an unknown place on the other side.

After David opened her car door, he had to force himself to release her hand as she slid onto the front seat. Except for the familiar sound of the boys wrestling over a video game in the back, we drove to church in silence. David clutched the steering wheel, his fingers white with strain. *I'm still not sure what I'm going to say. But you'll be there, right? Please give me the words.* When he glanced over at Laura, the tightness in his chest eased a little.

Years late, David had obeyed and offered everything that was important in his life to the One who had given it all to him. *You are enough.* He shot another glance at his wife, knowing in his heart that if she had gone he would not have been alone. But he was incredibly thankful that she didn't go, that she was still there in spite of everything.

David steered into the parking lot of the church. I readied myself to jump out of the car when he opened the door. Instead, he turned off the engine and sat, both hands frozen to the steering wheel. I settled on the seat and studied his face, listening in on his thoughts. Knowing what he was about to do, they were completely understandable.

We don't have to go in. We could drive away, spend the day together as a family. The people would understand. You would understand, wouldn't you?

A slight trembling started in my arms and legs. While I did get why he was going there, the direction he was heading was doing nothing for my health.

"Come on, Dad." Cody—bless him—grew impatient in the back seat. "We're going to be late."

David met Laura's gaze.

"No more hiding, David. You can do this." She gripped his arm. "You're not alone."

Releasing his breath, he nodded and opened his door.

Laura walked the boys to their Sunday school classes. David staggered to his office and closed the door. He sank onto the chair behind his desk. An anguished groan escaped him.

Why was it always so hard for him to do what he was asked to do? Every time he'd obeyed, God had shown him that He was faithful. And every time he hadn't, he had suffered because of the distance he'd put between them. Why was that such a hard lesson for him to learn?

David clasped his hands behind his neck. *I told you once that there were certain things I couldn't sacrifice, even for you. I forgot then that you had sacrificed far more for me than I could ever give back. Help me to let go. I've had to carry around what I've refused to give up, and I can't do it anymore. The load is too heavy for me. Please take it.*

I almost never cry—it's not in my nature—but I'm not embarrassed to admit I wiped a tear from my eye at the words of his heartfelt prayer. Mainly because, like David, I often find myself carrying around a load I was not meant to bear, and I know the joy of giving it up. I'd wished that joy for David for years. Now that he would finally experience it—regardless of what would happen in the next hour—I believe a few tears were completely justified.

The door opened and Laura stepped into the office. "It's time."

David picked an envelope up off his desk, folded it, and slid it into his shirt pocket. Laura took his arm. They walked out the door and up the aisle of the church. I snagged a seat in the front row where I could see everything that was going on.

Laura's hand slipped from the crook of his arm when she reached her seat. David paused at the end of her row. His resolve was weakening. The shaking in my limbs intensified, but he managed to keep moving toward the front.

The walk up the stairs to his chair behind the pulpit seemed to take forever. *I can't do this alone.*

You have never been alone.

The tension in his neck and shoulders eased.

Everyone was singing, but David couldn't focus on the words. When the song ended, he rose and walked to the pulpit. He grasped hold of it with both hands to support his trembling legs.

Raising his gaze, he studied the small crowd of men and women he'd come to know so well over the last three years. He had loved being their pastor, but he needed to let that go and follow whatever path lay ahead of him.

"I don't have a sermon prepared for you this morning. Instead, I have a story to share. It's a love story, although maybe not a traditional one. It's the story of a man who was raised to know and believe in a God who loved him. As a teenager, however, this man turned against everything he believed in. So far it's not that unusual a story, unfortunately. But this young man went down a path that was darker than most. He committed several robberies and spent time in juvenile detention." David scanned the faces in the room. Everyone looked serious, but no one appeared shocked. Knowing that was about to change, the weight in his chest increased.

He sought out Laura, drawing strength from her presence and her nod of encouragement. "The path he was on led him deeper and deeper into trouble. At the lowest point in his life, he committed a crime that nearly destroyed someone's life. He and another man were involved in the abduction and rape of a woman."

A few gasps rippled through the room. David didn't take his eyes from his wife, knowing he wouldn't be able to finish if he saw the horror on the faces of the people he loved.

"One of the men was determined to kill the woman, but something happened when he started toward her with a knife. She began talking to God—talking to Him as though He was right there with her. And all three of the people in that room suddenly realized that He was.

"This is the love part of that love story—God, coming into that room and giving the woman strength and peace during the worst moments of her life and showing those two men that no matter how hard they tried to run from Him, He wanted them for Himself. He was not willing to let them go. And that affected every person there. Because you can't be in the presence of such unconditional, indescribable love and not be changed somehow.

"The man who intended to kill her fled the building, clearly haunted by that encounter. The second man, after a momentous battle of wills, surrendered to the God who had never stopped pursuing him.

"My friends." David stepped away from the pulpit, walked down the stairs, and stood before them. He had to clear his throat before he could finish. "That second man was me."

He drew the letter of resignation out of his shirt pocket and laid it on the altar. "I no longer have the right to lead this congregation. I've kept from you a terrible secret and shattered the trust you placed in me. And I'm so sorry."

Someone was weeping, but he couldn't bring himself to peer around the room.

Laura stood to join him as he walked toward her row, and together they started for the door. Right before they reached the exit, David stopped. *What is that sound?* Turning, he gazed at the altar. One of the men of his congregation stood at the front of the church, one half of the resignation letter in each hand. He set the pieces on the altar and returned to his seat. Another member of the church, an older woman with a pale blue hat perched on her silver hair, rose and walked to the front, picked up one of the pieces, and tore it in half again.

Standing by the door, tears welling in his eyes, David watched as nearly every person in the room walked to the front and tore the envelope into smaller and smaller pieces.

He had never forgotten how he'd felt that day in the cabin, like God was so real and so present that David could reach out

353

his hand and touch Him. Kathryn had shown him God that day, in the midst of her own terror and pain. Then in prison, the darkest place he'd ever been, He'd come to David through Tiny and the boys. Now, in the face of his betrayal, the people of his church were revealing God to him once again. What had he ever done to deserve these gifts?

It's not what you've done—it's who you are. You are mine, and I will never let you go.

The presence was so real that when David closed his eyes he felt strong arms surrounding him and holding him close. He drew in a deep breath and realized it was gone. The load he'd chosen to carry for so long had been taken away. The peace that settled over him in its place nearly made him weep. It was the peace he'd felt that night in the motel and again on the plane to Toronto. *What I gave up that day, when I refused to tell Laura the truth, you've given it back to me, haven't you?*

Laura squeezed his hand. David gazed at her through a shimmer of tears. "Grace," she murmured, her eyes shining.

"Absolutely." Overwhelmed by wonder, he pressed her hand over his heart and held on as though he might never let it go.

I shook my head as Wonder danced in circles around me. Grace. Of all the beings in my world, I admire her more than any other. She is so strong. And her presence and influence are felt so keenly that I am always surprised the human she has draped her arm around can't see her as clearly as I can.

I smiled now, watching her with David. Her being in the room always meant that my chances of being found were greatly enhanced. And I had been, finally, by him. For the first time since he had been that small, carefree child, pushed on the swing by his mother, I stamped my feet on the ground beneath us and felt the solid, immovable strength of it. I started for the exit. Everything was okay. David and I would be together for good. He was going to be fine.

Now I had to go to another. My chest tightened as I realized that, as of this moment, I couldn't with any degree of certainty say any of those things about her.

Chapter Sixty-Nine

Sunday

The fire leaped and danced, fed by David's last two letters and the program from Halyna's funeral. Kathryn stuffed the small cream-colored shoebox through the door after them. Flames licked up the sides until they collapsed inwards and turned black before dissolving into ash. It was done. The past had been relegated to the past. Drawing in a deep, cleansing breath, she closed the door with a clang for the last time.

The screen door rattled. "Kat?"

The hope that leapt in her chest settled as she crossed the living room to the kitchen. "Hey, Aaron." She held the screen door for him as he came into the house.

"I'm heading into town to run a couple of errands and pick up a few things at the store so Josh and Rachel have food to eat while we're gone. Do you need anything?"

"I don't think so. I'll shop when we return from Wyoming."

"All right." He cocked his head. "You and Tory okay?"

Ah, the real reason for the visit. I had guessed as much.

"We're fine. Tory is freaking out a bit about seeing Dylan. So am I, but we're keeping busy today, trying not to think about it too much. She has an exam at the end of the week, so she's studying."

"And you? Expecting any company?"

Kathryn wrinkled her nose at him. "I don't know when Nick is coming by. When he was here on Tuesday, he said he'd be back in a few days. I'm not sitting around waiting for him to show up, if that's what you're asking. I've been finishing a few things, closing a few doors that still needed to be closed."

"So it's all good?"

"It's all good."

"Good." He grinned. "I'll see you tomorrow. Unless you need me before then."

She slipped a hand through his arm and directed him to the door as I settled onto a kitchen chair. "I won't. Everything's fine here. Nice and quiet. I don't expect anything to happen between now and tomorrow to change that."

My head jerked. Not that I wasn't enjoying this calm, controlled Kathryn, but a lingering trepidation, the nagging sense that something actually could still go terribly wrong, might have kept her senses sharper. I had no desire to invite Fear back into the thick of things—not that he had gone anywhere—but someone a little less toxic, Wariness maybe, would have been good. His presence might have at least given her an edge in the coming confrontation.

Kathryn held open the screen door. "I'm going out to the barn to take care of the horses then I'll make dinner for Tory and me. We'll likely call it an early night. It's been a long week."

"I'll bet." He reached for her and she ducked, thinking he was going to muss her hair again. Instead, he brushed a strand away from her face, his knuckles lightly brushing her cheek. "Get some rest, Kat."

"I will." The screen door closed quietly behind him. When he reached the top of the stairs, he glanced at her. A shadow crossed his face, sending a spate of chills shooting across her skin.

Aaron opened his mouth, then closed it and lifted a hand before clomping down the stairs.

Kathryn propped her shoulder against the doorframe, her eyes on him until he rounded the corner of the house and was gone. *What was that about?* She pushed herself away from the frame and started across the kitchen, but the coolness still shivering across her arms and neck sent her back to the door to hook the lock, something she never did during the day. She shot one more glance in the direction her brother had disappeared before going to check on her daughter.

For my part, I breathed a silent thanks to the Creator and to Aaron. Because of that parting glance, Wariness had shown up to join the party.

"Tory?" Kathryn tapped lightly on the bedroom door and waited. After a few seconds, she rapped again and opened the door slightly. Through the crack she could see her daughter lying on her stomach on her bed, an open textbook in front of her. Her head bopped to the beat of a song Kathryn could barely hear coming through her iPod ear buds. She grinned and walked over to the bed. "Tory?" She tapped her daughter's shoulder gently, not wanting to startle her.

Tory tugged the bud out of one ear. "Sorry, Mom. I didn't hear you come in."

"It's okay. Can you really study with those in your ears?"

"Yes, better actually. Silence drives me crazy, and I can't think at all."

I grinned in spite of the anxiety attacking my system like a virus. My kind of girl.

Kathryn settled on the edge of the bed. "Are you okay, honey? You were pretty quiet on the drive to and from church."

"I'm okay. Better if I don't think about tomorrow. It's easier if I'm studying. My mind doesn't go all kinds of places I don't want it to."

"I'll leave you to it then. I'm going out to feed the horses, and then I'll make dinner, okay?"

"Sounds good." Tory started to replace the earpiece.

"Tory?" Kathryn rested a hand on her shoulder.

"Yeah?"

"I'm sorry I kept the truth from you for so long."

Tory sat up and pulled her knees to her chest, wrapping both arms around them tightly. "No, you were right, Mom. I think it would have been better not to know. I shouldn't have pushed it, although I never imagined that the truth would be so horrible."

"I know. Kevin Dylan is a sick and twisted man, I'm afraid."

Tory bit her lip. "It's so sad, isn't it?" Her voice broke. "Such a waste of a life." She hesitated, staring at her knees. "You said he attacked and killed other women, right?"

"Unfortunately, yes."

"But he didn't kill you. Why?"

Kathryn's throat tightened. "He planned to. He said that he was going to, and he came at me with a knife. David didn't want him to, but he didn't stop him either. I think because he wasn't sure what to do. I had seen their faces, even knew their names."

Tory reached for her hand and clutched it tightly. "It's okay. You don't have to talk about it. I didn't mean to upset you."

"No, I want to help you understand. It's just that I've spent so many years trying to forget that the last few days have been extremely difficult. A lot of memories have been dredged up."

"And burned up, it seems."

Kathryn let out a short laugh. "That's right. That's helped me a lot." She tucked a strand of blonde hair behind her daughter's ear. "I want to try and answer all your questions. I don't want any more secrets between us."

Tory nodded. "So what happened? What stopped him?"

"I'm still not exactly sure. When I realized I was going to die, I started talking to God. He was so real to me in that cabin, Tory. When I was attacked, I felt him right there, suffering with me. Then when I saw the knife—" She swallowed, remembering the glinting steel blade she'd seen that day and so often since, in her nightmares. "I felt him with me again, and I wasn't afraid. I only wanted it to be over. I prayed out loud, 'God help me. Let this end.' And then I stared at Kevin Dylan, at the cold hatred in his eyes, and said, 'God help you too.'"

Tory studied her, emotions roiling in her eyes. *Help her to see, to understand what happened that day.* "I can't explain what occurred next. Dylan glanced at the ceiling and this look of terror crossed his face, as though he saw something there. He dropped the knife and backed away. David grabbed a gun and told him to get out or he'd kill him."

359

I remember that day like it was yesterday. What Dylan saw in the corner of that cabin terrified him and saved Kathryn's life. Only I knew what it was for sure, and that knowledge had saved my life as well. Until that moment I had experienced everything Kathryn had—the terror, the pain, the violation. I knew as certainly as she did that we were both about to die. And then I looked up.

"What happened then?" Tory's eyes were wide.

"He took off. David let me go, and I went straight to the police. Right after I set the cabin on fire and burned it to the ground."

"Mom!" Tory choked out a laugh. "Did you really?"

"Yes. I wasn't thinking too clearly at the time, or I probably wouldn't have destroyed evidence like that. Or I might have, since I couldn't stand the thought of knowing it was still there, that anything else evil could ever happen in that building."

"I would have done the same thing." Tory let go of Kathryn's hand and wrapped her arms around her knees again. "What do you think he saw when he looked up?"

"I have no idea. But after feeling God so strongly in that room, I've always believed it was him revealing himself to Dylan somehow—sending an angel, maybe—to stop him from killing me."

Tory pursed her lips. "I still don't understand why God didn't stop the attack from happening."

Another good question. Tory was full of them. If only Kathryn, like most humans—and most of us, for that matter—didn't suffer from such a shortage of good answers to go with them.

"I don't either. I've asked him that many times over the

years. What I do know is that, no matter what the circumstances, I've always been thankful to have you and never doubted you were a gift from God."

"I've always been grateful for you too." I leaned in as Tory's voice dropped to a whisper. "I hope you haven't thought for a second that because I've wanted to know about my father you haven't been enough."

"Oh, Tory, no." Kathryn cupped her daughter's knees with her hands. "I never thought that. I understand your need to know about your father. It doesn't take anything away from you and me." She brushed her hand against her daughter's cheek, wiping away the tears that continued to fall.

"You don't have to come with me to see him, Mom. I'll understand."

"Thank you for saying that, but I do need to see him. I've been closing doors on the past all week, and this is the last one that's still cracked open. I've been afraid of Dylan for so long, I need to see him one more time. I need to put an end to all that pain and terror for good."

The plan was so good, it made me ache. Mostly because I knew it would never be put into effect. While Kathryn would in all likelihood see Kevin Dylan one more time, it wouldn't be in Wyoming. And the chances that the encounter would put an end to all the pain and terror were slim. Well, ultimately it would, one way or the other. Sadly, not the way she meant and probably not before she experienced both all over again.

"Okay." Tory reached for the ear bud dangling on a white wire around her neck. "At least I'll be there for you this time."

"We'll be there for each other." Kathryn squeezed her daughter's knees before standing up. "I'll call you when supper's ready, okay?"

"Okay, thanks."

Kathryn stepped into the hallway and started to shut the door behind her. Before it closed completely, she regarded her daughter for a moment. When Tory's head started bobbing again, a small smile crossed Kathryn's face.

Feeling like a prisoner being led to her execution, I plodded after her as she descended the stairs and headed outside.

Chapter Seventy

Sunday

A black pickup sped along the gravel road toward the ranch. Kathryn stopped in the yard, her heart rate picking up speed, until it passed by the end of the laneway. She shook her head and started for the barn, kicking at a stone in her path with the toe of her work boot. *You're the one who sent him away.*

She didn't regret that, but now that she was ready to see Nick again, not knowing when he might show up was driving her a bit crazy. For my part, I knew exactly where Nick was, and I suspected, from what he was doing, that he was planning to come see her sometime in the next hour or two. I had a sinking feeling that his arrival might be a little late, but I grasped Hope's hand on one side and Faith's on the other as though my life depended on it—which it very well might—as I followed Kathryn to the barn. She hauled one of the heavy wooden doors open wide enough to slip inside.

Kathryn smiled as she picked up a bag of feed and dumped a pile into the trough in front of Tory's horse. Nick would come for her, she didn't doubt that. She'd seen that promise reflected in his eyes whenever they had been together over the years.

Setting the bag on the cement floor outside the next stall, she reached up and scratched between the horse's ears. "Sometimes you know that you know. Right, Diamond?" The horse tossed his head as if in agreement. Kathryn laughed, so caught up in her own thoughts that she didn't hear the barn door slowly opening behind her.

I caught the movement and swung my head toward it. This time I didn't move quickly enough as Fear lunged toward me. Stabs of pain shot up my arm as he sank his pointed teeth deep into my hand.

Chapter Seventy-One

Sunday

The man in line in front of him at the grocery store looked familiar, but it took Nick a moment to place him. "Aaron?"

The man glanced behind him.

"Nick Lawson." He reached around the large bouquet of Gerbera daisies he was holding to stick out his hand.

"Nick. Of course. I'm sorry. It's been a long time." Aaron shook his hand.

"Seventeen years."

The line moved forward and the two men moved with it. "I've heard a lot about you over the years. I was sorry to hear about your sister."

"Thank you."

Aaron glanced at the flowers. "Someone's birthday?"

Nick's neck warmed. "They're for Kathryn, actually. I was hoping to come by and see her this afternoon. Is she home, do you know?"

"Yes, I saw her earlier. As far as I know she's planning to be home all day."

"Okay good, maybe I'll—"

"That'll be 24.57." The cashier had finished ringing in Aaron's purchases and stood gazing at him expectantly. He grinned an apology and reached into his back pocket for his wallet. After paying, he grabbed his bags and waited at the door for Nick to finish.

Nick followed him outside to his truck. Aaron tossed his bags behind the seat. "So you're coming over now?"

"I thought I might, if you think it's a good time."

Aaron started to answer, but the shrill ringing of the cell phone in his shirt pocket stopped him. "Excuse me." He dug the phone out of his shirt pocket. "Hello?"

Nick transferred the flowers to his other hand and pressed a palm to the hood of Aaron's truck.

"Hey, Olivia. Everything okay?"

Nick's chest tightened a little. Olivia? Wasn't that the name of the woman investigating Kathryn's abduction?

He took a step closer as Aaron listened to the voice on the other end for a few seconds. "She's out in the barn with the horses, I think."

Nick frowned. Why would a cop want to know where Kathryn was?

Aaron narrowed his eyes. "Tory is home, but she doesn't usually answer the phone when she's studying. Meg and Josh are at our place. Why?"

Whatever the woman said in response to that, Aaron stiffened and glanced at Nick. "When?"

Nick rounded the front of the truck. Something was wrong and he was going with Aaron to find out what it was.

Aaron kept the phone pressed to his ear as he opened the truck door. "We're heading there now."

Another pause, then, "Nick Lawson is with me. Do you think Dylan would come after her?"

Nick's fingers froze on the door handle he'd been about to lift. Dylan? Kevin Dylan? *God, please don't let him have escaped.* He threw the flowers into the truck bed and yanked open the door of the truck, his heart pounding.

Aaron slid behind the wheel. "We're ten minutes away. We'll get there as soon as we can."

In the stillness of the cab, Nick could pick up the words the woman on the other end of the phone was saying. "The police are on their way too, and—"

"And?"

The cop drew in a deep breath. "And an ambulance."

Nick's stomach lurched.

"Okay, thanks." Aaron ended the call and dropped the phone into the cup holder between the seats.

"What's going on?" Nick slammed the door.

Aaron shoved the truck into reverse. "Kevin Dylan escaped

from jail Thursday morning. The police think he might head this way."

"Are they sure?"

"Olivia, the investigating officer on the case said that one of the men who escaped with Dylan was taken into custody this morning." Aaron backed out of the parking space. "He said Dylan had one thing with him when he left the prison—a newspaper clipping with a picture of Kathryn. Olivia thinks that's probably why they finally got around to letting her know he'd escaped."

He pounded the steering wheel. "I knew something wasn't right. I felt it today when I was leaving her, a kind of cold shiver passing through me. I should have stuck around, made sure she was okay."

"There's no way you could have known." Nick hesitated. "You said you were with her a few minutes ago, right? You don't think he could have been there, waiting for you to leave, do you?"

Aaron didn't appear thrown by the suggestion, so he'd clearly been thinking the same thing. He pushed the gas pedal to the floor, spewing gravel across the parking lot. "Let's just get home."

Chapter Seventy-Two

Sunday

"Hello, Kathryn."

Every drop of blood in her body solidified into ice. The voice that had haunted her for twenty years still had the power to take away her ability to breathe. She turned around slowly.

Kevin Dylan leaned against the doorframe of the barn, casually cleaning a fingernail with a sharp blade, similar to the one he had once held to her throat. His hair was darker and shorter than it had been the last time she'd seen him, but she still could have picked him out of any line-up. Kathryn glanced at the shotgun hanging on the wall above the door. It was intended for coyotes or cougars, but it would end the life of a man as easily as an animal.

Dylan pushed himself away from the frame. "You'll be dead before you get to it."

The ice-cold emotionless tone of his voice threatened to take her legs out from beneath her. Like he did in the nightmares she'd woken up screaming from for months, he took his time advancing toward her, drawing out her agony.

Think, Kathryn, think. Everything in her compelled her to cry out for help. But Aaron was gone and yelling might bring Tory or Meg. She couldn't put either of them in danger. She pressed her lips together to stifle a rising scream. *It's you and me then. Help me.*

A length of bailer twine hung on a nail on the side of the stall, and Dylan reached out and grabbed it as he walked by.

Kathryn's stomach clenched. This was not happening to her. Again. The fear subsided a fraction as heat billowed in her chest. Her fists clenched. She waited until he got close enough, fighting the urge to move backwards. As soon as he moved within range, she struck, pounding his chest with her fists. Dylan sheathed the knife in the holder at his belt and grabbed her wrists. Furious,

Kathryn kicked wildly. He grunted when her heavy barn boot connected with his shin. Letting go of one wrist, he smashed his fist into her jaw. Kathryn's head cracked hard against the wooden stall behind her. She closed her eyes as pain and light flashed behind them. She stopped kicking, concentrating on regaining her breath and staying on her feet.

In seconds, Dylan had wrapped the twine around her wrists. Before she could gather the strength to fight him, he shoved her against the boards and yanked her arms above her head, knotting the bailer twine over the wooden beam that hung low over the stall. A deep groan of fear and frustration escaped her as she strained against the twine, only managing to draw it tighter around her wrists.

Dylan crouched in front of her and removed one of her boots, tossing it to the side. Kathryn fought the overwhelming desire to kick him in the face with the other one before he tugged it off, knowing it wouldn't help her and would only make him angry. Although that might be better than the cold, machine-like demeanor he maintained now.

"My brother will be home any minute." She ground the words out between clenched teeth, her face throbbing where he had struck her.

Dylan straightened, a cruel, humorless smile twisting his face. "I don't think so. He only left twenty minutes ago. I've been watching you. I know he won't be home for at least an hour." He trailed his fingers along the side of her face. "Which gives us plenty of time to get reacquainted."

She cringed and jerked away.

I had stumbled and fallen when she was struck, but now I struggled to my feet. I had to get to her, to let her know I was still there.

Hope grabbed my arm and held me until I stopped fighting and sagged against her. Others crowded around Kathryn— Courage, Terror, Horror, Strength—but it was our place to wait and watch and be there for her when she needed us. If she needed us.

Dylan walked a slow semi-circle in front of her. "I've been dreaming about this for a long time. Dreaming about finally putting out the light."

Her eyes narrowed in confusion.

He drew his knife out of the sheath. The swishing sound constricted her chest. The sight of the sharp blade cut her breath into short gasps. He ran the flat side over his palm. "You know, the one that's been haunting my dreams for years? The way I hope I've haunted yours."

"What light?" Her voice shook and she pressed her lips together.

He rested his foot on a bale of hay as though they were two old friends discussing the weather. "In the cabin that day. That light up near the ceiling. You must have seen it."

Kathryn shook her head then inhaled sharply as pain shot through her skull, making clear thought almost impossible.

Dylan dropped his foot. "It doesn't matter. The point is, I've had a lot of time to think about it, thanks to you. I finally figured out how to make it go away. You're the one who caused it in the first place, so there's only one way I can see to extinguish it."

He held the knife up to the light, the glow of the dim bulb glinting off the metal. When he lowered it, his eyes were ice cold again. Kathryn's knees turned to liquid. *Don't leave me.* Strength returned to her legs, and she pushed herself up straight. *Even though I walk through the valley of the shadow of death ...* She'd learned that verse in Sunday school when she was eight years old, even won a small gold New Testament for memorizing the whole chapter. Not until this minute had she understood the power and truth of the words. Kathryn met his gaze steadily.

Dylan's eyelids flickered in confusion.

She needed to keep him talking, buy some time. "How did you get out of prison?"

He let out a cold laugh. "Anything's possible if you have enough cash." The steel returned to his eyes. The tip of the knife slid under the collar of her shirt. "Whaddya say, sweetheart? Once more, for old time's sake? It's been a few years since I've been around a woman, you know."

She struggled to breathe. *I will fear no evil.*

"Mom?"

Dylan whirled around at the sound of Tory's terrified voice. Kathryn's heart plunged downward. "Run, Tory. Go!" Tory didn't move.

Dylan sheathed the knife and snatched a pistol from the back of his jeans. "Good decision. Come in, join us." He gestured with the gun, and Tory stepped forward, her eyes on the weapon. When she got close to him, Dylan grabbed her and wrapped his arm around her neck, pressing the barrel of the gun to her head.

"Tory!" Kathryn cried out as her daughter gasped.

Dylan spun Tory around until they both faced her. "I didn't realize you had a daughter, Kathryn."

Tory struggled in his arms, and he tightened his grip around her neck until she stilled. A mocking smile turned up the corners of his mouth. "All these years I've been focused on taking your life, like I should have done in that cabin. But maybe I can take something even more valuable from you."

The safety came off with a soft click, and Kathryn's heart thudded erratically. "Dylan, no. She's … she's your daughter too."

He blinked. Tory's eyes were filled with fear and confusion when they met hers. As Kathryn watched, the fear cleared like a dark cloud swept away by a strong wind, leaving calm sky beneath. With one swift movement, Dylan removed his arm from her neck and whipped her toward him, holding both shoulders in a tight grasp. Tory lifted her chin. A flash of pride rippled through Kathryn at her daughter's strength. It gave her new courage, although the fact that Dylan's eyes bored into her child, that his hands touched her, threatened to rip it from her again.

Dylan studied Tory's face. "Mine?" He let out a short laugh. "Well, what do you know?" The hand with the gun came off Tory's shoulder. Kathryn tensed then relaxed slightly when he clicked the safety on again. Then his arm shot up and he brought the weapon down hard on the side of Tory's head.

Kathryn bit her lip to keep from screaming as her daughter dropped to the ground.

Dylan stepped over the prostrate body, shoving the pistol into his jeans as he strutted toward her. "Aren't I a good dad? I thought I'd save my daughter from having to watch her mother die."

She drew in one short, heavy breath after another, trying to push away the terror making it so hard to think. At least he wasn't going to kill Tory. That was all that mattered.

"Sorry, gorgeous. I guess we're going to have to cut this rendezvous short." Dylan slowly withdrew the knife again, then reached behind her and grabbed a handful of hair. With a hard yank, he tilted her head back.

Kathryn closed her eyes as the tip of his knife dug into her throat. *For you are with me.* Peace filled her. She was not alone.

She opened her eyes, blinking away the tears that had welled up so she could see his face. The knife dug deeper into her skin. Kathryn groaned as warm blood dripped down her neck.

The sound of a vehicle roaring up the driveway startled them both. *Aaron's back.*

The cold steel slipped from her throat as Dylan swiveled his head toward the sound.

When his gaze shifted to her again, her chest squeezed at the desperate determination in his eyes. Dylan raised the knife high above his head, blade pointed downward. For the second time in her life, Kathryn knew she was about to die.

She screamed.

Chapter Seventy-Three

Sunday

Kathryn flinched, unable to draw a breath as the blade arced through the air. From the corner of her eye she caught a movement by the open barn door.

Nick lunged toward them. Dylan pivoted and drove the knife into his shoulder.

"Nick!"

He dropped to his knees in front of Kathryn. Dylan still gripped the handle of the knife, and with his good arm Nick reached across and grasped hold of his wrist. For a few seconds the two of them struggled then Dylan kicked him in the stomach with his boot. Nick slumped forward. He groaned as Dylan yanked out the knife and raised it again.

A deafening explosion rattled the windows of the barn. Dylan froze, his arm still in the air. His eyes met Kathryn's, and time seemed to slow to a crawl as she watched what was happening. The machine-like demeanor was gone. Fear flickered, then pain. She forced herself to look past the physical pain of the gunshot wound to witness the raw pain of a little boy, forced to endure horrendous suffering at the hands of the ones who should have loved and taken care of him. She latched onto the child in his eyes. Despite the fog of terror and confusion that swirled around her, she knew that if she was ever going to forgive Kevin Dylan for all of this, as she'd promised to try, it would be for the sake of that tormented little boy.

His glance darted up to the ceiling, and she waited for the fear to surface. Before it could, a veil dropped over his eyes and they went completely blank. She gasped for breath under the weight of him crumpling toward her.

"Aaron? What's going—?" Meg ran through the barn doorway, her cry cut short as she clapped a hand over her mouth.

"Meg, help Tory." Aaron threw the shotgun onto a bale of hay and ran toward Kathryn. He reached down and grabbed the knife, covered in blood—Nick's blood, she realized with a sickening twist of her stomach—then shoved Dylan aside with one foot. He toppled over slowly and lay, face up, staring at the ceiling. Nick steadied himself against the side of the stall and pushed to his knees.

Aaron sliced through the bailer twine around her wrists. "Kat, are you okay?"

"I'm fine." She could barely push out the words, her throat was so tight with fear and shock.

"You're covered in blood." Aaron's voice shook.

"I don't think it's mine, except for my throat."

The twine snapped. "Aaron." She grabbed hold of his arms and waited until his eyes met hers. "I'm okay."

He let out his breath and nodded.

Kathryn sank onto the straw in front of Nick. Fear clutched her chest at the crimson stain spreading across the front of his denim shirt.

His fingers brushed her swelling jaw line. "I'm all right, really. Go see Tory."

Aaron helped Nick sit with his back to the side of the stall, then grabbed a blanket hanging on a nearby nail and pressed it against his shoulder. Nick winced then attempted a smile, obviously trying to ease her mind. It helped a little, but not much.

Leaning heavily on the stall, she struggled to her feet and stumbled over to her daughter. On her knees, Meg bent over Tory, brushing the hair away from her face. Kathryn knelt on the other side of her and stroked her cheek. "Tory." Her daughter's eyelids fluttered before she opened her eyes. Kathryn took her arm and helped her sit up. "Are you okay?"

Tory touched the side of her head gingerly. "I think so."

Kathryn wrapped her arms around her and held her tight, rocking back and forth. Over her daughter's head, her eyes met Meg's, who slid an arm around them both. For a moment, silence draped itself over the barn. Then the haunting wail of sirens broke the stillness.

Aaron set the knife on the bale next to the shotgun. "I'll go tell them where we are."

Thirty seconds later, two paramedics carrying a stretcher burst into the barn. They started for Nick, but he waved them over to Tory. The EMT closest to him hesitated. Then the wail of another siren filled the air and he nodded curtly and shifted his attention to Tory. They set the stretcher next to her on the ground. After asking her a few questions, they assisted her onto it. Kathryn took a step toward the door, but Tory grabbed her arm. "Stay with Nick, Mom. Aunt Meg can come with me."

Meg touched Kathryn's back. "Yes, I'll go with her. We'll meet you at the hospital."

Torn in two directions, Kathryn bit her lower lip. "We'll be right behind you."

"Another ambulance is nearly here," one of the EMTs assured her as he and his partner wheeled the stretcher toward the door.

Tory lifted her hand. Kathryn watched the four of them make their way across the hay-strewn floor. She waited until they had disappeared through the heavy wooden doors before turning to Nick.

He was watching her intently. One arm was slung across his chest as he pressed his hand against the blanket covering his shoulder. She hurried over, dropping to her knees in front of him. "How are you doing?"

Nick let go of the blanket. She replaced his hand with hers. Blood hadn't seeped through the cloth, which was a good sign. The knife must have gone in and out cleanly and not hit any major arteries. Kathryn repressed a shudder.

Nick ran his thumb lightly along her bruised jaw. "I'm okay. I don't think it's too bad. Just enough to give me a nice sexy scar."

Kathryn bit back a laugh, shocked that it was even possible. She hadn't thought she would laugh for a long time.

He covered her hand with his. "I'm more worried about you. You must have been terrified." The tremor rippling through the quiet words revealed his own fear.

"I'll be fine. Eventually." She attempted a smile but felt the sadness in it and let it go. "It's ..." She stopped, almost afraid to say it in case verbalizing it made it not true.

What she had forgotten, as human beings tend to do, is that Truth is a lot stronger than that. And speaking him out loud only tends to make him stronger.

"What?" Nick squeezed her hand, his gaze probing hers.

"It's over."

The bright light she'd seen when he'd knocked on her screen door—could that have been only five days ago?—flared in his eyes again.

Her breath caught at his intense gaze. Nick let go of her hand and brushed the back of his fingers across her cheek. Electricity sparked across her skin. "No more *as if* days. This is for real now. And it's forever."

In spite of everything that had happened in the last few minutes, a thrill shot through her. "Got it."

His hand slid to her neck and he pulled her toward him and touched his lips to hers. Kathryn closed her eyes. The warmth that flooded through her dispelled the cold that had gripped her since the moment she'd seen Kevin Dylan standing in the doorway of the barn.

She was free. After days spent letting go of the past and then confronting Kevin Dylan face to face, nothing stood in the way of her and Nick being together.

Forever.

I had to work to draw in a breath—my heart was still pounding so wildly. I shook Fear off of me and grasped my wounded hand tightly in the fingers of my good hand as he loped out of the barn.

Two hands reached for mine and tugged me from my knees where I had fallen when the blade drove into Nick's shoulder.

When I was reasonably steady on my feet, Faith moved to stand beside me, sliding a strong, reassuring arm around my shoulders. "You did it, my friend. And I'm so glad. If anyone deserves to find Happiness, it's the two of them."

I contemplated the pair in front of me. Faith was right, as always. After everything they had been through, these two definitely deserved Happiness, if I did say so myself. And I was—to use a well-worn but always-a-crowd-pleaser-at-our-parties joke—*happy* to be here for them.

I worked at evening out my breath, not wanting Faith to see that she had nearly slipped from my grasp when Kevin Dylan raised his knife. Still, she knew. She squeezed my shoulder, letting me know that everything was okay between us. The gentle reminder of her presence, and the knowledge that Kathryn had made it to the end of the path, to me, sent strength and healing through my badly bruised body and psyche. I managed a weak grin before turning my attention to Nick and Kathryn. The two of them gazed at each other, not speaking.

This time I didn't mind so much. In a moment, the barn would be swarming with EMTs and police officers and enough noise and chaos to satisfy even me. I leaned against Faith and watched the two of them in each other's arms, for once in my very long existence content to simply bask in the beautiful sound of silence.

Author Note

Dear Readers,

The Watcher was my debut novel, and although it has been largely rewritten and added to in this new, tenth-anniversary edition, the central theme remains unchanged: Grace. As David Henley says, in the shadow of it I feel small. God's grace is truly the most incomprehensible and life-transforming gift a human being can receive.

In this book, I have striven to demonstrate how grace—whether from God or from another person—can change someone at a heart level. I am deeply aware that the relationship between David and Kathryn will be controversial, even offensive, to some. Yet the question *The Watcher* poses is this: if God's grace is limitless, should the grace extended by a follower of Christ toward someone who has committed an egregious offense against them be any less, particularly if the offender is truly remorseful, asks forgiveness, demonstrates transformation, and no longer poses a threat?

Please note that I would never, under any circumstances, encourage anyone to return to a situation or to be in contact with a person when it is not safe to do so. But since Kathryn is assured by God and by David's own words and actions that he is no longer a danger to her and that he is a changed man, should she place limits on how much grace she extends to him or on what that grace looks like as it plays out in both their lives?

I leave it to you and God to decide.

My hope and prayer for all of you is that you experience God's overwhelming grace, love, and peace in your lives and that you remember you are never alone, whatever circumstances you may find yourselves in.

Sara

If you enjoyed this story, I'd appreciate if you'd consider leaving a review on any of the book-selling sites.

I'd also love to connect with you on the following sites:

Website (where you can sign up to receive my short, once-a-month newsletter): www.saradavison.org
Facebook: www.facebook.com/authorsaradavison

Also, if you aren't aware, I have a number of other Christian romantic suspense books in print. You might be interested in checking out the following titles:

The Seven Trilogy - The End Begins, The Darkness Deepens, The Morning Star Rises

The Night Guardians Series - Vigilant, Guarded, Driven, Forged (September 2022)

The Rose Tattoo Trilogy - Lost Down Deep, Written in Ink (August 2021), Sharp Like Glass (coming in 2022)

Acknowledgments

What a journey *The Watcher* has taken me on. For as far back as I can remember, at least from the age of eight or nine, I longed to write a book. The idea was so daunting, though, that after obtaining a degree in English literature, I signed up for every creative writing course, seminar, and workshop I could find. Basically, I did everything but actually sit down and write.

Then one Easter Sunday morning about fifteen years ago, the idea for a romantic suspense novel came to me. I hurried home and set to work, and a few months later I had a draft that I thought was pretty good. Then I showed it to an editor who quickly disabused me of that notion. So my first thank you goes to Krysia Lear, whose kind but honest feedback sent me to the drawing board to begin over with this book, then titled *UnBroken*.

Five years and countless drafts later, I believed the novel might be ready for publication. I received a lot of great feedback from editors and agents but no actual offers. On the strength of the unpublished manuscript, I was nominated for a Best New Canadian Christian Author award with The Word Guild, but still no contract. Even so, my second thank you goes out to every agent, editor, and judge who rejected *UnBroken* but graciously provided me with enough feedback and encouragement to keep me from giving up on it. You were right—something still wasn't working with the story.

When I decided to submit it to a publishing contest with Word Alive Press in Winnipeg in 2010, I needed to figure out what that something was. The answer finally came to me—the problem was the timeline. As fans of the TV show *24* well know, with a thriller or suspense a tight timeline is key. *UnBroken* took place over a span of twenty years, sort of a suspenseful epic novel, which doesn't always work particularly well. I'd read a couple of novels, including *The Book Thief*, that had a non-human narrator, and the idea intrigued me. Days before the deadline for the publishing contest, it occurred to me that a spiritual being, a watcher, could work as a narrator, and that other beings could be included as well to represent activity in the spiritual realm. At that point, *The Watcher* was born.

Re-writing the novel in less than two weeks by adding in all the Beings was certainly an experience—I have a vivid recollection of rarely showering, barely eating, and catching snatches of sleep here and there as I reworked the manuscript. Although my husband and kids may tell you differently, the self-sacrifice was worth it. By telling Kathryn's story from the viewpoint of The Watcher, I was able to shorten the timeline of events from twenty years to six days. I finished the rewrite on the day of the deadline and sent it off without having time to show it to one other person, which meant that I literally had no idea whether the story worked or if it even made sense.

The Watcher won the contest and was published by Word Alive Press in 2011. So my third thank you goes to the judges and to all the wonderful staff at Word Alive for believing in this crazy story and for being the first to send it out into the world. I will always be grateful for your support and encouragement.

Now, on the tenth anniversary of the release of this book, I offer deepest thanks to Miralee Ferrell, Alyssa Roat, Nikki Wright, Cindy Jackson, and everyone at Mountain Brook Ink and Mountain Brook Fire for their interest in and support of this project. As I have prepared the story for its re-release, I've been able to revise and update the book as well as add in a number of new chapters. Thank you for loving this story, for breathing new life into it, and for providing the opportunity for it to reach a whole new group of readers

.

More thanks than I can put into words go to my family, friends, fellow authors, and members of my writers' groups and organizations. Each of them has spurred me on and accompanied me every step of this wild, disheartening, thrilling, discouraging, exciting, growth and learning-filled ride. I would have quit a few paces past the starting line if it hadn't been for you.

And finally, a thank you from the bottom of my heart to readers who have honored and humbled me by taking the time to read this book and to let me know that God has used it to impact their lives in small or big ways. You are why I write.

May God send Peace, Grace, Joy, and Hope to bless each one of you for walking this road along with me.

Discussion Questions

1) The Watcher maintains that Faith doesn't dread storms, that in fact, "She usually comes out of the battering wind and rain stronger than ever." Have you found this to be true in your own life? Looking back, can you think of an extreme situation you faced? How did your faith weather that storm?

2) Is there anything from your past that you are holding onto like Kathryn did with the memories in her shoebox? Are you willing to let go of it? How would you do so and what do you think would happen if you did?

3) Do you struggle with fear in your life? Can you identify what you are afraid of? God tells us over three hundred and sixty times in Scripture not to be afraid, so clearly this is not how He wants us to live our lives. What do you think you could do in order to overcome the fear that robs you of joy and peace in your life?

4) Even in the worst moments of her life, Kathryn feels God with her and experiences peace. Have you ever had this experience? Share how you knew that God was there and how that made you feel.

5) Do you believe that God pursues people as relentlessly as He pursued David? Have you experienced this personally? Is there anything a person can do to move themselves outside of the reach of God's grace?

6) When Kathryn tells God that for His sake she will try to forgive David Henley, God responds that it is for her. Do you agree with that? Have you ever struggled to forgive someone? How did holding on to unforgiveness make you feel? If you were able to bring yourself to forgive, what was the impact on you and on the other person?

7) David feels strongly that God is calling him into full-time ministry, although he obeys very reluctantly. As he does, he eventually finds that being the pastor of his own church has become his heart's desire as well. Have you ever felt God calling you to do something you didn't want to do? If you obeyed in spite of your feelings, what happened?

8) When she goes to see David at his church, Kathryn insists that God had brought good out of the trauma she suffered. Do you believe that God can always bring good out of our circumstances? Have you seen this happen in your life or the life of someone you know?

9) Although Kathryn loves and trusts God and tries to serve Him the best she can, she still experiences a horrific attack that changes her life. Why do you think terrible things happen to good people? If God is sovereign and in control, why doesn't He stop bad things from happening?

10) Kathryn calls God her shelter and safe place, as He is referred to in the Bible. When you are facing difficult circumstances, what Scriptures speak to you the most strongly about who God is and what promises He has given to those who trust in Him?